THE TWELVE STRIPPERS OF CHRISTMAS

A Collection of Naughty Holiday Treats

LULU M. SYLVIAN

GRIFFYN INK

Holy crap guys! I wrote a book!
I want to thank everyone who listened to me,
encouraged me, supported me, put up with me.
This list is by no means complete.

In no particular order:
My husband, my children, my parents, my sister, Dana, Heather,
Sarah, Ella, Jody, Eli, Alana, Victoria, Kat, Suzanne, everyone in the
Music City RWA chapter, Holly, Miki, Bill, Grace, Sam, Liz, Mina,
Lisa, Nina, Leslie, Kassie, Jenny, Janae, Nicole, Samantha, Andrea,
Cyndi, Natalie, Heather, Tracey, Salem, Laura, the Muse, and all the
dancing boys including: Adam, Sergei, Mikhail, Channing, Laurent,
Larry, Eric, Sam, Ronnie, Alex, Saulo, Gene, Fred, Hugh, Christopher,
and John.

Dear parents: let your sons take dancing lessons!
To all the dancers, everywhere, keep dancing.

1

PARTRIDGE IN HER PEAR TREE

"*M*adge, seriously, I think this could be a real problem for us." Bethany Poirier trailed after her boss, picking up scattered bits of detritus from the work day.

Madge danced back and forth between the file cabinet in her office and the larger one in the hall. She bopped in time to the grinding music coming from the lounge.

"Bethany, relax. How is this going to be a problem?"

"It's an HR nightmare." Bethany loved her boss. She loved this company. She didn't have to dress up for work, she didn't have to wear shoes. It was just that sometimes they pushed the boundaries of HR-appropriate office behavior. "This is a lawsuit waiting to happen. You can't hire strippers for the office Christmas party."

"Oh, why not?" Madge turned to look at Bethany. Her brow furrowed. "You're shorter."

Bethany directed her gaze to her stocking feet. "I took my shoes off."

"Right." Madge continued. "How many women work for this company?"

"Five," Bethany responded.

"Of those five, how many are married, and how many are going to find this offensive?"

"You're the only married one, and I guess no one is going to find this offensive."

"See? I mean, who is in charge of all things HR?" Madge asked.

"I am."

"And how many in this company are men?"

"None since Charles left."

"Exactly." Madge stared at Bethany. She began bobbing her head again to the *um-cha um-cha* of the music pulsing through the office. "Who is the office prude?"

"Charles," Bethany replied.

"And after Charles?" Madge prodded.

"That would be me," Bethany replied.

"Are you going to sue me, Bethany?"

"No, but—" Bethany started.

"But nothing, it's a party. Have some wine." Madge picked up a bottle and began looking for a cup. She found a coffee mug. She poured the wine and handed it to Bethany. "We're having design issues with the Thruster 2000, but I'm not going to spend my time stressing over designs I can't do anything about right now until I hire a new engineer, and I can't do that the Friday before Christmas. I'm going to enjoy myself, and I want you to do the same."

"But we've got a little person dressed like an elf dancing around in there and handing out candy canes to bow-chikka-wow-wow music," Bethany whined.

"Only one? I hired two strippers." Madge quickly scurried to the lounge and the party. Bethany followed in her wake.

Through the door, Bethany could see the man dancing on the coffee table in the middle of the room. Her coworkers hooted and shouted as he twisted and posed. In a single swift move and with the help of velcro and snaps, he pulled off his green elf shirt. The green and red stocking hat bobbled on his head. She closed her eyes, the image of the well-defined little person cavorting in a red G-string and red and white thigh-high striped stockings forever seared into her brain.

Bethany sighed and turned back towards her boss. This was ridiculous, but Madge was right, no one in their office would lodge a complaint. Bethany was still adjusting after eight months of being with As You Like It after years of being in corporate HR departments. Years of filing complaints, years of documenting innuendo and off-color humor. AYLI was a completely different beast. Madge took good care of her employees, made sure they had what they needed, listened when there was a problem, and let loose with the inappropriate fun as she saw fit. Madge would have never have hired the strippers if Charles was still around.

This party was not only to celebrate the impending Christmas holiday but to let off some steam after Charles left. He had been Bethany's personal hell. From day one, Charles lodged some form of complaint against AYLI. Most of which were ridiculous, after all the man was a design engineer for a sexual pleasure device company. A company that catered primarily to the sexual needs of women and gay men. Apparently after nearly three years of employment, Charles began having a personal moral crisis, designer's remorse, and religious anxiety. And he made everyone else's work life miserable.

Madge patted her on the shoulder. "Chill, it's a Santa-gram, it's fun, relax."

Bethany sighed again, she faced the party and grabbed onto the mug in her hand with a death grip, lest it fall and spill wine everywhere.

She retreated into the hall with a spin, her breathing labored, "Oh, shit, we are so going to get sued."

"What?" Madge asked as she looked up from filing the last job folder into the long line of purple cabinets.

"Jonsey is on his Johnson. This isn't happening." Bethany moaned. She had thought the sight of the dwarf dancing was going to give her nightmares, but that was nothing compared to the vision she had just seen. Through labored breathing she managed to say, "The dwarf guy is standing on the table, and Jonsey is sucking him off. I cannot handle how completely nonpolitically correct this whole thing is."

"Really? How big is he?" Madge quickly scurried into the lounge.

Bethany groaned.

She heard Madge join the party with a loud whoop followed by, "Jonsey, that is not a candy cane. Put that away!"

The music changed again. Bethany slunk into the lounge, keeping to the edges of the room in case an orgy or something broke out. She wanted an escape route.

Santa made his entrance. He threw the doors open and strode in like he was the man in charge. He was larger than life, tall and round with a commanding presence. The costuming was fantastic, all red velvet with soft white fur trimming. It barely looked like a fat suit at all. Of course, she hadn't really expected the elf to be a little person when Madge had confessed to hiring the strippers, so it was possible this man was actually a big guy. He moved more fluidly than Bethany expected from a man of real girth. It didn't matter, so long as there were no more blow jobs in her presence at this party, she could handle it.

A hearty "ho, ho, ho," passed through his lips. He stopped in front of Jonsey, letting the large sack on his back fall to the floor. "So you're the ho?" he asked in a booming voice.

Jonsey cackled and clapped with delight. She was probably more than a bit tipsy. She was certainly enjoying herself.

Santa rummaged in his bag and pulled out a large lump of coal. He presented it to Jonsey. "Since you have clearly been naughty, naughty, naughty."

Jonsey grabbed the coal and continued to howl with laughter.

Santa placed the bag next to Sue, and then caressed her cheek. "Watch this for me," he said with a wink. He whipped himself around in a fast turn. "And no peeking."

Of course, Sue immediately tried to peek in the bag. Santa playfully smacked at her hand and waggled his finger at her. Bethany rolled her eyes, this was going to get so much worse as the night went on, she could just tell.

Santa's music changed again, and in his full suit, he began bumping and grinding. Sue got the first lap dance. From Bethany's perspective against the back wall, it looked like a giant Santa-shaped dog was humping her co-worker.

A complete HR nightmare.

Santa continued to dance, and then articles of clothing began falling off First to go was the belt, he removed it in a slow tease before draping it around Madge's neck. Under the jacket, he was round and wore a Henley-style long sleeved shirt with three small buttons at the neck. Suspenders held his pants up. One at a time he lowered the suspenders. The dance was more ridiculous than sexy.

Bethany wasn't exactly sure how he did it, but in a series of spins, he removed the shirt and all the padding. When he stopped he was shirtless, and the overlarge pants, no longer supported, fell to the ground.

A tall wall of muscle stepped out of the pile that was the Santa suit. His muscle groups had muscles. Bethany's jaw hit the floor. Before her, thrusting his crotch at Madge and Jonsey, was a perfectly sculpted bronze warrior. Bethany was instantly brought back to her Art Appreciation class in college, this man was a Greek God. He was perfection, at least in her eyes. The only detractor from all of this male glory was the thick white beard. The large skull and crossed candy canes tattoo emblazoned across his chest was humorous, as was the G-string that had a gift box with a large bow perfectly situated in front of his privates.

Bethany's attention was pulled away from the dancing Santa when Monica let out a loud whoop. The dancing elf pulled giant phallic candy canes from Santa's bag. He and Santa began what looked like a well rehearsed choreographed routine that involved a lot of rubbing and humping along the giant candy canes.

Bethany finally relaxed, this last number was too much. She started giggling and approached closer to the dancers and the rest of the party.

Santa had noticed her, she squealed when he grabbed her, pulling her into a sweaty embrace. He began humping and grinding around her. She couldn't help it, she began dancing to the music. She reached up and tugged the hat off. The dancer had longer hair than she expected.

Sue bounced up and began dancing with them, then they were joined by Monica. The elf danced with Jonsey and Madge. Bethany wasn't sure who removed the beard, but one minute she danced with a snowy-bearded man and the next, it was a face she recognized.

Bethany's muscles seized up, she froze, and then scurried danced away to a safe distance. She stared. That beautiful face and perfect body belonged to Seth Partridge. Seth had been a thing of beauty in high school, majestic and unattainable. And here he was more beautiful, more sculpted, and just as unattainable. Drama boy, track team, she had a crush on him for three and half years.

And now look at him. His sixteen-year-old body had given her some of her first sexual thoughts. His current body was giving her some seriously dirty ideas.

She needed to remember to thank Madge on Monday for hiring the Santa-gram.

"I recognize you, don't I?" Seth asked. Bethany had to brace herself against the sound of his voice. It was deeper, smoother, and sexier than she remembered. She nodded.

"Buccaneer County High, right?"

"Class of 2006. Go, Pirates. Arr," she replied.

Seth's face broke into a wide grin. Bethany had always liked his grin, that certainly hadn't changed. Only now it pulled at her and opened a chasm of longing deep in her core. In high school, his grin had made her giddy and flustered more than once. "So you remember Colin McIntry?"

"Yeah, I tutored him, I remember you, you're his friend Seth?" Bethany was glad he was the one to bring up their mutual past. It made her feel less like a stalker.

"Yeah, that's me. So, wow. What are you doing here? I mean, this isn't exactly the logical place to move to after Rock Falls."

"College, then work. How 'bout you?" Bethany kept staring at the checkbook in front of her. It was that or openly drool over Seth as he stood in front of her with no shirt and drops of sweat glistening between perfectly formed pecs.

"Moved here to get out of that town, it got smaller after high school. Met a girl who knew a guy who… and next thing I know

I'm doing the stripper fireman thing for bachelorette parties." Seth pulled a faded T-shirt on. It pulled across his chest and strained at his biceps.

"Who do I make this out to?" Bethany indicated the check with her pen. She leaned in and whispered, "I really hope your dance partner isn't going to sue us."

"I'm really sorry about that. R and D Entertainment, pronounced Randy, like on the invoice." Seth pointed to the piece of paper on the desk in front of Bethany. "Ricky isn't supposed to do that. I'm just glad you're still willing to pay us. Some of the guys take it too far, we're legally not allowed to do that. I actually hate the Santa gig, but it's good money."

Bethany shivered as his fingers slowly ran along hers when he took the check from her hand.

"When we get paid. Ricky has cost us getting paid more than once. One of these days he's going to get us into serious legal problems."

"Why don't they fire him?"

"He's the R of R and D. We get more Santa-grams and St. Patrick's day gigs because of him. We've even added some Ren-fair type numbers with dragons cause of that cable show. He works his angle hard. We've been doing this Santa bit twice a night all week, and practically every night since Thanksgiving."

"Sounds like he's really got something going on there. And work is work. It looked like you were enjoying yourself."

"I admit it, it's fun. I like to dance. Just never really thought I'd be a stripper."

"Does anybody?" Bethany asked.

"Point taken. It was good to see you again. Maybe I'll see you around town sometimes?" Seth picked up his duffle bag full of costume and pushed his way out AYLI's front doors.

Beth sighed and slumped into her desk chair. Seth Partridge. He was gorgeous. And he had remembered her. She had his work number, maybe she should call him for a private showing?

"Wow, Santa was hot!" Madge exclaimed as she walked past Bethany's desk. She paused. "I can't believe I boogied with a midget."

"Little person," Bethany corrected.

"Elf," Jonsey added, her bag on her shoulder. "He's in character, so it's okay to call him an elf. Man, he was one little hot package. And hung for a short dude."

Bethany groaned. "Good night, Jonsey, if he sues us, it's all on you."

"You know it!" Jonsey yelled as she left the building.

"Go home, Bethany. The party was a hit, and no one is suing anyone." Madge directed.

Bethany slogged her way out to the parking lot. The adrenaline rush of the party and seeing Seth again drained from her body. She felt beyond exhausted, she felt used up and wrung out.

Loud shouts from across the lot caught her attention. Seth waved his arms about. Ricky was bawling him out. Ricky kicked Seth in the shin, jumped in the van, and then slammed the door. Tires squealed as he pulled out of the lot at high speed. Seth stood staring after the van as it drove away. He looked silly and cute standing there in his oversized velvet Santa pants and hoodie. His breath made small puffs of steam. However, it was too cold for him to be out dressed the way he was. She rolled down her window as she pulled up next to him.

"You need some help? Looks like you got ditched."

Seth slicked his hair back with both hands. "Yeah, that asshole just fired me. I told him you were nervous we were gonna sue you for him not keeping it in his pants. He doesn't get it. He's gonna get into trouble someday. Someday that's gonna happen, and the girl will turn out to be underage." Seth stomped in a circle, shaking the aggravation out of his arms.

"You need a ride?" Bethany asked.

"Naw, I'm good." Seth started searching for pockets. He looked up sheepishly. "Yeah, I need a ride. My wallet, keys, phone—all of it are in my bag in Ricky's stupid van."

Bethany nodded her head to the side, indicating that Seth should climb in. "Come on, where do you live?"

"I'm on the other side of Mount Wash. It's kind of far, sorry."

"It's the least I could do since I feel kind of responsible for getting you fired," Bethany said.

"Hey, no, you didn't get me fired. I got me fired. Ricky has a good schtick, he just needs to learn to reign it in. This way I'm not around for when the shit hits the fan, and it will."

"You don't mind if we swing through a drive through, do you? Party snacks do not a dinner make."

"My treat..." Seth started. "If I had my wallet. Shit. You don't mind spotting me for a burger, do you? I'll buy next time."

Bethany melted at the grin he gave her. "Sure."

"I wish you hadn't remembered me from high school," Bethany said, shoving fries into her mouth.

"Why not? You remembered me."

"Yeah, but I was a mess." She cut herself off before she added *and you were hot.*

"We all were. It was high school."

"Bad hair, braces, total ugly duckling. High school was not a good time for me."

"I don't remember you being ugly. I remember you being smart and tutoring Colin. Well, you grew out it if you were an ugly duckling."

Bethany blushed like a traffic light the rest of the drive.

She pulled into the driveway behind Ricky's van.

"Good. Ricky's back. I can get in," Seth exclaimed.

"Why would Ricky be here?" Bethany asked, confused.

"He's my roommate. And boss. I guess it's going to be a little weird now, and he's going to actually start charging me rent instead of taking it out of my pay." Seth got out of the car. He walked around to the driver's side.

Bethany rolled down her window. She handed Seth a scrap of paper with her hastily scrawled phone number. "Call me sometime. We can catch up some more, or not." Her insides felt like they were curling in on themselves. She had just handed her phone number to Seth. She couldn't believe how nervous the whole thing was making her. She wanted to scream in excitement, more importantly, she wanted to be cool enough that Seth would consider calling her and not think she was still the same dork from high school.

Seth took the paper. He looked at the number. "Thanks." He waggled his eyebrows at her. "I will call. I owe you a hamburger. Thanks again."

He waved as he walked into the house.

She wanted to die. The cute boy from school said he would call her. She felt sixteen all over again. She was transported back to being Bethany, dweeb dork supreme. The only reason any boy, let alone a cute one, would talk to her was because she tutored English.

Bethany sat in the driveway much longer than necessary, gathering her wits. She wasn't sixteen anymore. She was an adult, for Christ's sake. Just because she was currently single did not make her desperate, but she yearned for more of Seth. Hell, she wasn't some shy virgin, and she worked for a vibrator design company. What was wrong with her?

She shifted into reverse and pulled out of the drive.

Less than a mile away her phone started ringing. She punched the answer button on the car's dash.

"Bet...sshole...can..." The unidentified caller kept breaking up.

"I have no idea if you can hear me, cause I can't hear a thing you're saying. Try calling me back." She ended the call.

Her phone rang again. "Hey Bethany, it's Seth. That asshole kicked me out of the house."

"What?" She pulled over and picked up the phone so she could hear Seth better.

"Ricky kicked me out of the house. I hate to ask this of you, but I'm stuck, my car is in the shop, and that asshole is refusing to pay me, calling it back rent and utilities. Fuck!" Seth yelled. "It's snowing." A fat white fluff splattered against her windshield, confirming his weather report.

"I'm coming to get you." She placed the phone back in the cradle and turned the car around.

Seth stood huddled under the front door overhang, staying out of the snow. He tossed a duffle bag into the back seat of Bethany's car before hopping into the passenger seat.

"I don't have money for a hotel. Can you take me to a shelter for tonight? I should be able to get my car back on Monday, and I guess I'll live in that until I can find another place."

Bethany shook her head. "You aren't staying in a shelter. You can sleep on my couch. I feel responsible. First, you're fired, and now you're kicked out of your place. It's the least I can do."

"Thanks, Bethany. This year has sucked. What more can it throw at me in the next week?"

Bethany glanced over at Seth, his head reclined on the seat. He looked completely defeated. Sexy as hell, but defeated.

Bethany padded out of her bedroom, the smell of hot chocolate and pancakes welcomed her. The sight of Seth standing in boxer shorts and socks in her kitchen thrilled her. He was a beautiful sight to wake up to. He turned and smiled at her.

That was when she panicked. Her pajamas were old and shabby, her head hosted a rat's nest of bed-head hair, and she hadn't brushed her teeth.

She dashed into the bathroom and slammed the door. When she entered the kitchen again, Seth wore jeans that hugged his hips and backside in a manner that made Bethany jealous of the denim fabric.

"I know I'm not very pretty in the morning, I just didn't think I would scare you." He laughed.

"It's not you, it's me," she mumbled into the mug of hot cocoa he handed her.

"Naw, you wake up pretty." She grinned. Seth was a master flirt. She knew she was still a morning mess, even in a robe with freshly brushed teeth and her hair pulled into a quick ponytail. But she'd take it. It had been a very long time since someone bothered to flirt with her while she looked like this. Actually, she couldn't really remember if any of her past boyfriends had. To the best of her memory, there had been that one kid in the dorm, but he flirted with everyone, that was never personal. This was very personal, and Bethany enjoyed it completely.

"How was the couch?"

"My feet hung off the edge, but it was comfortable enough." Seth leaned back against the counter, his breakfast plate in his hands.

"So what's the plan?" Bethany sat on her one kitchen chair and began eating. "Hmm, these are good."

"The least I could do. You kept me off the street last night." He looked at her over the rim of his mug. "The plan is to make some calls to find a place to stay tonight and go back to Ricky's today or tomorrow and get the rest of my stuff. Hopefully, pick up my car on Monday when the shop opens and start looking for a job."

"How many strip-o-gram places are there in this town? I mean—" Bethany cut herself off as she realized she had firmly planted her foot in her own mouth.

"As far as I know, Ricky has the market cornered on that one. But I can wait tables, change tires, stock shelves. I've been trying to get a job as a mechanical engineer ever since I graduated last year. I'm finding out around here it's not what you know, it's who you know. And a lot of places seem to hold the fact that it took me eight years to get a degree against me."

Bethany knew the pain of being between jobs and on her own. A random comment while waiting in line at the coffee shop had introduced her to Madge and her current job. "What about your family?"

Seth shook his head. "That's not an option."

Bethany nodded. She knew that one too well too. Gears in her head whirled to life. "Can you make more than just pancakes?"

"You mean can I cook? Sure, but I'm not interested in being a line chef."

Bethany shook her head, "I'll make you a deal, short term until you can get back on your feet and find a proper place to live. You can stay on my couch as long as you cook for me."

"You want me to be your live-in personal chef?" Seth cocked an eyebrow.

His expression gave her butterflies. She would love for him to be her live-in anything, especially if he did everything without a shirt on. "Sort of. But there's more."

"Cooking, cleaning, laundry, personal masseuse?" Seth asked jokingly.

She bit her lips, how to say this without sounding like she was coming on to him? She wanted to come on to him, but this wasn't the time. Sometimes her job could be embarrassing. Right now, getting ready to discuss it with a man as hot as Seth was definitely one of those times.

"How to you feel about the sex entertainment industry?" she blurted out.

"I'm a male stripper, what do you think?"

"I was thinking more along the line of sex toys." She could feel her own blush wash over her face.

"What are you getting at, Bethy girl?" Seth put his mug down slowly. To Bethany, he looked like he'd turned from affable house guest to super sexy predator. Maybe she just liked that gleam in his eyes.

"Are you familiar with As You Like It? The company that you danced at last night?" She began talking fast, this conversation was heading straight into the realm of innuendo. She didn't want to piss him off or insult him. Or lead him on, just yet. "We design and oversee the manufacture of personal pleasure devices. Our primary client base is women and gay men. Our engineer walked off the job a little over a week ago in a fit of moral righteousness."

"And here I hoped you were coming on to me," Seth sighed. "So you have an opening for a mechanical engineer who isn't ashamed of designing vibrators?"

"Basically."

Seth grinned widely. "Would you prefer to see my LinkedIn profile or a resume?"

"Hey Madge, I may have solved our engineering problem." Bethany stood in the door to her boss's office.

"You get a technical education over the weekend?"

"Better. I met a techy guy who has zero issues with the industry," Bethany tilted her head, indicating Madge should follow her. "C'mon."

Bethany led Madge into the conference room, where Seth stood looking out the window. Bethany sighed inwardly, he presented a glorious view, front or back facing. And he filled out dress shirts beautifully.

"Madge, I'd like to introduce you to..." Bethany gestured towards Seth. He turned around.

"Santa!" Madge cried out. She extended her hand to take Seth's. "So you possess beauty and brains?"

"Yes, ma'am." Seth nodded.

Bethany handed Madge a folder with Seth's resume on top. Madge glanced over the document before sitting. "First, don't call me ma'am, second tell me how a Santa-gram dancer can fulfill my Christmas wish of hiring a competent design engineer who isn't going to freak out that the dildos and vibrators he's working on are bigger than his ego?"

Bethany quietly closed the door behind her, leaving Madge to interview Seth. She kept her fingers crossed that this worked out for him. She would enjoy seeing him every day. Unfortunately, it would mean he was out of her apartment soon. She didn't know if she could actually handle him staying on her couch too much longer without throwing herself at him. His friendly flirting, and knowing his broad shoulders and tight ass slept on her couch, had driven her to some first-hand product testing of AYLI devices last night.

A light tapping behind her pulled her attention from the emails she scanned.

Seth leaned nonchalantly against the wall. His physical demeanor was calm, but his expression beamed. "She's giving me a trial run. After lunch, I sit down with the plans for the Thruster 2000 and see if I can figure out why it's not working. It's not really called that, is it?"

Bethany nodded. "Welcome to inappropriate yet accurate project names. Sue over in marketing already has a list of potential product names. While it's in production we typically go with a descriptive title. You should have been here when we created the Lick-her one-oh-one." Bethany snorted, her thoughts and her words were going to get her in trouble around this man. She would definitely like to have him lick her. Her hand flew to cover her face, and she continued to giggle. "And before lunch, what are you supposed to do?"

"I am supposed to impress the head of HR and have her go over paperwork and contingency hiring forms."

Bethany swiveled around in her chair. "Have a seat." She began handing sheets of paper to Seth, indicating which forms needed to be filled out and how.

Seth leaned back in the passenger seat as Bethany guided her car through evening rush hour traffic. "I'm sorry about my car not being ready. They didn't start working on it until today. I swear they've had it for over a week. I can't thank you enough, Bethany. You not only saved my butt from being on the streets, but I'm pretty sure you got me a job. And you're driving me all over the place."

"You think you can fix the design?"

"Yeah, it's really close, and I can see why it should work. Madge gave me until the end of the year to see what I can do with it. But if I can actually make it work before then, she's going to offer me a permanent position." He shifted to look at her. "Why don't we have a Christmas tree?"

"There is a big one in the lobby at work, what do you mean?"

"I mean at home, your apartment. You don't have a tree."

She shrugged. "I don't know. It doesn't seem worth it."

Seth leaned back. "Oh, you go home for Christmas? Get all the holidays you need there?"

Bethany shook her head. "There is no home. I mean, the apartment is home."

"What about your family back in Rock Falls?"

Bethany sighed loudly. "I don't know if you knew this, but my parents died in a car crash a few years after high school. My grandparents took care of me after that."

He hummed in understanding.

"And then they died a few years ago, so it's just me and a

distant aunt who I have vague memories of having met when I was really little."

"Sorry, I understand. I don't have family there either. Everyone either moved away or refuses to admit I exist. So what are we doing for Christmas?"

"You think you want to hang around with me for Christmas?" Bethany was shocked. She would have expected Seth, if not to have family obligations, to at least have plans with his friends.

"I couldn't think of a better way to spend my time. We should hit the grocery store tonight or tomorrow to stock up on snacks and supplies. We can make a cozy feast for the two of us. How does that sound?"

It sounded more than nice. It sounded romantic. "That sounds great, Seth. We can pick up a small tree while we're out." She blinked back unexpected emotion. This would be her first Christmas tree and the first time she'd really celebrated the holiday on her own. If she wasn't visiting a boyfriend's home or invited to some work-based lonely hearts group, she never bothered.

Bethany stared mournfully at the remnants of Christmas tree selections. The live trees were all dead and brown, and, of the pre-lit trees, the only choices were too big and expensive or unnatural colors. She was not convinced this was going to be a good idea.

Seth tossed another box of frozen appetizers in the cart. "I don't know about you, but on Christmans Day I think snacks and movies all day sounds perfect." His smile faded when he looked at her.

"Whats wrong, Bethy girl?"

Bethany sighed, the sweet and the bitter all mixed up into one. Seth already had a nickname for her, that made her heart soar. But the lack of tree options felt like a holiday kick in the backside. "No trees."

"What do you mean no trees? There's this one over here." He gestured broadly at the huge example.

"Too big."

"Okay, then we go avant-garde and get the white one and do all black and silver ornaments."

She giggled. "That sounds too chic for me."

"Then we do white with candy colored ornaments. It will be festive."

"A white tree? Will it work? Maybe no tree is best." She shook her head skeptically.

"Of course it will work. It will be Whoville meets Willy Wonka. Ridiculous and sweet. C'mon." Seth spun a pirouette in front of the tree then slid across the floor on his knees to be right in front of Bethany. "I'm begging, can we can we can we? Huh?"

Bethany's face felt like it was going to crack in half with her smile. An older lady paused and said, "When a boy that good looking is on his knees in front of you, you had better say yes."

Bethany started laughing. "Okay, okay, we can get the white tree."

He jumped up and kissed her on the cheek. "You'll love it, trust me."

Bethany closed her eyes as Seth wrangled the sample tree from the display. That kiss had been so soft, so unexpected. She was going to need to get more batteries for her personal collection of AYLI products, and soon, if he kept acting like this. Hell, if he kept acting like this, maybe she would find guts and make a move on him first.

Bethany pushed the overladen cart out of the checkout stall and towards the front sliding doors. They were well stocked for a fancy steak dinner, complete with pie and ice cream, along with several days' worth of snack food. On top of it all sat a snowy white tabletop Christmas tree and boxes of brightly colored ornaments.

"Damn, I forgot razor blades," Seth said. "I'll meet you back at the car. Sorry." He quickly disappeared in the direction of the pharmacy. Bethany sighed. He'd kiss her cheek, he begged nicely, he cooked, but he vanished as soon as she needed help with the heavy lifting. Typical man.

Bethany's fingers tapped out an impatient tattoo while she waited for Seth. He slid into the passenger seat in a rush, bringing the cold air with him.

"I thought we got all your stuff from Ricky's yesterday?"

"We did, just I just forgot how fast you go through razor blades when you have to shave your chest every day. That's going to be a nice little savings right there. These suckers are expensive. And if Madge offers me this job, I can stop shaving my chest."

The thought of Seth with dark curly chest hair caught her completely off guard. She gulped as she felt a blush wash over her entire body. She would love to get her fingers tangled in that while running them over his chest. She flushed harder.

"Are you okay? You're pink." Seth placed the back of his hand against her cheek and then her forehead. He pulled the glove from her fingers and placed her hand against the side of his face. "Your fingers are cold. Here." He reached for her other arm and pulled it across to him. He softly placed his lips on her wrist.

Bethany's blood felt as if it evaporated.

"Shhh, I'm checking your pulse."

Her pulse was through the roof. Her heart had taken off the second his lips were on her. When they brushed against her wrist, her toes curled and fires of lust sprang up all over her body. She leaned into his grasp, wanting him to put his mouth on the rest of her.

Stupid winter coats, stupid below freezing weather. She was bundled up and couldn't crawl into his lap as she wanted. Of course, her brain wasn't functioning. She was frozen in space, and Seth was checking her pulse with his lips.

"Your heart rate is up. You feeling okay?"

"Yeah," she answered, her voice soft as she fought to catch her breath.

"It must be the cold, and I didn't help with the groceries. You probably got a little chill unloading the cart. When we get home, you should rest. I'll bring everything in."

Bethany couldn't focus. What was she doing? Allowing Seth to stay at her apartment, getting him a job, and wanting him more with every passing second. Her high school crush on him had been bad enough, but this was infinitely worse. She felt like walking, talking nerve endings. This morning at breakfast he had eased past her, and the smell of clean Seth and his aftershave, combined with remembering what he looked like in a G-string, caused her to have to hide in her bathroom and cool down lest she maul the man.

Why couldn't she just tell him her feelings, invite him into her bed? Because she looked at Seth now with his broad strong shoulders and long flowing hair and saw the tall, lean kid with dark brown eyes she'd had a crush on, and she was sixteen again. She tripped over words, became flustered by a grin, no longer knew her left from her right. Bethany's inner dork ruled her body when Seth was around. Hard to be seductive when you're derping your way through the day.

Loud cheers emanated from across the office. Bethany kicked off her heels and padded over to the printer room to see what was up. Everyone was gathered around the 3-D printer watching it as it whirred and extruded bright orange plastic. With each humming pass, the Thruster 2000 began to take shape.

"Did you get it to work?" Bethany asked joining the group as they watched the excitement.

"We think so," Madge answered. "We should be able to tell if the mechanical motion is right on this model, and then we can send it to the guys in Spain to give us a functional sample."

"Spain?" Seth asked.

"Yeah, that's where all of our manufacturing is done. We haven't found a place in the US that is willing to work with us professionally," Jonsey explained. "They get all sexist and piggy when they have to deal with women."

"Or they don't want to touch our product expectations. The guys in Spain have provided excellent quality and don't seem to mind that this is a woman-owned business. That's kind of a big deal for me," Madge continued.

Seth nodded in understanding. His focus was on the device being extruded to life before their very eyes.

"This is going to take a while, well done, Seth. When it's ready, come get me. We need to talk." Madge patted him on the shoulder and left.

One by one the other team members returned to their desks. Bethany watched Seth's face. He looked like a kid in a candy factory. Awe, joy, and a single tear crossed his cheek.

"You okay, Seth?" Bethany asked.

He nodded and wiped the tear from his cheek. "It's been one hell of a roller coaster week. The highs are high, the lows are low. I'm just processing all of it, ya know." He turned to Bethany. "There goes my macho image, working for a bunch of women and crying."

"Seriously? You're gonna go all misogynistic asshole on us now?"

"No. But I don't want you to think that I'm overly emotional or that I'm losing it."

"There's nothing wrong with a little emotion, Seth." She rested her hand on his back.

Seth spun on her. Before she knew what was happening his arms were around her. "A little emotion is okay?" he asked before his lips descended onto hers.

Bethany froze, shocked to feel Seth's warmth enveloping her. Her senses reeled. Warm hands caressed her face as his lips continued to explore hers. She melted against him, pulling him closer, opening her mouth to feel his tongue lick against hers.

He pulled back. "That might have been a bit more than a little emotion." He continued to hold her. "Like I said, the highs have been really high."

She stared up into his face, not sure what to do or say. She wanted to preserve this moment in memory.

"Hey, Seth, whoa, sorry, I'll come back." Bethany turned to see Jonsey backing away from the print room.

Bethany stepped back, giggling nervously. "I...I should get back," she stammered.

Seth stared at her blankly.

"And Seth, that's a really good high. Really good."

Her pulse quickened as she watched his face break into a full grin. This Christmas was not going to suck, she decided on her way back to her desk.

Bethany still had problems focusing, and it was still Seth's fault. Now she couldn't help but think about his lips and his kiss. His embrace had been strong and not tentative. He had wanted to kiss her, he was assured and confident. And she wanted more.

Staring at the computer monitor in front of her did not make comprehending the email any easier. All the words said, "Seth kissed me."

"Hey, HR, are we going to have a problem if I hire your boyfriend?" Bethany jumped as Madge walked in.

"He's not my boyfriend," she blurted out.

"Not according to Jonsey. She said she walked in on one hell of a lip lock."

"I think he was just happy it's working. He said he's had a very manic week. That was just part of it. That's all." Her voice said one thing, but her brain was still screaming, "Seth kissed me!" She couldn't imagine that he would want to be her boyfriend. She could only hope.

"In any case, I'm not going to have a problem with the two of you if I hire him, am I?"

"You're going to hire him?" Bethany perked up. This would be perfect.

Madge nodded. "He's proven his worth in three days. He's easy to work with, and he seems to make my HR person very flustered, yet happy. Pull up the paperwork. I'd like to have it on my desk when he brings me the model for show and tell."

Bethany spun in her chair. Seth was right. This was one hell of a roller coaster week.

Bethany sat at the single chair in her kitchen. Next paycheck she needed to change that, especially if she was going to have Seth with her for a week or two more. She watched as Seth quietly chopped onions in preparation for their dinner. The scent of hot apple pie filled her apartment with a warm homeyness. Now if it would only spread to her as well. Seth had been uncharacteristically quiet on the drive home.

She wasn't sure if the Thruster 2000 had worked or if Madge had hired him. She was afraid to bring it up in case everything had gone south. She'd felt awkward around Seth after that kiss. She wanted more, but every time she got anywhere near him, she was overtaken by shyness.

Leaving Seth alone, she went into the living room. Bethany slid a Christmas CD into the DVD player and hit play. She tossed a shawl over the bouncing DVD logo on the TV while the speakers let the holiday music fill the apartment. She padded back into her bedroom and changed out of her work clothes. An overwhelming sense of dread filled her. Maybe this Christmas was going to be crappy after all. The music changed and picked up rhythm.

When Bethany returned to the kitchen, Seth's hips were twitching in time to the music. A smile crossed her lips as she watched him swivel and shuffle his feet. She giggled in delight as he spun all the way around.

"Come help me. These walnuts need pulverizing and you don't have a food processor." Bethany joined him at the counter. Seth's mood seemed significantly less somber than earlier.

"What do I do?" she asked.

He placed a bowl in front of her. "Pour about half a cup of these in." Seth handed her the bag of walnut pieces. "Now take the back of a large spoon." Seth reached around her, trapping her between his arms, his chest and the counter. He guided her hand in crushing the nut fragments between the wall of the bowl and the back of the spoon.

Bethany closed her eyes and leaned back against him as his warm breath caressed her ear.

"Hey, look up."

Bethany glanced up. Seth held something leafy and green over her head. "What's that?"

"Mistletoe." Seth's eyes twinkled at her. He spun her to face him and his mouth was on her before she had time to tell him it looked more like celery.

His lips were soft and exploring. A gentle quest against her own mouth. Bethany's soul did a flip, the kiss in the printer room had not been a fluke. She pulled Seth closer, wrapping her arms around his head and sucking his tongue into her mouth. She consumed him, and it felt like he consumed her back. His arms felt like vices around her.

Seth ran his hands down her back and scooped under her ass, lifting her. A clatter of dishes tinkled through her brain as Seth placed her on the counter. Their lips could not get enough of each other. Bethany wrapped her legs around his waist. She was lifted again as Seth began moving.

She barely noticed as her back collided with a door jam. Then she was on her back in bed. She tugged on Seth's clothing, completely ignoring buttons and zippers. In her haste to undress him, she forgot how clothing worked. Seth broke the kiss and pulled back. In a well-practiced dance move, he ripped his shirt open. Buttons flew across the room. Bethany fumbled with his belt and the waistband to his pants. Seth slapped her hands away and backed up.

Bethany watched wide-eyed as Seth began gyrating. She giggled. "I get a private show?"

"Only if you're good."

"I'll be the very best I can be," she said.

"Come here." Seth dragged her off the bed and into his arms. He began rocking her back and forth with a slow, side-stepping action. "I want to dance with you, Bethany."

She looked into his eyes as he caressed the side of her face. Her gaze followed his hand down her arm. He wrapped his long tapering fingers around hers. With a gentle pressure against her back, Seth guided her in a slow waltz. Bethany leaned into his shoulder, and he danced her around in the small space of her bedroom. Seth lifted her arm over her head and lead her around in a slow spin. Her cheek twitched, an involuntary tic, as the muscle wasn't sure if she wanted to smile or cry. She slapped her hand to her face, pressing against the muscle. He carefully removed her hand and began kissing her fingertips and then her palm.

Their eyes locked together. She shivered as Seth pulled her sweatshirt over her head. She traced the lines of his cheekbones, admiring how long his lashes looked as he gazed down. His fingers tickled trails over the tops of her breasts. Her abdomen clenched in an instant low self-esteem moment. When she'd changed clothes earlier, she should have put on sexy underwear. Of course, at the time, she hadn't dreamed this was an option for tonight.

But she relaxed within seconds. Seth didn't seem to care or notice her lack of matching undergarments. Her bra followed her shirt.

He pulled her in against his chest, pressing her breasts skin to skin with him. Their lips found each other again. Tongues, teeth, lips, breath. Bethany welcomed Seth into her mouth, and she gave him all of her desire. He lowered her to the bed. Bethany didn't want to let go of him, she wanted to hold him close, keep his warmth for herself. She felt empty and alone when Seth stood, leaving her on the bed. "Don't go anywhere." His voice was low and gravely.

In Seth's absence, Bethany shucked the rest of her clothing and slid under her covers.

Seth returned with a box, he ripped the top off and removed a foil square. "I really didn't need more razors." He smirked.

Bethany's mouth dropped open. Seth had been thinking about this, too, only he was more prepared to take action than she was. Bethany threw back the covers. "Get in here."

Seth kicked off his shoes and dropped his pants. He climbed in next to her. His smooth, warm skin slid against hers. His hardness pressed against her hip. Seth pulled her into his arms once more, legs twining together. He kissed the tip of her nose. "You aren't still in contact with Colin, are you?"

"What a weird thing to ask me right now Seth. I haven't thought about Colin since graduation."

He shook his head. "Bro code. I never asked you out in high school because Colin liked you. I just wanted to confirm I wasn't going to break any unspoken agreement."

"You honestly wouldn't continue with this if I was on speaking terms with Colin?"

"Hell, no, I wanted to be aware of whose toes I was about to crush." Seth grinned. "I've waited entirely too long for this. Bethany, I cannot believe you are back in my life."

A loud *beep beep beep* alarm and the smell of burned pie rolled into the room.

"The pie!" Seth sprang from the bed.

Bethany followed him pulling the top blanket along with her.

Seth stood nude under the fire alarm in her small hall, fanning the device, so the incessant beeping would stop. "Will you see how badly we killed the pie?"

Bethany pulled her admiring gaze away from his firm body to check the oven. She pulled out a smoking, crispy, dark brown pie. "It's dead, Jim."

Seth laughed as he approached her. "Thanks, Bones. Well, that's a fail."

"No, you were distracted," Bethany corrected.

"I was, wasn't I?" Seth grabbed the edges of the blanket and pulled her towards him. Bethany welcomed him back into her arms. "Shall we continue?"

"I think you need to tell me more about how you didn't ask me out in high school. I didn't think you even knew who I was. Would you have asked me out if you knew I had a crush on you back then?"

"You had a crush on me? I was such a skinny geek. My Adam's apple was bigger than my head."

"Yeah, but you certainly grew up nicely."

"So did you, Bethany Poirier. You know I always wanted to be the partridge in your pear tree."

Bethany's mouth fell open as she recognized Seth's double entendre. "You know the meaning of my name?"

"I had a crush on you, I did stupid things, like looking up your name on the web, comparing astrology signs. All that stupid shit."

"But you didn't ask me out?"

Seth shook his head. "One of my best friends at the time had the hots for you. I couldn't ask you out without destroying that relationship. And c'mon, in high school it's bros before hos."

Bethany smacked Seth across the chest. "Are you calling me a ho?"

Seth slipped into his Santa impression."Ho ho ho." His gaze softened as he looked at her. "Never, but I was seventeen and kind of stupid."

"And now?" Bethany asked.

"I'm twenty-eight and exceptionally stupid, but I finally have a chance to do something very much not dumb."

"This is very much not dumb." She pulled his face down to her and began kissing him.

The kiss deepened, the blanket dropped and forgotten. Seth scooped Bethany into his arms and carried her back to the bed. "Touch me," he said, laying her down and kneeling before her. He guided her hands across his chest.

"Didn't you have a tattoo the other night?" Bethany asked as she trailed her fingers back and forth across Seth's firm pecs. The hairs growing back in on his chest tickled her fingertips.

"Temporary, part of the costume."

"Hmm."

Seth returned the gesture and traced his fingers across Bethany's breasts. When he caught a nipple between his fingers, she gasped. She moaned when he replaced his fingers with his mouth. Seth's hand trailed lower across her belly and wrapped around her hip. She shivered.

Seth pulled his mouth from her. "What's wrong, Bethany? You're shaking."

"Nerves. What if this sucks?" Bethany wanted Seth so badly, but she couldn't stop quaking.

"It won't. It doesn't have to be perfect the first time, but it will be, because it's you and it's me."

Bethany smiled. "You're letting emotions show again."

"A little emotion is good, remember?"

"Remind me," Bethany said as she pulled Seth back down to her breast. She lifted her hips to him when his fingers found her folds. Her own hand found his shaft, hot and hard.

More touching, and then Seth slipped a condom into her hands. She dressed his length before guiding him to her core.

Bethany forgot her worries as Seth rocked into her. They pounded lust and passion and years of want into each other. She cried out as he pushed her over the edge of her own desires. A groan from him followed soon after.

"That did not suck." Bethany sighed as she curled up into a ball with Seth wrapped around her.

Bethany woke with Seth gazing at her. "What?" She smiled.

"I was so focused on how to thank you that I forgot to tell you Madge offered me the job." He leaned in for a kiss.

Beth turned away. For a second there she thought she was developing some seriously heavy feelings for Seth, and that all collapsed into a pit of despair in the middle of her gut. That hadn't been mutual emotion and lust. That had been a thank you fuck.

"Congratulations." Her voice was flat. She struggled to keep it as even as possible, suppressing the pain that tried to overwhelm her. "Go back to sleep."

The next time she woke, Seth was wrapped around her in a warm cocoon. His chest against her back, legs tucked up under hers. His soft, even breathing caressed her ear. She closed her eyes and let the good emotions remind her that this, right now, was something she had wished for, for years. Seth holding her. Seth as her lover. Seth.

But the memory of his confession last night returned like a sharp pain. This hadn't meant anything to him. This had merely been an elaborate thank you. He was paying her back with his body. No wonder he had no problems with the sex entertainment industry.

She couldn't relax against him anymore. The hurt was too poignant. Bethany started to get out of bed, but Seth's arm tightened around her middle.

"Merry Christmas, Bethy girl," he breathed against her ear.

"Yeah, merry fucking Christmas," she grumbled.

"What's the matter, hon?"

Bethany turned a sharp glare on Seth. "Congratulations on the job."

Seth hummed pulling her closer. "Thank you for your help with that, and thank you for giving me a place to stay, and..."

"Don't thank me for the sex, just don't." Bethany cut him off. She pulled away from him and sat up.

"Why not? It was wonderful. You are wonderful." Seth trailed his finger up and down her arm.

"Why not? Because I don't need to be your pity fuck. A card, a bottle of wine, something like that would have been just fine as a thank you." She stood and stormed off into the bathroom.

The hot shower didn't wash away the pain. She cried until the water ran cold. Good, Seth would get cold water for his shower.

Dressed, Seth sat on the couch, a present in his lap. Clearly, he had been waiting for her. He held up the box. "This is the thank you gift for letting me stay. Last night had nothing to do with me thanking you." He spoke tersely, biting the words through his clenched teeth. "Last night was because I was in love with you in high school, and I might just be falling in love with you again. Last night I was so nervous after kissing you that I didn't know how to speak. If you honestly think that last night was nothing more than a cheap gratitude fuck, then whatever you do, don't open the box."

Bethany stared at him, her wet hair dripping water onto the back of her shirt. Tears dripped from her chin onto the front of her shirt. "I...I'm sorry. I..." She stopped, unable to form words. She wiped at her face with her sleeve and tore into Seth's present.

Vibrant colors glowed from the ornate German glass ornament. A partridge in a pear tree. She looked up at Seth. This had deeper meaning for him than just being a fancy tree ornament. He'd let it slip last night, that he knew what their last names meant. She began sobbing. "I'm so sorry, I'm so uncertain. I jumped to the wrong conclusion."

Seth pulled her onto his lap, wrapping his arms around her. "I thought this could be our first Christmas together."

Bethany nodded enthusiastically. "I would like that very much. I'm an idiot. I've wanted you for so long. I guess I couldn't believe it was really happening. Forgive me?"

Seth stroked her hair. "It's really happening, and it's really wonderful."

Bethany pushed up, gazing deep into Seth's eyes. "I didn't get you anything. I don't have a box for you to unwrap."

Seth grinned. "I got my present last night. You were the best present to unwrap. And I'm going to keep you."

2

PERFECT CUP

*A*lexa wrapped her hands around the steaming mug, closed her eyes, and allowed the scent to enfold her. The fragrance was distinctly Middle Eastern. However, she couldn't clearly tell exactly what made it so. There was a hint of something floral like jasmine or rose, something sweet like honey, something tangy like orange peels, and something earthy like frankincense, but nothing definite, nothing clearly identifiable. That would be tricky later. She liked to be able to identify what in the tea made them special. Maybe this one was magical, or just a lovely new blend to share with her readers.

Alexa inhaled deeply, cleared her mind, and realized she had no clue what she was supposed to be doing. It was a planning day, she needed to map out the content for the next three to six months for her blog, but she wanted to bang out content. She wanted to bang.

She needed fresh air. This apartment-office-tomb was stuffy and closed in, having been shut up with the onset of the freezing winter months. She couldn't focus enough to determine what she needed to develop for her blog. The next six months needed to be fresh, and not more of the same 'cuddle up and keep warm with this blend.' There had to be a reason for people to keep coming back to her blog. Her blog was her livelihood, no readers, no income.

She shoved her feet into warm boots and pulled her parka on. She grabbed the first hat within reach, a ridiculous orange and red striped creation with a large pompom on top. The hat declared her position regarding a popular cult-status TV show, she was a fan.

She hit the sidewalk in front of her building and set off, destination clear-the-brain-and-begin-thinking-again.

I need a real live hero who drinks tea. I need someone to come in and save me from my brain. I need to interview some hottie British tea drinker. Oh Tom, Ben, Collin. Ben and Tom. Yeah, I could totally be the biscuit in that afternoon tea party. I need...I NEED TO GET LAID!

Alexa's brain meandered in too many different directions, never landing on one consistent concept for very long. Her internal stream of consciousness persisted until she realized she had stopped walking. She wasn't certain how long she had been standing, watching the action in front of her. She hadn't meant to stare. Her brain, being so distracted with various topics, hadn't exactly registered what her eyes had been doing.

"How're you doing?" The man she'd inadvertently ogled had a square jaw lined with a thin beard, nice lips, and a voice like liquid chocolate. He gave Alexa a little upward nod of his head. It was a shapely head with close-cropped, tightly curled hair. He had everything nice, and that was why Alexa figured he had mesmerized her as he carried cases of beer and water from a delivery pallet on the sidewalk into a building.

"No, no, I'm good," she stammered. *Oh my God, wrong answer stupid. And he's wearing a Santa hat.*

Red stocking cap with white pom-pom, tight jeans, and a T-shirt with the long sleeves pushed up. He didn't seem to be bothered by the cold. Alexa sighed as she watched him pick up another box and disappear into the dark of the building. His jeans displayed his ass to perfection. He even whistled. *Could he be any cuter?*

"You sure you don't need anything?" he asked again. This time she registered hints of a British accent.

"Just enjoying the show," Alexa gushed.

"By all means, enjoy away." He rolled his shoulders, did an

extra flex of bicep, and carried another box into the building.

Alexa's brain, not firing on all cylinders, took a moment to realize that she had just come across as the vilest, most sexist pig ever. Had she been a man doing that to a woman, she should have been slapped. Instead, he flexed for her.

"I just objectified you in a very demeaning manner, and you don't mind?" she asked him after he jogged down the few steps to the sidewalk.

The man paused. Damn, he was tall. Then he shrugged. "It's all part of the job. Look, if you want to objectify me without guilt and enjoy a real show, come by tonight. Doors open at eight." He pointed to the marquee on the building behind him. *Manfred's Manly Male Review.*

"Oh. Right." Alexa felt a little awkward, but she smiled. Alliteration always made her happy. *Manfred should have used manifestation instead of review...more Ms that way.* She had been ogling a stripper in his day wear, and he had just invited her to ogle him some more. "I think I just will."

"Bring a toy. We're having a charity drive." He smiled, flashing a set of dazzling white teeth. "See you tonight, Jayne."

Ung. Alexa put her hand on top of her hat. *Fandom.*

Alexa blended into the dark of the club. Sparkle and glam would have been the wrong fashion choice. She was glad she'd stuck with basic black. Glitter and sequins better served the women who arrived in groups and appeared to have already been drinking before attending the show.

Alexa purchased a local microbrew from the bar before finding a seat tucked into a corner. For some reason, she felt the need to hide once she arrived at the club. Could she really openly ogle the performers? Half of the current crowd was more than ready to objectify the men based on their rowdy behavior.

Well, she was out among people. She went out among people regularly, writing in coffee shops and tea parlors across the city. How was this any different? Yet again, she was alone in a crowd. This hardly qualified as human interaction.

The stage lights dimmed, and the woman next to her grabbed her arm. "I'm so excited!"

"Me too." She replied rather awkwardly. Well, that was definitely interaction. Alexa smirked. *That's two people today. I'm up 200%.*

Sound screeched and crashed, and lights swarmed around the club without focus. The music changed dramatically from loud and booming to tinkling and lilting. A Christmas carol filled the air, and the woman next to Alexa started singing along.

The stage curtains slid open, revealing a man half dressed in a Santa suit, lounging on a throne. Two ripped men costumed as elves pushed the throne forward, downstage. The audience squealed with excitement and delight.

The throne was elaborate: tall, gilded, ornate with gothic architectural detail; it was everything a throne should be. The "Santa" was not. He defied anyone's preconceived notion of what that jolly old elf was. There was no body fat on the man. He was lean and muscular. His long limbs betrayed his extensive height. His full-length scarlet robe of velvet, lined in ermine fur, cascaded around his frame, open, displaying an impressive collection of chest and abdominal muscles. Matching red britches and knee high, black leather boots completed his costume. There wasn't a gray or white hair anywhere on his head or face. Thick wavy ginger hair graced his head under a crown of holly leaves and berries, no stocking cap with a ball of fluff on the end for him. The smirk across his face denoted his withering scorn for the scene before him. He kicked lazily in time to the music.

Now that's a bad-ass man who clearly drinks tea. Holy crap! Alexa covered her mouth in an excited silent scream as she realized she could leverage tonight's show for her blog. She let out a particularly loud catcall to celebrate that this evening had just become a tax write-off.

The elves slid the throne back and out of the way. Alexa recognized her morning ogle-victim as one of the elves, and her jaw dropped. He'd looked hot and cute wearing jeans and a T-shirt. Now, shirtless with an open vest, poofy pants, and curly-toed shoes, he made the ridiculous costume look sexy.

The Santa looked around and deigned to stand. He tossed his long velvet cloak out of the way, the elves flanking him. He continued to act as if this was all beneath him.

Three sexually intimidating, ripped, with more abs than should be legal, Christmas characters stood poised ready to thrill.

The woman next to her leaned over and yelled over the music.

"That's one elf that can be on my shelf anytime."

"Seriously! I'll take the one on the left." Alexa laughed along with her new friend. The one on the left. He hadn't minded her watching him this morning and had even invited her to watch him tonight. She sighed. He was gorgeous. His skin glowed under a layer of gold shimmer body paint, making his dark tones warmer. Alexa wanted to touch all that rich skin that looked smooth and hard with muscles.

The triumvirate of hotness ground out their thrusts and poses as a boom-chakka-boom bass line turned the innocent Christmas carol into a soundtrack for soft-core porn disco dancing. Santa lost more of his clothes. When the first number finished, Santa was left in nothing but his boots, a holly wreath crown, and a bright red thong. Much to Alexa's disappointment, her elf was still mostly dressed, having only lost his vest.

The required holiday number out of the way, the show became grittier, the dancing sexier. The men hotter, if that was even possible. Alexa had to wait for two more numbers before her elf-crush returned to stage. He quickened her pulse. He made the nerves in her entire body scream out to be caressed. And he was nothing like any of her thin, delicate, pale, British, tea-drinking fantasy men. Her elf was solid and earthy, his strength was not hidden under refined clothing but out on display. There was something very visceral about her desire for this man.

Last night had been a complete success. Not only had she gotten out of her regular routine, which she clearly needed, but she had interacted with people and been inspired for an entire series of articles. She would have content for months.

Alexa focused, trying to return to the moment, enjoying the process and ceremony of making the tea. She placed the loose leaves into her rather boring, functional, stainless mesh tea ball. She had received hundreds of cute and clever tea infusers, however, none worked as well as this particular style. She placed the infuser into the pot, and then poured the boiling hot water. Once the tea began to steep, Alexa's brain cut loose from the process and contemplated how to find the right bad-asses to interview.

The walk in the brisk cool air yesterday had helped her brain find focus for work, so she decided to repeat it today. That, and she wanted the phone number from the door of the club. She knew she could search online for it, but the desire to possibly see her stripper-elf-crush inspired her to go in person.

She put her warm boots on, wrapped up in her parka, and skipped the striped hat before heading out. The front of the club was quiet, the windows dark. No hot stripper-elf loading in the morning's delivery. She took a picture of the front door focusing on the phone number, and with less enthusiasm, made her way back to her apartment.

"Hi, my name is Alexa Haywood, and this is going to sound like an odd request." She had waited until the afternoon when someone might be around to answer the phone. The gruff voice on the other end of the line confirmed that her timing was right and that her request was odd. Could he find out if any of the men from the performance the previous night considered themselves to be tea drinkers, and could she interview them for a series of articles profiling modern tea drinkers? He promised he would check and have someone call her back after she convinced him she would liberally sprinkle the name of the club throughout the interview. Free advertising was still free advertising.

"After all," she concluded, "it was one of your dancers who

inspired this idea. And I do want to give credit where credit is due."

To her surprise, the gruff voice called her back and told her to be at the club in twenty minutes. He had an interview for her.

Expecting the haughty ginger Santa for her interview—since she had made up her mind he drank tea—Alexa was shocked when elf-crush man walked in and approached her.

"You're my interview?" She gaped at him.

He smiled and gave a short laugh. "Yeah, this is about drinking tea, right?" She heard the slightest lilt of an accent in his voice again. It sent shivers down her spine. Her brain forgot how to form words.

"Yeah." Alexa sat back down after shaking his hand. "So, um, right. I'm tea. I'm Alexa and I have a blog on tea."

"Hi Alexa, I'm Tom and I drink tea. Sounds like a good match." He smiled. "Not wearing your cunning hat today?"

Alexa's insides slid all together into a formless goo. Her brain turned to mush. Moisture left her mouth. She licked her lower lip, trying to remember how to talk. His name was Tom, he was British, and he knew her fandom. *Could he be any more perfect?*

"So, Tom, why do you drink tea?" She groaned inwardly. That was the stupidest question. She had a notepad with a list of potential questions, and that was not one of them. She closed her eyes in abject humiliation at her own idiocy. She had better get the dumb unscripted questions out of the way, so that maybe, she could focus on the task at hand.

She held up her hand to stop Tom, elf-crush, hot man, and tea drinker from talking. Slowly, without opening her eyes, she pointed to the empty space above her head where a hat was not. "You watch?"

"I even cosplay the pilot. Cargo pants and tacky shirts make a comfortable costume, and I like to shake things up with a little interracial crossover."

Alexa couldn't open her eyes, she melted inside even more. Her eyelids cracked open and she peered at Tom. Trying not to blush, she began questioning Mr. Perfect, name of Tom, plays with dinosaurs, drinks tea, stripper. "So, Tom, you're a leaf on the wind?" *If he's gay, I'm going to walk into traffic and kill myself.*

"I typically quote Shakespeare to impress women, but if sci-fi movie quotes are your thing..." Tom chuckled.

Perfect, completely. "Will you marry me?" The words were out of her mouth before she realized what she was saying.

Tom laughed. "How about we go out for dinner first?"

Alexa gazed at Tom over the now cleared table. Tom had a warm smile, a hardy laugh, and his voice with overtones of a British accent made Alexa quiver.

"They want to close and go home for the night. Would you mind continuing this conversation at my place?" She blushed at the reaction Tom gave her. His look said that was too forward. His look did not say "hell yes."

"Or we could pick this up another time. If that's all right with you?" she said, talking fast to cover her embarrassment.

Throughout their evening Alexa had gotten much more than the interview material she needed for her bad-ass tea drinker profile. Tom was half English, and his mum drank tea every day. Since he stayed with her, he also drank tea. Alexa didn't chide him for still living with his mother. This city was expensive. More and more multigenerational families were going back to old traditions because of the financial climate.

If Alexa's tea blog hadn't hit it big, with good timing and what she considered sheer dumb luck, she would be living with roommates or back in Wisconsin with her parents.

"Why don't we pick this back up over breakfast?" Tom suggested as he stood and pulled his coat on.

Distracted by his long arms, Alexa didn't catch his next words. "I'm sorry what?"

"Oh, nothing," Tom mumbled and focused on his coat's buttons.

"No, really, what did you say? I didn't hear you." She asked as she stood.

"Should I call or nudge you?"

Alexa's jaw went slack. So, she hadn't been too forward. Her lips pulled up into a smug grin.

"You think your mom with let you spend the night?" Alexa used her best teasing voice.

"I'm a big boy. I don't think my mum is going worry too much." Tom stepped around the table and stood in front of Alexa.

Her nerves went haywire at his proximity. This was looking like a "hell yes." She stepped in, closing the gap between them. Her hands wrapped around the front edges of his jacket, pulling him in. "So you're a big boy? I can't wait for you to show me."

"The lady likes a little show and tell?" Tom cocked an eyebrow at Alexa.

Tom looked at Alexa's wall. It was covered in displayed teapots. Some sat on customized shelves, others seemed to just float in front of the wall. She had an extensive collection, ranging from traditional Japanese ceremonial pieces to traditional English service sets and everything in between and beyond. Tea paraphernalia lined bookshelves. Her kitchen counter was stacked with boxes and small cloth bags, the labels indicated it was all tea.

"You weren't joking when you said you were a professional tea blogger, were you?" he asked, his voice raised so she could hear him from the other room.

Alexa came out of her bedroom. "No, I wasn't."

He had thought her cute the first time he saw her all mismatched and bundled up. Her verbal fumbles when they'd met again this afternoon had been endearing.

But now?

He gulped. She stood before him in a pale slip and matching satin robe. Her light brown hair was brushed smooth and flowed around her shoulders. He could make out the shape of her pert nipples through the thin fabric. She was sexy as hell.

"I don't want to talk about tea anymore tonight." Her voice had taken on a sultry husky tone.

"I don't think... I can't... form coherent words with you looking like that." Tom was the one fumbling over his words now.

"Then don't."

He pulled his shirt off over his head and then crushed Alexa to his chest. She was soft in his arms. He slid his lips over hers, tasting peppermint.

Her hands tickled across his chest as she explored his skin. Tom hadn't realized how petite she was until he wrapped his arms around her, delicate. He wanted to merge her into his skin, but he was afraid if he pulled her any closer she might break.

He deepened the kiss, exploring her mouth with his tongue, sucking her breath into his body. He slipped the robe over her shoulders. It slithered to the floor, cool and sensual when it pooled against his bare feet.

Alexa had invited him to get comfortable when they'd entered her apartment. She had kicked off her shoes, so Tom had followed suit. They had cuddled on her couch watching an episode of a popular cable show. The plot turned particularly sexy, and the next thing Tom knew Alexa's mouth was on his and hands were groping body parts, hers on him and his on her.

When she excused herself for a moment, Tom paced, inspected her tea collection, and mused at how strange life was. He had just met her, thought she was cute, and now...

Now he was going to make love to her. He was thinking too much, he knew it. Alexa skimmed her hand down his chest and tickled below his bellybutton. Thoughts turned to need as she pulled at his zipper, and blood left his brain.

"Oh, that's lovely." She purred, reaching in through his open jeans and stroking him.

He couldn't think. She had laughed at his jokes over dinner. His physique clearly impressed her, now her hand was on him, caressing his skin. Tom lifted her easily, crossed her living room, and entered her bedroom.

He eased her down onto her bed. "What do you want from me, Alexa?" His voice sounded like gravel to his own ears.

"For now, just you. I don't need anything fancy, just you."

She deserved fancy. She deserved silver settings and Shakespeare quotes. For now, he would give her what she wanted. He removed the condom he kept in his wallet and shimmied out of his jeans before sliding into the bed next to her.

Her body was pliant, her skin tasted like ambrosia. She was warm under his fingers and hot and wet under his weight. They moved in a rhythm that guaranteed enjoyment and crashed together when their bodies could no longer stand the pleasure of it all.

Pancakes? Alexa smelled pancakes.

She needed to keep this man. He quoted her favorite movies, his body did amazing things to hers, and he was making breakfast.

"Morning, beautiful," he said as she shuffled into the kitchen. She had wrapped up in a thick robe to ward off the chill.

Tom looked better than the pancakes smelled. Even fully dressed, he sent shivers through her body. Or maybe that was a leftover memory from last night.

"You cook?" she asked. She relaxed into a chair at the table. Tea was already steeping in one of her functional pots. He hadn't just tossed a tea bag into a mug. She was impressed, then again, he had admitted his English mother had trained him properly.

"My mum didn't raise me to be a slacker. Speaking of, I need to go home and check on her birds." Tom placed a plate with a short stack of fluffy pancakes in front of her.

She tilted the pot and filled the tea cup waiting for her. Tom sat across from her, his own plate stacked high.

"Birds? Can't she do it?"

"Mum's in England. Visiting her sister over the holiday. You want to come? I'd like it if you would."

The earnestness in Tom's expression and tone when he asked her to come with him melted her. Alexa already was in emotional peril from this man. Spending more time with him was the utmost thing she wanted to do. Tom and emotions were a positive combination. Her stomach did a flip.

"Sure, sounds like fun. Birds." Alexa didn't typically like birds, unless they came with a knife and a fork. This was going to be interesting.

A large white cage took up as much space as the couch did. Alexa hovered back by the door when Tom led her in.

"C'mon. They're over here."

"I can see them fine from here." Rats with wings, why would anyone want to keep them in their apartment?

"Alexa, what's the matter? You're a bundle of nerves. Mum's not here, and if she were, she doesn't bite."

"I'm not worried so much about being bit, as I am being pecked," she admitted. And getting the bird plague.

"What? You have a problem with the birds?"

She nodded, still not moving further into the apartment.

Tom strode back to her, slipped his hand under her elbow, and guided her to the couch. "Sit."

Alexa sat. Still nervous, she twisted her fingers in her scarf. She stared at the birds, they were kind of pretty, and that cooing sound they made wasn't horrible. Tom left her to make noises in the kitchen. Cupboards opened and closed. Water ran and was shut off. He reemerged and began fussing with the large bird cage.

When he turned around, Alexa saw he held a tannish-gray pigeon cocooned in his large hands.

She breathed deeply and squirmed as he brought the bird over to her. She did not want to touch it.

"Would you like to hold it?" Tom asked.

His raised eyebrows and little grin said please. Alexa acquiesced, against her personal prejudices.

Tom guided her through how to hold the bird and then carefully transferred the animal into her hands. Alexa could feel its heart beating rapidly. Its small warm body quivered in her hands. It was more afraid of her than she of it.

She cooed at the bird, attempting to calm it. It was fascinating, and amazing, and not nearly as frightening as she had assumed it would be.

She smiled up into Tom's face. "What is it? It's not a typical pigeon. It's a dove, right? Dove gray, the color, is because of the bird."

Tom made motions to claim the bird from her.

"Oh, let me." She stood and met him by the cage. Tom opened the door and Alexa released the bird back in.

"Turtle Doves," he said. "As in the second day of Christmas my true love gave to me..."

"Two turtle doves, and a partridge in a pear tree," Alexa finished for him.

"Dad gave Mum two of them their second Christmas together, she's kept doves ever since."

"That's sweet."

"Not really," Tom scoffed. "Bastard ran off before he could make good on five golden rings after five years together. I always thought it was something I would do properly. The whole lot over twelve years."

Alexa's smiled at the idea, twelve years' worth of gifts already planned out. "What did she do with her pear tree?"

"Oh, that. Mum has this wicked recipe for braised pheasant with poached pears."

Alexa nodded. It sounded divine.

"I was thinking." Tom pulled her into his arms. "Unless you have other plans, I could make it for you for Christmas dinner."

"The braised pheasant?" Alexa wrapped her arms around his waist and smiled into his eyes. "Why would you do that?"

"To properly start the tradition, of course. It wouldn't be nearly as meaningful to start with our second Christmas together."

"You want to start a tradition with me?" Alexa blinked. Her insides quivered in excitement.

"I do, what do you say?"

"I guess I'd better make sure I don't have other plans." Alexa lifted onto her tiptoes and pressed a kiss against Tom's lips.

3

THREE FRENCH COCKERELS

*T*he parking lot was already full with vendors and other participants for the Ladies Auxiliary's First Annual Winter Chicken Festival as Tyler guided his pickup and trailer through the back gates at the county fairgrounds. Not bothering to find a place to park, he pulled up next to the side entrance for vendor check in. He jumped out and walked around to open the passenger door and help his grandmother down. "Nan, why can't this just be a Christmas market like we've done every year since forever?"

"Move into the twenty-first century already, Tyler. Christmas is not inclusive. Not everyone celebrates Christmas or the holidays. But everyone loves chickens." Nan grasped Tyler's hand and leaned on him, as he helped the five-foot-nothing President of the Ladies Auxiliary down from his truck. "Just because we're a little backwater town in rural Kentucky doesn't mean we aren't progressive. It's time to show the rest of the world how great this state really is. Southern hospitality doesn't cut out anyone. When Jesus said 'love thy neighbor,' he didn't specify which ones, now, did he?"

"No, ma'am, he did not." Tyler escorted his grandmother over the gravel and onto the paved sidewalk.

"Should I sign you up for the charity strip-off?" she asked in all seriousness.

"Nan!" Tyler hoped he wasn't blushing. She always had to point out when he blushed, and that made it worse.

"We can't have a sexist Cutie Pie contest for the women without something equally racy for the men. Your cousin Ash will most likely win. But you should sign up. Represent."

Tyler shook his head. His grandmother embraced modern living, the Internet, and its ideas. Sometimes hearing the words coming out of her mouth made him wonder if it was a good idea for her to have a computer and satellite TV.

"Of course Ash will win. He's a fireman. I think it's a job requirement to be built that way." Tyler shrugged. Ash was definitely the winner of the gene pool in their family. Tall, ripped, and athletic, he had a fan club that seemed to follow him everywhere.

"Or that good looking Darren Halpern might win. He can do a mean two-step, so he might have smoother moves," Nan said without a hint of irony or giggle in her tone.

"Darren is better looking than Ash. But Ash knows how to show off more. Both of them are pretty buff."

Nan stopped and gripped Tyler's hand. She had impressive crushing power for a seemingly frail, ninety-year-old woman. Technically his great-grandmother, but since no one spoke of the controversy surrounding her daughter, everyone ignored the great part. She gasped. "Tyler, are you gay and coming out to me?"

He chuckled. She'd been waiting for a moment like this for years. To have an openly gay grandson she could dote on would prove her hipness to the rest of the Ladies Auxiliary. She would have to wait for another generation for that possibility. "No, Nan, I'm not gay. But you would be the first person I told."

She reached up. Tyler had to bend over so that she could pat him on the cheek. "You know I will love you no matter what."

He patted her hand as it rested on his face. It was moments like this that made him hope she would live forever. She loved her grandchildren better than their own parents did. "I love you, too, Nan. But I like girls...a girl...a woman," he corrected himself. Damn. He hadn't meant to say that.

Her laser keen eyes sparkled at him. "Hmm?" The noise

seemed innocent enough, but Tyler knew Nan wouldn't leave him alone until she knew who it was.

Tell her now and get it over with, or spend the rest of time being pestered until he confessed? Tell her now. "Please don't say anything, Nan. It's Kolby Devin."

"She's a pretty thing. Good hips. Breeds chickens out past Traitor's Ridge. Why haven't you asked her out yet? She's not a tramp like that Justine Smith, is she?"

"No, ma'am. But she is out of my league," Tyler confessed as he rubbed his middle.

"Don't give me any of that twaddle. You are a nice looking hunk of a man. Any woman would be proud to have you."

"Not when Ash is my cousin. She doesn't know, so please, Nan, just don't say anything." He gave her his best puppy dog eyes and hoped she would take pity on him.

"I'll give you until the end of the week before I say something. I think that's reasonable. Now go set up those fancy chicken coops of yours at the entry booth so we can get this party started."

Kolby hauled her third fowl cage onto the display table as the rooster inside scrabbled on the tilted surface. He complained low in his throat, warbling in his distress. If he could cuss her out, he would. He would add extra choice words to what his two brothers already on the table would have said if they could talk. "I know baby, I know," she cooed at the large orange and black French Copper Marans.

Natalie Cleary pulled a cart laden with her own show bird into the tent.

Kolby watched as a large black rooster rolled past. "Hello, gorgeous. That is the gothiest bird I've ever seen. You finally got one of those Thai birds!"

"You mean Indonesian. Ayam Cemani. This is Hercules. He's pretty but..." Natalie groaned, indicating the headache the show bird was giving her.

"I thought once you go black, there's no going back?" Kolby laughed.

Natalie shook her head. "Seriously. Either I switch over my whole flock, or I put this guy on a time out. His flesh is black, which freaks people out entirely too much. No one wants to eat black chicken meat. He's useless for breeding. That's how I managed to get him so cheap."

"What about cross breeding? We could hook him up with one of my Marans." That extra level of glowing blue and green plumage would be beautiful in her already dark feathered hens.

"You don't want him getting jiggy with your girls. Dominant hyper pigmentation, and if the offspring don't come out all black, they're funky through and through. No one wants to eat funky chicken."

"Funky chicken is for dancing, not for frying." Justine Smith bounced in between the two women. She wiggled her finger between the bars of the crate. "Hey, pretty fella. So next time someone presents you with a big black cock, you're going to run screaming in the opposite direction?" She tilted her head at Natalie.

Natalie held up her finger, poised to pontificate, and then she froze. She stroked her chin, deep in thought. "Are we talking birds or Sheriff Addams?"

"So that's how it is?" Kolby laughed.

"Uh huh. I'm really hoping he joins in that charity strip-off." Natalie's voice went all soft and squishy around the edges.

"That's like one step to the side of a bachelor auction. I'm not sure if this is better or worse." Kolby commented.

"Does it matter? He's dreamy." Natalie's eyes clouded over.

Justine ignored Natalie's drift off into fantasy land. "Did you see the backyard chicken hutches Tyler made? They're like little fairy cottages for urban chicken keepers."

"Which Tyler? Briggens or Weiss?" Kolby asked.

"Tyler Weiss," Justine clarified.

Kolby sighed. "Oh, now he's cute. He bails the hay on my front acreage."

"Did you just sigh over Tyler Weiss? He's tubby," Justine added.

"So? I don't mind a little girth on a man. He has the nicest eyes and sweetest smile." Kolby momentarily got lost in her own Tyler-induced fantasy. She'd been hoping Tyler would ask her out. Apparently taking drinks and snacks to him whenever he was mowing or doing other handyman chores she could do herself—but hired him for anyway—wasn't an obvious enough hint that she liked him. She didn't think her flirting skills were that lacking. She wouldn't mind seeing him up there for the strip-off. If she tossed enough tips his way, maybe he'd clue in.

"Are you registering for the Miss Baked Chicken?" Justine twisted side to side, swishing her skirt around. "I want to be queen of this festival." She spun in place.

Kolby blinked and focused on her friend's dress. She hadn't even noticed that Justine was all dolled up. Her hair and makeup were always spot on. Between loading the birds and dodging the innuendo, Kolby hadn't lowered her focus below Justine's neck.

"You look fabulous. I'm not, but I'll walk over with you. The boys are set for now. You coming, Natalie?"

"Nope, I gotta get my big black cock settled. He's being fussy." Natalie twitched a smile at her friends.

"She's going to have so much fun with that one today, isn't she?" Kolby asked Justine as they left the rooster display tent.

"It's so going to bite her on the ass if she says it around Brett Addams."

"Naw, I think she wants him to hear her saying something like that. Maybe it will give him an excuse to ask her out, or…"

"Or for her to jump his bones without the pretense of a date."

Kolby hovered as Justine filled out the single page form required for her to enter the pageant and talent competition.

Mrs. Weiss pushed a form across the table towards Kolby. "Aren't you going to fill one out, sweetie?"

Kolby shook her head. "No, ma'am, I don't go in for pageants. I don't have the poise."

"Nonsense. You have nice hair, good cheekbones, perky boobs, and a good waist to hip ratio. That's all the judges are ever looking at anyways. Okay, not the Miss Baked Chicken pageant. How about the Cutie Pie contest?" the little old lady asked. "Les Unmentionables is providing the lingerie."

"I didn't bake anything," Kolby explained. Tyler's elderly grandmother was making her nervous. The old lady had a reputation as a matchmaker. Kolby had a sinking feeling she was lined up in Mrs. Weiss's sites like Bambi on the first day of hunting season.

Justine handed over her entry form. "I don't understand why we can't call it the Miss Kentucky Fried…"

"Copyright nonsense and fast food, that's why," Mrs. Weiss replied. "I was hoping when they changed the name of the restaurant to the letters we could get our name back."

"It's just as well we call it The Baked Chicken Pageant, and since we're being inclusive with this event the title is split between Miss and Mister," the other lady working registration added.

"That's right. We'll have one young man and one young lady with a half Baked title," Tyler's Nan confirmed with a nod.

Tyler held the puppy for his cousin while Ash copped a feel from the latest cute girl who had asked him for a photo. *Pics with a Fireman and a Puppy* was raking in the charitable contributions. Ash had been on duty, and shirtless, for the first hour with one of his coworkers. The line of women wanting their picture with a shirtless fireman and a random puppy had to include every woman in a three-county area. Tyler killed time by hanging out and playing with the puppies. Not only was the photo booth raising money, they were also adopting out the puppies for the local animal shelter.

Only an hour into the First Annual Winter Chicken Festival and three puppies had already been adopted.

"Thank God tight jeans came back in fashion," Ash muttered loud enough for Tyler to hear as they both watched the most recent female ass sashay away.

"You doing the pageant, man?" Tyler asked.

"Pageant and strip-off. The chief encouraged us to participate in at least one as part of our civic duties. You?" Ash picked up one of the floppy-eared puppies and scratched it on the belly.

Tyler shook his head. "No way in hell, man. Nan said I should, but nuh-uh."

"How is your Nan?" Mrs. Hepple asked as she stepped into the booth. She picked up a fluffy brown and white mop of a dog and handed it to Ash.

"Nan is spitting fire as always, Mrs. H." Ash put an arm around the woman's shoulder and posed with the dog.

She paused in her conversation long enough to smile for the camera. "Did I hear you say you were doing the pageant? Good for you. It's a shame we couldn't go back to calling the pageant its original name. We live in Kentucky. We fry chicken here. Secret recipe, my tushie. Everyone knows it's the buttermilk."

Ash placed the puppy in her arms. She passed it back to Tyler.

Kolby and Justine swept into the booth. Tyler forgot how to move. Kolby stepped right up to him and began petting the puppy in his arms.

Any blood that might have been left in his brain immediately headed straight for his groin when she smiled and batted those big honey brown eyes at him.

"Hey, Tyler," she purred between making cooing sounds at the puppy.

"Get over here, Kolby," Justine demanded. "We're gonna have a three way with Ash..." She left the rest of the sentence hanging.

Ash chuckled. "For the picture, Justine."

"Are you going to be the mister to my miss in the Baked pageant?"

Justine's words faded as Kolby returned the puppy to Tyler's arms. She was all he could see, all he paid attention to.

"You going to enter the pageant?" Kolby asked him.

He couldn't form words. Whenever she spoke to him, he became an idiot.

Ash seemed to sense his awkwardness and butted in. "No,

but my man T is going to enter the strip-off. How 'bout that, ladies?"

"I can't wait." Kolby's eyes seemed to get wider and brighter, but Justine's voice cut through, killing his momentary joy.

"That will be good for a laugh." Justine cackled and walked arm in arm out of the photo booth with Kolby, along with any semblance of self-esteem Tyler may have had.

"Why the hell did you say that?" he fussed at his cousin.

"Did you see the look on their faces? They think it's going to be a hoot! You have to do it now, man." Ash laughed and slapped Tyler on the shoulder.

His cousin might have more obvious muscles, but Tyler was taller than the brash firefighter by a solid inch and outweighed him. Tyler considered punching Ash in his rock-hard abs before realization struck. He was going to have to sign up for the strip-off.

Kolby sat on a display table in the rooster tent swinging her legs back and forth. A gaggle of small children ran through the area, knocking into one of the tables and jostling the bird crates.

"Hey! No running," she called after them. Kids shouldn't be allowed loose around like that. Where were their parents?

She jumped off her perch and approached the crate with Marmalade, her prize French Copper Marans, making shushing noises at the riled-up bird. A snick and a grinding noise caught her attention. She turned to see one of the little miscreants unlock the cage holding a very large Brahma rooster. The freakishly large bird was fluffy and the size of a medium dog—and could do a lot of damage with his talons if he put his mind to it.

So could she, but the bratty kid scampered as she cussed at him. The now-freed rooster skittered around the tent. She felt like a fool chasing the big ball of feathers around the tables. She finally intercepted him. The bird calmed as soon as Kolby gathered him into her arms, but she still got a face full of fluff.

Natalie sauntered up with a bag of cotton candy in her hand.

"S'up? It's candy cane flavored," she declared as she shoved it at Kolby.

"Some idiot tried to set the big guy free." Kolby reached in and pulled off a piece of the spun sugar.

"Stupid kid, but I am loving this fair. They're sneaking in bits of Christmas here and there. You know what? I think the Ladies Auxiliary had a great idea by ditching the whole Christmas theme. I mean, there's still tons of shopping, tons of food, but I'm glad of the break. It's been non-stop Christmas carols since before Thanksgiving."

"I hear you. I'm enjoying not having to see all the ugly sweaters—"

"Did you see the one on Maisie Hepple?" Natalie made gagging noises.

Kolby shook her head. "No, but her mom had something pretty hideous on."

"Speaking of wearing something hideous, did you and Justine hit the *Pics with a Fireman and Puppy* booth?" Natalie asked.

"What was hideous about that?" Kolby furrowed her brow. Everything in that booth had been really cute, including the blushing Tyler.

"Nothing. I just wanted to know if you saw them. Hubba hubba." Natalie sucked in her breath and shut her mouth. Kolby followed her gaze, Laverne and Maisie Hepple had entered the tent.

"…and then can you believe Barbara Jones is walking around spouting off about how the secret recipe is baking soda," Laverne said to Maisie as they strolled by.

Natalie and Kolby watched as mother and daughter, in matching ugly Christmas sweaters, passed through the display tent, without paying any attention to the roosters, or the two women staring at them.

Kolby lost control of her laughter first. It burst from her like water escaping a damn.

"Come on, let's get out of here." Kolby grabbed Natalie's wrist and dragged her out of the tent. "The strip-off is starting soon."

✳

One tent over from the roosters housed the "sexist contests," as Nan had called them.

Tyler sat sweating like a hooker in church on a Sunday in August without air conditioning as he watched the Cutie Pie auction.

Civic-minded single women modeled revealing underwear supplied by a local lingerie boutique while auctioning off home-made baked goods.

It was a county fair favorite, so of course, Nan and the other ladies of the Auxiliary felt it should be included in the Winter Chicken Festival.

There were some fine young women in Belvoir County. And some fine older ones, too. And they were on display, all their glorious jiggly bits and all their smooth bits. He couldn't help but watch. Ash, Darren, and a few other guys from the fire department made inappropriate catcalls. But that was the whole point, right? A little cheesecake now and some pie later? Of course, Ash kept nudging Tyler in the ribs asking if he was interested in the hair pie that each cutie was hiding.

Tyler was mortified by his cousin's behavior and at his own thoughts. None of the women present had the pie he wanted—that belonged to Kolby.

The last of the Cuties left the stage. The MC jumped in front of the mic and began his banter about legs, breasts, and baked goods. "Okay, okay, bidding on the pies is now over. All you men in the audience, it's your turn now to show off the goods. Time to show these ladies we know how to bring home the bacon and dish it out, too! The First Annual Winter Chicken Festival All Male Strip-off has begun!"

On cue the people in the tent whooped it up with hollers and whistles.

"Come on, guys, it's first come, first served." The MC swept his hand, indicating the side table where Nan and her cronies sat, ready to sign up the hapless men willing to remove their clothes in the name of charity.

"Okay, ladies out there, can I hear you?" The MC pointed the mic out into the crowd. This time the women present catcalled and hollered.

Tyler cringed. He wanted to fold in on himself, disappear, and walk out the door. But Ash would see that as chickening out and would razz him about not having balls for the rest of his natural life. Some days he hated his cousin. This was one of them. At this point, Tyler just hoped he survived the rest of the afternoon with the ability to reclaim the dignity he was about to hand over to Nan's sign-up sheet.

A quick glance around confirmed Kolby wasn't here to witness this. That would be entirely too much.

As the men lined up to compete, the music in the tent changed. Light country pop had accompanied the Cutie Pie contest, and now bow-chicka-bow-wow porn thump and boom filled the air.

"We have some rules. First rule, no touching the participants. They can't touch you, ladies, and you cannot touch them. At least while they're performing. I don't care what you get up to out back afterward. But please remember this is a family event." The MC hunched over the mic. "So don't get caught."

He held up a finger with each new rule. "Second rule, skivvies, gentlemen. You must keep them on." The audience responded with loud boos. "Third rule, have a good time, and remember this is for charity. All tips collected today will be donated to the local Angel Tree and the Belvoir County Food Bank to help out those less fortunate this time of year."

The MC stopped and indicated the sign-up table. Darren and Ash were jostling with each other over who got to be first. Nan slowly made her way onto the stage.

Tyler groaned. There was no way this was going to end well.

She took the mic in her tiny, firm grip. "We're gonna start this show with a twofer. I expect you young ladies out there to double down on the tips. Ash and Darren, you boys get up here and start us off right." The MC escorted Nan off the stage.

Ash sauntered up on stage, his thumbs hooked in the front of his yellow fireman's pants. Darren followed behind, nodding in his cocksure way with arms out stretched, palms up, and fingers beckoning in a 'bring it on' motion.

The shouts from the spectators drowned out the music. Both men began gyrating on stage.

Ash made good use of his suspenders while Darren played with his belt, turning it into a phallic prop.

When T-shirts went flying, the whoops got even louder. Both men put their well-developed muscles on display.

Tyler groaned and tried to edge his way out of the crowd. His escape was foiled, he crashed into Kolby and Natalie as they pushed their way into the tent.

"Where you going, Tyler? Aren't you going to get up there and shimmy for us?" Natalie's voice was a tease.

He slid his gaze to Kolby. Was she blushing? She didn't look at him but focused on the stage.

"Oh, Tyler, will you?" Why did her voice sound like she had been running hard, all raspy and trying to catch her breath?

Tyler shook his head. "No one wants to see me."

"That's not true." Kolby's eyes locked on his. The look she gave him now made him want to do anything she asked. Deep in his gut, he just hoped she wasn't encouraging him to be mean.

He returned his attention to the men on stage. Ash had successfully dropped trou and was cavorting about in plaid boxers, much to the delight of the crowd. And much to the delight of the Ladies Auxiliary, dollar bills littered the floor like snow.

Darren still had his jeans on. He slid his torso around and grabbed the button at his waist. He undid the button, pulled the jeans forward and looked down at his crotch. He shook his head in an exaggerated gesture.

The music ended, and the MC jumped up on stage. "I think our winner for this little strip-off is Ash. So Darren, why'd you freeze?"

Darren leaned into the mic. "I didn't freeze, Johnny. Remember the rules? I ain't wearing skivvies." He emphasized the last word with a crotch thrust.

The decibel level in the tent blew out Tyler's ears. Dollar bills rained down.

Tyler glanced over at Kolby, whose hands were clapped to the side of her head. She laughed with a wide smile. He would do anything for that smile. If that included making a complete ass out himself for the next ten minutes, so be it.

He shuffled his feet, not sure if he should say something—wit was beyond him in Kolby's presence—or if he should head for the sign-up table. His decision was made for him as he heard Nan's voice crackling through the mic.

"Tyler Weiss, get your butt up here and show this halfwit cousin of yours what a real man looks like."

Hands pressed him forward. Tyler was in front of the crowd in what felt like no time. He wasn't even certain if he used his own legs to propel himself onto the stage.

He stared out over the crowd, at first unable to see much because of the stage lights There was music playing. He could sort of hear it under the cacophony of sound bombarding him. Not a comfortable dancer, Tyler twitched his hips side to side.

Roars of laughter crashed over him in waves.

Great, this was all a bad joke. And he was the butt of it. Tyler paused and spun away from the audience. He needed to think.

No, he was a dumb ass. No one was going to think he was sexy. He didn't need to try. Hell, he wore a similar outfit to Darren, plaid shirt, and jeans. The clothes looked completely different on the two different men. Darren got women. Tyler got laughs. Laughs. If he attempted to shake it like Ash or Darren, he would be humiliated. But if he did something entirely different, if he hammed it up and encouraged these people see him as a big goober, he would be in charge.

And maybe he could make some money for charity along with impressing Kolby with his sense of humor.

Tyler relaxed. He twisted his upper torso and peeked at the audience. He gave them a little finger wiggle of a wave. Another crashing wave of roaring cheers.

But it was okay. Goober was in control now.

He did his best sashay, mimicking every woman he had ever seen in high heels, over to the edge of the stage. He leaned over, making sure to push his ass out, and snatched the cowboy hat from the MC, which he cockily placed on his own head. More laughter crashed around him.

Tyler unbuttoned his plaid shirt, one button at a time. He

made sure to struggle with the third button and untuck the shirt halfway in the process. Dollar bills filled the air. For a moment he paused and watched the money flutter around him. He followed a few of the bills down. His gaze landed on Kolby. She was smiling and laughing.

He felt his balls tighten at her grin. Tyler swallowed hard, trying to find moisture in his arid mouth. It's a show, so give her a show.

He bent his knees and stuck his butt out in the most pin-up girl, cheesecake pose he could think of, and then gave Kolby a big saucy wink.

He stumbled trying to right himself when she clasped her hands to her heart and rolled her eyes toward heaven.

She was just playing along, right?

Tyler finished unbuttoning his shirt and again turned his back on the audience. He slowly opened the shirt wide and then closed it. He pulled the shirt off one shoulder, following the move with a glance back at the crowd. They already knew he was wearing a gray T-shirt underneath, as it had been clearly visible from the unfastening of the first button. The folks in the tent still responded with catcalls and whoops of encouragement as if he were exposing flesh and not another layer of clothing.

A few more teasing shimmies and he removed the plaid shirt. He faced the audience with a spin and was greeted with a loud crash and screams.

His audience was screaming, but not with laughter. Everyone focused at some commotion around knee level. People scattered. The entire audience was either running toward the walls or chasing after objects he couldn't detect past the stage lights.

Finally his eyes adjusted. Tyler trotted to the edge of the stage, where a large bundle of flapping, squawking feathers flew up into his face.

Instinctively, he reached for the object—and grabbed onto the warm body of a very irate rooster. The beast pecked him on the nose, and Tyler dropped the bird. The bird lunged for him again. Eight pounds of angry fowl jumped up his legs, clawing and pecking at him. Tyler ran back to where he had dropped his shirt, the rooster attacking him the entire time. He tossed his shirt, and covered the squawking beast. The hell was going on?

Someone yelled, "Who's the idiot that set all the roosters free?"

Roosters scattered everywhere. Kolby couldn't believe her eyes. There were roosters in the strip show. It took her a long moment to reorient herself to what was happening. One minute Tyler was on stage hamming it up in a mocking strip tease that felt like a performance just for her. Did he realize how sexy his sense of humor was? Next birds were running wild around her knees.

One kid dove for a bird and caught him by the feet. "Don't hurt the birds!" Kolby yelled at him. Some of these show birds were worth more than that kid.

Kolby didn't see her Marans anywhere in the throng.

She wrapped her arms around the same Brahma who'd been set free earlier. The docile bird let her soothe him as she carried him back to the rooster tent and his crate.

It wasn't much better in there than it had been in the show tent. Mayhem ruled the roost—literally. People and birds yelled, noise and feathers filled the air. Roosters squared off and flew at each other, beaks and talons poised to do damage to each other and to the people trying to capture them. Others birds strutted around squawking with exasperation and annoyance. Crates were open and knocked off tables. Some crates were on their sides with the birds still inside.

Uprighting the Brahma's crate, Kolby cooed at him as she locked him back inside. Her heart pounded in her throat as she located her three crates.

Credence huffed at her with indignation. His crate was on its side and he was not happy. Kolby opened the cage and lifted her prized rooter out.

"Are you okay, baby?" she cooed and snuggled him. He wriggled but soon calmed down to the familiar sound of her voice.

"Where are your brothers?" she asked as she placed him back inside his righted crate.

She clicked the latch and returned her attention to her surroundings. Other bird owners were re-crating their birds. A few roosters still raced about. No sign of her other two boys.

Kolby scooped up one of the smaller birds in a fortuitous catch as he ran past, and placed him in an empty crate. The owners could sort him out later.

She ran back into the show tent, hoping to spot her other birds. What she saw was red. Darren held Capricorn upside down by his legs, and her bird was warbling and thrashing around.

"How dare you touch my cock like that!" she screamed at the man as she scooped up the bird away from his grasp.

"Hey, just trying to help," he retorted.

"Then learn how to properly hold a bird, you big lout."

"It's just a chicken, Kolby. Geez, get a grip," Darren scoffed. "I thought you'd be a little more grateful for the man that rescued one of your birds."

"Thanks," she snapped.

"What, no kiss?"

She shoved past Darren and back into the other tent. Once Capricorn was in his crate, Kolby scanned the tent again. No Marmalade.

She did see Brett Addams carefully holding Natalie's prize Ayam Cemani like a baby as she hung off his elbow, gazing up at his face as if he were her hero.

Kolby huffed. She rushed back to the show tent. Empty—no more birds.

She raced out of the big tent and frantically looked around. Not a sign of any other roosters. She dashed back inside. No Marmalade. Where was he? What was she going to do? She slumped onto the stage and let tears fall.

She wiped at them angrily. She was at a complete loss.

"Hey Kolby, are you all right?" Tyler's soft drawl asked.

She looked up at him. His handsome face with broad cheeks and a short nose was full of concern.

"You don't look okay. What's the matter? Did your birds get hurt in all this ruckus?"

Kolby grabbed his still unbuttoned shirt and buried her face against his chest. She felt his hand brush her hair and down her back.

"I can't find Marmalade," she sobbed. Tyler felt so solid and strong. She was falling apart, and he was the only thing holding her together.

"That's your really big cockerel, right? Big orange neck, black tail?" Tyler remembered her birds. That made her start to cry even more.

"Did you bring others for the show?"

Kolby nodded into his chest.

"Why don't I go look for him? You go wipe your face with some cool water and check on your other birds. I'll come find you in the rooster tent, okay?"

Tyler was right. She needed to calm down, and washing her face would help. She also needed to check Credence and Capricorn over, make sure they didn't sustain any injuries from all of that hullabaloo.

"You know how to carry a rooster?" She asked.

"Sure, like a dog or a cat. Hold them close, keep their wings down, make them feel secure."

"Right, and don't hold him upside down." She sniffed.

"What kind of idiot would do that?" He shook his head.

"You're my hero." Kolby stood up and gave Tyler a kiss on the cheek. She knew he would treat Marmalade with care.

He blushed. "I haven't earned that yet. Let me find your bird then you can thank me."

When he walked away, she realized just how soothing his embrace had been. Then again, she had shoved herself into it. Maybe he really didn't think of her in the kissing way.

But that wasn't important right now. She needed to take care of her distressed birds. She could worry about the hopelessness of her crush on Tyler Weiss later.

❄

Tyler's stomach churned. Kolby had crawled into his arms and sobbed on his chest. His T-shirt still bore a small damp spot left by her tears. He was never going to wash this shirt again.

She had called him her hero. He wasn't feeling very heroic at the moment. There wasn't a hint of that damned bird anywhere.

The Winter Chicken Festival had been designed to protect people from the cold with a series of large tents lashed together and an open entry into one of the fair ground's permanent structures. This setup provided heat and access to running water and real bathrooms.

Tyler stalked through every last tent, and he literally crawled between them as well. Still no bird. And no one had seen any more roosters running around.

He checked out the main entrance and wished he hadn't left his jacket in the pickup. A fine drizzle and diminishing light were going to make the next half of his search miserable. For Kolby, he would do this in his bare feet in the snow. She had kissed his face, and her lips had felt like clouds. Determined not to let her down, he stepped out into the weather.

After a fruitless search that took longer than he wanted, and probably not half the time that was needed, Tyler returned empty-handed to the rooster tent.

Kolby sat on the table. Her torso and arms draped over the crate holding the smaller of the two roosters. Her dark hair, in a thick braid, hung limply over her shoulder. She wiped at her nose, still sniffling.

His heart broke to see her so sad. He had watched, from too far away, as she established herself as a Marans breeder. Her birds consistently produced the desired dark brown eggs. Her hens were full and fluffy with dark feathers, and the roosters were picture-book quality. To lose her spokesmodel and top show bird had to feel like a kick in the teeth.

And here he was again, watching her from too far away.

He would give anything to be her hero, but he'd failed miserably.

"Kolby?" He didn't want to startle her, didn't want to cause her any more grief.

Her puffy red eyes lifted to meet his steady gaze. When she

saw he had no bird in his arms, she didn't smile the way she usually did when she saw him.

He shook his head and opened his empty arms. He was so sorry, so unbelievable sorry. He would give anything to see her smile again, but he was only able to deliver bad news.

Kolby rushed into his arms, holding onto him as fiercely as if he was the only person who could save her.

The twist of nerves in his guts melted into goo. He carefully wrapped his arms around her warm, soft body. He loved the scent of farm in her hair, fresh grass, feed, and a hint of leather. It was better than the most expensive Parisian perfume in existence.

Parts of his body that had no business reacting that way in this situation tightened as she burrowed her face into his neck. She cried with small hiccuping pulses.

His body should not be responding to the feel of her breasts rubbing against him. She was in distress. This was not sexy. His body disagreed. This was the hottest contact he'd ever had with her, and his groin was standing at attention.

Tyler cleared his throat. "Why don't you take these two fellas home? Practically everyone else has already left. I'll stay here and keep looking. I'll get a pocket full of cracked corn, and he'll come find me to get the goods. Right?"

Kolby shuddered. Tyler couldn't tell if she was laughing or was crying harder.

He tucked his finger under her chin and pulled her face from his neck. Damn, he really liked the feel of her nuzzling him. But that bird wasn't going to get found if they just stood here holding each other.

Teardrops glistened on her lashes. Emotion had spotted her cheeks with bright pink. And her lips. Damn her lips. The full lower lip quivered ever so slightly. He couldn't think how to make anything better. The only thing better would be...

Uncertain exactly how, Tyler slid his lips onto Kolby's. He stilled her shaking by pressing his lips into hers. She tasted like peppermint and salty tears. Ambrosia. A brief second of shock at his own forward actions paused his kiss.

Kolby snaked an arm around his neck and pulled him down

more, amping things up. Tyler stopped thinking and returned to kissing. Her lips were soft as they slid over his. He pulled her lower lip between his teeth. Her tongue found his. Tyler fisted his hands into the back of her shirt and then began caressing her sides. When she coiled her fingers into his hair and tugged, he cupped one of her breasts stroking a thumb back and forth until he could feel the hardened nub of a nipple through her clothes.

She moaned into his mouth. Reality flooded back into his awareness.

He broke the kiss. "I...I shouldn't have taken advantage of you."

Kolby wiped tears from her cheeks and stared up into his face. "Damn it, Tyler. What's it gonna take for you to take advantage of me? If not me all over you, then what?"

Tyler stared wide-eyed at the words coming from Kolby's perfect lips. Was he hearing her clearly?

She ran her hands over her hair and stomped in a circle in frustration. "Lordy. Tyler, do you even like me? Or did I just throw myself at you and you're not even interested? Did you mean that or are you just being nice about Marmalade?"

Tyler tried to speak but words wouldn't form.

He stuttered after a few false starts. "Did you...am I...we?" He pointed at her and then poked himself in the chest.

She stared at him. "We what?"

"You like me? But you're so beautiful and I'm...well, I'm not. You should be with someone like Darren or Ash."

"Why would I want to be with either of those meatheads?"

"Because...you're the most beautiful woman I've ever seen. Everyone knows beautiful people belong together. You kissed me and I'm still a frog."

Kolby stepped back into Tyler's personal space. She poked him in the chest but left her finger on him. That one touch made his body roar with desire. "First of all, thank you for calling me beautiful. Second of all, you are handsome, smart, and funny. You are a cuddly, sexy, teddy bear of a man. There's more going on in your head in a single day than either of those muscle-bound jerks have in a year. I like you, I like you a whole lot. And

I'd like to kiss you again sometime, cuz, damn, boy, you know what you're doing."

Her finger twisted into the gray fabric of his exposed undershirt.

"Yes, ma'am, I'd like that, too." He reached an arm around her and pulled her against him. He stroked her tearstained cheek with his thumb. "You go home. I'll find your missing boy and bring him out to your farm. Maybe then we can kiss some more. I'll feel like I earned it by then."

"You come over to my place tonight and we'll do more than some kissing."

She was sexy and more forward than he expected. Tyler blushed.

"I made a grown man blush? Tyler, this is exactly why I like you." She lifted on her toes and gave him a quick smack of the lips.

Hot, bothered, and flummoxed, Tyler wandered off into the drizzly evening to find her prize rooster. Kolby was going to be waiting for him. Tonight.

Kolby stared at the channel guide on her TV. It was late, the rain heavier, and no sign of Tyler or Marmalade. The twinkling lights on her Christmas tree, which normally cheered her up, annoyed her. She reached under the tree and yanked the plug from the wall. Tonight the only things that could improve her mood weren't around. And it looked like they wouldn't be here at all.

She'd given up trying to look sexy over an hour ago and changed from the "take me now" lingerie purchased from the Les Unmentionables booth at the festival. Purchasing that outfit had taken forever. Not because she couldn't decide, but because everyone else dragged her into the argument the cooks of this county had whenever they got together—the secret of the secret recipe. Claudette Farnsworth effectively ended the argument by loudly declaring the secret was frying in a pressure cooker and then swept out of the booth. Kolby honestly didn't care. The colonel and his fast food joint made better fried chicken than she had ever managed, so why bother figuring it out? He could do it cheaper, faster, and tastier.

Now cuddled up in warm fleece jammie pants, a tank top, and a zippered hoodie, Kolby was looking to start a third movie. Two movies watched, one pint of ice cream devoured. She'd even had time to listen to Justine prattle over the phone about her Miss Baked win, with Ash Weiss winning Mister Baked, so they were going to see what they could cook up together.

She had to accept that Tyler wasn't into her. Booty call be damned. She had been obvious enough, hadn't she?

Time to break out the booze. She'd lost two cocks in one afternoon. One prize show rooster, and one love interest. It was too much.

She poured Kahlúa into the remaining ice cream in the carton. The chocolate and cream colors swirled together in a mesmerizing pattern. She was just about to glug it straight from the carton when a loud honking pulled her out of the soon-to-be hang over. She slid the container onto the table and pushed out her front door to watch as a large truck pulled in with three fancy urban chicken coops lashed onto the trailer behind it. Tyler had finally showed up.

Ignoring the cold rain, she ran down the stairs and leaped into his arms as he descended from the truck. He laughed as she peppered his face with kisses. "I haven't even said anything yet."

"I didn't think you were coming." Kolby felt his hand slide under her ass to hold her up. Her arms locked around his neck and her legs wrapped around his waist.

He carried her toward the back of his trailer. "I had to find something first. Remember?"

Kolby slid out of his grasp. "Did you find him?"

"Sure did. Look." Tyler lifted a latch on the last of the hutches. He shone his flashlight into the small enclosure.

Tucked up on the top shelf of a small ladder, placed for just this reason, a large orange and black bird huddled, roosting for the night.

"Marmalade!" Kolby covered her mouth, not wanting to disturb the sleeping bird.

"He must have gotten in when it was getting dark. And put himself to bed." Tyler clicked off the flashlight and closed the hatch.

"How did you find him?" Kolby held onto Tyler's forearm and bounced with joy.

"I didn't. I looked for him for hours, Kolby. I couldn't face coming over here to let you know I had let you down. I finally gave up and loaded up the hutches. When I was loading that one up last, I heard a scrabbling noise and a warble that sounded like a pissed off chicken, and... I had located one pissed off chicken. He was not pleased to be woken up."

"I don't want to disturb him again. Can we leave him in there until morning?" Kolby's eyes were bright, she bit her lower lip and willed Tyler to figure out what she was saying.

"But that means I can't unload, and I'll have to drive, and—"

Kolby shook her head. Tyler wasn't getting the hint.

Tyler slowly closed his eyes. "I'm being stupid. You are inviting me to stay. I thought you had maybe meant that earlier. I didn't want to make any presumptions. I'm not cluing in very fast right now, am I?"

Kolby nodded this time.

She let out a whoop and a giggle as Tyler scooped her into his arms and carried her up the stairs and into her house. He spun around once inside. "Which way to the bedroom? It may take me a minute longer to get there, but I'm not dumb."

Kolby pointed him through the kitchen and around a corner. Tyler took the stairs two at a time. He didn't even seem to be struggling to carry her. Her insides were a riot of butterflies.

Tyler was large and strong—and her hero. She pointed to the last room off the short hall.

Tyler kicked open the door and carried Kolby through. Her bedroom was bright yellow and her furniture was big, dark, old stuff. It suited her, traditional and feminine. He lowered her to the mattress.

"You sure about this? I want you to know I'm not like my cousin. I don't mess around."

He couldn't believe he was standing in her bedroom, and not because she needed him to fix something. As many times as she had him over to tinker on things, he had never poked around. Never invaded her privacy and looked for her bedroom. It would have been too much a kick in the balls to see where this woman slept, where she made love, and not be a part of it.

"I don't fool around either." Her lips curved into a small teasing smile.

His breathing became labored. "If we do this tonight, I'll probably wake up in love with you. You'll have a hard time getting rid of me. I might even expect you to marry me at some point."

"Is that so bad? Sounds like a good thing to me." Kolby lifted onto her knees and wiggled to the edge of the bed. The tank top she wore did nothing to hide her natural form. He needed help from heaven if he was going to survive this night with her body jiggling like that.

She wrapped her hands up in the edges of Tyler's damp plaid shirt. She lifted the sides and pulled back, peeling the shirt over his shoulders and down his arms. Kolby ran her fingers over the muscles in his arms.

"I love watching these muscles bunch and flex as you work. It's why I'm always calling you for stupid little projects."

Tyler gently ran the back of his knuckles over her hair, afraid to actually touch her, afraid she would disappear in a puff of a dream.

"I never figured it out, did I? Are you sure you want me, big oaf that I am?"

She smiled at him. The smile he wanted to see for the rest of his life.

"You talk too much." She dug her fingers into the hair on the top of his head, tugging it, pulling his head down to hers and pressing her lips to his.

Tyler slid an arm up under her shirt. He couldn't touch the skin of her back enough. Warm and smooth under his rough fingers, he wished for bigger hands so he wouldn't miss an inch.

Kolby pulled at his shirt, untucking it from his jeans. Tyler reached down and pushed her hand away before she had a chance to run it over his middle.

"You sure you want to do that? I'm not some hard body." It was hard to talk with her constant kisses.

Kolby pulled back, her gaze holding his. She removed her hoodie and pulled her tank off over her head. Tyler forced himself to look into her eyes, not at her breasts—yet—though the rest of his body was rampaging against the restraint of his clothing.

"Stop worrying, big guy. I want you. All of you." She held his gaze for a long moment of silence. "Are you gonna look at my boobs or not?"

Tyler smiled. "Yes, ma'am, I will. But once I do, I don't think I'll be able to contain myself, so I wanted to be perfectly clear first."

"Make love to me already." Kolby lunged for Tyler and pulled him down with her onto the bed.

His face was surrounded by the soft bounty of her breasts. He didn't know where to put his mouth. So much skin, so much he wanted to taste.

Kolby yanked at his shirt, finally getting it over his head. This wasn't the feeling of a kid in a candy shop. This was better, a man being touched by the woman he'd loved from afar for too long. This was rain in the desert, this was sun after a long dark night, this was bird song after a storm.

Her skin felt like silk against his. His mouth finally decided on one nipple. The peak elongated as he pulled at it with his lips. She arched her chest and cradled his head to her flesh.

His hands roamed, looking for a new part of her to touch. He slid one under the waistband of her pants and dug his fingers into the flesh of her butt.

Kolby squirmed and touched him. She stroked his back, raking her nails down his arms.

She kicked, Tyler shoved, and her fluffy pants were down around her knees. His hands wrapped around her hips and brushed her lower belly.

Kolby groaned. She made a high keening sound when the back of his hand brushed the soft curls covering her sex.

"You are amazing," he said as he lifted up on his arms to look at her. Her lips were red and swollen with his kisses, her gaze hooded. "Can I taste you?"

Kolby closed her eyes and thrust her hips up to him. "Yes." Her answer was breathy and more moan that word.

Tyler asked permission every step of the way. There was something undeniably sexy about his requests. "Can I kiss you?" "May I look at you?" The last one, "Can I taste you" about sent her over the edge. His lips on her breasts had already wound her up, and he did amazing twirly things with his tongue. She wanted his mouth on her everywhere he was willing to put it.

She dug her fingers into his curly hair, giving him a slightly more than encouraging push toward her sex.

She levitated when his tongue licked her folds. Tyler knew what he was doing. Why hadn't anyone ever told her this man was the cunnilingus master of Belvoir County?

She cried out when he introduced a single finger to the party with his tongue. He was going to take her to the edge and beyond with what he was doing. He added a second finger, and she tightened up, preparing for the ultimate exploding release. Kolby bucked.

Sucking tongue, thrusting fingers, and he made a growling noise as he consumed her. Tyler had skills. She wanted him to use all of them on her. But Kolby shoved his shoulders and pushed him off. "I want you inside me properly when I come, and I'm close."

"Yes, ma'am." He stood and pulled his belt off.

He was taking too long. The strip show he gave her now was pure torture. He leaned over and shucked his boots, one at a time. Next, his jeans. Finally he stood before her. The tent in his shorts did nothing to hide his desire for her.

Tyler picked his jeans back up and fished a pack out of his back pocket. He tossed the condom to Kolby. "I picked some of these up on the way over. I wasn't sure exactly if that was the hint you were giving me. Damn if I'm not glad that it was.."

Kolby chuckled as she ripped the pack open. Tyler climbed back on the bed.

"You forgot to lose the shorts, hon." She touched his shoulder and ran her fingers down his chest.

Tyler rolled away from her, pulling her to lay across his chest. "I thought you might like to take care of that."

She hooked her fingers under the elastic. "Like opening a present on Christmas morning."

She pulled the cotton down his legs. She let her gaze trail up past his knees, stopping on his aroused manhood. His body was beautiful and strong, and he had been holding out on her. She licked her lips.

"You're staring." He laughed.

Kolby ripped her gaze away from his crotch and looked Tyler in the eye. "You've been hiding that all this time? Damn."

Tyler was a big man, tall, broad, and proportional. She wrapped her hand around the hot appendage and leaned her body against his. She peppered his face with kisses while stroking him. She loved how he asked her permission, so it was only fair that she ask him. "Will you please share this," she begged with a squeeze, "with me?"

"I can't think of anything I'd rather do at this moment, darling."

Kolby pushed up and faced Tyler's impressive member. She rolled the condom down his substantial length. She was glad she hadn't stopped to buy a box on her way home, because she would have gotten the wrong size. She always figured Tyler was packing an impressing organ but had never expected it to be quite this impressive.

She straddled him, positioning herself in front of his erection. It caressed her ass with its warm length.

"I'd like these here." She picked up his hands and placed them on her breasts. She rocked against his hips before lifting up and settling back, impaling herself on his length.

She let herself settle and accept all of him. Tyler moaned and his eyes rolled up into his head.

"You okay there?"

"Kolby, you are heaven. I can die a happy man now."

"Don't say that. I'm just getting started." She pressed her hips down and began rocking, stroking against him. She leaned into his hands, letting him hold her upright as she focused on directing her legs on how to move.

Her body wanted to seize. Her body wanted to riot. She needed to thrust and push, but at the same time, she forgot how to do any of it.

Tyler grabbed her hips, his fingers biting into her skin. She wrapped her hands around his and let him take over, thrusting up into her.

Her body erupted in fireworks as passion drove her over the edge. Tyler growled and began thrusting harder, faster. Kolby found her muscles and pushed back into him. They crashed together in a burst of shouts and physical explosions.

Tyler sank against the mattress, the grip on her hips lessening as his entire body relaxed. Kolby collapsed onto his chest and sighed with happiness.

She had her prize cock back and she won another cock she suspected she'd prize even more.

Tyler woke up as weak sunlight tried to stream in the window. The loud crowing of several roosters made sleeping impossible. Kolby, on the other hand, must be used to it. She lay collapsed against him, breathing softly in sleep. She had shared her gorgeous body with him over and over again. It was a miracle he could remember his own name, let alone where he was. Of course, how could he forget with her snuggled into his embrace?

He hadn't lied when he'd said there was a good possibility he would wake up in love with her.

Without disturbing her, he unwrapped her arms and slid out of the nice warm bed, leaving her to sleep. He had things to do.

She found him an hour later.

"Tyler Weiss, what do you think you're doing?" She wore muck boots and a thick fleece robe.

He stared back at her. Her hair was in complete disarray, and he could tell she was nowhere near awake yet, but she was even more beautiful than she'd been last night.

Yeah, he was in love. How could he not be?

Tyler nodded to a bowl of eggs on the top step near her feet. "Taking care of your chickens. What does it look like?" He continued to toss feed around the enclosure. Marmalade and the other two cocks strutted around, making sure all the hens were accounted for.

"I didn't think you would want them out wandering around too much this morning, what with the weather and our plans for the day."

He tossed the last bit of feed on the ground, wiped his hands, and crossed the yard to the porch.

"And what plans would that be?"

Tyler climbed the steps and wrapped an arm around Kolby's waist. "I'm gonna keep you in bed and burn through the box of condoms I went out and bought this morning."

She wrapped her arms around his neck and laughed. "Sounds like the best idea ever. Hey, Tyler."

"Yes, ma'am?"

"What would you say if I told you I woke up in love with you?" Kolby smiled at him. His heart pounded in his chest so hard it felt like it would burst.

"I'd say funny, cause that happened to me, too."

"Good. You gonna marry me now?" She pierced him with her gaze.

"That may be the best idea I've ever heard." When she pressed her lips to his, his insides melted. He swung her up into his arms and carried her inside.

"Honeymoon first?" he asked.

"Yes, sir!" She laughed and pointed the way back to the bedroom.

4

CALLING BIRD

*W*hen the bartender told me that some guy over there wanted to buy me a drink and vaguely nodded toward the other end of the bar, I thought, why not?

"I'll have a skinny Shirley Temple. No, make that a skinny Roy Rogers."

"Sure thing." The bartender disappeared for a moment before a tall glass of fizzy mock-tail appeared before me. For the two or three bucks my fancy soda cost, I was under no obligation to my benefactor.

Without looking for who bought the drink, I picked it up and then spun around on the stool to watch the beginning of the show. Predominantly a male-base cabaret review, *The Saturday Night Show* had gained a strong following because of its variety of performers including Thorne, one part rock-star, one part stripper. All parts hot. The audience consisted of every orientation, we were all here for the spectacle. The sheer number of bachelorette parties with future brides in mini veils explained one of the reasons why the club's popularity had grown. This club was lousy with bridesmaids.

In fact, it was why I was here. My cousin and her other bridesmaids swarmed the edge of the stage. My feet were bothering me after a long week at work, so I'd opted for a seat at the bar over the mosh-pit crowd at the base of the stage.

Points lost for sitting so far from the stage, but points gained for sitting at the bar and not having to wait for service.

"You're in a club, twenty-one and over, and you're drinking a kiddie drink. Designated driver?" a gravely male voice, low and somewhat sexy, asked me.

I turned, tilted my gaze up, and froze. Any semblance of a witty retort evaporated from my tongue. Long black hair, dark eyes, heavy eyeliner, full lips, square chin. My idea of the quintessential rockstar stood smirking at my drink.

I dropped my eyes and stared at his hands. Tattooed knuckles bedecked in heavy silver rings gripped a steaming mug. I couldn't look directly at him, he was too perfect. I already felt the wobbles of turning into once-human-ooze deep in my gut. My eyes followed his hand to a wrist wrapped in leather and chain bracelets and a few dripping scarves.

"Coffee?" I managed to say.

"Yeah." He held the mug up in salute before taking a sip. That 'yeah' was really quite a sexy sound.

"You're picking on me for drinking a Roy Rogers, and you're drinking coffee? Trying to get sober?" I'm not sure how I was able to form words. My throat was dry, and my tongue felt swollen. I always lost the ability to speak coherently around good looking men. It was a good thing I was sitting down, because I know my knees had forgotten how to work.

He huffed. "Trying to stay sober. You?"

"I just don't drink." I shrugged. "What are the odds that you would buy a drink for the only other person in this whole place that doesn't imbibe?"

His response rumbled with humor. I'm sure he was smiling or something, but since I couldn't look at his face, I couldn't be sure. "I'm sure there's at least one other person in here not drinking tonight."

"True, but seriously, c'mon."

Mr. Gorgeous Rocker nodded in agreement. I risked a glance at his face and caught him smiling. He was really hot. I felt like I should recognize him, but my brain was jelly. His sleeveless vest revealed swirls of tattoos and muscular arms. *Drool.* I couldn't tell if he had a tank on or not with all the necklaces and scarves that hung from his neck. He accessorized better than I ever did.

"What's a guy like you doing in a place like this?" I asked.

"Isn't that supposed to be my line?"

"Sorry, beat you to the punch. Thanks for the drink, but why?" More like how was I managing a conversation with the hottest guy in the building?

"You have a great smile, Roy. I thought, now there's a girl who's already having a good time. She'll be fun to play with."

I reached over and tilted his face up until he made eye contact. "The smile is up here. Those are boobs." Oh my God, I couldn't believe I'd actually done that. I should have let him keep ogling my boobs. They were enjoying it, my nipples were standing up begging for more attention.

He smirked. I melted. The embodiment of every teenage sexual fantasy I'd ever had from the tattoos on the biceps to the labret piercing under his lower lip stood in front of me. He had the grin from the singer in that one band, the jawline from the bass player from that other band, the hair from the drummer in that other-other band. He was the whole package, as if he'd reached out and taken the best pieces from hundreds of different men and wrapped them all up into an Ava-approved concept.

The best part was that he didn't seem like he was faking it, either. A real live rocker. A real live, super amped, sexual fantasy of a man.

Rocker Boy turned, set his coffee on the bar, and nodded at the bartender. He handed over a mic. It was festooned with even more draping scarves.

Oh, fuck me, no.

Rocker Boy lifted my purse from my shoulders and handed it to the bartender.

"Hey!" I protested, but he grabbed my hand, dragged me off my stool, and headed into the crowd before I could seriously complain. Besides, I was still in shock, how had I not recognized him?

"Come, Roy." He began vocal cartwheels into the mic as he walked towards the stage. The audience parted for him like a clingy ooze. Several women stroked his arms, or otherwise tried to reach for him as we passed. I was on the receiving end of some serious death-ray glares.

He pulled me up a few steps and then we were on the stage. We were on the fucking stage.

Coffee Rocker was Thorne. I couldn't believe I hadn't recognized him from the posters. If only he were leading me into a bedroom like this instead of onto a fucking stage.

"Everybody, this is Roy. Say hello to Roy."

I couldn't decide if this was going to be fun or if I should just die now from embarrassment. There I was, under the lights where everyone could see me. No drooling in my own little world over the show tonight. Nope I was in the spotlight almost as much as Thorne.

"Wave to the good people, Roy." I followed his instructions and waved at the audience. I think. I couldn't see anything past the stage lights.

Thorne led me to a chair and had me sit. Then he began singing. The music was loungey and very 1950s, and I'm sure when Old Blue Eyes sang it back in the day panties disappeared and poodle skirts flipped up. The lights created a figurative wall. I felt as if we were alone and he really was singing just for me. His voice was swoon-worthy, all creamy soft, with an edge of teasing sex. Panties were disappearing tonight. I'm pretty sure mine had already evaporated with the heat of being near him.

He crooned, he caressed my cheek, he sat in my lap, he held my hand. I could almost forget it was part of a show. But with the hand he wasn't using to stroke me, he held a mic. I wasn't special; I was a victim. But I ate it up anyway.

As soon as I'd decided I was actually enjoying myself, the song ended. With a loud crash of drums and guitar, the music throbbed harder, louder, and the lyrics changed from sweet nothings to raunch and raw sex.

He ran to the edge of the stage clapping high over his head, building up a frenzy in the audience. Now that he'd turned his attention to his adoring fans instead of me, I felt deserted, a puddle of human goo in my chair.

When he came back to me, he crawled between my legs,

spreading them apart so he could stand completely in my personal space. I was glad I'd picked lace tights under shorts instead of a skirt, or the audience and Thorne would be getting a flash of my sopping wet panties right about now, assuming they hadn't actually disappeared.

Even with several layers of fabric between us, I was having a hard time remembering how to breathe. *In Ava, out Ava.* Oh gods, his belly button was right there. He definitely wasn't wearing a shirt, thank the lords of heaven and earth. His perfect abs and exposed happy trail were within licking distance.

I gasped in shock when he grabbed a handful of my hair and began thrusting his hips at my face. *Why, yes, let me unzip those for you. I have no problems with a little fellatio at the moment.* I had to keep telling myself the lights were not a wall and people were out there watching him do this to me. The man was sex on legs. And I wanted him.

I've been to enough strip shows to know that male strippers aren't about tantalizing the audience so much as teasing and embarrassing them. And I was the target. But damn, if it wasn't fun to be this close to Thorne's crotch, getting a very personal lap dance from him.

The actual removal of clothing began as Thorne began singing about stripping. The scarves that draped and dripped from his body were tossed out to the invisible audience, while others were placed around my neck. As Thorne removed more and more of the scarves I cheered and screamed along with the rest of the crowd. It didn't matter that he was performing for the audience now, giving me his back. I enjoyed the view.

His long vest fell to the floor, revealing muscles that looked like perfect examples out of one of my anatomy books, and a super tight ass. I'm pretty sure I moaned loudly. His body was amazing. I wanted a close up of that belly button again, and next time I'd lick it. I would.

He danced around and over me as the song continued. I enjoyed watching him perform from this vantage point. It was better than front row of any concert I'd ever been to. But I was feeling tortured, being so close and not having the guts to reach out and touch him. I couldn't decide if I wanted my status as hapless stage victim to end or not. If it ended I would no longer have his attention.

When the tear-away snaps on his pants went pop. I lost it. The pants flew, the screams from the audience grew louder, and Thorne's naked ass cheeks were right at my chest, with a fluffy tail in my face. He moved, and I dropped out of the chair sobbing with laughter. A fluffy tail, I was not expecting that.

"Looks like we broke Roy. You okay Roy?" He changed his focus from the audience to looking down at me

I nodded. "You're really hot, but..." I was overwhelmed by laughter again. I could barely move, I was laughing so hard. I pointed at his crotch. Instead of a spiked leather G-string like one would expect from a stripper-rocker, the man wore fuzzy cat drawers, complete with ears and a tail. "You have a pussy on your dick."

"Kris, have you seen my purse?"

"No Ava, I have not." My roommate yelled from the other room.

I tossed pillows onto the floor, tearing apart the living room couch. Typically after a late night, I would stagger in the front door, dump my shit on the couch, and head down the hallway to my room. Car keys: check, jacket: check, but no purse. I ran out to the driveway and cleaned my car out in my frantic search.

But no purse. I drove home, so I must have put my keys in my pocket. What did I do with the damned purse?

I trudged back to my bedroom and began rifling through the dirty clothes from the night before. I was knee deep in dirty laundry when the doorbell rang. After Kris announced she would answer it, I ignored it and went back to searching

"Ava, it's for you," she yelled.

"Who is it?" I asked as I passed her in the hallway on my way to the door.

"I don't know, some guy. He's waiting on the porch."

Gee, thanks, how about asking for his name? I rolled my eyes at the closed front door. "You could have at least left the door open." *Rude.*

I opened the door, saw Thorne, and shut the door again.

Holy shit! Why is he here?

Realizing what I had just done, I opened it immediately. Thorne stood looking at me. He still looked like a rocker boy, leather jacket, ripped up jeans, long hair spiked up on top, unshaved scruff. I felt my pulse quicken.

"Hi, Roy," Thorne said, looking perplexed.

"What are you doing here?"

"Having doors slammed in my face. Is that really how you treat the guy who returns this?" He held up my purse. "You left it at the bar last night."

"I've been going insane looking for this." I hugged my bag, happy to see it again, happy to have my wallet and ID back.

"The purse gets a hug, and I get nothing?"

"I'm sorry, Thorne, thank you." I leaned forward and gave him an awkward half-hug. *I am so fucking lame.*

He shook his head. "I want something as enthusiastic as the purse got."

"Seriously?" I cocked an eyebrow at him and held up my purse "My bag and I are in a long term relationship, but I just met you and your penchant for animal themed G-strings last night." Besides, I'd probably do something truly embarrassing if I touched him again.

He laughed. "You got me. Can I buy you a cup of coffee?"

I wiped down the table on the patio as I nervously waited for Thorne to come outside with the drinks. How had I gotten so lucky as to have Thorne, known locally for his singing, not only return my purse but take me out for coffee? I should have worn something cute this morning and not my basic yoga pants cause I'm too tired to deal with zippers. I could at least have put make-up on. Or brushed my hair. At least I showered last night and applied fresh deodorant this morning. I'm pretty sure at some point I brushed my teeth. I did a quick pit sniff and breathed into my palm just make sure minimal hygiene requirements had been met.

Well, it wasn't like Thorne gave me any warning. He was stuck with me in my standard Saturday-morning slouch.

He placed a paper cup of hot coffee in front of me. He looked rocker perfect this morning. "So, Roy, why don't you drink? Is that a good girl thing or what?" The man certainly knew how to open a conversation. No comments on the weather or if I had a good time last night. I may have giggled like an idiot.

"You don't drink, either. Is that a bad boy thing or what?" Two could play this game.

"Touché. Call me Lonnie. Thorne's just a stage name. As for not drinking, it's more of a how-to-not-be-a-dead-boy thing." Lonnie lifted the plastic lid and blew on his drink. Damn, he had nice lips.

"I got really stupid when I was young, did some shit I shouldn't have, combined drugs I shouldn't have, and I got really dead for something like three to five minutes. So not drinking is a living thing."

I didn't really know how to respond. "Whoa, really? You look really healthy now." He looked fit. Beyond healthy, and that was a professional opinion. I'm a nurse. I should know. I pretended to fuss with my coffee, trying to cover my lame-ass response.

"I am, obnoxiously so. I work out, I take vitamins, and I even eat vegetables. Why am I telling you this?"

"Because I asked." I laughed, and I may have batted my eyelashes at him.

"But didn't I ask you first?"

I nodded. "But you jumped in on the whole good girl thing, so I artfully redirected the conversation."

"Successfully, I would say. I don't typically reveal the whole *was-dead* thing right away. It is public record, but not something I typically advertise." He air quoted around "was dead."

"So, did you see a light?"

"I honestly don't remember a damned thing. I'm actually missing a few days there."

"Damn, how long you been…" I was curious. I wanted to

know more. I had never met a dead guy before. But as soon as the words flew out of mouth, I realized I was rude.

"Sober? Two thousand six hundred sixty nine days. That's seven years, three months, and twenty-two days."

"You keep track?"

"I count every fucking day. Each day is a new chance to live, and I remind myself of that. Even though I effectively killed myself, I didn't take the cosmic hint right away. I didn't die, so my dumb ass thought, hey, maybe that means I can't." He gave me an epic eye roll, clearly he thought younger Lonnie was an idiot. "Someone else I knew died about six months later, and I fucking got woke."

I wasn't sure how to process that. I couldn't imagine. "I'm so sorry. I don't drink because it tastes nasty, end of story. It's not some moral high ground. If my friends drink, whatever. I'm good as designated driver as long as nobody pukes in my car."

"So you are a good girl?" He gave me a sexy smirk. Oh hell, his breathing was sexy.

"What does that even mean? I'm a good girl because I do the right thing, like not letting my friends drive drunk? Everybody should be good that way. Or are you asking if my views of drinking reflect my virtue?"

Lonnie cleared his throat, and shifted in his chair. "Which do you think?"

Oh I had gotten that question before. I don't drink therefore I'm uptight. What was he trying to get at? It almost felt like he was teasing me, goading me on, but why? Was he flirting? Shit, he was flirting and I'm too dumb to catch it.

"You might as well ask why girls like horses. It's all loaded with innuendo. Do good girls really like bad boys, or is it bad boys who are obsessed with good girls? What's wrong with bad girls, and what makes a girl bad?"

Lonnie shrugged. "Why do girls like horses?"

I ignored him. "I think men are just obsessed with how freaky a girl is in bed. A *bad girl*," I made finger quotes around bad girl, "in the sense of virtue, is an antiquated ideal and completely sexist. A woman can have sex and know her way around in a bedroom and be the nicest, kindest person in the world. She can wear sweater sets and pearls and still be a super freak. She could also be Miss Virgin Mission Control and dress the same way. I think men are just interested in what's underneath the clothes, and not much else. They don't care if you are actually a good person or if you're a bitch and slap your kids around."

"So which are you? Virgin territory or a freak in sheep's clothing?"

Here we go.

"You are self-proclaimed bad boy, Lonnie." I pointed at his chest.

"How so?"

"Seriously? Your stage name. Thorne. Spiked leather jacket, black nail polish, eyeliner before noon, all says bad boy. But does that say you are a bad person?" I could have included addict, but that would have been a low blow, and I did like him. I liked him a little too much. He made my body all quivery. His name Lonnie felt nice on my tongue. I wondered if he would as well.

"How do you know I'm not a nice guy in douche's clothing?" he countered.

"Oh, don't be a nice guy." I whined. "Nice guys are basically assholes trying to convince you they aren't. They are the guys who hang around you even after you tell them you aren't interested, and get mad when you tell them you do not have any romantic feelings for them. They wave the friend-zone flag around like you did something other than tell them the truth. They are the same guys who will describe their ideal mate to you, and you meet every last one of their bullet points—eye color, age, boob size—they may even kiss you, but then they put you on the back burner until something better comes along. You friend-zone yourself cause you're a masochist. And when you finally realize you can't be friends with them for all that mental abuse and neglect, and you tell them you can't be friends, no blame, just I can't do this to myself anymore, they get mad at you and profess it's because they're a nice guy that you are walking away from them. They blame you for finally finding the strength to get yourself out of that unhealthy situation. They think girls only want bad boys, and that's not true." So not true. I could go on forever on this one. I could write a fucking thesis on the friend-zone. I've lived there entirely too long.

"What do girls want?"

Talk about a loaded question.

"Not an asshole. I can't speak for all women everywhere, but I want a good guy, a boy scout, a guy who does the right thing for no other reason than it's right. He gets out and helps push someone's broken down car through an intersection instead of honking at the poor person. He's not afraid to back down from a fight and never fights just to fight." I took a sip of my coffee. Lonnie was still watching me, still listening. "If he's in a relationship, he's all in and isn't looking for something better to come along. He doesn't act like you're friends and then bitch about being friend-zoned when you say you've only ever thought of him as such. He doesn't whine that he's a nice guy. And he owns his shit. If he fucks up, he admits it and doesn't try to put the blame somewhere else."

Lonnie opened his mouth to say something.

"And don't you dare say I've put some thought into that. Any girl who has ever had to deal with a boy has put some thought into it. It seems to me most guys are just wondering if some chick will suck his dick. They don't really care about the whole good girl bad girl thing."

Lonnie closed his mouth and took another sip of coffee.

"So what do these good guys look like?" he finally asked.

"Uh uh." I shook my head. "That's like saying good girls only ever dress a certain way, and any female with boobs in a tight T-shirt is a bad girl. Boobs make T-shirts tight and it's no indication of a girl's predilection for virtuous behavior or kindness. And let's be honest. I've met some outright bitches who were virtuous as fuck."

Lonnie smiled at me. It was wicked the way his mouth spread and revealed gleaming perfect teeth. He reminded me of a big bad wolf. Damn, I was horny and he was setting all of my hormones on edge.

"What?" I asked, a little annoyed. I figured he wasn't flirting with me anymore. Why would he bother after my tirade went a little off the deep end?

"You're very passionate about this. I touched a nerve."

"As someone whose been judged because T-shirts run a little tight on the girls, yeah, I am. I am neither a good girl nor a bad girl, but I do try to be a good person."

Lonnie shrugged. "I've met some very good people who most people would write off as being bad simply because of their personal style choices." He waggled his tattooed knuckles at me. "But you sound like some of that is a little too close to home."

"You have no idea." My phone buzzed, and I checked the screen before tossing it onto the table. It was a text from my roommate. She'd just run into Matt. She told him I was out having coffee. "I am the back burner queen." *Thanks, Matt.*

Lonnie picked up my phone.

"What are you doing?" I watched him man handle my phone and wished I could trade places with it.

He held up a finger for me to wait. He focused on my phone, picked up his own phone, took my picture, and kept typing on his phone.

A honking car caught my attention. It sounded like Matt's old fashioned ah-oo-gah horn sound, but I didn't see his pickup. I turned back to Lonnie. "Done?"

He gave a brief nod.

"Hey, babe."

Matt. Not someone I wanted to see right now. He was the antithesis of Lonnie: clean cut, clean shaven, wearing a polo and khakis. And he only called me babe when he was up to something, like figuring out how to break my heart again. He pulled a chair over from another table and sat next to me. "Did you see me drive by?"

He draped an arm across my shoulder. Twenty-four hours ago I would have gone all twitter-pated with that gesture. Physical contact from Matt was typically high on my list of panty evaporating actions. Not today.

"Matt." I shrugged his arm off.

My phone buzzed again and I picked it up. I didn't particularly care how rude I was being. Ranting at Lonnie had made me start to realize a few things.

"Let me guess, this is Mr. Back Burner?"

I smiled at Lonnie. Smart man. "Lonnie, this is Matt."

I quickly returned Lonnie's text.

"Himself."

"So what are you two doing?" Matt asked.

Lonnie lifted his cup in a salute. "Coffee. How about you?"

"When I saw Ava, I figured I'd stop by, see if you wanted to grab a pizza tonight or just Netflix and chill?" Matt asked me.

What the hell? I'm having coffee with another man and Matt, who I've been after for eons finally asks me out again.

My phone buzzed again.

"You want him?"

I texted back, *"yes."*

Truth be told, I was drawn to them both, but in reality, Matt was a good guy and a realistic choice: stable, no recovery issues, assistant manager at a big box store. He had "father" and "provider" written all over his aura. Lonnie was a fantasy: rock-star attitude, hot body, sobriety. That was a lot of baggage I didn't need to help carry. Lonnie would be good for a romp, but he wasn't Mr. Long-term life plan.

"Play along."

"Too late, bro." Lonnie pushed away from the table, his chair making an ungodly screeching noise. "Ava's going clubbing with me tonight. You can't sleep in and ask for Netflix and chill when Ava looks this fine in the morning."

"It's past noon..." Matt didn't finish, but his expression finished for him. *Asshole.*

Lonnie stood up and stretched. I smiled, it was a pure power play. 'Look how big I really am, and I'm clad in leather.'

It worked on me. I was pretty sure my panties went poof. He bent down and nuzzled my ear. I closed my eyes, and leaned into him. I know my panties evaporated with that contact. Oh hells bells, Lonnie smelled good. "Call me. We need to plan the rest of this." He whispered in his low, raspy voice.

Why was he helping me get Matt? Sure, I had wanted Matt for years, but did Lonnie not realize that after staring at his lips for over an hour, if he said boo I would do stupid shit for him? Wasn't that whole good girl bad girl discussion leading up to something? I slumped in my chair and looked at Matt. It was the closest he'd been to me in a long time.

I looked over at him. "What?" My panties were firmly back in place.

"Matt," I sobbed into my phone. "He ditched me. Will you come get me?" I hung up knowing Matt was on his way to rescue me.

So far Lonnie had been right. Matt had played right into the plan. Call Matt and coo over Lonnie. Get mad at Matt and hang up. Wait several hours, get dressed up, call him to come rescue me from a night gone wrong. When he came to get me, I would smear my make-up and look like I had been crying and shivering in the chill just enough so Matt would have to wrap an arm around me.

Matt would think he was my hero and finally notice me outside of the friend zone. Move me off the back burner. It felt so middle school, but apparently seeing me with Lonnie had put me on Matt's radar, something I had been trying to do for a few years. The problem was, I was no longer certain that was what I wanted.

Off and on Matt had acted interested, and I know I was. We'd even talked about dating, but he'd started dating a friend of mine instead. Said it was for mutual protection. What did that even mean? He needed a petite brunette chick to protect him from the busty wench who could picture having his babies?

Okay, maybe I was a bit more than interested in Matt. After they'd broke up, he'd even kissed me, but soon thereafter started dating someone else. Stupid me, forever hopeful. I let him friend-zone me. I let him put me on the back burner.

But I wanted the guy who did the right thing because it was right, not because there was a reward. Lonnie had driven by my house to deliver my bag. Lonnie had devised a cunning plan to get Matt to sit up and take notice. Lonnie made my panties go poof. But Matt was a long term goal.

Matt pulled up to the curb in front of me. I hopped into the cab of his truck. One look at his clothes told me he came straight from work. "Thanks, Matt. I guess it's too late to take you up on some pizza and a movie, huh?" He had the heater on and handed me a hoodie that smelled of his Old Spice.

When he grinned sheepishly at me, my heart did not skip a beat like it usually did. Matt and his clean-cut good looks always made my toes curl, especially when he smiled. I had dreamed of licking the corners of his mouth when he smiled at me like that. "Not tonight, Ava. Let's get you home. How about tomorrow?"

Matt was being noble, and not trying to crawl in my pants for an instant reward. Why wasn't I melting?

The next morning my phone rang. I slapped around until I found the evil device and looked at the number. I couldn't focus on it, the name wasn't registering. I stared blearily at the screen. Well, I was awake now. I checked the call directory. Nothing from Matt. Lonnie had explained that if Matt was hooked, Matt would call super early.

I scrolled back and stared at the most recent call. Lonnie Rose. Oh, duh. I needed to ask him about Matt anyway, so I hit return call.

"Hey," I groaned into the phone.

"Did you get your man, Roy?" Lonnie sounded entirely too chipper for an early morning call.

I rolled onto my back and watched shadows on my ceiling. "I don't know. He hasn't called. You said he would call." I sighed. Matt had come to the rescue, but nothing happened. "I'm not sure what's next."

"Come over to the club before lunch and we'll work something out. You still want him?"

"Sure." I had wanted Matt for so long that I didn't know what not pining for him was like.

"We'll get you your man. I'll be there by eleven. Show up some time after that."

"Okay, see you then." I hung up. Lonnie was hot but clearly not interested. I did not need to put myself into that position again, lusting after someone who couldn't care less. Been there, done that entirely too many times. Didn't want the T-shirt or the tears. I had plenty of male friends, they just don't give me the female equivalent of a hard-on. It was the ones my body wanted to share fluids with that gave me issues. I wanted to be near them, but I'm the one who always got hurt. I needed to walk away, not walk into that night club.

Without the bright lights, the flashing disco globe, or the throbbing music, the dark interior of the night club seemed drab, dull, and lifeless. In only a few hours, energy would surge back through the doors, and this place would thrive with a beat all its own.

Lonnie's crooning voice would reverberate from the walls. Fire eaters would tantalize and thrill, along with a team of more traditional male strippers. Z-Club Sound certainly provided a variety of male flesh for entertainment, and audiences were thronging to watch it all.

"Roy!" Lonnie's voice echoed through the large, empty space.

Today when Lonnie came in for a hug, I did not deny him. It wasn't as enthusiastic an embrace as I expected, but I did feel his hard body press against mine, and, well, damn. The man gave good hugs. Really good hugs.

But I was officially after Matt. *Focus, girl.* Lonnie was extra hot in his tight T-shirt that showed off his well-defined pecs and shoulders. I had to stop myself from drooling over his ass in his form fitting jeans.

"I'm thinking of adding some different songs. Tell me what you think." He trotted off towards the sound booth to start the music.

I found a chair next to a table covered in random junk and cleaning supplies.

A ticking countdown of drumsticks from prerecorded music bounced off the walls before a reverberating crash of drums and guitar chords kicked off the song. Loud guitar and a steady beat indicated this one as solid rock'n'roll. No ballads or crooning would accompany this song. Lonnie strutted onto the stage and tossed his head, letting his long hair bounce around. He then told me to talk dirty to him.

I cackled. If he wasn't practicing for a strip show, I would have sworn he was flirting with me.

"Hey, asshole." A thick British accent cut into Lonnie's song. "If this is the new number, let me see it."

Lonnie squinted toward the sound booth. "I'm not dressed for it."

"You don't have to take shit off, but this is the bondage piece, right? How's that gonna work? You've got a bird here, show me."

Lonnie tilted his head in acknowledgment. "Hey, Roy, see that rope?"

I pushed around some of the junk on top of the table and picked up a cable. I held it up for Lonnie to see.

"Grab that and come on up."

I climbed the steps and handed Lonnie the rope, more like a red silk cord. He fumbled around with it and began talking through his performance. Describing his planned actions. "Ok, I'm going to pull the mark up on stage like I did last time. Then I'm going to take a scarf and tie her hands together." Yep, I was the mark, in all my targeted glory.

Lonnie wrestled with the rope and the microphone.

"Here give me that." I took the microphone and set it on the floor.

Lonnie muttered to himself. "Good point. I'm gonna have to start off with the earpiece." He draped the rope around his neck.

The booming voice from the sound booth cut through the music again. "See, this is why you do walk-throughs, asshole."

Lonnie lifted his middle finger and waved it about over his head.

"Let's try that again." The sound booth guy said.

Lonnie started singing, not loudly, but enough to give him the pacing of the number. "This is where I take the scarf and bind the mark's hands." He pulled the rope from his neck as if it were a scarf, slowly dragging down and off. I'd never really put too much though into being tied up before. But now, with the way Lonnie had just slid the cord from his neck, I was all for some tie-me-up tie-me-down action.

Stop it, Ava, he's not into you. But I still giggled as Lonnie bound my wrists together.

"That okay? Not too tight?"

"That's fine." *More, please?* The voice in my head was not helping.

Lonnie grabbed my bound wrists and looped them over his head. His face was right in mine. Perfect for kissing. *No, Ava, no.* He scooped his hands under my ass and lifted.

I wrapped my legs around him. I wasn't going to survive this. He felt so good. Lonnie paused, staring into my eyes. I couldn't breathe. He held me like that for a moment, not singing, before he slowly put me back down. "That's not gonna work," he murmured, his voice barely above a whisper.

"I'm too heavy," I managed, all too aware that I was pressed against him. "Pick a smaller mark."

Lonnie just looked into my eyes. "No, you're perfect. It was the wrong position." He lowered himself down so I was forced to sit on his knee.

Lonnie continued to lower me to the floor so that I lay on my back, he held himself above me like a lover. He started singing again, mostly to himself. "Do you wanna touch, do you wanna touch?"

Yes, I want to touch! I forced myself to hold still, no wriggling. My natural instinct was to wrap my legs over his hips, and rub against him. *Damn, girl, it's just pretend. An act. Be professional. This is not personal.*

Lonnie rolled his body in a wave over mine, his chest skimming along my breasts. A chill swept over my skin, goose pimples covering my arms as I shivered. My nipples hardened, longing for Lonnie to brush up against me again. I hoped he hadn't noticed, because that would be embarrassing.

He lifted my bound hands and moved them from his neck to over my head on the floor. With one hand holding my wrists, he proceeded to do one-armed push-ups over me. Did he not realize this position thrust my breast out at him? My nipples trained on him like little hard homing beacons. He brought his face close and continued to sing. To the audience it would look like he was nuzzling my neck. His hair and breath tickled my cheek, but he didn't touch me.

Hold it together, girl. I closed my eyes, only opening them again when Lonnie shifted.

He sat back on his haunches, pulling me into a sitting position, and hooked my hands back over his neck. He rose, lifting me with him. He pressed into my hips with his as he gyrated to the song.

If my panties hadn't gone poof by now, they seriously did this time. When the song ended and he dipped me, our faces were a breath apart. I thought for a split second he was going to kiss me. If that happened, I'm pretty sure I would make my panties disappear for real and I would do all the bad girl things he could possibly dream of, and maybe more.

We were both breathing heavily. *It was a bit of a work out, that's all.* This was hard. If I kissed Lonnie, would I forget all about Matt? But Lonnie was helping me to get Matt. There was no way he was even mildly interested in me. Men don't help the women they are interested in to land other men. They don't. Do they?

I closed my eyes as Lonnie stood us up. I was doing it again. Falling for a guy who didn't see me the same way. Why did I always do this to myself?

"Does that work for you?" he asked.

"That should work," I whispered. *One hint, Lonnie, just one, and I'll forget I ever had a crush on Matt.*

"Hey, asshole." The voice from the sound booth no longer boomed through the sound system, as the broad man who commanded that voice climbed the stairs. "That's going to have panties wet like nobody's business. Hell, it might be so damp in here Keith's flames won't light." He clapped Lonnie on the back and extended a meaty hand to me.

He was right. Panties were wet.

Lonnie slapped the larger man on the chest. "This is Jeremy, our sound guy and one of the owners. He makes sure the shit I sing sounds better than when it comes out my mouth."

He reached to shake my hand, and had an awkward moment

figuring out how to shake while still trussed up. Jeremy shook my hand.

Jeremy huffed, "so how you gonna get the mark out of the bondage job?"

I thrust my hands toward Lonnie. He began unwrapping my bonds. "How about I deliver her back into the audience and let her friends untie her? She can keep the scarf."

Jeremy scrunched up his face, "definitely not. You need another song."

"I'm trying to reduce how much time I spend with each mark, so I can get more of 'em up on stage. More marks mean more tips."

"You need to charge them," I said.

"What? How?" Jeremy asked.

"Sell tickets. If you have a red ticket, you have Lon...Thorne's undivided attention. If you have a blue ticket, then five of you to get a personalized show. You know that lap dance you gave me?" I faced Lonnie and began gesturing wildly. "Put five chairs up here and do five lap dances in the course of one or two songs. Also, with the tickets, there's your tip guarantee. And you don't have to just limit the tickets to his numbers. Have the other guys figure out how they can do that, too. Sell tickets for on stage viewing. I mean, I wouldn't with the fire guy, but at least one other number could easily have VIP onstage seating."

"You're a smart one, Roy," Jeremy said.

"Nuh-uh, she's Ava to you," Lonnie corrected him.

"I though you called her Roy?" Jeremy asked.

Lonnie thumbed himself in the chest, "I get to call her Roy, you don't."

"Why do you call me Roy?"

"You were drinking a Roy Rogers. Isn't that obvious?" The expression on Lonnie's face screamed, "duh!"

"Good thing I didn't order the Shirley Temple."

"Let's get out of here, Roy." He glared at Jeremy. "We have to catch you a man. Have you called him yet?"

"You said he would call. He's the kind of guy who does the calling and doesn't think girls should call," I complained.

"Girls call guys all the time. It's the twenty-first century. Call him."

I shook my head. Matt was old fashioned that way. Or at least that was what I told myself. I never had good luck placing that first call. Truth is, I wanted to be called.

"That's complete bollocks," Jeremy said. "If a bird likes a bloke, she should call him."

I turned to face Jeremy. "So you wouldn't mind if a girl called you and asked you out if she didn't think you were moving fast enough?"

"That's how I got my wife, or I should say she got me. Met her at the pub. She was leaving for America the next week and wanted to make sure I knew that she wanted me to come with her."

"You met your wife, and the next week you moved to the States with her?"

"I followed about a month later. But if she hadn't called, I would've been too slow, and I would have missed out on the best damn thing that's ever happened to me."

I was being a wimp about Matt, hoping that Lonnie's prophecy would come true. "So I should call him?"

Both Lonnie and Jeremy nodded.

"Fine, I'll call. Nice to meet you, Jeremy." I waved as I followed Lonnie off the stage.

"You too, Ava. See you tonight, asshole," Jeremy called after us.

In response Lonnie waved his hand in the air, middle finger lifted again.

Lonnie looped my arm through his as we walked to the coffee shop at the end of the block. I loved how he pulled me in. Why wasn't he interested? Why was he helping me get Matt?

"Lonnie, why do you do this? Why aren't you in a band?"

"Bands are bad for my sobriety. I was in a band when I OD-ed. I was in a band when the drummer choked to death on his own vomit."

"I'm so sorry." I felt guilty for bringing up those memories.

"There are fewer distractions doing this. Plus, I don't make money if I get puffy and out of shape, and that's the first thing that's going to happen if I'm not sober." He shivered. "I've seen pictures from back in those days. I thought I was hot shit. I was pasty and had zero muscle tone. It was not pretty. Now I'm sober and handsome."

"And so modest." I punched him in the shoulder.

"Don't forget wise and talented."

"And old." I needed something to jab at him with, age was the first thing I could think of.

"Damn straight, and every day I get older, so listen to this old man and call that boy you like."

"Calling doesn't go so well for me. I'm always too nervous," I confessed.

"And you think guys aren't? We hide it better."

"What if he says no?"

"Then he says no. And you have to ask yourself if you're willing to stay Miss Back Burner, or if you're going to move on."

"Why should he pick me?"

Lonnie stopped and glared at me. He grazed me with his assessment, looking up and down, and then walked in a slow circle around me like I was a prize race horse.

"Why wouldn't he pick you? You are opinionated as fuck, and I bet you even know the difference between your with one R and you're with an apostrophe R-E. You're cute, in a curvy girl kind of way. Boobs are always good, and yours are a nice size, round and more than a handful. You're short, a good height to lean against. You have healthy looking teeth, and you give off that sweet but freaky vibe."

I laughed. "I should take that all as a compliment, right? And I'm not short. You're tall."

Lonnie chuckled.

"I'm not really a bad girl. I think I'm more a vanilla in freak's clothing than the other way around."

This is nice. It had taken a couple of days, but I was snuggled under a blanket on the couch, my feet in Matt's lap. I did call. I called more than once, and Matt invited me over for movies and pizza. The second movie of the night lulled me into a drowsy state. Matt began rubbing my feet. His hands felt soft and warm, and I loved that he instinctively knew I needed my tired feet massaged after the day I'd had at work. I closed my eyes.

I need to thank Lonnie, he's brilliant.

Calling was the right thing to do. Yes, this is what I wanted, to just chill with Matt. To know I was worth his time.

A jump scare in the movie freaked me out, and I flailed, kicking poor Matt in the process.

Matt groaned and doubled over, cupping himself. I had nailed him in the junk, hard.

"Are you okay? What'd I kick? I'm so sorry." I rested my hand on his shoulder, leaning in to comfort him, and to see if he needed my assistance in a professional capacity.

"Back off would ya." Matt growled.

"Get over it, I'm a nurse."

Matt shifted, and I caught a glimpse of his exposed, semi-erect penis. That was not what I was expecting to see. He hadn't unzipped himself to make sure all parts were still there... it had been hanging out already.

"Oh gross, you put your dick on my feet?" He hadn't even kissed me yet tonight, and his junk was on me. He skipped over way too many bases to get to this point.

"Don't pretend you didn't like it."

"Matt, you didn't ask. I wasn't ready for that yet." Not tonight, not this week. Not this time of the month, especially not the first time. I let out a heavy sigh.

"God, don't be so shrill."

Shrill? He said I was shrill? He hadn't heard shrill yet.

I jumped off the couch. My shoulders tried to climb into my ears, escaping the cooties my feet had obviously been infected with. I slammed my cootified feet into my shoes.

Matt sneered. It twisted his face into a caricature of a grouchy old man. "You've been jonesing after my dick for years. Deny it."

"That's not the point. You didn't ask. Just when it looks like we're finally gonna get together, you go and put your dick on me before you even kiss me?" Damn, he thought I was just some random booty call, and I… was stupid to have ever thought he would actually care for me. *I'm a fucking idiot.*

"You would have gotten to it eventually. I just got the party started."

"Not tonight. I wouldn't have. You are such an ass." He just needed to ask. Why hadn't he asked?

"You liked it, so stop acting like it's a big deal."

I halted my rush to escape Matt's apartment. This needed to be a clear fuck-off. I was done with him. I was done being stupid. I looked him in the eye, making sure he didn't miss it when I changed to staring at his crotch. "You're right. It's not big. I'm outta here."

Lonnie sat on my front stoop flipping a large, bronze coin in his fingers. I climbed out the back of the cab and approached him. The one person I wanted to see and there he was.

"I'm not a good man," Lonnie said as he stood. "I manipulated you." He continued watching the coin. "Seven years sober." He leaned down and picked up a brown paper bag.

I took the bag and pulled out a bottle of whiskey. This didn't look good, but it could have been worse. The bottle was new, the cap still sealed.

"I had a hard time not opening that tonight," he confessed.

"How long have you been here waiting?"

"For you? Thirty-two years. Show ended an hour ago. I came straight here."

"To wait for me?" I'm so fucking dense. Lonnie was waiting for me. He nodded.

"How did you know?" I asked.

"To wait? Or that you'd be coming home tonight?"

"Either." I was confused. Hurt by Matt's insensitivity but excited that Lonnie was here.

"I knew he'd fuck it up. That's actually my problem. I realized too late that I was responsible for putting you into a bad situation. He had asshole written all over him, and instead of warning you, telling you what I wanted, I sent you to him because it's what you wanted. I made him want you, but I had to check in, see you were ok, so I came here."

My heart thudded hard. *What do you want, Lonnie?*

"That's so… Lonnie." I went to hug him.

Lonnie placed a hand on my shoulder, holding me back.

"It's not noble, it's chicken shit. I couldn't deal with the possibility that Matt might do something to you, and instead of facing it head on and calling you to check, I lurked here like a creeper waiting for you to come home."

"Is that why the booze?"

Lonnie nodded. "There are moments in our lives that irrevocably change us forever if we're lucky enough to recognize them for what they are. The first time I was too doped up to clue in, and it took me another five months and thirteen days to realize I was given a second chance at life. Nine nights ago I faced another one of those life-defining moments. Eight days ago I found out the girl didn't want me, so I decided to help her get what she wanted. Her happiness was worth more than my own. Just over a week of knowing you, Ava, and I've been living in hell. So, yeah, I'm a coward."

"You seriously considered putting your sobriety at risk over me?" I was still not wrapping my brain around this. Lonnie was in hell? I was in hell. Did he want me, too?

"I am having a hard time coming to terms with putting you in Matt's arms, even though that's what you want."

"Turns out it's not what I want. I'm just now figuring out he's a total douche, not a good guy. He put his dick on my feet. He thought it was a sure fire way to seduce me. He hadn't even kissed me yet. How'd you guess?" I stood close enough that his chest brushed against mine when he took deep breaths.

"Matt's easy. He only wants someone if he thinks someone else finds them desirable. The more desired they are, the higher their worth in his eyes. He's blind to being able to see you for yourself. He fell right into your plan because he thought I was a threat."

"I want you to be a threat, Lonnie. What do you want?" I inched closer, and lopped my fingers into the front of his shirt.

Lonnie crushed me against him, and my air dissipated. His

arms bound me to him, and I did not want to escape. I wrapped my arms around him and pressed into him. Our lips found each other and I sucked on his tongue. He tasted like mint gum and coffee. He smelled like sweat, stale cigarettes, and too many different perfumes. I didn't care. He'd come straight here after the show to wait for me. *For me.* I dug my fingers into the mass of his black hair, while he grabbed onto the back of my blouse.

I was breathless when he finally broke the kiss. "You asked me what a good guy looks like, Lonnie. You. Good guys look like you."

"I'm not good. I have jealousy issues, I'm a recovering addict, I—"

"Shut up. And kiss me again."

I pulled his head to me and consumed his lips and mouth. He nibbled on my lip and I seriously considered asking him what he thought about period sex. No, not tonight, but soon.

"Roy, does this mean I can put my dick on your feet now?"

I snorted. At least he asked. If my arms weren't wrapped around him, I would have punched him. "Seriously? Don't act like a jerk. Maybe in a week or two. But, really, is that your kink? I'm not a fan."

He sighed long and slow. "Ava, I want to see you tomorrow, and the day after, and the day after that. I count every day I'm alive, and so far the days with you in them have been the most important ones," Lonnie said, his tone waxing serious. He kept touching my face and stroking my ear.

"I like that. I want to count days with you, too."

5

FIVE GLOWING RINGS

$\mathscr{T}$he lights dimmed and strobes of color danced around the venue. Amy bounced in anticipation She turned a crazy grin to Jackie, her cousin's friend who had stepped up to take the second ticket when Karen had been called into work.

"This is insane!" she shouted over the loud music. The energy in the nightclub was palpable, causing Amy's heart to race with excitement.

Jackie leaned closer to Amy's ear to talk. "So your grandmother really bought tickets for you and Karen to see a strip show?"

"Yeah, she thought it would be fun and distracting," Amy yelled back.

"I think I like your grandmother." Jackie's shoulder bumped hers as the house lights went black.

The stage lights slowly increased from nothing to glaring bright.

Six chairs lined the stage. The music grew louder. The people around Amy shifted restlessly in their seats. Nothing happened on the stage.

Whoops and cat calls from the crowd rang out, and still nothing but chairs. A billow of fog crept around the chairs.

"There are supposed to be men, right?" Amy asked. She always hated the teasing buildup of concerts. In theater it was lights out, music on, curtain open, show starts. Clearly these guys thought of themselves as rock stars.

Jackie laughed, tossing her hair over her shoulder. So far all of Karen's friends had been super glamorous, with perfect clothes, perfect nails, perfect hair. Amy would love to have hair that never needed to be ironed and didn't understand the concept of frizz. Karen also had the looks and the luck. Except for tonight. Her luck hadn't held and she was missing the show.

"Maybe they've stripped so far down there's nothing left."

"You're saying they're invisible? If that's the case, I like that long-haired one over there." Amy pointed randomly at the stage. If she was going to fantasize about a man, he was going to have long black hair.

The music grew louder. Colored lights swirled over the audience.

After several minutes of building anticipation, the lights dimmed again. The darker the lights faded, the louder the audience yelled in response.

Total darkness. The music stopped. A hush swept over the crowd.

Nothing but whispers. Amy's heart thudded as she nervously picked at the polish on her finger nails. She would never have perfect nails, not with this bad habit. At least she no longer bit them.

Impatience for the start of the show was killing her. These guys certainly knew how to build audience expectation, and she hoped they didn't disappoint. The only time she'd seen male strippers had been in movies or daytime television, and none of those men could dance. They just humped their crotches at women. They were pretty to look at, but Amy wanted to see dancing.

With a cacophonous blast, the music boomed and the lights blazed.

Six men stood in front of the chairs. From the hips down, they wore faded denim. Their chests were covered by zippered vests with hoods. The only things exposed were their well-defined arms and their chins. They appeared to be similar in height—posture could make up for slight differences— and quite tall. A few chins were covered in facial hair. For all intents and purposes, they were six identical men.

A loud crash of music, and moving as one, they unzipped their vests midway.

Another burst of noise, and the men shifted, showing off the size of their bulging muscles with a classic arm bend. Each time the music changed, so did the dancers, freezing with a new pose until the phrase of music changed. Zippers moved down further, and then back up. The poses became more athletic in design. The audience ate it up and showed their appreciation in screams and hoots of laughter.

The real dancing began with another eruption of sound. Spins, jumps, and the typical thrusts of male exotic dancers dominated their repertoire. So far the dances were just like every male stripper Amy had seen on television. It was entertaining, but nothing special.

Then the nature of the performance changed. The chairs became partners as the men used them to twirl and toss and even dance on. This was the stuff they never showed on TV. Amy grinned with the thrill of watching the men move. Finally. This is exactly what she wanted, a good fantasy about a man built like that.

The number ended, and the six dancers left the stage without ever exposing their faces. Their skills as performers and athletic gymnasts, along with plenty of pecs and abs, were all the crowd got to see.

They were replaced by four men in black trench coats carrying umbrellas.

Amy sang along to "It's Raining Men" as the dancers spun their umbrellas before tossing them aside, followed by the clothing they removed in a flash. There was barely any tease, hardly any finesse to the stripping. One moment they were clothed, and the next, thanks to break-away snaps and Velcro, they were not. Whoa! Anything that had been in hiding during that first number was now out on display. Well, almost everything.

With tight black satin booty shorts and gyrating hips, the men on stage strutted their way down into the crowd. Dollar bills filled the air like snow as women threw tips at the dancers. The women on the aisles were the first victims of the undivided attention of each dancer. The men thrust and humped at their targets while the victim's friends cackled in delight. Some of the women were bold enough to stroke the dancers' chests and thighs.

Oh crap, I'm on the aisle. Nope, I can't.

"Switch places with me!" Amy yelled at Jackie. She grabbed the other woman by the shoulders and squeezed past her, placing her companion on the aisle.

The rain routine ended, and those dancers were replaced. Jackie threw dollar bills and was rewarded with the gyrating attentions of a stripped down fireman. Amy couldn't stop laughing. Jackie hooked her arm around the dancer's neck and counter-thrust. Amy's jaw fell open at her brazen actions. She felt more like a voyeur than someone enjoying a raunchy dance show. Other women in the audience were also hanging off the dancers, and some of the dancers were groping their audience right back.

Once the dancer retreated, Jackie pulled Amy back to the end of the row. "Your turn. Karen said to make sure you get the full experience!"

New music, a new number, and cowboys boots scooted out to "Kemosabe."

Amy groaned. *This is going to be bad.*

Three men dressed like B-movie Native Americans emerged next. Amy closed her eyes against the atrocity. She cracked her lids just a enough to peek at the dancing. It was a train wreck, a stereotypical, beautiful, gyrating, dry humping, culturally insensitive train wreck.

But her peek was enough to show her that one of the Native men was possibly the most handsome man she had ever laid eyes on.

Her eyes popped open and stayed on the middle dancer. His hair gleamed long and black. His chest was well defined, as all the dancers were, yet his proportions seemed more perfect to Amy. He couldn't have been more beautiful if he'd tried.

She didn't recognize him from any of the previous numbers.

She would have remembered seeing that hair before. Most of the other men had short, clean-cut hairstyles, and the other man with long hair had a goatee.

She hadn't been joking when she'd told Jackie she preferred a man with long hair.

After Kyle, Amy wanted someone who was his polar opposite. She wanted thrilling instead of business conservative, and to her that meant tattoos and long hair. The long-haired dancer singled out an audience member and began the ubiquitous lap dance of grinding and laughter.

Damn, she didn't really care anymore about how inappropriate this number was. She could not take her eyes from the man. Of all of the dancers tonight, she wanted a lap dance from this guy. She wouldn't be opposed to a little sweat and embarrassment at his hands. Something about him drew her like a moth to a bug zapper.

She waved around her fan of dollar bills and whooped as he danced down the aisle. Their eyes met. Amy would have sworn she saw his dark eyes flash bright blue. He stalked towards her, coming closer than she anticipated.

Close enough to touch.

His jaw was strong with a square chin, his nose long and straight, and his lips... They were soft.

Amy melted into him as he held her face and kissed her. Her ability to see and hear the world around her disappeared. She wrapped her arms around his broad shoulders and held on as he deepened the kiss, biting at her lower lip, licking her and finding her tongue with his.

The world tilted sideways.

Amy righted herself in the hard wood chair. This was hauntingly familiar. Ah yes, the smell of antiseptic and dying flesh. The hand in hers tightened its grip.

She made hushing sounds as she stared into the bright blue eyes of her fiancé.

The mad, evil irony of it. She'd become a nurse to help wounded young men recover while she waited for the return of hers. She hadn't realized being a nurse meant easing their pain in their last few days of life. So many succumbed to their injuries no matter what the medical staff attempted.

This war was the devil incarnate, hell on earth. She had watched so many young men die. Too much blood had spilled onto the pinafore of her uniform. She had held so many hands, sat watch up and down this long row of narrow hospital beds for so many deaths. All the while she had waited for him to come home, waited and prayed. This was not what she'd meant when she said she needed to see him again. She wanted him whole, wanted him well.

His breath rattled through his lungs.

No.

She promised him it would be all right. Assured him he was home now, that he was safe and loved. That he should focus on recovering. His wounds could be overcome, and they could still get married.

She didn't cry. She couldn't cry, at least not anymore. All her tears had long been spent over the boys she didn't know.

And here was the one she loved so well, the one who was to be her husband, and he didn't even recognize her. His blue eyes stared blankly through her. His chest stilled.

NO!

Noise and bright lights rushed back into her consciousness.

The soft lips were pulled from her. Two men in G-strings and cowboy hats dragged her dancer back onto stage and behind the curtains.

Amy tentatively placed her fingers against her lips. She had felt the kiss for a mere second of time, but the smell of the hospital ward lingered in her nose.

What had just happened?

"What the hell was that all about?" Jackie yelled, shaking her arm.

Amy shook her head and looked at her companion in bewilderment. "I honestly don't know."

Amy followed her burrito down the line as it passed from one worker to the next. She pointed at the various salsas and toppings. Yes, she would like queso and an extra side of sour cream, please.

When Karen had left for work this morning, she had not been in a good mood, especially after Amy had come crashing in late after the strip show. Amy hadn't remembered the coffee table in the middle of the room, and several cuss words and one bruised shin later, she had woken her exhausted cousin. She'd known Karen had to work some, but she had assumed it wouldn't be this much. They had barely seen each other at all yesterday between sleeping and Karen getting called in for the night shift.

Today, Amy had spent the morning contemplating the rest of her life. She had several days left on her week-long vacation, time she had originally planned on spending with Kyle, and after that fiasco, with Karen. Now she was alone. Alone in a city she didn't know very well.

Dumped on Christmas Eve by her fiancé, Amy had been at loose ends with vacation time to burn. Karen had invited her to drink and party away her woes in Las Vegas for a few days following Christmas. It wasn't a tough decision. Play and forget Kyle, or hide on the couch at her mother's house? Karen's offer of libations and no explanations easily defeated tea and cookies. So she'd driven to Vegas, following behind Karen's car in her own, the day after Christmas. Their grandmother had even funded the strip show and some shopping excursions they had yet to take.

Karen's offer was for a place to stay and a base to return to after nights of gambling, drinking, and general debauchery. Karen's work schedule meant she couldn't party all day, but she'd promised they would have a few evenings to hang out, which for Amy meant margaritas by the inch and walking up and down the Strip taking in the free fountain and light shows. When Gran had offered to pay for tickets to a highly popular, expensive male revue, they'd decided it was a great way to add the debauchery quotient to Amy's vacation.

Now that debauchery was checked off, Amy had a few more days to cleanse the memories of Kyle from her system before she had to return home, go back to work, and get on with her life.

She paid for her burrito, picked up her tray, and scanned the seating area. Just a few seats away, a grin spread across the face of the most handsome man she had ever seen.

She froze. He had kissed her last night, and now he was here, eating a burrito and winking at her. Her blood pressure dropped the second before she let go of the tray.

Her burrito and chips crashed to the floor.

"Whoa there." A hand on her elbow prevented her from following her lunch down.

Gentle hands guided her to a chair. "You'd better sit before you fall over."

His voice was smooth as silk.

Amy couldn't see him because she was having problems focusing on what was in front of her. Her vision blurred in and out. The lights were fuzzy, and different faces kept flashing before her.

"Hey, Bud, get her a new burrito. What did you have, sweetheart?"

Was he talking to her?

"Huh? What?" was all she managed to mumble.

"What did you have?" He knelt down and looked her in the eyes. She could focus on those eyes. Those dark, familiar eyes. Last night they'd been blue. Hadn't they been blue? Amy's head began to swim again.

"Here, you'd better drink this."

A cup of cold water pressed against her lips.

Amy could hear the conversation as if it were behind a wall of cotton. They remembered her order. They wanted to charge her again, but this man insisted that they not. He spoke. Voices muttered.

She rested her hands against her eyes and propped her elbows on the table in front of her.

A tray slid in front of her, and the tangy, warm smell of queso-covered burrito filled her nose.

She moved slowly, lifting her head to see the man before her. "Thank you. I'm not sure what happened."

"You almost passed out." The light behind him cast his features into shadow. She shifted her gaze to the table in front of her. Two burritos, two drinks. He took the seat across from her, the light no longer behind him. She could see him clearly. He was gorgeous.

She looked into eyes of a rich, dark brown, in a face with high cheekbones and the dusky skin of a Native American. He smiled again, showing off the gleaming white teeth of a showman.

"I'm sorry about that," Amy muttered, embarrassed that she'd lost it after one wink and confused that he seemed to have different faces in her memories of him. And Amy had many memories of him, despite never having met him before last night. But why?

"I don't think you had much choice in the matter. Are you feeling better?" he asked. To Amy his soothing voice sounded as if it were full of genuine concern. She could listen to him murmur to her for the rest of her life. Maybe she had already, in a different life..

"I am, and I'll be even better after I eat something." If she could eat. Her stomach twisted with nerves. The stripper who'd kissed her was sitting across from her at the burrito shop around the corner from her cousin's apartment. What were the odds?

She hoped she wasn't blushing.. Of course it would take passing out in public to get the attention of a guy like this. Last night would have been part of the show. He probably kissed a hundred women a week. Despite his kindness, he wasn't treating her like she was special, because she really wasn't special at all, to anyone. Look at Kyle. And her family's response to the break-up. And Karen, inviting her to Vegas but working the whole time.

And just like that, the adrenaline rush of seeing this man again was replaced with the despair of being unwanted. Amy shoved a forkful of burrito into her mouth. At least food loved her.

"I recognize you from last night," he said in his deep, sexy voice.

Amy choked on her bite.

She swallowed and wiped a napkin across her mouth. "I

didn't think you would remember me. I mean, you dance for so many people. I guess that's all part of the routine, huh?"

He shook his head slowly. "Oh, no, I definitely remember you."

"How? You must kiss so many women. Oh, have you got one of those photographic memories, never forgets a face?" Amy asked. There was no way this guy just happened to remember her. She couldn't believe that. Not her. Maybe her cousin. People remembered Karen. Karen was tall and athletic with silky, long hair, and always dressed to impress. Amy was the polar opposite —short and curvy with some extra weight and curly hair. On a good day Amy considered herself to be fluffy and cute. And this wasn't really turning out to be a good day.

"I never remember faces. But I remember you. How could you think that I wouldn't? I don't kiss just anyone. And I never kiss anyone in the middle of a show. So trust me, I remember you."

Amy dropped her gaze to her food, her cheeks heating with the telltale flush of embarrassment. His lips on hers, the warmth of his skin, the smell of his sweat, were all somehow etched in her long-term memory. That hadn't been the first time he had kissed her, but it had. He remembered her. She remembered his lips. She remembered them as soon as he'd touched her with them. She peeked at him through her lashes, and yes, his mouth was perfectly formed, and she wanted to kiss him again.

"So what are you doing here? This isn't the Strip. Tourists don't typically wander into the neighborhoods for lunch." He grinned before taking a bite of his own food. She wanted to lick the dollop of sour cream from the corner of his mouth.

"You have something…" She reached over and delicately wiped the edge of his lips. He grabbed her hand and sucked the food from her fingertip. Her core melted into molten lava as his lips wrapped around her finger.

What had he asked her again? *Breathe, remember to breathe.* "I…I…I'm visiting my cousin," she stammered.

He let her hand go. The ability to form cohesive thought returned.

"She's at work today so I'm just hanging around. I've done

the Strip for the past two days, and that's plenty for me. I'm pretty much waiting for her to get off work and poking around until she does. I didn't want to be trapped inside all day." Amy wiped at her mouth. "At this point, I'm good just to hang out and watch movies while I lick my wounds.."

"Wounds?" he asked.

"I recently got dumped. Instead of house hunting with my future husband, I'm entertaining myself in Vegas." Amy cringed as she failed to stop her runaway mouth from offering too much information. This guy didn't care about the nitpicky details.

The pity in his gaze as it landed on her ring finger was almost a physical touch. "You were engaged?"

Amy nodded. "Yeah," she said with a mournful sigh. "For almost five years."

He rested his hand on top of hers. The touch travelled through her system, a tingling buzz as if she had licked a battery. "You need a friendly ear?"

His kindness, his pleasantness, overcame her normal shyness. Not knowing what possessed her, Amy proceeded to tell this beautiful man about how her ex-fiancé, Kyle, had wanted to exchange gifts on Christmas Eve instead of Christmas Day. She was eager to start new family traditions with him, so she'd agreed. She gave him the rechargeable power drill he'd been dropping hints for since they were hoping to purchase a house in a few months and get married in September. Their future was coming together, power tools and home ownership.

But she'd been wrong.

She toyed with the straw wrapper, rolling the paper into a tight spiral before unwrapping it. "Then Kyle handed me a small box. I thought maybe he had gotten our wedding bands, but it was a roll of cash. He was giving me back the deposit money on our wedding site. He'd never paid it, and he no longer wanted to get married." Amy blinked tears from her eyes. The acute, hollow agony she'd felt that day returned in a rush. "My early Christmas present was him returning my half of the deposit money to me."

The dancer reached across the table and wiped tears from her cheeks. "Please tell me you didn't let him keep the drill."

"He left it behind, so I still have it. That happened and I was numb. Had to tell my family the next morning. 'Merry Christmas, the wedding's off.'" *Yeah, that was fun. Not.* "The look my grandmother gave me. She clearly blamed—"

Amy's phone pinged, alerting her to a text. She picked it up, a welcome distraction from the pitying expression on her companion's face. "Well, crap."

"Are you okay?" he asked.

"I'm fine, just left to my own devices for tonight. My cousin picked up a second shift at the hospital," Amy explained. "She did a great sales job on the glam of Vegas, and so far I've been out on my own, hung out with a friend of hers I don't know, and stared at every single inch of her apartment. She's always at work. Hell, maybe I'll head home tonight. Get out of Karen's hair, let her sleep." Sadly, she hadn't seen enough of her cousin to know if they would make good roommates, an idea that had been tickling Amy in the back of her mind.

"Why don't you come with me? I only have one show tonight, and then we can go out."

Amy started to protest that she needed to...what? She needed to do nothing. Her cousin had left her on her own again, and a very good-looking man wanted to take her out. No, a gorgeous man wanted to take her out and was willing to be seen in public with her. Why the hell not?

"I didn't really bring clothes for night out," she protested weakly.

"You look beautiful as you are," he said.

This man—his grin, his voice—she wanted to wrap up in him. She knew why she wanted to go out with him—those lips, and maybe to figure out more about the strange memories she had of him. But why was he smiling at her like that? Why had he kissed her?

"I don't even know you."

"My name's Jason." He clasped her hand and shook it in a proper introduction. His hand was warm, his grip firm. She wanted to feel his hands hold her face again. "And we know each other. I think we've known each other for a very long time."

All the hairs on her body stood on end, and shiver ran up and down her spine. He was right. They knew each other. But how?

"Then who am I, Jason?" she teased, trying to ease the quaking she felt in her gut.

"I know who you are. We have had lives together. I just don't know your name." It felt true to Amy, but was it really the same for Jason? Or did the man have one hell of a smooth pick up line?

Amy rose and followed Jason out of the burrito shop.

"My name is Amy. And I would really like to go out with you tonight."

"Great!" Jason's smile weakened Amy's knees. "I have to head over to the gym before the show. I'll have a ticket waiting for you at will-call. Be there for the seven-thirty show?"

Amy nodded. "Yeah, I'll be there."

Jason leaned down and kissed her on the cheek. He was taller than she'd realized. She liked tall men because they made her feel petite. Something she didn't experience every day.

Amy placed a hand over the spot where his lips had brushed her face. He sauntered off, silky black hair flowing halfway down his back, long legs encased in faded denim. She blew air, slowly, out of her mouth. What had she stumbled into? Was this an alternative universe where buff, good-looking men paid attention to short, pudgy women?

Amy glanced at her phone. She had just enough time to go back to Karen's apartment and try on every single outfit she'd brought with her to see if she owned anything cute enough to wear on a date with a guy like Jason.

Amy picked up the ticket her new friend had promised would be waiting for her at will-call. She found a seat in the back of the venue, not interested in being up front in the thick of the action. The nerves in her stomach were dancing enough with the crash and boom of the music without adding the possibility of stripper lap dances to the mix.

As it had last night, the show heightened the audience's

anticipation with the music and the empty stage. When the lights came on to reveal the hooded dancers, Amy spotted Jason, second from the right. She recognized his square chin and the shape of his lips after staring at them over lunch. His movements displayed a fluid grace and a hard lock action the other dancers lacked.

When the "Kemosabe" number started, it felt like a punch in the gut. Jason seemed like such a noble guy, or maybe that was her hormones talking. Yet this number was so politically incorrect. She watched as Jason thrust his hips at the paying customers. A stab of ridiculous jealousy replaced all other feelings in her breast.

However, she couldn't help but notice he didn't kiss anybody.

Hoping that meant something, Amy watched the rest of the show alternating between amusement and territorial resentment. The next time Jason appeared on stage, Amy sucked in her breath and licked her lips. He was so sexy that it was almost unfair. He and the other two men on stage were dressed in fluorescent colors. LED lights twinkled throughout their costumes, splashes of bright body paint decorated their arms, faces, and exposed skin.

Jason twirled several hula hoops on one wrist. So did the other back-up dancer. In addition to the hoops, Jason's costume included an open vest that looked like a skinned puppet. Bandoleers crossed his chest, but instead of bullets, tiny lights dotted the belting. Something that looked more like a mini skirt than a loin cloth covered his ass, while neon chaps wrapped around his legs.

When the lights turned off, black lights illuminated the men. Their costumes glowed. The hula hoops Jason and the other man twirled left streaking trails of color from their internal LEDs.

They moved like ghosts, spots of colored paint identifying their location, the rest of their skin purple velvet against the inky black background. The hoops flew across the stage as the dancers tossed them to each other. The center dancer gyrated, and a spot light found him.

The stupid spot light was getting in her way. She wanted to

focus on Jason. Hoops in air, the fuzzy vests fell to the floor. She scooted to the edge of her seat as the audience reacted with louder shouts and catcalls. The men on stage continued to remove articles of clothing, and all she could see was the one spotlighted man and the hula hoops. She had to squint to see Jason.

Jason was down to just the chaps and the bandoleers. His G-string didn't glow. Dear God, was he even wearing one? She could hardly see him.

The chaps disappeared next. Then one by one Jason caught all of the hula hoops. All Amy could see of him were the glowing streaks as the hoops whipped around his body. The other two dancers left the stage and were now on main the floor, humping and grinding for the crowd. Amy ignored them, her eyes on Jason, as he continued to spin the hula hoops.

How the heck was he doing that? The hoops traveled up and down his body, turning him into a column of spinning color. The lights mesmerized her, as did Jason's dancing skills. As sexy as he was, the hip thrusts and humping weren't necessary. Then again, she wasn't on the receiving end of those thrusts. Up close and personal, perhaps she'd have a completely different perspective on Jason's movements.

He controlled at least one hoop with his feet. His hips and his hands spun the other hoops. The music ended on a loud crescendo. Jason held up five hula hoops like an illuminated fantail of a proud peacock. Amy's jaw hit the floor. She had problems getting one hula hoop to swing around her hips, and here was Jason manipulating five of them at once.

After the lights dimmed for the last time, Amy approached the bouncer by the backstage curtain. She handed him the note Jason had left with her ticket. The man nodded her over to some chairs before he disappeared behind the curtains. He returned a few minutes later and grunted, "He said to wait, he'll be right out."

Amy thanked him. While she waited, she watched the night-club empty, the house lights go up, and a crew of workers speed through the rows of seating, gathering garbage and getting ready for the next show.

Amy caught her breath when Jason emerged from backstage. She'd expected him to be in the same jeans and shirt he'd worn earlier, but he was clearly dressed to impress. He wore a tight black T-shirt, which shimmered just enough to suggest silk, tucked into dress slacks. Over this he'd donned a collarless black leather jacket. His hair was slicked into a braid, and his face glowed with a tinge of pink from being scrubbed clean of make-up, though remnants of dark eyeliner still ringed his eyes.

Amy considered the short black dress and floral leggings that had been the cutest of her suitcase's offerings. She hadn't come to Vegas to date, so she'd made do with what she had. She just hoped it was appropriate for his plans.

"You look good enough to eat," Jason said as he leaned in to kiss her cheek.

"Does that mean I'm okay to be seen in public?"

"You are too pretty to share." Jason enclosed her hand in his and led her out the back door of the club and into a parking lot.

"So now what?" Amy asked.

"Late dinner, then you let me seduce you."

Amy laughed. She didn't actually believe he was serious, as much as she wanted him to be. Jason seemed a little too good to be true. Maybe he flirted with everyone, and maybe he was setting her up. Maybe he was just a really nice guy, and a pity date was his good Samaritan action for the month. If it weren't for the strange memories she had of him, she'd never have agreed to this. "Dinner sounds great. I guess we'll play that other one by ear."

Amy spent all of dinner smiling and blushing. Jason made her laugh, and when he called her sweetheart she felt giddy.

"Where did you learn to hula hoop like that? That was amazing."

"I used to be a competitive hoop dancer."

"You were a competitive hula hooper?" Amy asked.

"No, Native American Hoop Dancer."

"About that." Amy cleared her throat. She didn't understand how he could debase his culture. She really liked him, yet this aspect of his career bothered her. "How can you to that whole cowboy and Indian thing?"

Jason's expression went flat. "Money, bills."

"Okay." She wanted to be enraged, but she realized her privileged upbringing did not give her the right to judge what others needed to do to survive.

But Jason wasn't finished. "People have prostituted themselves for less. I do the whole Tonto shtick because my tips more than double. The hoops let me show off. Those are what I love. I can't afford to do the hoops and not the rest. I make zero tips hoop dancing because I don't leave the stage."

Amy squirmed. She'd brought up the topic, and clearly it was something she didn't fully understand. Something she wanted to, and possibly never would understand.

"I'm sorry. I just wanted to understand. I didn't mean to come across so judgmental."

"It's hard sometimes. It kills my soul, yet I tell myself the money is worth it. I want to be a dancer. I don't want to learn a trade and get a day job." Jason gestured air quotes around the words *day job*. "Fortunately not too many of my family have come to my show. My mom knows about it, because there are some nights I just can't face myself. But I have to or lose my job."

"Hula hoops are really in right now. You could teach a hooping class."

"I don't want to teach aerobics. I want to dance."

"So you teach hoop dancing. Look, Jason, you're hot. I know you know this, run with it. Become the hot hoops instructor. Women will flock to you." Amy certainly would.

"It's not about the women, Amy, it's about the dance. But I do hear what you're saying. Find something that doesn't kill my soul that lets me do what I love. I'm working on that. I go to auditions, I coach other dancers. Being a stripper is a stepping stone on the way to a bigger goal. It's not my end game."

Amy shrank in her chair. "I'm sorry. I was rude."

"It shows you care." Jason's grin melted her. "It shows how big your heart is. You are concerned about the culture of others, of my culture, and you care about how it affects me. No one has really called me on my shit for a very long time. I didn't expect that of you."

Amy started to apologize again before Jason cut her off. "I like that." He paused. "I like you."

She blushed. She was drawn to Jason, more than she had ever been drawn to anyone she had known for such a short time. But did she care? Yes, she cared what he thought of her, but did that mean she cared about him? Too many emotions swirled in and around her skull. Whatever she felt, she hoped he did make good on his offer to seduce her. She wanted it more than anything she could imagine.

Jason led Amy out of the restaurant. He dropped her hand and then spun on the ball of his foot, completing several full turns. He stopped with a jump, planting his feet. "Whoo!"

"I guess you enjoyed your supper?" Amy ran after him as he danced down the street.

Ignoring the crowded sidewalk, Jason leaped onto a planter before landing with another spin.

"If you were singing, I would think I'd been transported into a musical," she said, looking up at Jason as he spun around a lamp pole.

He smiled down at her.

"Why do you say that?"

"Because you're dancing up the street like a mad man." She laughed.

Jason twirled and executed an undulating body wave before coming to a stop in front of her.

The breath caught in her throat as he merged their personal spaces. "You are music that makes me feel like dancing," he confessed in a low whisper.

Amy expected her face to burst into flames with the heat of her flush, but instead it was suddenly cold and wet. She lifted her face to the sky to watch the downpour overtake them.

She smiled into the rain. "It is like a musical, and now it's raining."

"You know what that means, don't you?" Jason asked. She shook her head and looked into his eyes.

"It means the hero gets to kiss the girl."

"Are you my hero, Jason?" Amy asked, focusing on his lips.

"If you let me."

Amy closed her eyes as Jason's mouth covered hers. His lips felt hot in the chill of the rain. She leaned into him, tasting his lips and his tongue. His kiss pulled at her core, her entire body flaring up like liquid fire. She wanted to feel all of him. His lips and arms were not nearly enough. Her entire being shook with need, with want. His arms tightened around her.

Her brain disengaged, and her perception of the world went fuzzy.

He stood towering over her. His long dark hair was pulled back and tied in a sleek top knot. She watched as he fastened his armor over his shoulders. He wouldn't let her help. She should never sully her fingers with the work of a solider. She stretched and rolled over languidly, enjoying the feel of the rough bedding against her sensitive flesh. Her silken robes lay scattered, discarded on the floor without regard for the expense or the fine workmanship. Her husband would always buy her more.

He kept her draped in finery, as if that was what she wanted from life. No, she wanted what she shouldn't have, what she had to sneak, and lie, and cheat to have. She wanted to be a soldier's wife, not merely his mistress. But that was not her life choice to make. That option had been taken away from her when she'd been married off to one of the Emperor's younger sons and not to the man whose bastard son she would bear and raise as her husband's.

She reached one of her lithe arms up to him, wanting to draw him down for one more kiss. Instead he grabbed her and pulled her from the sheets, pressing her nude flesh to the hard leather of his gear.

"I love you," she whispered.

His kiss was fierce and filled her with longing, even though he was here, in her arms.

"I'll return to you."

With those last words he turned and walked out of her life forever.

Amy gasped. The lights of the Strip twinkled in her peripheral vision. Jason's warm arms were still wrapped around her, holding her close. Her fingers bit into his skin for support.

"Tell me you felt that, too," he whispered against her lips.

Could he be referring to the memory that assaulted her, or did he think it was one hell of a kiss?

"Take me home with you," Amy replied.

They rode in the back of the taxi in silence. Had he seen a vision like hers or something else? She didn't know where to start, how to ask without sounding nuts, and she didn't want their driver to overhear. This felt beyond personal. This would expose her completely.

Nerves bunched in her stomach as Jason led her up the stairs to his apartment.

She stepped through the door into a sizable loft.

She turned to take in the apartment but found herself spinning into his arms.

Jason held her hand in his, tucked in under his chin, and began swaying back and forth. The music was in his head, and he guided their steps. She studied his face. Long dark lashes rested against high cheekbones, a straight, long nose, full, sensual lips.

What was it about those lips? Why was it that every time she kissed him, she became someone else?

"When I kiss you..." she started.

"It feels like you have kissed me a thousand times before, and even then it's not enough," he finished for her.

"Something like that," she replied softly.

Jason's lips found her neck.

"Oh." The flutter in Amy's core that had been building all night blossomed into a frenzied riot of need.

His kisses trailed down her throat. He unbuttoned the top of her dress and placed a kiss delicately on the flesh beneath. Blazing a trail of heat down her breastbone, Jason followed each button with a kiss.

His mouth felt hot, sharp, and soft all at once. Amy couldn't remember another time when anyone's lips had done this to her. Kyle had never done this to her, physically, emotionally. She didn't want to think about Kyle, she didn't want to think. She just wanted Jason.

He lifted her dress over her head and tossed it. She stood in his embrace in her bra and leggings. He towered over her, his gaze predatory. He stepped back enough to remove his own shirt.

Amy licked her lips. She'd seen his perfectly muscled chest

before, yet in this new context, he was even more sexy, more exquisite since he was hers.

He pulled her against him, her breasts crushing into his chest. Her nipples hardened as his warmth spread to her.

She played her fingers across his collarbones, tracing down and around his muscular pecs. She looked up into his eyes as he stroked the side of her face.

"I want to seduce you," he whispered.

Her breath caught in her throat. "It's working."

"Let me make love to you, Amy."

"Please." She wasn't begging. That didn't need to happen tonight, because this was a prayer for her desires. She needed to feel Jason's body pressing down on hers. She wanted to know what happened beyond the kisses.

Jason dipped, catching her knees with his elbow and lifting her into his arms. In a few long steps, he placed Amy on his bed. She laughed.

"What?" Jason paused to look at her.

"I halfway expected you to rip off your pants as if they had break-away snaps," she confessed.

"I don't think Armani makes stripper slacks," Jason said as he sank onto the side of the bed and shed his pants.

"Those are Armani?"

"I wanted to look good for you."

"Color me impressed." She shifted so she could wrap her arms around his chest, pressing into his back.

Jason swiveled and pulled her to his bare skin. "If you think that's impressive, wait until I make you scream." His mouth descended on hers.

The kiss didn't take Amy out of her body this time. Instead she became incredibly aware of all of her senses. The way Jason's manly scent filled her and heightened her yearning; the smooth, silken fall of his hair over her arms; the burning, hot press of his manhood against her belly.

The rest of her clothes found their way off with Jason's help. Finally, skin on skin. Hands petting and stroking. Lips everywhere.

Jason lowered her to her back. Amy gripped his shoulders as his mouth sucked in one taut nipple.

She gasped aloud as teeth scraped the sensitive peak.

Amy dug her fingers into Jason's hair, letting the strands twine around her fingers, gleefully and wonderfully captured. She giggled as he extricated himself from her grasp long enough to sheath himself in a condom, only to allow her to grab fistfuls of his hair again.

His knee pushed between her legs and against her core.

She moaned.

She needed friction. She needed penetration. Amy ground her hips against his thigh. Jason's fingers bit into the soft flesh of her ass as he lifted and brought her hips up to his.

A piercing thrust, and Amy cried out. That did not feel good, not at all.

Jason jumped back, removing himself from her body. He sat on his heels and reached for her. "Are you ok? That didn't sound good."

Amy shifted uncomfortably. "That's not exactly how I expected that to feel."

"What?" Jason looked down at his lap. "I'm not deformed."

Amy followed his gaze and stared at Jason's penis. Nerves bunched in her stomach, clenching with the reality of what they had done. Here he was in all his naked glory. He wasn't trying to hide from her, no shame or embarrassment. "No, you are not. That's actually a lovely specimen. I just hadn't realized it was going to be that pokey."

"Amy?" Jason drew out her name.

Amy stared into Jason's eyes and then quickly looked away. "Until about sixty seconds ago, I was a technically virgin. That's what's going on here. I thought it would be pressure and rubbing, not sharp and stabbing."

Jason ran a hand through his hair, brushing it back from his brow. "Well, fuck. Why didn't you say something? Why didn't you tell me I was about to be your first?"

Because I wanted you to like me. "Why? So you could turn me down?"

"I wouldn't do that." Jason shook his head. "I thought you said you had a long-term fiancé."

"Yeah, I did. Long-term. I was a virgin when I met him, and he liked the idea of having a virgin bride. But he kept dragging the engagement out longer and longer. Didn't seem to want to have sex, with me, anyway. And stupid me, I let him string me along."

"You aren't stupid. Don't say that."

"I am stupid, Jason. He was sleeping with other women the entire time. Just not with me. And that's not because I didn't want to. I did. He didn't." Amy turned her back to Jason. She didn't want to rehash the humiliation of Kyle not loving her, not while she was here with this beautiful man. Jason made her feel desirable in a way she never had before. She couldn't face him. She didn't want to watch him change his mind.

"Amy." He stroked her back, his fingers eased the tension that gathered in her shoulders. "That doesn't make you stupid. That makes you trusting. Why didn't you say something?" She leaned into Jason's warm and comforting touch. Perhaps she wasn't a pariah if he wasn't already rushing her out his door in horror. But she had to know.

"Because guys aren't interested in old virgins. It's like after a certain age you become some sort of freak. 'What's wrong with you that you never had sex before?' Guys wouldn't date me when I was a twenty-three-year-old virgin because they were afraid I would get clingy. Now I'm twenty-eight. I didn't want you to change your mind."

Jason continued to stroke her back, letting his hands caress her from shoulder to behind. He wouldn't keep cuddling her if she had freaked him out to the point of not wanting her. His touch and the soothing murmur of his voice reassured her.

"I wish you would have said something so that I could have done things better. I was in such a rush just to touch you that I had no finesse. I figured we were going for a marathon, and I was in a hurry to get started." He pulled her around and into his chest. "You need this done right. You need quality, not quantity. Let me make it up to you. Let's start again, from the beginning. Let me make love to you knowing I'm your first."

Amy relaxed, melting into Jason's touch. She found herself blinking tears from her eyes. "You still want me? Even though I didn't tell you?"

"Of course, I want you. My God, I've wanted you since I first saw you."

"Me, too." She had wanted him before he kissed her. After that, he was all she could think about.

"Are you okay? I mean, you weren't hurt badly, were you? You think you still want to do this tonight? I'm going to make love to you whether it involves penetration or not. There are other things we can do that will make you feel amazing." Jason spoke against her hair, his hands continued to stroke, tickling her sensitized flesh.

"Really? You're asking me if I'm okay?" She longed for him to touch her. Everywhere. The unexpected sharpness between her legs had already subsided. With Jason's coaxing, she would soon forget about it.

"I want you to enjoy this. You aren't if you're hurt. Unless you think pain is gonna be your thing?" Jason leaned back to look at her. He ran the back of his fingers down the side of her face.

She hooked her hand around his neck and pulled him close. "Make love to me," she whispered against his mouth.

Jason sucked her lips into a passion-fueled kiss. "My pleasure," he groaned back.

Again, his kiss didn't transport her to another place, another body. He grounded her in this reality.

She lay back and tried to pull him with her, but he shifted out of bed.

"I should have done this to begin with." He placed one last kiss against her lips before he moved across the large room and turned on music, low and slow R&B, with crooning voices. Once he lit a few candles and clicked off the overhead lights, the ambience changed drastically.

He slid back in next to her.

"Uhm, condom?" Amy asked, noting that he had discarded the earlier one.

"I'll get a fresh one when it's time. Roll over."

Amy complied. She looked over her shoulder. Jason rubbed lotion between his palms.

"It's okay," he said. "I'm just going to rub your back."

Grabbing a pillow for support, she lay as flat on the bed as her breasts allowed. She closed her eyes as Jason's warm hands pressed into her back. His thumbs drew circles into her muscles as his other fingers kneaded. He worked from the middle of her back, up to her shoulders, and down her spine.

She clenched her butt muscles when his hands began massaging her ass.

"Relax." His voice soothed, and Amy allowed herself to melt even more into the bed. He kneaded over her hips and down the backs of her legs, dragging any tension she had in her body out through her feet. He spent time on each foot—digging his thumbs into her heel and over her arch.

"Hey!" she called out when his teeth scraped over the ball of her foot. Amy twisted to watch as Jason began sucking each one of her toes into his mouth. The sensation of his lips liquefied her body. His tongue darted between toes and back over the arch of her foot. She couldn't form words, so she just moaned and muttered incoherent sounds of pleasure and encouragement.

"Come here." Jason lay down next to her, then coaxed her to throw a leg over him until she straddled his hips. "You touch me, too."

Perched on her knees, she looked down into his handsome face. "How?"

"Do what I do," Jason directed. She leaned forward and ran her hands over Jason's chest as he caressed hers. Up the center of her breastbone, over her collarbone, down the side of her ribs, he massaged the skin surrounding her breasts. Gently, he cupped each one and began squeezing at the supple flesh. Amy mimicked the motion across Jason's firm pectoral muscles.

When his thumb found her nipple, she felt as if he'd actually traced his thumb over her clit. Her internal muscles fluttered with want.

She scooted her haunches further down on Jason's leg. She had felt his erection press against her stomach earlier, and now she wanted to see it, to touch it.

"My turn." She spotted the bottle of massage oil on the table next to Jason's bed. She nodded at it, and Jason reached over for her, handing her the bottle.

Amy poured the oil into her palm and rubbed her palms together as she had seen Jason do earlier. Slowly she ran her hands over the tops of his thick thighs and into the thatch of curling hair around his manhood. His erection mesmerized her —how it throbbed and pulsed as she caressed him. With each pass of her hands, she grew bolder, touching him more and more, until she traced her thumb from the base to the tip of his shaft. She was surprised at how smooth and solid it felt. Like suede-covered marble. And warm, so warm.

"What do you like?" Amy asked as she petted his shaft.

Jason hummed. "The usual."

"I don't know what that means."

"Haven't you ever given a hand job?" Jason asked, concerned.

"When I said virgin, I meant virgin, completely. No hand jobs, no blow jobs, no fingering."

Jason groaned.

"I'm sorry, I'm sorry." Amy pulled her hands away from his groin and scooted back further.

He reached for her. "No, I'm sorry. This feels good. You touching me feels good. I want to show you how to give a hand job, and a blow job, and all of it. But if I do, there won't be as impressive a showing for the actual deed."

Amy raised her eyebrows. Jason wanted to impress her? Didn't he know that just being himself was impressive enough?

Jason chuckled. "Round two is never as remarkable as round one. If you keep touching me this way, round one will end prematurely. Tonight needs to be about you, not me. There's nothing to be sorry about." He pulled her down on top of his chest. His skin was smooth and warm, and feeling him against her breasts and belly fanned the flames burning in her core.

Jason rolled with her until he was back above her. He lowered his head and sucked a taut nipple into his mouth. The more Jason played with her nipple, the less she could think. When he caught her other nipple between his thumb and finger, she practically levitated off the bed. Jason lowered one hand to the curls at the juncture of her legs, Amy thought she might die. Her body felt so tight. Her need pulsed beneath his fingers.

She cried out when his fingers found her clit and began stroking rhythmically. The long tapering digits continued to slide over her, and then they were thrusting into her. At first it stung like he rubbed against a cut. The more her body reacted, the less she noticed any discomfort, only euphoria and need. Her body was on fire. She felt as if she would literally burst apart if he didn't stop. But if he stopped, she would die.

"Oh, Jason, whatever you're doing, keep doing it," she managed.

He paused, his mouth leaving her breast.

"No," she pleaded. "Don't stop now."

"Condom." Jason smiled down at her.

He shifted between her legs, his hand returned to toying with her folds and clit. "You ready?"

Amy shut her eyes and nodded.

Jason kissed her, plunging his tongue between her lips. Amy sucked on him as if he were life itself. She arched against him as he thrust into her fully. Their bodies merged into one. Amy couldn't tell where she ended and Jason began. Pressure, stroking, urgency, she didn't cry out but pulled harder on his tongue. She wanted all of him inside her.

She had to stop kissing him as her breathing grew more intense. Was this passion or a heart attack? She held her breath, before screaming as everything burst apart at the seams. She couldn't see, and she didn't want to. She couldn't control her movements, yet she felt as if she continued to counter-thrust against Jason.

Stars exploded above her. Visions of different lives played across her mind's eye, lives from World War I, an African tribe she recognized but couldn't name, the Russian steppes, the Pacific Islands, feudal Japan. Hundreds of lives that had all been shared with Jason. Her body continued to burst with convulsions from her core as he thrust into her over and over. She finally reformed into her body, her internal muscles continued to clench and hold onto her lover. He pushed his hips against her one last time and stopped moving. He growled and moaned all at once. She strained against him as he held tight onto her.

With a shudder Jason fell against her.

Amy panted, trying to catch her breath. Jason rolled to the side and pulled her into his arms.

"You okay?" he asked, stroking her hair away from her face.

"Uh-huh." She whimpered. "That wasn't what... Oh... That's... Wow. Did I do good? Cause I think that was ridiculously amazing."

Jason kissed her brow above her eye. "You did better than good. It felt like you truly enjoyed it."

"You can feel it when I explode?"

"Of course. All those muscles, and I'm right there in the middle of them. It's incredible."

"No, I exploded. I turned into dust and sparkle, and I saw my past lives. I knew the secrets of the universe, and then I was sucked back into my body. And there you were." She smiled. "It was glorious."

Jason kissed her again. "That's one hell of an orgasm."

"That was an orgasm?" Amy asked in disbelief.

"Virgin with a capital V," Jason muttered. "Didn't you ever play with a vibrator or anything?"

Amy shook her head. "Nothing up and in, especially not after I got engaged and it became an issue. I mean..." Amy blushed and tried to tuck her head into Jason's chest to hide. "I've rubbed on things, and I've gotten the ooh I'm done twitches. I figured those were orgasms. Oh my God, I can't believe we're talking about whether I've ever masturbated."

"I thought it was more about if you'd ever experienced an orgasm before."

"Well, definitely not like that. How about you?"

"I've made women scream before, if that's what you're asking.

Amy stiffened. "That's not what I'm asking."

"Right. Sorry." He caressed her arm. "For me it's not an explosion, it's more of a black hole, and I collapse into it before bursting free."

"Do you get visions?" Did he see what she had? Did he know they had experienced all of those shared lives before this one?

"Not typically. But I do get very tired. Shhh, we can talk more later. Right now, sleep." Jason pulled blankets around Amy's shoulders.

She relaxed into his even breathing, falling asleep soon after Jason stopped talking.

"Hell, I don't know."

Amy rolled over and rubbed her sleepy eyes. She could hear her cousin talking loudly on the phone from the other room.

"She came in like a herd of wildebeests in the middle of the night. It's like she doesn't care that I have to get up and go to work." Amy held still and focused on what her cousin was saying. When she'd tiptoed into her cousin's apartment just before one a.m., Karen hadn't been off work yet. She was the one who'd stomped in like a herd of wildebeests about forty minutes later, waking Amy from dreams of Jason.

Amy didn't want to wake up, she wanted to go back to her dreams. She had no intention of eavesdropping on Karen. Amy thought they had gotten along great since she'd come to Vegas— but the conversation she was hearing indicated something very different.

"No, she's out cold now, snoring. She's probably drunk off her ass. Oh my God, Jackie told me she's a total slut. I totally believe it, too. She just broke up with her boyfriend like days ago. She's not even interested in hanging out with me. Like, what am I, a Motel Six? Jackie went to that strip show with her, said she was groping the men at the strip club. She said they had to pull Amy off one guy. It was embarrassing. Seriously. Ha. She would have blown that guy then and there in front of everybody, she was that bad."

Amy rolled onto her back and frowned at the ceiling. What the hell? Why did Karen think such a ridiculous thing about her? Jackie must have lied to her about what had happened at the strip club, but why? And now Karen was spreading rumors about her, which was stupid, because it's not like Amy knew anyone else in Vegas. Who was Karen trying to impress with how horrible Amy was?

Karen dropped her voice. Amy heard her walk past the door to the office where Amy slept and into the small kitchen. Karen's whispering sounded like hisses. "She's a total cow, low self-esteem and everything. My grandmother made me invite her. You know, a pity thing since she just got dumped. No, no. She goes home tomorrow. It's not soon enough. I'm going to have to disinfect my entire apartment from her skank." Now that sounded more like Karen was telling the truth. "No, I'm not stuck with her today. I get to go to work instead. It's a tossup, really, work or hang with my cuz? At least I get paid at the hospital." So much for considering a move here.

Amy felt like an elephant had stepped on her chest. Cow? Wildebeest? She thought her cousin liked her. She thought they were friends. This hurt worse than Kyle; this was her cousin. She didn't dare move, doing her best to pretend to be asleep. If she had to face Karen at this moment, she didn't know what she would say, or do. Rage collided with hurt in her heart. How were you supposed to behave when everything is a lie? The sound of the apartment door slamming spurred her to action.

Amy jumped out of the bed and shoved her things into her bag. Her hands shook with frustration and rage. Skank?

She has to clean up my skank? She mockingly imitated Karen. "Come hang out with me. Come get drunk and get laid. I live in Vegas. You'll have fun forgetting that douche. We know how to party here. Oh, I have to work. Oh, go to the club with this total stranger who is my friend. Oh, I took a double shift. Fucking hypocrite."

She dumped her cousin's makeup box onto her bed. That lipstick looked expensive. Perfect.

In large, looping script Amy wrote, "Your friend is a fucking lying bitch," across the bathroom mirror. She set popcorn in the microwave and pressed start. After changing out of her PJs, she lugged her bags out to the car. She came back inside to the stench of burning popcorn. "Here's your skank." Amy looked at the lipstick intending to write on the microwave with it, grabbed a paper towel, wiped off what was left, capped the tube, and popped in into her purse. She liked the color.

Amy drove over to Jason's. What was she going to tell him? Would he let her stay?

She'd just met him, but she didn't want to leave yet. Until overhearing her cousin's overstressed tirade, she'd actually thought of proposing that she pay half the rent and move to Vegas. Now she didn't even want to be in the same city with that two-faced workaholic.

Amy bounced on the balls of her feet as she knocked on Jason's door. She was nervous as hell to see him again. She had wanted to stay with him all night, but silly adult that she was, she'd figured she shouldn't stay out when she was Karen's guest. She hadn't even told Karen about her dinner date, let alone that she was spending time with the stripper from the show who had kissed her. She hadn't even gotten a chance to tell Karen about Jason kissing her at the show. No, Jackie had taken care of that, turning it into Amy almost blowing the man right there in front of everyone.

Jason was taking forever. She could hear him moving around inside. She knocked again.

The door flew open. "God, what already?"

The annoyed voice belonged to a beautiful woman with high, broad cheekbones and the same long black hair and coppery skin of Jason's heritage. The woman was in her bra holding a shirt in front of herself.

Amy couldn't breathe. The elephant on her chest was joined by the rest of his herd. Jason hadn't wanted her to leave a few hours ago, but he already had another half-naked woman in his apartment.

"Is Jason here?" she managed in a whisper.

"Yeah, but he's busy." The other woman sneered. "He just stepped out of the shower, should be getting dressed."

Amy followed her gaze. She could hear the rumble of Jason's voice but couldn't hear what he said.

"It's one of your women," the lady yelled back to him.

One of your women. One of. One of.

Amy's vision dimmed. She turn and ran. She bolted down the

stairs, gulping for air. Her foot slid, she stumbled on the last few steps, and sat heavily before she fell.

She couldn't breathe *One of. One of. Not even someone special, just another one in a line. One of.*

Amy held on to the handrail above her head. She sucked in gulps of air and sobbed. She closed her eyes, but all she saw was Jason's face clenched in passion above her. Grinding the heels of her palms into her eyes, she tried to rub out the visions of him. She saw his cold, dead blue eyes staring past her. She saw the warm, fathomless depths of black eyes that loved her. She saw his chocolate brown eyes smiling at her. Visions of Jason, or any of a hundred other faces that she had loved in a hundred other lives, wouldn't go away

She fell forward as strong, warm arms pulled her into an embrace.

"Amy, what's the matter? What happened?" Jason stroked her hair back from her face.

She tried to struggle and shove away from him, but she had no strength left. It had drained completely. Her cousin thought she was a skank, and to Jason she was just another woman.

"Go away," she cried and weakly pushed against him. "I'm not just one of your girlfriends. Go back to your latest woman."

"What the hell did Heather say?"

Amy shook her head. She didn't want to talk to Jason. She hadn't asked to fall for him, but she had, and this hurt. The betrayal from her cousin had felt like a hard squeezing, but this felt as if her cells were being shredded. How much more rejection could she take in a week and still survive?

"Come on, Amy, what did my sister say to you?"

His sister. Amy stopped railing against Jason and clung to him. She gulped, trying to stop crying.

"Not another lover, but your sister?"

"My sister."

Amy looked up at Jason for the first time since he had found her. His face was full of concern, his eyes red as if he had also been crying.

"Come on." Jason helped Amy to her feet. "I'm happy to see

you. I thought it wouldn't be until later, but these tears are making me sad. Why are you so unhappy?"

"Your sister," Amy managed to say as she trembled. She held onto Jason, her nerves still raw and frayed from the emotional beating.

"Is this just about Heather?"

Amy shook her head. "My cousin. She hates me." She sniffed, trying to stop her crying. She lost against another flood of tears.

Jason led Amy back to his apartment.

"Amy, this is my sister Heather."

Amy looked up, but Heather was focused on the project in her lap. She probably thought Amy was an idiot.

Heather sat cross-legged on the floor surrounded by fabrics and sewing supplies. She stitched small silver cones to light blue fabric, trimmed with white and bright yellow. "Oh, hey, it's you again. Jason, do I really have to knot each bell?"

"If you don't, and one breaks off, it will drag the rest of them. I thought Mom showed you this?"

"It's been years since I competed. Give me a break." She returned her focus to her stitching.

Jason led Amy past the kitchen area and back to his bedroom. "Heather is putting together her regalia for a pow wow next week."

"Is that why she didn't have a shirt on earlier?" Amy sniffed and wiped at her nose.

Jason chuckled. "Probably. So let me see if I figured this out. My sister answers the door in her bra, makes a crack about you being another woman, and…"

"And I ran away," Amy finished. "I came over early because my cousin doesn't want me there."

"What happened?" Jason sat next to Amy on the bed and pulled her into his chest.

She leaned against him and played with his fingers, finding solace in touching him.

"She thought I was asleep. Her friend lied about me, and I heard the whole thing. Karen believed the lies and said mean, vicious things. I thought we were friends. She left for work, so I ran away and came here. When I saw Heather, I thought, oh

God, Karen is right and I am just a slut. I slept with you and never even thought about anything else."

"Don't say that. There is no shame in what we did. There is no shame in enjoying sex."

Amy swallowed down the rest of what she wanted to tell Jason. He had just said this was about enjoying sex without shame. No mention of emotions or connections. So Amy wouldn't bring those up, either.

Instead she said, "I thought I'd ask if you wanted me to stay again tonight or if I should just head home to Riverside." The drive wasn't very long, just about four hours, depending on traffic. She could use an extra day to resettle back into life, go grocery shopping, but she would much rather stay with Jason.

Jason lifted her face with a finger under her chin. "Please stay." He lowered his head and pressed his lips against hers.

The world swirled, and Amy saw the man she loved in horsehair pants and wool jacket chasing after a giggling child in a bright red robe. She looked down at her own robe wrapped loosely around her expanded belly.

The vision didn't last long before Jason pulled back from the kiss. Amy blinked several times to reorient herself to the here and now in Jason's apartment. He wanted her to stay. Her heart soared.

"I promised to help Heather this morning, and then we'll go grab lunch. I have to work both shows tonight. Do you want to come, or do you just want to hang out here and watch TV?"

"I don't know. I'm so tired right now." Amy whimpered, suddenly overwhelmed by exhaustion.

"Why don't you lay down and rest while Heather and I get some work done? I'll check on you later."

She felt like a complete loser, and Jason was being so nice. He kissed the center of her palm and pulled a blanket over her shoulders.

She didn't remember falling asleep.

Amy sat in front of Jason on the bed. His legs wrapped around the space she occupied. Her legs were over his thighs as they faced each other. She had watched both of his shows earlier tonight, enjoying the thrill that at the end of the night, no matter how many women shrieked at him or threw money at him, he was taking her home.

She traced around his features with her fingertips, wondering how was she going to be able to leave him in the morning. She shook her head. Afternoon. She wouldn't head out until he had to go to work. The drive home would take a chunk of her day, but not all of it. She didn't want to think about it, yet leaving was nagging at her. How could she tell him she didn't want leave? Should she tell him? She hadn't been ready for a rebound affair. She wasn't looking for one, and that wasn't what she wanted from Jason. She'd only known him three days, but she wanted him, he was vital to her. And when she kissed him, she saw all of their pasts together.

She didn't think she had it in her to write this off as a two-night stand. But admitting this to him took more courage than she possessed. If he didn't feel the same, she would crumble apart.

The small smile on his lips and his physical reaction told her that he enjoyed this moment, but did he want more than this moment? Though this moment was...wonderful. He had invited her to touch him anywhere and everywhere, to discover a male body with her hands.

It didn't bother him in the least that he was her first. He was gentle and patient with her as her fingers explored the planes of his body. She trailed up his perfect abs, defined even in their relaxed state. She circled his belly button and played with the crisp hairs trailing down. He giggled, grabbing her hands away from his stomach. "Hey, that tickles."

He smiled into her eyes, and Amy melted.

"I don't want to leave," she confessed, her breath catching in her throat.

"You don't have to leave for a few hours. Let's not think about it," Jason said as he leaned in and kissed the palm of her hand.

"What should I be thinking about?" she asked.

"This." Jason kissed her neck. "And this." He placed her hand on his thickening cock. "And this." He palmed one of her breasts.

He was right. She needed to ignore tomorrow and just enjoy right now.

"I can't think at all when you do that," Amy murmured as Jason licked and sucked at her. Her fingers fumbled as she attempted to reciprocate and stroke him.

"Hmmm mmm." Jason hummed against her delicate flesh, causing her to inhale sharply.

He started to fumble for something on the side table. She leaned over and grabbed the foil packet he blindly reached for.

Jason lay back, letting Amy take the lead. Rolling the condom down his engorged length felt odd yet sexy to her. Safe sex, something she had never put much thought towards before meeting Jason. She had just assumed Kyle would know what to do when the moment came. It was time for her to take control of more than a few aspects of her life.

Jason reached up and tuggedat one of her nipples, and any thought process Amy was engaged in dissolved into raw energy and hot need. His strong hands gripped her ass and lifted her. She let him guide her down until she was impaled on him. She didn't try to suppress the moans as she rocked against him. The reciprocal noises he made drove her in her passion.

All the nerves in her core caught fire as her body shattered. Jason called out and clutched her hips with a bruising grip. She continued to push onto him until her thigh muscles seized up and her body dissolved into star dust.

She slumped against him, panting as she came back to awareness of their joined bodies. She twitched and shuddered as her body continued to thrum with ecstasy.

Jason pulled her down into his embrace and brushed the hair from her face. She was mostly asleep when she heard him mutter about "forever" and "this life."

Amy hoisted her bag into the trunk of her car. She wanted to confess her feelings to Jason.

"Amy." Jason's voice saying her name was almost enough to stop her in her tracks. Almost enough to make her turn around and tell him how she felt. Almost. She did hesitate before slamming the trunk. She fought against it. She didn't want to say goodbye. She didn't want to leave.

Despite the fact the night they'd spent together was earth shattering, Jason hadn't said a word indicating this was anything other than a fling, a couple of wonderful nights while she was on vacation. She knew the saying, this was over and never to be spoken of again. She didn't want to burden him with her sticky needs and emotions. She wasn't going to be a clingy virgin. She wasn't...

Until she saw sadness in his eyes.

"I really like you, Jason. I'm sorry. I know I'm supposed to be cool and all...but...you...this. I know you must have other women and everything, but... I'm so bad at this," Amy blurted, her resolve gone.

Jason pulled her into his embrace. "No one is saying this has to be the end. Riverside is only a few hour's drive away. You can come back on weekends. I can drive out when I have two days off in a row."

She didn't have words to express her enthusiasm, so she kissed him. At first it was merely a hard pressing of lips, but then she softened her pressure, and Jason slipped his tongue to twine against hers.

The world tilted.

All the men preened and pranced. Proud as they could possibly be. He smiled, but only for her. She knew his ochre makeup, black lips, and beaded adornments were for her. He had made sure she would be there. The dance tonight would take forever before she could run away with him.

She felt abandoned as Jason's lips left hers.

"Are you serious?" she asked when they finally came up for air. "You aren't just saying that?"

When he grinned, she had to fight even harder not to yank her bag out of the trunk and lug it back upstairs for good.

Jason brushed hair back from Amy's face. He smiled into her

eyes. "I'm not just saying that. I don't want to be your what-happens-in-Vegas-stays-in-Vegas."

Amy laughed as she led Brian down the sidewalk toward her apartment. She flipped her keys around in her hand. They had spent a long day in training. Spreadsheets and flowcharts crowded in her brain. After a group outing for dinner, Brian, one of the accountants from the Portland office, asked if there was a nearby movie theater to fill his time. Needing to catch up on all of the holiday releases, and knowing Brian was married, Amy asked if she could tag along. No one else decided to join them. She wanted an escape from the seeping darkness in her soul from missing Jason. A movie seemed like a perfect platonic distraction for them both.

"Amy." A low voice caught her off guard.

"What? Who's that?" Amy stopped. Her heart jumped to her throat. Brian placed a hand on her shoulder. "Jason, is that you?"

Jason emerged from the shadows near the front of her apartment. "Amy, what are you doing?"

"What am I doing? What are you doing here?" Her heart thudded even faster. Jason.

Brian stepped in front of Amy. "She's on a date, asshole," he responded.

Amy pushed back in front of Brian to stand between him and Jason. "This is not a date. You're married," she explained.

"You left two days ago and are already dating? I thought we were going to try to work something out?" Jason asked.

"It's not a date," Amy repeated, her voice rising in pitch. She needed Jason to understand .

"So you just needed me to get past your little situation." He turned to Brian. "Were you going to sleep with her?"

Brian chuckled. "Well, yeah."

Amy pursed her lips and glared from one man to the other. "No, we were not going to have sex. You're married. This is not a date. Oh my God. I was just going to lend you a fucking book because you couldn't wait for me to bring it in tomorrow."

Jason continued to address Brian. "What's your take on sleeping with virgins?"

"Jason!"

"Naw, man, virgins don't know what they're doing," Brian replied, ignoring Amy.

"What the hell, Jason? Why are you here?" Amy asked.

"Dude, what is your problem?" Brain asked. He stepped forward and looked at Amy as he puffed out his chest.

"Get away from her," Jason growled. He loomed menacingly and stalked toward Brian. Brian was taller and thicker than Jason, but Jason had muscles and the fluid movements of a dancer.

Amy watched as the men squared off. "Would the two of you stop?" Now they were annoying her with their display of macho bullshit.

"Back off." Brian shoved against Jason's chest.

Jason staggered back.

"Get away from her," Jason countered, pushing his chest against Brian.

"Get off me, asshole." Brian shoved again.

"You still gonna sleep with her? Even if I told you she's a virgin?"

Jason would not back down.

Amy was torn inside. Part of her was furious at the spectacle these two assholes were making of themselves. Part of her could not have been more happy to see Jason. If he hadn't startled her so badly, she would have leaped straight into his arms. Instead, her coworker thought this was a date, and testosterone poisoning filled the air.

Brian paused and then turned to Amy. "That true?"

Amy rolled her eyes. "No."

"Because I took care of that for you," Jason snarled.

Brian chuckled. "So you do virgins?"

"I do her!" Jason yelled and swung at Brian's jaw.

Brian's head kicked back. When he reoriented himself, he lunged at Jason, tackling him to the ground.

Amy danced around as the men punched at each other. "Stop it! Stop it."

She pulled on Brian's shirt, finally catching his arm to prevent him from successfully punching Jason in the face for a third time. "Get off him!" she yelled.

Brian jumped up and huffed as he glared down at Amy. He started to reach for her. She pushed at his chest. "Go away. I can't believe you thought this was a date."

Brian brushed her hands away from him. "Get off me, bitch. The only reason I was gonna sleep with you was for a pity fuck. You're nothing but a fat cow. Good fucking luck doing any better than this loser."

Amy's chest lifted and fell with her heavy breathing as she glared at Brian's retreating back. What the hell had just happened? She knelt beside Jason and lifted his shoulders onto her lap.

"What are you doing here, Jason?" She stroked his hair away from his face, looking at the bright red marks that were going to develop into nasty bruises. She was so happy to see him, but this whole situation was messed up.

Jason lifted his hand up to touch her.

"You know how you said guys didn't want to sleep with virgins because they were afraid the girl would get clingy?" He gave a derisive chuckle. "Apparently it's not the girl who gets clingy. The guy is afraid he will." He pushed himself into a sitting position and then stood. He extended his arm for Amy, pulling her into his embrace.

"I couldn't even make it a full forty-eight hours without you. Amy, you're going to think I'm mad. I've known we belong together since the first moment I saw you. I know because I had a weird past-life flashback of some sort. I kissed you because you were my wife and I loved you completely. I've had several of these flashbacks at different times."

"Me, too," Amy whispered. "I was afraid to say anything. I thought you would think I was crazy."

"I'm so glad you've had them, too. That means neither one of us is crazy."

Amy nodded. "I've had several. Most were good, happy memories. Some were horrible."

"In Japan, I was a warrior and you were married to the Emperor's son. I was executed to protect you."

A sob caught in Amy's throat. "How?"

"I have no idea. But what I do know is that I am in love with you and have been many, many times in hundreds of lives before this one."

"I didn't know how to tell you. When you first kissed me, I watched you die in a hospital bed. I've seen you with our children. You took me away from my husband because we loved each other." Amy smoothed his hair away from his brow. Now that she had him again, she did not want to stop touching him.

"All those past lives can't be wrong. We belong to each other. Come back with me. Marry me."

"That's really sudden, Jason." Amy paused. It felt right in a way that marrying Kyle had never been. "How is that going to work?"

"I don't know. We'll figure it out. For now you'll stay here and work, and I'll be in Vegas. We'll have weekends until I find something here or you find something in Vegas. Or, hell, we'll both find something somewhere else—as long as we're together. What's important is that I love you and I need you."

Amy couldn't breathe. Her heart threatened to burst out of her throat. Tears spilled down her cheeks.

"And here I was thinking that I was a fool for having fallen in love with you so fast." She pulled his face to hers and slid her lips over his, kissing him as if he were the air she needed to survive.

"So?" Jason's eye bored into her. "Will you marry me?"

"I love you, Jason. I have loved you for so many lives. I want to love you for a thousand more. Yes, I will marry you."

This time when Jason kissed her, Amy saw this life, this love, their children, and their happily ever after.

6

BLAZE AND GLORI

*A*lone in a ridiculously long line, Glori felt awkward, obviously on her own. The stuffy terminal induced sweat and her glasses slid down her nose. It would have been nice to already be with family, she could have had help with her bags, but no. Everyone had agreed to meet on the boat at dinner time.

The line moved, and she hauled her stuff another four feet and shoved her glasses back up. The attendant had said to have passports and tickets out and ready. Glori had stood like a statue with papers in hand for a good fifteen minutes before she realized she was at least fifty feet and thirty minutes away from being asked for her documents.

She began to think she had over-packed, and underprepared for this check-in process. Even worse, she might need to pee. No, no tinkling thoughts. She was not about to give up her place in line. She could hold it until she made it past the desk attendant.

So she inched along, holding it in, for what seemed like hours. When she finally leaned against the counter and handed her documents to the check-in clerk, the lady had the gall to set the papers down and walk away.

"Hey, come back!" Glori called after the uniformed woman.

She slowly banged her head against the counter. "I have to pee, come back."

Someone chuckled behind her. She glared over her shoulder at the culprit. Who would dare laugh at her obvious misery?

A hot guy, that's who. He was staring right at her, eyes crinkled in mirth. Why did the good-looking ones always have to laugh at her? Cute-and-douchey. So much for a cute but, sweet guy. Why didn't those exist?

The clerk finally returned, asked Glori a few questions, stamped papers, and directed her to the nearest restroom.

Glori couldn't move fast enough, her teeth were about to float away. In her haste, she stumbled, spilling the contents of one of her bags. Small, wrapped Christmas presents scattered across the floor.

Glori slumped. Defeated.

"Go, I'll pick all of this up for you," a friendly male voice said.

Glori looked up, expecting to see an older guy—but it was Cute-and-douchey.

He waved a hand toward the restrooms. "Go. I promise I won't steal anything."

Glori adjusted her glasses, afraid she was going to start seeing yellow, and managed a "thanks," before dashing to the restroom, leaving her bags with maybe-not-douchey guy.

Glori lugged her bags up the gangplank and onto the cruise ship. She had really thought Cute-and-douchey had been Cute-and-nice there for a moment. When she returned from the restroom, he'd been chatting with an older, sensuous beauty whose looks Glori could only dream of having.

"Thank you so much." Glori tried not to gush, but her bladder was more grateful than her brain.

Cute-and-douchey nodded in acknowledgment but continued to talk with the rich cougar.

"Are you not going to introduce me?" The woman purred in some kind of odd accent.

"Sure. Chick-who-had-to-pee, this is..." He paused to let the cougar fill in her name.

"You are not with her?" The fake-sounding accent grew thicker with every word.

Before she could say anything Cute-and-douchey laughed. "Hell, no, I was just watching her stuff so she could go to the restroom before she embarrassed everyone and herself." The blush of shame heated Glori's face. She grabbed her bag handles, doing her best not to touch Douche-boi.

"I'm sure everyone is grateful to you for saving them from the embarrassment of my massive bladder failure."

She stomped away, her belongings in tow, ignoring the laughter of Cruise Cougar and Douche-boi.

So far, this cruise sucked hairy donkey balls. She lifted her unwieldy case over another bump in the gangplank and fumed. On such a huge ship, the odds of running into those two again was minimal. Once the cruise was underway, things would be better.

Blaze heard the entire thing, the exasperated young woman struggling and the asshole frat boy who stepped in to help. At first, Blaze had been taken in by the kindness of the man. But the words coming out of his mouth didn't match his actions. He wasn't trying to help the poor frazzled girl, clearly on her own and with more baggage than she could manage. He was showing off for a group of posh women who looked to be shopping for a cruise romance.

He wanted to deck the guy when he introduced her as "girl-who-needed-to-pee." Blaze couldn't miss her flush of embarrassment as she ran away—or the flash of comic book panties as her skirt flipped around in her hasty escape.

He also didn't miss that she left one of her bags behind. The large tote still over Jerk-boy's shoulder matched her pop-art floral luggage.

"Hey man." Blaze reached out to shake the jerk's hand. "I saw what you did for that lady."

"Some of us are cut out to be heroes." Jerk-boy smiled at the cougar next to him. She was attractive, and rich, based on the jewelry and designer clothing. She sized Blaze up as if he were an option for her main course. He was too used to the game from women like her. On the job, it was one thing, but on his own time, he didn't play.

Still shaking Jerk-boy's hand, he reached up and removed the bag of gifts from his shoulder. "Well, you missed one. I'll just take it for you so you don't have to interrupt your chat."

Blaze strode after the frazzled woman, whose raw need had become his problem. He'd spent the last year trying to figure out what was wrong in his life, and a big part of it was his apathy. For months he'd been trying to be the change he wanted to see in the world, to do good because it was right, not for a reward. He tried to convince himself returning her bag had nothing to do with the flash of her shapely ass or her pert little nose.

Blaze sucked in his cheeks and bit the inside flesh of his mouth. Not too long ago he had been that jerk-boy: high maintenance professional boyfriend for higher maintenance divorcees. Until he met Leanne. She wasn't a divorced older woman, but she was the daughter of one. She wanted a man with money like daddy and a body like a stripper. Blaze had the body because he had the job. Unfortunately, strippers don't make the kind of money that pays for Jaguars, condos, or Louboutin shoes.

Blaze spotted the woman ahead of him right before she disappeared into the ship, her long pigtails easily identifying her. Faced with a welcoming crowd of smiling ship attendees, he lost sight of his goal.

"Have you seen a flustered young lady with luggage that matches this?" he asked, holding up the tote bag he had rescued.

One of the cruise attendants, remembering the distinctive luggage, directed Blaze to the port side of the ship, down a level and forward in the bow.

Once in the long hallway, Blaze wove through other passengers, catching a glimpse of her pigtails. As the hall zig-zagged he lost sight of her temporarily. The next time the hall jagged, she had disappeared.

Nobody there. She had to be behind one of the closed doors. Blaze took a deep breath and prepared to knock on every door in this section. Right before he began, his quarry popped out of a cabin and headed straight toward him.

The donkey balls this cruised sucked on were getting bigger and hairier. She'd left the gifts with Douche-boi. How the hell would she find him? Glori raced out of her room and smacked at full speed into a wall of solid muscle. The rebound knocked her onto her backside.

"I am so sorry," she began before she got a glimpse of her victim. She pushed her glasses back and looked up. Her mouth dried and her tongue turned to sand. An angel with unruly dark red hair and a square chin smiled down at her. She blinked, expecting the vision to clear and the countenance of the man in front of her to fade into average, or even into the basic good looks that Douche-boi sported. If anything, the more she looked at him, the better looking he got. He radiated light.

She gaped up at him as he held out her tote bag. "You forgot this."

"My bag!" Relief overwhelmed her, and then gratefulness. The vision in front of her held out his hand to help her up.

When she slid her hand into his, a warmth spread over her body. He hauled her to her feet and offered the bag. Which she couldn't take because she was clinging to his hand like a weirdo. Awkwardly she let him go and accepted the tote.

"I… ah… actually came out to go look for that."

"At rather high speed," the man noted as he rubbed his chest.

Wowza, and what a chest it was. He made the guy back in the terminal look like a marshmallow. Glori had a hard time peeling her eyes away from the way his faded T-shirt framed broad shoulders and strained at his strong arms. And to think she typically wasn't attracted to muscles. She considered herself to be a mind over matter kind of girl.

She managed to refocus on his smile. It was dazzling and

seemed genuine, as if he were amused with the situation, and not laughing at her.

"How did you get it? I thought I left it with…"

"That jerk? You did. I saw the whole thing and figured he wouldn't make sure you got your bag, so I took care of it."

"You saved my Christmas." Glori rummaged through the tote, ensuring all the presents were accounted for.

"I'm sorry. I'm being rude. I crash into you and don't even ask your name. Glori." She stuck out her hand again.

The man took her hand and held it—didn't shake it, just held it. "Blaze."

She stared at his hand then at his luggage.

"I really am sorry. You came after me before you got a chance to put your own stuff away."

He shrugged. "I didn't bring nearly as much stuff as you did. Traveling with family?"

"I'm meeting everyone later. They drove down day before yesterday, but I flew in this morning. I'm supposed to room with my cousin, but she's not here yet."

She realized she was babbling as Blaze nodded, the red curls around his collar bobbing with the motion.

Glori's mouth went from the Sahara Desert to flood of drool. Who knew hair would do that to her? She thought she could deal with the muscles without being affected. But his grin and that red hair? No wonder his name was Blaze. Damn.

Glori continued to babble. "My mom decided this would be a good distraction for the holidays, seeing how this past year has been pretty crappy all around."

Blaze nodded at her comment. "That it has. I'm glad I was able to find you and get your bag back to you. It was nice to meet you. I hope you have a good cruise."

"You have a good cruise, too, and Merry Christmas." She watched as he made his way down the long hallway. She certainly hoped she would see that smile and hair again on this trip. It seemed things were finally looking up until she tried to go back into her room.

Locked.

Glori beat her head against the door. She could picture the key perfectly, sitting on the table next to the bed.

Big, pulsing, fat, hairy donkey balls.

Glori leaned back in her deck chair and tried to read. She pushed her glasses up her nose but the words continued to blur. A loud, attention grabbing laugh did its job, it caught her attention. Douche-boi and his entourage of slimy friends walked past. Why had she thought he was good looking yesterday? The clean cut hair? How could that compare to some unruly copper curls? The broad shoulders? The smile? He was chesty but mushy. Top heavy. Did he not know you should never skip leg day? Glori didn't work out and even she knew that you never skipped leg day.

What had Blaze called him? Jerk-boy. Full of himself. Clearly, he and his friends all had over-inflated egos. No need to acknowledge him again. Besides, how could she keep a straight face if she had to speak to him? He wore a yellow speedo, a banana-yellow banana hammock.

She snorted at herself. When had she gotten so judgmental on looks? Oh right, when she ended up on a cruise that was clearly more about appearances than relaxing. This morning her mother admitted to having purchased a new wardrobe for this vacation, right before berating Glori on her outfit. There was nothing wrong with it—a tank top, a polka dotted skirt, and a men's dress shirt with the sleeves rolled up to protect her from the sun. A straw hat topped it off. Her mom hadn't commented on her smiley face panties, only because she hadn't seen them.

A group of middle-aged women with off-season tans got out of their deck chairs and sashayed in the same direction as the douche patrol. If she lurked behind them, she could call it obser-vation in the name of anthropology. The study of the cruise cougar, yeah science not curiosity—and better than this boring book. And her boring family. She could hardly tell that this was some special family trip, her cousin was a no-show, and everyone else was ignoring her, doing their own thing. Other than the gifts stashed in her room, there were no tell-tale signs that Christmas existed on this boat.

Glori made it to the bar before she chickened out as cruise anthropologist. Her small glimpse showed her a television quality soap opera with cougars and gigolos, when she was more in the mood for a comedy. Glori began wandering the decks. People-watching on the upper deck was less entertaining. Away from the pool and the bar, people seemed intent on their winter tans, but at least there was a breeze. And a view. The ocean stretched out as far as the eye could see, no sight of land or other ships. It was kind of eerie, and kind of cool.

She heard the beat of dance music and followed it to another bar, one featuring dance lessons on an outdoor dance floor.

Glori swayed to the music. It was her favorite jazzy swing, but she was too late to join the lesson. Plus, she was alone, it was hard to participate in social dancing without a partner.

"You want to dance?" a deep voice behind her asked.

"Love to," she answered before she turned to see who her dance partner might be.

She let out a small "eep" when she recognized Blaze. "You dance?"

The sun caught his hair and it lit up like curling flames. His name fit him even better in the sunlight. She wanted to reach up and get her fingers caught in his curls.

"I do. The question is, do you?" He smiled down at her.

Glori set her book inside her hat and place both on a deck chair. "I Lindy and swing a little."

Blaze picked up her hand and twirled her onto the dance floor. Her skirt flew up and out—then again that was why she wore this style and the crazy undies. She never knew who would see them when the skirt went flying.

They started with a light two-step that Blaze quickly led into the more typical side-by-side steps and kicks.

He pulled her back into a closer embrace. "Do you flip?"

Glori nodded. Blaze placed his hands firmly on her ribs and swung her behind and around his back before putting her feet back on the ground.

She laughed in delight.

"Again?"

She nodded, this time Blaze flipped her up and over his arm.

Glori, winded but enthused, stumbled a little upon landing. Blaze halted, steadying her. "You okay?"

"That was fun, just lost it a little there at the end. You weren't kidding when you said you danced." Blaze confused her senses and made her tingle. She pushed her glasses back into place and smiled at him. He smiled back. It made her toes curl.

"Excuse me Miss 'I swing a little'." Blaze mocked her earlier words.

"I used to dance more, but nowadays it's a little. I need water. Want something?"

"Water." Blaze nodded.

Glori returned to find Blaze resting with his legs stretched out in front of him. His shorts showed off slim but muscular thighs that had not missed leg day. Under his loose shirt, he didn't appear to be bulky, just well muscled and flexible. She breathed in the sight of him. The past twenty-four hours had turned her shallow, ogling a man because he had great legs and red hair.

She handed Blaze a bottle of water and grabbed her hat. She dumped her book on the table and put the hat back on top of her head.

Blaze took one look at her book and began laughing.

Glori snatched it out of his hands. "So what? I read. You should try it sometime."

"It's not that." Blaze retrieved something from the chair next to him—a copy of the same book. Then he slid his sunglasses on. "How far in are you?"

"No way." His copy of the book had wear on the spine and a bookmark sticking out of the middle—and she was a jerk. "Well, I take back my reading comment."

Glori managed to escape her mother's clutches after a morning of shopping and eating entirely too much at the buffet. Strolling along the upper deck with a wrapped gift in her hands, she scanned the other passengers for a bright crop of curly hair. Most of the sunbathers this afternoon were couples.

And here she was, trolling for a guy. Was she stupid? Yesterday they might have danced a little and talked about the book they were reading a lot, but she didn't even know if he was single. The book she'd purchased him as a thank you for saving her Christmas was probably overstepping. If she saw him with someone, she could pretend it was for someone else. It was less than ten bucks, no big deal. Besides it was Christmas day.

She descended to the pool at the stern of the ship. Since this was a modest sized cruise ship, her ability to find Blaze was reasonable. She sure kept seeing Douche-boi everywhere, and she didn't *want* to see him.

Deep in the shade of an awning, Glori spotted her man. Was he alone? He lounged, book in hand, next to a table with a pair of sunglasses...and a single cocktail. Bingo. Her apprehension quelled, her feet took her to his side.

"Hi," she interrupted, blocking the sun from his face.

"Hey, Glori." His smile made his eyes sparkle and emphasized the shape of his lips.

Glori swallowed hard. She could swoon over that grin.

"I wanted to give you something." She held the wrapped present out. "It's a thank you. And you're almost finished with your book, so I thought... Well, you saved my bacon, and my nephews got to unwrap their presents this morning. That kind of thing is really important to kids."

Glori twisted self-consciously after Blaze took the gift.

"*On the first day of Christmas my new friend gave to me...*" Blaze sang a bit as he set the package on his knee. "What are you doing for the rest of the afternoon? Want to go swimming?"

"Yeah, no. I don't do water, and I'm stuck in family obligations. I snuck out cause I wanted to thank you." She pointed at the gift in his lap. "I'm expected soon or my mother will call the chief steward to conduct a ship-wide search." She turned to leave.

"Merry Christmas, Glori. And thank you."

"Merry Christmas to you, too." She gave him an awkward, flappy wave.

Because she was completely uncool, she couldn't stop herself from a last glance over her shoulder. He was grinning at her as she climbed the stairs to the upper deck. She stumbled, cursed, and waved again.

This time he waved back.

Sun, beach, barely a hint of Christmas, no worries. This was why his family had sent him away this week. They were concerned about him, even a year after the breakup.

His mom, convinced he was internalizing his pain, paid for him to go to therapy. He'd welcomed some perspective on aspects of his life that may have lead up to Leanne's explosive departure. It hadn't taken the therapist long to conclude he was well balanced.

While he may have seemed to have had a complete personality change when Leanne left, it was really her just taking all the superficial away with her. Now he felt like a new person, more caring for others, more responsible in the world. He'd starting spending less money, teaching more, and volunteering. The weight that had been lifted from his shoulders when Leanne, the culmination of a life of bad choices, had left in a fit of petty rage had allowed him to soar.

A familiar giggle caught his attention. He straightened in his lounge chair and scanned the area for Glori. There she was, dancing in the water as the waves licked her toes. She wore a vintage style sundress with wide straps and a short full skirt, a straw hat, and white tennies in her hands. She laughed and giggled as she dashed back and forth with two little boys, the nephews.

Blaze settled into a more comfortable position under his cabana shade and watched. No bathing suit—she'd said she didn't swim—but he was glad to see she put her toes into the water. Here was a woman who made no pretenses about who she was. Her hair was a natural light brown, no highlights or tell-tale roots. Her clothes said comfortable yet defined a personal sense of style. Glori and her tortoise shell rimmed glasses liked things a little retro, and a lot fun. Like her panties. Someone who knew their panties might be seen and still had a sense of humor about it was the kind of person he wanted to spend time with.

And, of course, there was her dancing. For just having met, they'd moved so well together. He couldn't remember a time when he'd danced so naturally with a new partner. He would love the opportunity to dance with her again—and other things. She was the kind of woman he could take out and show off. Not only was she adorably attractive, she could move. What was he thinking? She was sweet and funny, with lips that he desperately wanted to kiss, but this was a cruise. She could be from anywhere.

But it wouldn't hurt to find out more about her, would it? He headed for the water, determined to make his vacation even better.

"Hey, Glori."

He'd caught her by surprise, she jumped and gave a small scream.

"Blaze!" A smile lit up her face.

Blaze returned her grin.

Her eyes scoped down his shirtless torso. "Holy crap." She smacked her mouth shut. The look on her face indicated the words had escaped before she meant them to. "Are you wearing sunscreen?"

"I am. Are you?".

When she stepped closer to him, he felt a tightening in his groin. "Always, but then again, I don't sunburn. You're a ginger, and gingers fry."

"Like a freaking lobster. I wear lots of sunscreen. Right now I'm getting my vitamin D for the year. You look like you're having fun. I thought you didn't do water?"

A wave washed up Blaze's legs. Glori jumped against his chest as if the wave had goosed her. Blaze welcomed the cooling water. His body was heating up. She jolted out of his arms. "I can swim, I just don't particularly like it."

As the wave receded, she eeped and pulled the skirt of her

dress up around her hips, exposing her panties. Today she wore candy canes, a reminder this was Christmas vacation.

"We're in a bit deep for me," she confessed.

"I'll keep you dry." Blaze scooped her up into his arms and took two steps out to sea as the tide pushed him.

Glori began squirming and kicking. "No, I was serious. Stop it."

Blaze dug his feet against the current. "It's okay. The water is barely up to my knees."

"Take me back." It was a demand, not a tease. "I'm not kidding. I don't like water where I can't see my feet. This is too deep."

"Okay, whatever you like." Blaze forged back to where the waves dwindled to his toes.

Glori squirmed out of his grasp. "That wasn't funny, I have issues, and you just ignored them."

"I just... Look, I'm sorry." Glori skittered away from the waves. Blaze felt embarrassment heat him all over but realized it was the sun. He needed to cover up before he fried. "I need a shirt, hold on."

Blaze jogged back to his cabana and grabbed a shirt. Still at the shore, Glori was dejectedly kicking at the water.

He stepped back in front of her and pulled her chin up with a finger. "You okay?"

Glori smiled. "Sorry I freaked. I figured you were making your escape."

"Hardly. I'm just getting to know you." Blaze slid sunglasses over his eyes and turned his attention out to the water. "How'd you pick the book you gave me?"

"Aunt Gloreee! Aunt Gloreee!" A small boy ran towards them, stopping a few yards away. "Grandma said you had to come back now. The ship's gonna leave."

"Tell her I'm coming." The boy turned and ran away, and Glori sighed. "I have to go."

This was nowhere near enough time with her.

"What are you doing later tonight?"

She seemed to agree and flashed him a cheeky grin. "Mandatory family dinner. I'm free after that. Want to meet for dessert? I'll tell you about the book then."

"Wear your dancing shoes," Blaze called after her, watching her flip her skirt side to side as she returned to her family.

"So how was your Christmas yesterday?" Blaze asked.

Glori gazed up at him as as they strolled through the lower deck, watching overdressed passengers gambling. The highlight of her day had been him smiling at her, but she couldn't exactly say that. Or could she? "Boring, stressful, and expensive. We all had to hang around while the boys opened presents. I escaped long enough to find you, but the rest of it was pretty much eat too much and hang out in my parents' stateroom and watch my nephews play with shit and watch cartoons."

"Didn't you get anything good?"

"I didn't get a cruise. Ask me how much I love that. I got a gift card. Mom thought it would be better than giving me the cash to cover my ticket. Ask me," Glori gestured. Since her cousin hadn't shown up, apparently she was on the hook for the whole cabin. Financially, this was going to hurt.

Blaze grinned at her. "Okay, Glori, how much did you love that your mother gave you a gift card?"

"Arrrr" Glori stomped in a circle before stopping and pointing out through a window. "I agreed to take a cruise to support my brother because I would get to hang out with my crazy inappropriate cousin and my parents were paying for it. She didn't show, and they didn't pay. If you hadn't found my bag, I would have been totally screwed." Glori stopped and sighed mid-rant. "Thank you, Blaze, I don't know if I've said it enough but, thank you. You saved my family's Christmas, and my ass. Don't get me wrong, I love my brother and those little monkeys, just it would have been nice if this trip wasn't all about distracting my brother and keeping the boys happy. I mean Christmas is typically always about the boys, only grandchildren and all, but I can usually run away and go out. And it doesn't cut into my rent the way this trip has."

"Distracting your brother?"

"Nasty divorce and his ex is psycho. This was my parents' idea to prevent her from showing up and ruining Christmas."

Blaze let out a derisive snort and rolled his eyes.

"Was that for me, or the psycho ex?" She thought Blaze liked her, but she had a hard time reading his signals. Then again, she always had a hard time reading other people's signals. That was the nice thing about kindergarteners. They didn't have hidden signals. They were excited, they were cranky, they were tired, they needed to pee, they were hungry, they were bored. And all of those emotions and needs were out on display.

"Psycho ex is why I'm here, too."

"Oh yeah? What's your sob story?" Glori flopped down into an upholstered chair, crossing her ankles as she stretched out.

Blaze dragged a chair over to sit next to her.

"Last Christmas I was about to become engaged to a beautiful woman. Turns out she was pretty on the outside only. I was going broke trying to provide for her. She threw a fit, trashed our apartment, and vandalized my car. All on Christmas Eve after I came home late from a job."

As he frowned, obviously reliving some bad memories, she wanted to offer comfort and caress the side of his face. Instead, she pushed her glasses up her nose.

"What kind of job? Cat burglar? Drug dealer?"

Blaze scoffed. "I had a performance showcase where my partner and I went to a corporate event. We danced and showed off a bit, then we provided dance lessons for everyone, so they could have a grand ball, with everyone waltzing around."

"I take it your ex wasn't your dance partner?" Glori guessed.

"Nope, and she was convinced that I was having an affair with my partner. So when I came home later than expected, kissed her good night, and immediately fell asleep, she took a golf club to the living room. I woke up the next morning and all the dishes were broken, the sliding glass door was shattered, and the tree had taken a real beating. And she was gone. I seriously dodged a bullet there. Actually it felt more like I dodged an entire firing squad."

"I'm so sorry, Blaze. That's bad."

"Yeah, well, she didn't find the ring I had for her. I had a realization after she left. I was a complete egocentric douche. I decided it was time to change my ways. Grow up, figure out who I really was. Mom thought I was taking it really hard, and that I was going crazy. I like to think I was going sane. Anyway, my sisters and mom sent me away from all things Christmas, and put me on a boat for a week."

"Has it worked?"

"Nah. But I didn't need something like a cruise for Christmas. Leanne didn't ruin it for me. She gave me a terrific gift when she left. She gave me myself. And this year, you" Blaze paused staring into Glori's eyes, "gave me a book."

Glori's mouth went dry.

"Did you like the book?"

"I did. It was entertaining. Vampires who aren't vampires, and other things that go bump in the night save the day. I finished this afternoon. Why that book? All they had in the gift shop?"

"One of my favorite authors. And, yes, they had it at the gift shop. I figured we were already reading the same book, so I took a gamble and thought you might like this one as well."

"That makes it a special gift. You shared your favorite author with me." He leaned forward in his chair, staring into her eyes. "You know my deepest darkest secrets. Now tell me everything about you."

"I teach kindergarten. I'm not allowed secrets." Glori giggled. "If I have any and the kids find out, then it's no longer a secret."

Blaze leaned back and folded his hands behind his head. "Where did you learn to dance?"

This was not going to be impressive. There just wasn't anything impressive about her, but he seemed interested, so what the hell? "Okay, everything about me. This is awkward, you know that, right?" She eyed Blaze, whose eyes twinkled with mischief. Glori proceeded to tell Blaze everything from her choice of profession to how an ex introduced her to dancing. It felt a bit like an inquisition, and the words rushed out of her in a torrent.

When she slowed down, Blaze took her hand. "I don't mean

to make you feel awkward. I want to know all about you and I'm being profoundly uncool about the whole thing. Let me make it up to you." Blaze stood and offered her a courtly bow. "Shall we go find a dance floor and cut it up?"

Glori slipped her hand into his. "Absolutely."

The discordant ring of the cabin phone woke Glori. She was warm and comfortably wedged next to pillows. Until her wall of pillows shifted and grabbed the ringing phone.

"Hello? No, wrong cabin."

Glori's eyes cracked open. Pillows don't have groggy morning voices, and don't answer phones.

The phone rang again.

Glori clambered over the human obstacle in her bed and grabbed the receiver. "Yes?" she answered a little too brightly.

Her mother's voice pierced her eardrum. "Do you have someone in there with you? I just called and a man told me I had the wrong cabin, but I swear I dialed your number."

Glori glanced over at Blaze's sleepy form. Not quite awake, she couldn't exactly remember why he was in her bed. She put her fingers to his lips in a shushing gesture, hoping he wouldn't make a noise. His lips were distracting and soft to touch.

She had to focus on her mother's words.

"No, it's just me. Your finger must have slipped or something.."

"Meet us for breakfast at the buffet, and then we can all go to the beach."

"Um, I'm going on a coffee plantation tour with a friend."

"Friend? You didn't tell me you knew someone on the cruise," her mother chided.

"Just someone I met. We both love coffee, so, yeah."

But her mother wasn't having it. In the end, Glori agreed to meet her mother at the buffet first just to shut her up.

Blaze let Glori keep her finger on his lips until she hung up the phone. The moment she did, he pulled her close. "Morning," he said before kissing her.

The kiss was light but still flustered Glori. Why was Blaze in her bed, why were they still dressed, and why was he kissing her? She didn't mind; she just didn't immediately remember.

"I must be dreaming. I'm not awake." She lay back down and closed her eyes.

She felt Blaze shift against her. "Who was that?"

Glori kept her eyes shut. She knew she wasn't dreaming, but she wanted to stay pressed against Blaze's back instead of face her mother. "My mother. She expects me to have breakfast with everyone in forty-five minutes and then go to the beach."

"You told her you were going to the plantation with me." Blaze shifted again and pulled Glori into a spooning position.

Glori sighed. "This is nice. I don't remember you falling asleep here."

"Neither do I. We must have drifted off after I walked you back. Do you want me to leave?" He burrowed his face into the hair near her ear.

"Hmm. I'd like you to stay. Hell, I'd like to stay, but I have to shower and get dressed before I meet my family."

"You sound very much like you don't want to." Blaze's smooth voice in her ear made her melt. Their conversation last night had wandered over all sorts of topics, at times like rapid-fire Q and A session. They had danced, and they strolled the decks holding hands, and when she started yawning, Blaze walked her to her cabin.

"I don't, but Mom will guilt me with the nephew card. They love me."

"You have plans. Just say no."

"It's not that easy." He wouldn't understand. This was her mother.

"Then I'll go with you, and I'll say no." Blaze kissed the back of her head and sat up. "I'll go get ready and meet you there."

Glori's insides flipped in response to his kiss. She rolled over to look up at him.

Blaze extricated himself from her bed. The clothes he had slept in were a rumpled mess. He stretched.

Glori watched as he seemed to extend, and then extend some more. "Lordy, you're tall."

"And you're cute." He leaned down and came in for a kiss.

Glori's insides did another flip as his mouth descended on hers. Blaze felt like electricity against her lips. "Probably should brush my teeth before I do that again." He laughed.

Glori nodded enthusiastically. She wanted to kiss him some more but was not yet willing to share her own morning breath.

"Are you sure you wanna come with me today?" Her nerves danced. Even though they had spent the night together and nothing had happened, she couldn't believe he still wanted to spend the entire day with her, too.

Blaze lowered his lids and looked at Glori. She would have sworn it was a leer. "I definitely want to come with you."

"Terrific." She needed a buffer between her and her family. She hoped this would go well. "Meet me at the big buffet for breakfast and a showdown with mom."

Blaze stepped out the cabin door, winking at her before he left. "Forty-five minutes."

She flopped back on the bed in happiness. This cruise had improved exponentially since she'd met him. He had kissed her, he was meeting her for breakfast, he wanted to come with... "Oh God," she moaned loudly she clued into why he'd leered as he said that. She was such a dork.

They met in front of the eat-until-you-explode buffet to face Glori's mother. Glori wore another flippy little skirt. He had to admit he could hardly wait to see what today's panties looked like, and not because he wanted to dance with her. He wanted to remove them with his teeth.

After Glori apologized to him one more time for what was about to occur, they found her family at a table piled with dishes, indicating they had already made several trips through the buffet line.

"Hi, Mom." Blaze recognized her exasperated tone because he used it with his own mom. Glori was bracing for a battle.

At her greeting, her family all turned their eyes to Glori. He recognized the two boys as her nephews from the beach and assumed the man about his age was her brother. The two older couples had to be her aunt and uncle and parents. The older women favored each other, and Glori looked like both of them.

"You're late," said the lady with the large bouffant hair. That must be the mother.

"I'm not late. I'm not having breakfast with you." Glori indicated him with a hand wave. "Blaze and I have to meet our bus for the plantation tour."

The aunt looked over her glasses at Blaze. "Are you sure you wouldn't rather come shopping? Or go to the beach with the boys?"

Glori twisted the toe of her shoe into the floor, a gesture Blaze had come to recognize as discomfort. "I'm all beached out. Besides, I've had this planned, I bought the tickets a while ago. Need to use them."

Blaze didn't like the scrutiny they put her under. He rested his hand on her shoulder. "The tour's really popular. We're lucky Glori booked in advance."

"I'm sorry we haven't been introduced." Glori's mother stood, making a production of folding her napkin and placing it next to her plate. She extended her hand to Blaze. "I'm Gloria's mother, Mrs. Asher. What is Blaze short for? Is that your last name?"

"Blaisier, ma'am." He took her hand, noticing that she had a limp grip. Assertive woman with dead fish handshakes—must be a generational thing. His mother was the same.

"And what does your mother call you, young man?"

"My mother calls me Blaze, so that's what I go by."

Glori's mother grabbed Glori's upper arm. "You'll excuse us for a moment." She hauled Glori through a set of sliding glass doors to an outside deck.

Blaze smiled awkwardly as everyone could hear Mrs. Asher's screeching stage whisper. The doors blocked some of the words, but the cadence and the tone were distinctly a chewing out. Glori's father looked embarrassed.

Unable to stand by while Glori's mother berated her, Blaze nodded to the family and followed.

Glori twisted her foot, holding her arms around her body,

and kept nudging her glasses up her nose. Every time she started to talk, she was cut off by more tirade from her mother.

"Mrs. Asher," he began.

"You don't need to be out here right now. This is between me and—"

Blaze cut her off. "No, I think I do. First of all, we could all hear you in there. Glori has done nothing to embarrass you or your family. She is not cavorting around the islands with some stranger. This is a guided tour provided by the cruise company."

As he spoke, he positioned himself next to Glori and wrapped his arm around her shoulders.

Mrs. Asher's expression went from stern disapproval to shock and realization. "You were the man in Glori's room this morning when I called. That wasn't a wrong number."

"And if I was? That would be between your daughter and myself. She is an adult." Blaze turned his attention to Glori. "We should get going." He guided her away from her mother.

That was definitely not the way to win her mother over, but he cared more about Glori than her family. He needed to save his girl even if it meant saving her from her mother.

Glori leaned into him as they walked back towards the grill.

"You okay?" He could feel her shiver.

"She's not really this bad. She's stressed and wants this vacation to be perfect," Glori explained.

"So she's taking everything that's not perfect out on you? That's not acceptable. I have a strong minded mother, too. I get it. But that's no excuse to chew you out like that, not in public, and definitely not around me. I'm afraid I made a less than stellar first impression."

Glori eased away from Blaze's embrace. "She'll pretend it never happened, and by dinner time she'll be pleased as punch to have met you. Blaisier?" Her voice had the soft lilt of a laugh as she said his name.

"It's a family name. Blaisier William Gosling. Mom has called me Blaze since day one." He pointed to the top of his head. "So Blaze."

"Blaze suits you better anyway." Glori reached up to play with his hair. It was the first time she'd touched him like that.

Blaze wanted to skip the tour, take her back to the cabin, and let her play with the rest of him.

Their tour guide explained that they stood in a storage shed. To Glori, it was a roof, four walls, a floor, and no breeze. She zoned out. Between Blaze's comforting proximity and the tour guide's voice, she could have fallen asleep.

The guide's lilting accent made the dull information sound lovely, but that wasn't enough. Blah blah blah, coffee coffee coffee. Hopefully, the tour would get more interesting. Hopefully, it would be somewhere with air conditioning. Once out of the storage shelter, a light breeze improved things. She lagged behind, waiting for Blaze to join her, but he stayed in the shed.

She turned back to find him. He stood in the middle of the shed. She leaned against the door frame, crossed her arms, and watched him. He really was good looking, he seemed to like her, and he'd stood up to her mother. He stood poised in the middle of the room, focused on nothing. What was he thinking?

His posture changed, his knees softened, and his chest lifted. He lifted his elbows and then his hands to shoulder level. One sandaled foot slid out, and he spun. He executed a perfect pirouette. His arms extended, and he leaped, doing the splits mid-air. He took small running steps and then he leaped again, this time gaining air, and spinning at least twice. He landed in what looked like a lunge, leg extended behind him, knee bent, arms and focus reaching out.

Glori made an undignified "ungph" sound as he landed. She knew he could dance, but not like that. She had never seen anything so amazing. She was taken in my his display of grace, poise, and strength. And that extended toe point. And he did it all in hiking sandals and shorts.

Blaze, eyes bright with exertion, hair wild from the spinning, caught sight of her by the door and smiled. He looked like a sun god, with flames escaping from his hair and eyes.

She licked her dry lips. "You're a dancer. Like a serious dancer."

Blaze's smile widened. She leaned more heavily, letting the building hold her up since her knees were no longer able to support her weight.

"I couldn't resist the call of a wide open floor."

"You're like a ballerina," Glori said, still in awe at the way the man could move.

"Danseur," he corrected, emphasizing the second syllable of the word. "And yes, classically trained, the whole bit."

"Why did I think you were a ballroom dance instructor?"

"Because I am. I'm too tall for most ballet companies. They may say it's all about skill, but they're after a certain look. Musical theater isn't an option because I can't sing or act. Ballroom, Lindy, social dances, competition dances, I teach those and some others." Blaze held his hand out to her and waited for Glori to take it before they headed to catch up with the rest of the tour.

The contact with his hand sent electrical sparks up her arm, and when his thumb began stroking her skin, she couldn't think straight.

How had this happened so fast? He'd gone from handsome stranger to a friend she felt she'd known forever, in a matter of days.

Glori leaned her head against Blaze's shoulder on the bus ride down the mountain and back to the harbor. The touristy shops beckoned as they made their way back to the cruise ship.

"Mind if we poke around in the stores?" Glori asked. "I really want to get a T-shirt or something to commemorate my trip."

"You want to go home with more than a tan?"

"Exactly." She pulled on Blaze's hand and headed into a shop with shirts and knickknacks.

They drifted from shop to shop. Blaze pointed out Doucheboi as he shopped with a cruise cougar. They watched as she guided her escort into a designer jewelry shop.

"Now she'll buy herself something extravagant, and she'll get him a chunky gold necklace or bracelet," Blaze said.

"How do you know?" Glori asked.

"I used to be that guy, professional boy-toy. My ex was that woman's daughter and on her way to being a future rich divorcee." He chuckled. "She never quite figured out that I wasn't rich, and trying to keep up with her was making me broke."

Glori glanced over him. "You seem so non-douchey now."

"I like to think I'm making better life choices." Blaze looked into her eyes. A chill washed over her as he cupped the back of her head and lowered his lips to hers.

She closed her eyes and breathed him in as he slid his lips over hers. He knew exactly how to elicit a response from her. She moaned into his mouth as his tongue swept her lips apart. Glori reached up and buried her fingers into the mass of curls on Blaze's head.

"I've been wanting to do that all day." Blaze sighed as he broke off the kiss.

"You do that well. Would you mind if we went back to my cabin, and maybe did that some more?"

Glori stepped into her room and dumped her few shopping bags on the floor. She flopped back against her mattress and cast Blaze a coy look.

"I am suddenly exhausted. I think I need a nap," she announced.

"Sure, excuse me a second." Blaze ducked into her tiny bathroom. Glori heard water run before Blaze exited, whipping a washcloth across his neck and down his now shirtless chest.

"Oh." Glori's eyes popped out of her head at his ridiculously well-defined torso.

"A nap sounds like a good idea. Mind if I join you?"

Glori's insides bubbled in excitement. She scooted over to make room for Blaze, attempting to play it cool instead of squealing with delight.

When Blaze stretched out, she politely inched away from him just in case he didn't want to get overly friendly.

"What are you doing? Come here." Blaze gently removed her glasses before tucking her under his arm. The only place Glori had to rest her head and one arm was across his chest.

His skin was slightly damp from the washcloth. He was warm and smelled like sex. Blaze gently stroked her hair and the back of her arm. She resisted the urge to comb through the smattering of chest hairs and twirl her fingers around his nipples. Her body thrummed at his proximity, but she didn't know if she could bring herself to kiss him first.

But she did anyway.

She reached up and hooked a hand around his neck. "You sleepy? I thought we were coming back to my room to neck?"

Blaze grinned as he lowered himself to her lips.

Glori sighed against him. His lips were soft and seeking. She buried her fingers in his hair and held him close. Their lips slid against each other and parted in a timed choreography. He tasted rich, like the coffee they'd sampled earlier in the day. It was ambrosia. Their tongues danced, as their lips continued to taste each other.

Blaze trailed kisses along her jaw line, scraping his teeth along her chin. Glori pulled his hair, bringing his mouth back to hers. She held onto and dug her fingers into his shoulders. She ran her hands over him, touching his skin and kneading the muscles in his arms.

Blaze pulled her leg up to his hip, his hand caressing her thigh. He stopped when his fingers touched the edge of her panties, edged away, and back. His fingers bit into her skin

She was nothing but nerve endings, his lips on hers, his skin under her palms, his fingers near her core. When she moaned, he slipped under the lower edge of her panties to cup her ass. It felt entirely too good and, at the same time, one step towards a mistake. She tensed up and pulled his hand off of her.

It was now or never. She didn't want to regret having missed the chance to be with him more than she would ever regret having a holiday affair with him. It took a heart beat to make up her mind.

She relaxed into the kiss, and place his hand back. Blaze responded by palming her ass.

He groaned, "these unicorn panties of yours would look really good right now in a pile on the floor with the rest of my clothes."

Glori rolled out from his grasp. "Yes, I agree." She leaned over the edge of the bed and pointed to the floor. "In a pile right there, as a matter of fact."

Standing, Blaze unfastened the waist band to his shorts and dropped them on the spot Glori had indicated. She let out a small gasp of excitement.

His eyebrows lifted. "Damn, you are sexy. Come here." Blaze pulled her up in front of him.

"I've been wondering what your bra looks like. Does it match those unicorns?" Blaze snaked his fingers under the hem of her shirt and tugged it up and over her head.

"Nothing fancy. Sorry." Glori started to wrap her arms around her chest to cover the functional undergarment.

"Sexy has hell, just what I expected." Blaze licked his lips, his eyes on her breasts. His mouth descended back to hers.

She pressed her body to Blaze, feeling his warm skin against hers. "Are you sure about this? I stink after being all sweaty today."

Blaze walked backward toward the bathroom. "That's an easy fix."

He left her long enough to turn the shower taps on and finish disrobing. His entire body was as well sculpted as his chest and legs. The hair around his manhood was as vibrant as the hair on top of his head. He stood in front of her in all his fiery splendor.

She reached behind and unhooked her bra. Blaze hissed as she exposed her breasts. When she started to unfasten her skirt, he covered her hands with his. "Let me," he said, his voice rough with desire.

He kneeled before her and lowered her skirt to the floor. Glori placed a hand on his shoulder for balance as she stepped out of it. Blaze sighed and stared at her sex. He leaned forward and bit her hip, a growl low in his throat. To her surprise, he then nipped the unicorn panties with his teeth and pulled them down past her butt.

Glori giggled. He used his hands to push them the rest of the way off.

"Shower." He smacked her ass with a little push.

Glori gasped as they crowded in the small, steamy cubicle. "There's not much room in here."

"There's plenty." Blaze rubbed his wet torso against hers. Their slick skin slid together. "You wanted to rinse off, right? And I want to touch you."

Blaze grabbed her wrists and held her arms over her head with one capable hand. With the other, he touched her every-where—sides, back, neck, legs, ass. But then he dropped her arms and stepped closer. As he lowered his head and began kissing, Glori was trapped between the shower wall and the wall of muscles that was Blaze. He slid his torso across hers, rubbing against her breasts. He licked water from her neck and trailed kisses down to her collarbone.

"Oh." Glori's giggles were replaced with heavy breathing.

Blaze's tongue continued to lick and suck water from her breasts. Her stomach flipped as he attempted to kneel in the shower. Blaze growled and ripped the shower curtain open. He spun the tap, shutting off the water.

"I can't make love to you in this shower. Too fucking small." Blaze pulled Glori back out to the cabin and rushed her to the bed.

She sprawled on the mattress before him, and his eyes glinted.

"Is it still a yes?"

"Yes, please," Glori whispered.

Blaze practically fell onto the bed with her. His mouth was everywhere. She cried out when he sucked a nipple into his mouth. Teeth scraped against sensitive skin. He left a burning train of sucking kisses down her body. When he reached the rounded curve of her belly, he crushed his face into her soft flesh.

He lowered his head until he gently bit her inner thigh. Glori gasped. The tickle of chin stubble grazed her leg. She tried not to buck her hips, lifting them towards his mouth—and failed. When his tongue licked her delicate folds, she barely held back a cry. His tongue felt almost cool against her burning skin. Blaze. He set her on fire.

Blaze teased and coaxed whines and loud moans from her.

Glori coiled her fingers into his hair and thrust her hips to meet the rhythmic motion of his tongue.

Glori cried out in despair when his mouth left her and he leaned down to fumble through the shopping bags. "What are you looking for?"

Blaze turned, a triumphant grin on his face. "These." He shook a small blue box at her.

"When did you get those?"

He opened the box and removed a condom. "In that store getting bottles of water. I'd feel like a real idiot if I wasn't prepared." Blaze rolled the condom down his length.

"Thank goodness." Glori chuckled and dropped her thighs open. "I'm glad one of us came prepared"

Blaze lowered himself to her. His lips found hers again. "I'm prepared to make you come."

She threw her head back and stifled a cry as he slid into her, filling her. It felt like he belonged. When he eased back to begin thrusting, her body missed him. When he pushed into her fully, her body rejoiced at the contact. Glori wanted him deep inside her, where she could wrap around him and hold him close. The tighter she held on, the more her muscles throbbed and pulsed.

The throbbing took on a life of its own. Glori could no longer control her motions. She lifted her hips in sporadic spasms as an orgasm washed over her. She sucked in air, but it felt like her lungs forgot how to breathe.

Blaze roared and held his hips tight to hers. She continued to quiver around him. Spent, he lowered himself to rest against her breasts.

She toyed with his curls. "I'm glad I said yes."

"Me, too, sweetheart, me, too." Blaze kissed her one last time, rolled off her, and padded into the bathroom. He returned with two large fluffy towels. "We got your sheets all wet

"Housekeeping will remake the bed if I ask nicely." Glori folded the towel under her head.

"But not just yet. Now I want to take a nap." Blaze confessed. "I never would have been able to sleep. You and those rainbow unicorn panties were distracting."

"Oh, all distractions taken care of?" Glori teased.

"Wonderfully, gloriously, deliciously taken care of." Blaze's breathing evened out. Glori let his relaxed state lull her to sleep.

Glori leaned into Blaze's arm. Together they rested on the railing around the upper causeway. She looked out over the open air bar and dance club. Blaze's gaze was directed out to sea.

She didn't want to let go, but the cruise ended tomorrow. She would leave with her family back to small town Missouri, and Blaze would get on a plane back to Atlanta. She was sadder than she wanted to admit, even to herself.

She felt muzzy headed. Probably not getting enough sleep the past few nights. She nuzzled her face against his strength, breathing him in. She had never had a fling like this before. It was oddly liberating, yet scary. She would never regret having slept with him, only that it couldn't last longer.

They'd spent all of yesterday and last night in his room so her mother couldn't track her down. It was fabulous. And not just the sex. They talked and talked, and Glori felt like she knew everything about Blaze.

"What are they doing down there?" Glori pointed to the night club. Several uniformed workers carted a heavy platform and deposited it in the middle of the dance floor. "So much for dancing this afternoon."

Their shoulders brushed as they watched the workers assemble tall pole in the center of the platform. They followed up with a second platform and a pole.

Blaze laughed. "It's a stripper pole. Why the hell are they putting those up?"

As if to answer his question, the activities director made a ship wide announcement. "Starting in twenty minutes at the Under the Stars nightclub, we will have an areal pole dance demonstration. Come join the fun and take a twirl around the dancing pole."

Blaze grabbed Glori's hand. "C'mon, this should be good."

A crowd had already gathered by the time Glori and Blaze arrived. A woman with a headset—clearly the announcer in her cruise uniform of khaki shorts and red polo—conferred with the dancers, who wore substantially fewer clothes covered in sequins.

"Ladies and gentlemen. I'm Desiree," the announcer began. She paced between the two poles and introduced Ivan and Katiana, today's demonstrators.

Ivan climbed his pole like a monkey with prehensile toes. Everyone oohed and ahed as he proceeded to acrobat balance on one arm at the top of the pole. The pole swayed slightly under his weight but Ivan kept his balance. He lowered himself to the pole and swung around in a slow descending spiral until his feet were back on the floor. Katiana began her pole dance by swinging low around the pole, with her feet barely off the floor. She lifted her legs over her head in a fluid motion and hung upside down by the grip of her thighs. Several people, men and women, made cat calls at her skills.

The dancers then began a choreographed duet. They defied gravity as they rolled up and down the poles, pausing to pose in the splits or swinging their legs into various acrobatics. At the end of the demonstration, Glori felt the need to go home, join a gym, and work on her core strength. Blaze stuck two fingers in his mouth and whistled appreciatively.

When Desiree called for audience participation, a few young women goaded each other onto the dance platform. They spun around the pole without much skill and no upper arm strength. Desiree's call for more volunteers produced a few men, including Douche-boi, who jumped up on the platform in his yellow speedo and began flexing.

Blaze shook his head and crossed his arms. "This is going to be bad."

Douche-boi swung around and managed to lift himself almost perpendicular to pole, like some flesh and banana human flag. He dropped back to the floor before he fell.

The audience cheered him on with as much enthusiasm as they'd cheered the professional dancers.

Blaze handed Glori his sunglasses. "Hold these. I need to show that asshole a thing or two." He stepped up to the platform before Glori fully grasped what he was about to do. She knew he could dance, and she was quite familiar with his exceptional core strength as demonstrated in bed. Could he pole dance, too?

Well, why not?

She watched as he approached Ivan, shook his hand, and said something. Ivan smiled and nodded. Blaze pulled his shirt over his head to appreciative whistles from the audience. He stretched his arms and kicked his sandals off. Ivan approached the second pole. The music that had been playing grew louder, a heavy downbeat driving the electronic sound.

The two men looked at each other, nodded, and in a single motion, they both leaped, grabbing the pole about eight feet off the ground. Glori gasped. They pulled themselves up their respective poles, hand over hand, the rest of their bodies angling away from the pole.

Did Blaze know Ivan? They moved in almost synchronized movements. Climbing the pole, swinging around while holding with one hand, they matched. They did the human flag pose, but both men used a wide arm grip and held themselves perfectly perpendicular, before lowering themselves back to the pole slowly, muscles rippling.

She was aware that Ivan was doing the same moves, but she couldn't tear her gaze from Blaze. He gripped the pole and swung his legs up over his head as he rotated around the pole, as his legs swung down he hooked his foot and wrapped his torso around the pole, the tension between his shoulder and his leg held him aloft. He extended the other leg back, grabbed that foot with his hand and continued to rotate. The move reminded Glori of an Olympic ice skater performing a spin. Blaze contorted himself around the pole until he was almost upside down, this time doing the splits while he supported himself by an elbow. He rolled up the pole changing grips, and positions.

Muscles she explored with her fingers and mouth were flexing and bunching as Blaze moved and posed. No wonder the man was so well defined. He rolled higher up the pole, hooked one knee, braced against the other foot and stood. Extending his arms as he spun, Blaze and Ivan high-fived each other as they rotated around the poles and came to the center at the same time.

Blaze was barely breathing heavy by the time his feet hit ground. The crowd whooped and hollered. An overwhelming sense of pride washed over her. The pouty expression on Douche-boi's face was welcome pay-back after he had been so rude to her that very first day.

Blaze certainly had gained the attention of quite a few of the female spectators. He walked past all of them, and straight to Glori. The smile on his face declared his victory. He slipped both hands around her face and kissed her in front of everyone. She felt breathless and light headed. Her whole body blushed when her ears finally registered the roar of applause from those around them.

Desiree made another announcement, but Glori had stopped paying attention, her focus on Blaze. He pulled his shirt back on, wrapped an arm around Glori, and guided her away from the night club.

"Holy cow, that was…wow," Glori gushed. "You have to know that guy, you were too in sync to not."

Blaze slid his sunglasses back over his eyes. "Yeah, I know Ivan. We trained together for a local Cirque type outfit. I know that wasn't fair, but I couldn't help myself. I'm a show-off."

"And you move like a stripper," she said.

"I am a stripper. And you're a kindergarten teacher."

"I thought you were a dance instructor, and now you're a stripper? I don't get it. What is it exactly that you do Blaze?" Confusion begin to set in. Glori placed a hand to her temple hoping to massage her brain into clearer thinking. She sat on a lounge with a heavy thud.

Blaze leaned forward bracing his elbows on his knees. "I dance. Sometimes that means I'm doing ballroom exhibitions, while sometimes that means I'm trying to get hired by a company that needs aerial performers. Sometimes that means I'm halfway up a pole and pulling my clothes off. I also teach. Right now my most popular class is a pole dancing class. The thing is, I dance. I'm not trying to hide anything from you. I thought this was a perfect way to show you what I do."

Glori pursed her lips, she raked Blaze up and down with her gaze. He seemed to be going fuzzy around the edges.

"Are you objectifying me?" Blaze laughed

Glori ducked her head, ashamed. She was objectifying him, especially after having witnessed that display of talent. She huffed out a long breath, suddenly feeling nauseated.

Blaze placed a finger under Glori's chin and lifted so she had to face him. His eyebrows were lifted above the rims of his sunglasses. "Glori?"

Glori crossed her arms and leaned back into her chair, pretending that she was more mad at him than she really was. Pretending it didn't feel like the entire boat tilted sideways. "When were you planning on telling me about this particular skill set, stripper man?"

"I omitted the stripper thing at first because I wasn't sure how you would take it. This was my way of introducing the topic."

"Introducing the topic? Blaze, the cruise is over tomorrow." She didn't know what hurt more right now—knowing she only had a night left with him, her head, or finding out she really didn't know him.

"I know." Blaze pushed back away from her personal space. "That's another topic I wanted to introduce. When the cruise ends, it doesn't mean we have to, does it?"

Glori's stomach dropped out of her body. Her heart tried to pound out of her chest. Her head spun. Her vision tunneled. She couldn't catch a breath.

Blaze was wrapped around her, holding her steady. "What's the matter? You're white as a sheet." He placed a hand against her forehead. "And clammy. I'm taking you to medical right now." Blaze swept her up in his arms.

Glori leaned against him, her hands wrapped around his neck. He had said something wonderful, and then the world tilted. She wanted to focus on what Blaze had said. This didn't need to end. Right now focusing on anything was difficult.

Blaze set Glori down gently on the examination table. His heart was in his throat the entire trip into the lower levels of the ship.

The ship's doctor indicated that he needed to stand slightly to the back so she could examine Glori. Blaze did not want to release her hand, but Glori murmured that it was okay. He reluctantly let her go. He watched as they took her blood pressure and began a basic examination.

Now the doctor stood in front of Glori with a digital thermometer in her hand. Glori sat with the wand end in her mouth.

"I think, Miss Asher you are dehydrated," the doctor began.

The device pinged, and the doctor removed the thermometer from Glori's mouth. "Your temperature is a touch high, your blood pressure is a little low, and your heart rate is up. Let me look at you."

Glori pulled her glasses off so the doctor could flash a penlight into her eyes to check for pupil dilation and reaction. The doctor placed fingers near the scrape of Glori's cheek, and then various places along her skull, all while making "uh hmm" noises.

Blaze clenched and unclenched his fist, anxious to find out what was wrong, and what could he do to fix it. He hated this feeling of helplessness.

"I want to hook you up with some fluids. I'll be right back." The doctor stepped out of the small curtained area.

Blaze wrapped his hand around Glori's and stroked her forehead. "Not drinking enough water?" She looked so pale and frail resting in the medical bed.

Glori slowly shook her head. "I guess not. Maybe it was all the excitement of finding out I've been dating a secret stripper."

"Not so secret anymore." He smiled, she was taking the news better than he had hoped, of course, coupled with passing out, this was not how he pictured their last day together.

"Truth? Your ex left you for ballroom dancing? Did she know what you can do on a pole?"

Blaze laughed. Glori saw the irony in the situation that he had. "Yep, I got left over a waltz, and not because someone got a little handsy delivering a tip into my shorts."

"Women handle your goods a lot then?" Her eyes slitted as she looked at him.

"Only if I let them."

"I wouldn't leave you over dancing. It's what makes you amazing."

Blaze's heart lodged in his throat at her words. Before he could reply the curtain swished to the side. The doctor returned rolling in a tall silver table. "We're going to give you some fluids. And then you'll need to rest. You should feel better once we get all this into you." She patted the bags of saline on the table.

After she hooked Glori up with an IV and a bag of fluid. She rolled the cart out again. Leaving them with directions to let Glori relax.

Blaze returned to her side and stroked the arm that wasn't full of IV tubes. She was suddenly so small and fragile. He didn't want to let her out of his sight, out of his embrace. Letting her go back home was going to be the end of him. He tried to tell her that right before she started to pass out.

Her eyes fluttered shut. "I'm sleepy." She was beautiful. Peacefully resting. He could watch her sleep for the rest of his life. A brilliant plan exploded in his brain.

"You rest, I need to go check on something." He kissed her cheek, stepped out into the waiting area and leaned on the receptionist's desk. "Can I use your phone?"

"It only makes in-ship calls."

"How do I reach the captain?"

"Blaze, stop worrying over me." Glori wasn't really annoyed, she loved his undivided attention, but he was fussing like a mother hen.

"You heard the doctor. I'm supposed to take care of you. You have everything you need? I don't want to leave you alone right now, but I have to go do this thing."

"I'll be okay. I promise. I have a table full of drinks. I'm in the shade. I'm not going anywhere."

Blaze took two steps away, returned, and kissed her. "I don't want you to forget me while I'm gone."

As if she could. He'd been an excitable puppy ever since she woke up from her little snooze while they pumped her full of fluids.

She should probably try to find her mother, who had not been in her cabin when they called from medical. But Glori promised Blaze she wouldn't go anywhere. Odds were that her mother might actually walk past her at some point. It wasn't a very big ship.

She dozed, exhausted by everything, and bored with people watching.

"Gloria Asher." Her mother's voice woke her. "You have been avoiding me. My goodness. Are you alright?" She focused on the bruise and bandage on Glori's arm. "What happened? Did that man hurt you? I'll have him arrested."

"I'm fine, Mom." Glori pushed herself more upright on the lounge. She nodded at her father before pasting a fake smile on for her mother. "It's from an IV. I got dehydrated and passed out. Blaze did't hurt me. Would you please be nicer to him?"

"Why should I?" Her mother sat at the end of the lounger, leaving her father standing.

"Because she likes him, and the boy likes her."

Glori blinked up at her dad, surprised he had it figured out.

"Nonsense. He's only interested in one thing."

"Mom." Glori dragged the name out in exasperation.

"Honey, I've seen that look on a man's face before. And yes, he's interested in only one thing."

"Dad!" Glori shouted.

"It's not that, sweetie," her father corrected. "It's you. Everything about you."

"I don't know if he's that serious. But I might be. So yeah, can you please try to be nice to him?"

"Mr. and Mrs. Asher." Blaze's baritone voice caused them all to turn their attention to him. "I'm glad you're here. Glori. You feeling okay darling?"

Glori nodded. Blaze suddenly looked less tall, shuffling as if he were nervous.

"Can you all meet me in front of the Grand Stairs in half an hour? At the bottom, in the lobby. Don't be late." He leaned over and kissed her on the cheek. "Thirty minutes, all of you, okay?"

Blaze kept looking back over his shoulder as he walked away from her this time. Something was bothering him, and she wasn't in a position to soothe him, and it started eating her insides.

Her father chuckled. "That boy is up to something."

Glori walked slowly, explaining to her parents how she passed out, not realizing anything was wrong. She was fine, stable on her feet, just not moving quickly.

She stopped when she caught sight of Blaze speaking with the ship's captain.

Blaze beamed when he saw her. He didn't need the sun to radiate light and fire. He just needed to smile at her like that. He came to her, took her hand, and guided her to the captain who stood at the base of the stairs. "We're in international waters, and this ship is registered in Bermuda. We can do this right now."

Glori blinked uncertain what Blaze was getting at.

He lifted her left hand and slipped a delicate band of silver down her finger. "Will you marry me?" His question was barely above a rumble of sound.

"Right now?" Glori looked from the band on her finger into Blaze's eyes.

"Yes, right now. I don't want to go home without you. But I will, knowing we're secure with each other, committed to each other, and that at some point in the very near future we will make a home together." Glori's nerves were doing a fandango in her gut. Her heart pounded. She reached out to brace herself on Blaze's arm. "I don't think you'll find much work in Summerset."

"You okay?" He quickly steadied her.

"I've never been better. Atlanta needs kindergarten teachers right?" She laughed, nodding like she had no control. "Yes. A resounding yes. Hell, yes."

Her mother scowled, her expression sour. "This can't be legal."

"Hush, Martha, your daughter is getting married." Her father surprised her again.

Glori leaned into Blaze's arm as they turned to face the captain.

"Did Aunt Gloreee really get married? Does that mean she's not gonna be our aunt anymore?" Glori smiled at her nephews' incessant questioning, glad she wasn't getting in the van with them. She loved kids, sure, but right now, she had other things to do. She was staying with Blaze and flying home with him to meet his mother.

They stood on the walkway surrounded by people and their luggage lining up for airport shuttles and valets.

Glori had already hugged her aunt and uncle goodbye before they climbed into their car and pulled away. Her mother fussed.

"It's legal, Mom. The cruise line has all of their captains registered to be able to legally perform weddings." Glori let out a ragged sigh.

Blaze leaned down to whisper in her ear. "I love you. This was a good decision."

Glori turned to her new husband. "My mother is going to make us get married again. She's convinced that wasn't legal."

"I'll marry you again. I'll marry you as many times as it takes." Blaze smiled. "My mom might insist on another one as well. We can let them plan a wedding. That should make them happy."

"You want to have a June wedding?" Glori teased.

"Sure, I'll marry you again in June." Blaze rested his lips against her forehead.

She had always dreamed of a big wedding, but now, her shipboard surprise wedding seemed like it couldn't be more perfect. "How about we just let them plan a big reception or two? They get their big parties and we've already got our perfect wedding."

"You are amazing." Blaze chuckled.

"That is why you married me." She smirked.

A minivan pulled up the curb and honked. The back door slid open and Glori's nephews scampered inside. Her father climbed out of the passenger seat and began tossing their luggage into the back of the van.

Glori hugged her dad. "See you in a few days." She felt like her heart would burst watching Blaze shake her father's hand. They had his blessing.

Her mother wasn't so easy. "I'm never going to see you again. You're going to move away and—"

Glori cut her off. "I will be home in less than a week, and then we have to work out what we're doing next. Why can't you act like you've gained a son instead of lost a daughter?"

"I'm just going to miss you."

"I love you, Mom. Have a happy New Year. You're picking me up at the airport, remember?"

To Glori's surprise, her mother hugged Blaze. "You take care of my daughter."

"I plan on it, for a very long time." He gave her one of his dazzling smiles, certain to win her over eventually.

Glori leaned into Blaze as they watched her family drive away. He pulled her into his embrace, dipped his lips to hers, and made the world fade away.

"That was one hell of a cruise, huh?" He pushed her glasses back up her nose.

"It turned out even better than I dreamed. I got the best Christmas present I could have ever wished for," Glori confessed.

"I know what you mean. I got your unicorn panties in my pocket. What did you get?" Blaze asked with a smirk.

"Blaze!" She sighed. "I got you." Glori buried her fingers in Blaze's messy curls and pulled him down for another kiss.

7

BURLESQUE CYGNUS

SENT: 12/27 7:49PM
TO: I.GUTHRIE@THEPRESSPAPER.COM
SUBJECT: IDEAS

Iona,
I need your ideas ASAP for your next few stories.
George

SENT: 12/28 8:15AM
TO: G.WALLS@THEPRESSPAPER.COM
SUBJECT: RE: IDEAS

Gee, I tried to get pictures of that spider-brat, but no such luck.
Seriously, George, I've got nothing. My cousin wants us to
publish her leftover cranberry ham casserole again. I sent it off
to the kids in Culinary, I figured they could tell her no and she
might listen. Other than that, I've got nada.
Iona

SENT: 12/28 8:32AM
TO: I.GUTHRIE@THEPRESSPAPER.COM
SUBJECT: RE: IDEAS

Is she still trying to get us to print that? Every damned year.
You need to brainstorm. I need something. I don't care how
fluffy it is.
George

SENT: 12/28 9:43AM
TO: G.WALLS@THEPRESSPAPER.COM
SUBJECT: FOUND A HOT LEAD

Hey George,
Just found out that the high school kids who did the live nativity
weren't very well cast. Turns out Mary isn't a virgin at all. She's
knocked up, and the kid who played Joseph is the dad. Guess
they won't be reprising those roles next year. Maybe they can
supply the live baby for the baby Jesus?
Iona

SENT: 12/28 10:02AM
TO: I.GUTHRIE@THEPRESSPAPER.COM
SUBJECT: RE: FOUND A HOT LEAD

Iona,
I would hardly call that investigative reporting. And as enter-
taining and ironic as it is, nope, can't print that. It's gossip.
You've got until the end of the day to get me something interest-
ing, or I'm assigning you to pee-wee sports again.
George

SENT: 12/28 10:20AM
TO: G.WALLS@THEPRESSPAPER.COM
SUBJECT: RE:FOUND A HOT LEAD

Noooo!
You can't be so cruel! All those sniffling, snot-covered kids. I don't get why everyone thinks they are so cute. They are not cute. They can't kick a ball. It's like watching a herd of cats. I'll have something by the end of today, I promise.
Iona

SENT: 12/28 5:23PM
TO: G.WALLS@THEPRESSPAPER.COM
SUBJECT: BRILLIANT IDEA

George! George!
Burlesque Cygnus is in town! I heard a rumor that there is something not quite right about their act. I want to investigate. Will the paper reimburse me for my ticket?
Iona

SENT: 12/28 5:32PM
TO: I.GUTHRIE@THEPRESSPAPER.COM
SUBJECT: RE: BRILLIANT IDEA

Sure,
Turn in your stub at the end of the month. What's your lead? They aren't really brothers? Animal endangerment by hiding swans in G-strings?
If you don't find anything, I expect at least a review of the show based on the cost of the ticket.
George

SENT: 12/28 5:42PM
TO: G.WALLS@THEPRESSPAPER.COM
SUBJECT: RE: BRILLIANT IDEA

Thanks George.
Friend in Seattle said there was no way they should be able to do some of the stunts they pull off without wires and excessive rigging on the stage. Just some simple magic-trick debunking.
Iona

SENT: 12/29 12:16AM
TO: G.WALLS@THEPRESSPAPER.COM
SUBJECT: IT'S A SCOOP!

There is something seriously hinky happening at the show! I need access back stage and tickets to the last two nights of the show. My usual contact at the theater said these guys brought their own security detail, so I don't have an easy way in.

SENT: 12/29 8:07AM
TO: I.GUTHRIE @THEPRESSPAPER.COM
SUBJECT: RE: IT'S A SCOOP!

Iona,
What have you got? Those tickets are $150 a pop, and you're asking the The Press to cover $450 worth of tickets to some stripper/magic show. I won't give this the okay until you let me know what's going on.
George

SENT: 12/29 9:52AM
TO: G.WALLS@THEPRESSPAPER.COM
SUBJECT: RE: IT'S A SCOOP!

Hey George,
From what I could tell, they didn't rig the stage, but they had to have. The very last number, the big finale, all seven of the Cygnus brothers dive into this little pool that's maybe five feet deep, if that much. So they are hanging off their aerial silks, and one at a time they dive. But they don't come up. Instead a huge freaking swan rears up, wings extended. I had no idea those things could be so damned scary. As each brother dives, another swan starts swimming around. At the end seven swans are swimming in a circle, no men anywhere. The swans fly out of the pool, waddle through curtains, and BAM! Out pop the guys. Completely dry. I really need to get in there and see the show again.
Iona

SENT: 12/29 10:00AM
TO: I.GUTHRIE @THEPRESSPAPER.COM
SUBJECT: RE: IT'S A SCOOP!

You're the one who wants to be an investigative reporter. Channel Lois Lane and break in like I know you will. This had better be worth it.
George

SENT: 12/29 1:14PM
TO: G.WALLS@THEPRESSPAPER.COM
SUBJECT: HOLY WOW MUSCLES

As far as I can tell, there is nothing tricky going on with the pole dancing or the aerial silks. Just good skill and extreme muscle control. And I do mean extreme muscles. Got an eyeful sneaking around backstage. I can say with all seriousness and honesty they are not stuffing those G-strings.
Iona

SENT: 12/29 1:22PM
TO: I.GUTHRIE @THEPRESSPAPER.COM
SUBJECT: RE: HOLY WOW MUSCLES

Iona,
I did not pay $450 for tickets for you to be ogling naked men. I mean, I know that's what Burlesque Cygnus is all about, but I expect your professionalism to overrule your hormones on this assignment.
George

SENT: 12/29 4:42PM
TO: G.WALLS@THEPRESSPAPER.COM
SUBJECT: RE: HOLY WOW MUSCLES

Hey George,
When I'm through with this story, can I do a little investigating fluff on aerial silk dancing? I want to try it. Derrick guided me through some simple movements, and it's thrilling!
Iona

SENT: 12/29 4:50PM
TO: I.GUTHRIE@THEPRESSPAPER.COM
SUBJECT: FORGET MUSCLES WHAT ABOUT BIRDS

Iona,
Stop playing around. What about the swans? Do we have an angle on animal cruelty? Have you checked out the pool for trap doors? Who is Derrick? And Iona, where's my story?
George

SENT: 12/29 5:32PM
TO: G.WALLS@THEPRESSPAPER.COM
SUBJECT: RE: FORGET MUSCLES WHAT ABOUT BIRDS

Sorry George,
Derrick is one of the Cygnus brothers. He's the one I acciden-
tally barged in on while he was starkers. He's been showing me
around behind the scenes. They have a very intense workout
routine to keep up their strength for the show. Lots of upper
body work. Lots of well defined muscles, so no body paint to
fool the audience about six-pack abs. Those are real. And very
firm.
I might need to write a piece of the strength benefits of alternative workout methods for men. Derrick has the firmest backside. I mean, all of them do. But yeah.
I'm not supposed to kiss the mark am I? Is that going to cause a
conflict of interest?
Iona

SENT: 12/29 5:36PM
TO: I.GUTHRIE@THEPRESSPAPER.COM
SUBJECT: RE: FORGET MUSCLES WHAT ABOUT BIRDS

Iona Guthrie!
If you're kissing Derrick Cygnus, can you really be objective?
I'm already noticing a decided lack of interest in debunking the
magic portion of the show. Get into that pool, and find out
about the swans.
George

SENT: 12/29 7:53PM
TO: G.WALLS@THEPRESSPAPER.COM
SUBJECT: RE: FORGET MUSCLES WHAT ABOUT BIRDS

Hey Perry White,
I think the swans do a disappearing act every night. I haven't seen any sign of them or how they are taken care of. I promise I will get to that pool tonight after the show.
Lois Lane

SENT: 12/29 10:03PM
TO: G.WALLS@THEPRESSPAPER.COM
SUBJECT: RE: FORGET MUSCLES WHAT ABOUT BIRDS

George,
I can't find the swans. Seriously. I just watched them waddle off stage, and now poof, nothing. I will get into that pool, I swear. Derrick has been sticking pretty close. I'm going to have to distract him so I can sneak off and find those birds.
Iona

SENT: 12/30 10:15AM
TO: I.GUTHRIE @THEPRESSPAPER.COM
SUBJECT: IONA CHECK IN

Iona
You're being too quiet. It's been almost twelve hours.
Check in.
George

SENT: 12/30 10:55AM
TO: I.GUTHRIE @THEPRESSPAPER.COM
SUBJECT: IONA CHECK IN

Iona? Getting worried.

SENT: 12/30 11:21AM
TO: G.WALLS@THEPRESSPAPER.COM
SUBJECT: RE: IONA CHECK IN

Sorry about that, George.
I went to track down the swans. Derrick ended up distracting me. All night. Chemistry happened, if you get my drift. But I swear I can still be objective. My hormones will not get in the way of my story. You know how driven I am. Being a journalist is important to me. I'm like a spy on a mission. It's nothing personal. Emotions are not involved. I did manage get him to show me the pool. No trap doors. I'm kind of freaked out about those birds now.
Iona

SENT: 12/30 1:28PM
TO: G.WALLS@THEPRESSPAPER.COM
SUBJECT: I MET A SWAN

George ,
I met one of the birds. He's one fat, happy, mean son-of-a-bitch. There are seven swans, and each one has the same name as the brother he appears for. I met Tom. Funny thing is that Tom, the human, wasn't around, but the other brothers were. And I only got to meet the one bird. And I swear that bird gave me the stink-eye exactly the same way human Tom did when Derrick first introduced us. I tried to follow them when they went to re-crate the bird. There are no crates. None. I've been all over this building the past two days. And last night on the tour bus, there were no crates there, either.
Iona

SENT: 12/30 11:11PM
TO: G.WALLS@THEPRESSPAPER.COM
SUBJECT: FOLLOWING

George,
I'm going to follow them to their next stop. Derrick has invited
me. I can't miss this opportunity to investigate further.
Iona

SENT: 12/30 11:11PM
TO: I.GUTHRIE@THEPRESSPAPER.COM
SUBJECT: RE: FOLLOWING

Iona,
Has this story gotten too big for you to handle? The Press can't
cover travel expenses on what was supposed to be a fun fluff
piece reviewing and debunking a traveling magic male strip
show.
George

SENT: 12/30 11:38PM
TO: G.WALLS@THEPRESSPAPER.COM
SUBJECT: RE: FOLLOWING

I'll be fine, George. And no travel costs, I'm staying with Derrick

SENT: 12/31 12:18PM
TO: G.WALLS@THEPRESSPAPER.COM
SUBJECT: I MIGHT BE IN TROUBLE HERE

George,
I was wrong. I might have gotten in over my head. I think I saw
something that is not possible.
Iona

SENT: 12/31 12:20PM
TO: I.GUTHRIE@THEPRESSPAPER.COM
SUBJECT: RE: I MIGHT BE IN TROUBLE HERE

Get out of there, Guthrie! Where are you? Get a cab and leave.

SENT: 12/31 12:42PM
TO: I.GUTHRIE@THEPRESSPAPER.COM
SUBJECT: RE: I MIGHT BE IN TROUBLE HERE

Iona? Check in.

SENT: 12/31 1:29PM
TO: G.WALLS@THEPRESSPAPER.COM
SUBJECT: EVERYTHING IS FINE

Wow, George.
I was wrong, I was so completely wrong about all of it, especially
about Derrick. We're getting married!
Iona

SENT: 12/31 1:38PM
TO: I.GUTHRIE@THEPRESSPAPER.COM
SUBJECT: RE: EVERYTHING IS FINE

Iona,
Is that code for something? Are you safe? Can you call?
George

SENT: 12/31 2:13PM
TO: G.WALLS@THEPRESSPAPER.COM
SUBJECT: RE: EVERYTHING IS FINE

I'm perfectly safe, George. I overreacted to a trick they were practicing. That is all. Derrick and I are getting married is code for I'm in love and I'm getting married!

I won't be writing the story after all. I guess I owe the paper $450. Oh, and I quit.

George, sometimes the magic is real.
Iona Guthrie-Cygnus

8

MORE THAN WANT

*S*t. Cyr leaned back in her chair. She looked at her friends who she hadn't seen for over a standard rotation, happy to be in their company again.

"What? You don't want to see nude males in zero-grav?" Zora flopped her finger around mimicking male humanoid genitalia in no gravity.

"But this is how we celebrate when we get together. How is tonight any different?" Yaz blinked slowly, waiting for an explanation. "We meet on Fergus once every solar rotation. We imbibe too much. We enjoy. We celebrate."

St. Cyr looked up into her friend's large opalescent eyes. "It was just an idea Yaz. Something from old stories."

"And they burn trees. Right?" Zora added.

"I don't exactly know, I think it's just a log. I read about it once and it sounded nice." St. Cyr shrugged. "Company, food, peace, quiet."

"Logs are trees," Zora explained.

"You want us to burn trees?" Yaz blinked in amazement.

"No, we won't be burning any trees. Besides I seriously doubt they would let us do that here." Asteroid Station Fergus extended thousands of feet above them until it anchored to the other asteroid, Asteroid Alpha.

With the station's artificial grav fields and manufactured

atmosphere, large open flames would not be a good idea. St. Cyr returned her focus to her surroundings. Fergus, one station, two asteroids. Asteroid Beta, overcrowded, overpriced, covered in dirt. Beta was populated with the dregs of the nomadic space population. Up there on Alpha, the financial elite played, worked, and lived in interstellar luxury.

"So what is it you wanted to celebrate?" Zora's question grounded St. Cyr back on Beta.

"I think it was the return of light or the birth of a deity," St. Cyr explained. "Or some combination."

"Don't you follow your heritage?" Zora asked. "Don't you know?"

"I'm a space kid. Heritage is for grandmothers born on planets. Space stations and asteroid fields for me. Planets make me nervous. There are no ceilings." Wide open spaces made her nervous, how would she know the atmosphere wouldn't evaporate?

"Well this place promises live males, no mechs." Yaz continued to try to sell St. Cyr on an evening of look-don't-touch.

Not that St. Cyr was opposed to a little touch, but she was definitely tired of mech-men. Nowadays it was almost impossible to tell the difference with your eyes closed, almost. But mechs lacked the nuances a live man had while fucking. St. Cyr was in need of nuance, not mechanics. Yaz was talking about watching dancers, not having sex. The concept was the same, a good performance required finesse.

"Live? Actual humanoid flesh?" St. Cyr gave her friends a lopsided grin. "Fine, I'm in."

She tossed down the rest of her synthcaf, shivered at the bitter taste, and stood. "I'll meet you tonight out front. Off to pick up a job."

Zora's gaze locked on St. Cyr. "What gives? I thought our rendezvous on Fergus was a vacay?"

St. Cyr shrugged. She thought Zora knew they didn't all have rich daddies footing the bill for this trip. "It is, but I had to work my way here, and I have to work my way back. I got a ping for an easy transport. It would be stupid to turn it down."

"What will you be moving?" Yaz asked.

St. Cyr shrugged. "Won't know till I meet the client. I'm going up, girls." She pointed to the opposite asteroid. "I've got a pass to Alpha. Gonna take some extra time to scope out how the other side lives." She waggled her eye brows before patting Zora on the back.

St. Cyr stared through the wall of the transparent aluminum lift. This was just money showing off. Even so, it offered a spectacular view of the station. Asteroid Beta dropped away beneath her, and Alpha loomed ever more so the higher she traveled. At some point the lift would have to pause for the grav shift, wouldn't it?

Her feet slowly lifted from the floor. Here came the shift. She watched the sky tilt before she felt the pod rotate. Interesting— the entire pod shifted yet floor remained floor instead of making her reorient her body. She watched the ceiling of the lift, pristine and white. It had never served as a surface for feet. Definitely a lot of money.

The lift began descending. Gravity pulled her feet down to the floor. The Beta half of Fergus now loomed above her, with her destination in Alpha below. She blinked, reorienting her brain. Grav switches were always a little tricky. This rotating lift was a new one for her. At least she no longer hurled the contents of her stomach whenever she reoriented, and up became down.

The lift eased to a stop, she was still hundreds of levels above the second asteroid. Could she get away with traveling all the way down to the surface? She'd heard that Alpha was exorbitantly posh, wealth the likes of which she would never experience. Images never did a place like that justice. She wanted to see what commerce levels on Alpha were like, how were the rich catered to. Free travel between the two halves of the station was frowned upon. Residents of Alpha could travel to Beta, but residents and traders on Beta did not have the same liberties with traveling to the high rent districts. Classism and wealth still ran the system and probably always would. But she had docs, she had permission to be on this part of the station. The docs were in her arm, on her chip, ready for scanning at a second's notice.

St. Cyr stared down at Alpha. Someone clearing their throat caught her attention. The lift doors had opened without her noticing.

Disapproval radiated from the Enceladian female who stood on the other side of the lift doors. She slowly blinked her large opalescent eyes. St. Cyr hid a smirk. She looked just like Yaz with rebar shoved up her ass.

"You must be Saint Seer." The female sneered.

"Why must I be anyone?"

"Why else would someone of your ilk be arriving at an appointed time for a meeting with Bayrrune Anatha?"

"Then you have proven your ability to state the obvious. It's pronounced sincere." St. Cyr stepped forward, pleased when the Enceladian woman flinched away from her.

St. Cyr wasn't a high end transporter. The financial elite typically did not deal with her class. She wondered what was up as she followed the Enceladian female through a maze of corridors. While she might not get ritzy cargos, she refused to deal in contraband, so if this Bayrrune Anatha person thought she would smuggle for him, he had another think coming. As they walked under arches of glass two stories tall, St. Cyr had to remind herself to keep her mouth from gaping in amazement. To think all of this was hidden away on a measly little Asteroid Station like Fergus.

"Leave," a stern voice barked.

The Enceladian woman left St. Cyr standing in the middle of an auditorium sized office. The floor-to-ceiling wall exposed a full view of the asteroid field. More transparent aluminum.

"Sorry, what?" St. Cyr forced her attention away from the view and onto the man hidden behind a bank of holo-displays

"I said you'll do," the man repeated.

St. Cyr looked at him. She sucked air in through her teeth. Ma'achqwae, cerulean skin, four arms. She had yet to meet a Ma'achqwae who didn't stir her blood. She found them irresistible. If Bayrrune was the title Barron said with a thick accent, and not a name, this one was royalty. He was regal enough. St.

Cyr wiggled her finger over the translation implant behind her left ear. Typically, accents were not an issue, but occasionally the device would glitch on similar concepts. It was a damned good translator, it just wasn't perfect. None of them ever were.

His attitude said title. With a full head of blue-black hair, a distinguished brow and sharp cheekbones, he was extremely attractive. As a younger man, he would have been beautiful beyond belief. His attitude, however was an instantaneous turn off.

His eyes ignored her. With one arm he held a sheaf of documents out to her. A holo-display held his focus as his two primary hands directed visuals around.

"What am I transporting?" she asked, her eyes darting from his face to the papers in his hand.

"It's in the contract, nothing that someone like you would turn down."

"Don't assume things about me." She took the papers and began flipping through them. "Why hire me?"

"Discretion."

"Which is why we're using paper docs instead of the traditional transfer of info to my chip?" St. Cyr asked.

"Precisely," Anatha confirmed.

Bayrrune Anatha was a man of few words. St. Cyr huffed and returned her attention to the contract.

She began to read. Nothing jumped out at her from the paperwork. Undisclosed contents, but guarantee of system approved non-contraband, package to be placed in her care within twelve standard units of signature, delivery at specified location, her ship and berth named. Provisions supplied, fifty percent deposit, payment in full upon delivery.

Her eyes bugged out at the amount to be transferred into her account. And that was the deposit. "Within twelve standard units? You expect me to sit around and wait while you package up a shipment? That's a problem. I'll take delivery between 0900 and 1300 tomorrow."

Anatha harrumphed. "Fine, cross that part out. Anything else you object to?"

St. Cyr picked up a pen from his desk without asking. The

man didn't react at all, so he was either confident or completely unbothered by peons. She made a few changes before signing and placing the document down on the desk. His eyes flicked to glance at the paper before returning to the holo-display. Hello, peon.

"Show Morvora your chip, and payment will be deposited. Your package will be delivered at 0900 sharp." And with that St. Cyr was clearly dismissed. Anatha's assistant reappeared and led her out of the office. She scanned St. Cyr's chip before programming the lift to return her to the dregs of Fergus.

St. Cyr watched Alpha drop away as the lift sped her back to where she belonged, with the riffraff of the system on Beta. All thoughts of redirecting the lift to check out Alpha gone. She felt like she needed to wash their disapproval from her skin.

At that, she laughed. They were probably disinfecting the entire place after she'd been there. They deserved it, all the discomfort her presence provided. Classist jackholes.

She closed her eyes as the grav-field switched and she began descending towards where she belonged. She didn't have to worry about her employer or her job until tomorrow. That was enough time to party for hours with Yaz and Zora at the club with live nude men. Tonight they would celebrate, and she would pay. That deposit was nonrefundable.

The venue was more vertical than St. Cyr had expected. Six stories of tiered tables and chairs surrounded an anti-grav column. Partially dressed men and women floated up and down within the grav field. Eye candy to keep the patrons happy before the main performance started.

"I tell ya, girls, I want to get myself one of those Ma'achqwae men." St. Cyr sighed. "This guy was arrogant as fuck, but I'd have done him in a hot second."

"You are so bad. All you care about is a man's appearance," Zora scolded.

Yaz blinked slowly as her kind always did. St. Cyr could read her friend's blinks. Yaz agreed with Zora.

"That's not true. I'm also interested in how well he can use his dick." St. Cyr smirked. "We're sitting in a seedy club waiting for a live nude show, and you two are being all high and mighty about my attitude towards men. This is a special kind of hypocrisy, don't you think? All I'm saying is rich and powerful is sexy, and add on top of it those refined features, that blue skin, and four hands."

"When was the last time you got laid?"

"Zora, that is impolite to ask." Yaz scolded.

"With a live one? It's been too long. Mechs scratch itches pretty well, but I'd like a little cuddle and attention after. Mechs are shit when it comes to using their tongues."

"You need a better programmer." Zora laughed.

"Both of you are horrible." Yaz's natural pink skin darkened as her whole body flushed. The colors in her opaline eyes swirled.

St. Cyr leaned across the table accusingly, glaring at Yaz. "You, my tall pink lady, love it. After all, this is your favorite way to celebrate—admiring fine male flesh."

Zora giggled. "We aren't your sisters. Stop pretending you aren't as astroid-brained as we are."

Yaz shrugged, an awkward move as it wasn't a natural motion for the Enceladian with her triple jointed shoulders.

A delivery bar-bot hovered at the end of their table. Yaz removed their order from the serving mech. "Actual alcohol, not the synth stuff." She placed a green fluffy drink in front of Zora, a fluffy pink drink in front of herself, and a short, wide glass filled with a glowing amber liquid in front of St. Cyr. "And for you, gut rot."

Zora lifter her glass in salut. "Thank you, St. Cyr."

"No, thank that Ma'achqwae tycoon and that mysterious cargo he wants me to transport."

"Aren't you concerned? You don't know what you're carry-ing." Yaz asked.

"I'll get a manifest in the morning. I was able to add in a clause giving me final refusal. It's all legit. And the money is really good. Really good." St. Cyr replied.

Lights in the performance column flashed. The pre-show eye candy flipped their way to strategically placed exits.

"Oh, the show is starting." Yaz clapped in excitement.

St. Cyr picked up her whiskey and leaned back to enjoy the spectacle. Amused by Yaz's and Zora's enthusiasm, St. Cyr hid her own behind a firm clasp on her glass.

Live nudes, yes. Strip show, no. This was a zero-grav aerial ballet. The first dancer into the grav field, a Terran, spun up from the first floor. Clouds of blue and green hair swirled around her body. Her hair was died and the skin coloring was body paint.

"I wish my breasts looked that perfect." Zora sighed wistfully.

"All breasts are perfect in zero gravity," Yaz answered.

"Sure, they are. I just never have anyone with me to appreciate them when I'm in zero grav," Zora chuckled.

St. Cyr laughed. "Sex in zero grav is a whole lot trickier than anyone will admit. And then you end up with random fluids floating around."

"Ew, do you have to be so gross?" Zora complained.

"Not gross, honest." Yaz defended St. Cyr.

"Honest and gross," St. Cyr added with a smirk.

Grumbles from the next table over curbed their conversation. St. Cyr returned her focus on the show. Another Terran, this one a male, joined the performance. What zero grav did for the woman's breasts, it also did for the man's anatomy. Perky is the word that came to St. Cyr's mind.

The dancers floated and twirled, connected by a wide length of silk. This allowed them to more or less control the direction of their movement. It was lovely to look at, but nothing particularly titillating once you got past the performer's lack of clothing.

Additional dancers swirled into the space, including a Ma'achqwae male.

What was it about this race? St. Cyr felt the breath catch in her throat and her hands tremble. Carefully she set the glass tumbler on the table lest she drop it. Bayrrune Anatha had nothing on this dancer, and Bayrrune Anatha was an incredibly good looking man.

St. Cyr leaned forward, focusing all her attention on the blue male with four arms. He swirled, twining limbs and spinning around with the other performers. Terran bodies blocked her view of this ideal male. She swiped her hand when other dancers got between her and her view of the dancer, as if she could actually move them out of her way.

When he'd first entered the stage, she'd admired how zero grav enhanced his male attributes. Now she admired his long muscular legs, his narrow column of a waist rippled with muscles, his double pecs, and those arms. Those four arms bulging with muscle that she could imagine crushing around her, with four hands she could feel grasping at her flesh. Once she reached his face, she could not take her eyes from him. Large golden eyes, high cheekbones, and a strong square jaw with a prominent chin. His crop of blackest-black hair hung shaggy and licked down the back of his neck.

All of her attention was on the dancer when she felt Yaz yank the back of her vest. "You cannot just walk into the null-grav field, St. Cyr. Sit." Yaz tugged harder until the backs of her legs hit the chair and she sat with a thump.

St. Cyr blinked up at her tall pink friend in confusion. Her eyes moving rapidly in contrast to the slow sweep of Yaz's eye lids.

"You got up and walked to the edge of the platform like you were being pulled forward." Yaz explained. "Like you were possessed."

"More like she wants to possess someone inside that column." Zora added.

"What?" St. Cyr looked back and forth between Zora and Yaz.

Zora, with her arms crossed, glared down at St. Cyr. "You were going to try to swan dive into the null-grav field. Yaz pulled you back before you did something dumb and got hurt. The field is too far away from our platform. You wouldn't have made it. Odds are, you would have bounced off the field and fallen. It would have been a mess."

"Yes, you could have been badly injured. At the very least, they would have kicked us out. Who is so enthralling?" Yaz asked.

St. Cyr pointed. The beautiful blue man floated past, wrapped in silk cloth. "Him. I've never seen anyone so beautiful in my life." Her voice was barely a whisper. The nodig-sessu wanted him. She pushed that thought away even as she felt it contract in her core at the mere sight of him.

"Well, come on then. We need to get St. Cyr out of here before she tries something stupid again." Zora lifted St. Cyr from her chair with a guiding hand under her elbow. "We need to hit the stage door and wait for this one." She directed her attention to Yaz. "I've never seen St. Cyr like this over a man. Typically they don't faze her."

Yaz nodded. "She is most seriously fazed."

A team of private enforcers pushed past, entering the back stage door as their lift doors opened.

"Why are we waiting around like groupies?" St. Cyr asked.

"Because you haven't seen your face. You were going to kill yourself trying to get closer to that performer. The least we could do is find out more about him. This is the most direct way possible. That was the last performance of the night, and it was almost over—"

Zora was cut off when the door crashed open. A burly enforcer from the private force stepped through and, with a large sweeping motion of his arm, cleared a path. Behind him followed St. Cyr's beautiful blue Ma'achqwae with both sets of arms restrained behind him. Two flanking officers gripped his uppermost arms.

St. Cyr screamed a battle cry and leaped onto the back of the officer closest to her. She shrieked and pounded on the large man. He was Enceladian, so he was taller than the average Terran male. The Ma'achqwae belonged to her, the enforcers couldn't have him.

St. Cyr was vaguely aware of her friends yelling at her to stop.

Something about being arrested, something else about being kicked off station. All she knew is she had to free this man from custody. Common sense disappeared as hormones and physical *need* took hold of her body. Fingers bit into her arms and legs. One moment she was attacking and the next, the breath slammed out of her chest as she hit a wall. She lay in a heap, trying to fill her lungs with air.

Shit, the *nodig*. She thought she had taken her meds. Hadn't she? The nodig-sessu, a physical response triggered by a surge in mating hormones, had taken control. She should have recognized it when Zora and Yaz told her that she was about to throw herself at the performers inside the club.

St. Cyr blinked past the pain in her chest and back. Her man looked over his shoulder at her as he was rushed out of the passage and away. She dropped her head and tried to keep the keening wail in her head from escaping out of her mouth.

A cool hand stroked hair back from her face. "St. Cyr, are you alright?" Yaz's smooth voice calmed St. Cyr's prickly nerves.

She nodded. "Nodig-sessu. Didn't expect it."

"Your skin went all swirly and gold. You're a fucking Neryad? All this time I thought you were Terran. Why didn't you ever tell us? Deities abound, what the hell are we supposed to do now?" Zora's voice sounded screechy in St Cyr's ears.

"Nothing." St. Cyr pushed herself into a sitting position. "You don't have to do anything. On the other hand, I have to have sex, or I will stop being able to function. And I'm only a quarter Neryad. But I got the quarter with all of the nodig."

"I thought the nodig-sessu was only quelled by—"

"It's quelled by sex. It's driven by desire. Clearly my body thinks blue-boy is mine. I'll hurt myself and others trying to get to him. As you have witnessed. What I need right now are my meds, cause I must have missed a dose, and then a mech, in that order." Her voice sounded rough. The amount of control it took not to run after the man and those officers was taking its toll. If she couldn't have the man she needed, at least a mechanical man would take the edge off.

❄

Pounding rang throughout the ship. St. Cyr groaned and sat on the edge of her bunk, the bedding a mess of twisted blankets from last night's acrobatics with a rented mech. As directed, it had left her on her own, no additional interaction after the allotted time expired. Her body did not feel raw and satiated. It felt used. Used by her own damned genetics and a sex toy that could walk itself out of her cabin on its own two legs.

The thudding continued as someone or something banged on the hull. She slapped her hand against the back wall until her fingers found the comm switch. "Yeah?"

"I have a delivery from Bayrrune Anatha for transportation." The voice had a distinct modulation to it. Enceladian.

"Gimme a sec." St. Cyr flipped the comm switch. Damn, it was already time to take delivery. Shit shit shit shit. She had wanted to be ready to leave when the package was delivered. This was to be a quick trip, easy money, but sleeping in had already set her back half a day. She still had to shower, dress, and do a rundown of all systems before she could launch. She ticked off everything she still needed to do as she plodded to the hold.

She stared bleary eyed as the gangway lowered and bright lights from the landing bay flooded her cargo hold. She padded down the ramp, pulling her dressing gown around her. The landing bay had an unexpected chill to its atmosphere.

"Hey!" She waved down the group of men standing around her ship's main hatch. "Wheel whatever you have up in here. It'll be easier than wrestling anything in that way."

St. Cyr waited by the end of the ramp as the same private enforcers from the night before approached. Her brow knit together. Why were these guys here? They hadn't pursued her after she'd jumped one of them, so why now?

Her hand went to her mussed hair when she saw they had the Ma'achqwae man her body wanted so desperately.

"You contracted to transport a passenger home." A bruiser of a man with more knuckles than brains shoved the blue dancer towards St. Cyr. "This is your passenger." He glared at St. Cyr. "Do you accept delivery?"

"Uhm, I don't transport kidnap victims." St. Cyr struggled

against her inclination to fight and kick and scream and tear the bindings from the man.

The enforcer rattled a sheaf of forms at her. "No kidnap, agreed transport. Passenger and effects, including all provisions necessary for the duration. I have your signature."

She nodded in agreement. She signed a contract, beyond that her brain felt muzzy.

Two other uniformed men deposited wheeled crates on the floor of her cargo hold.

Bruiser held out a document on a board. St. Cyr looked at it. "What am I supposed to do with that?"

"I need your mark." Bruiser harrumphed. More old fashioned paper. Paper burned, no evidence left behind. She took the proffered pen and made her mark on the papers. He handed her one document from the stack. "Here's your manifest. Delivery location and date of arrival. Once confirmed, Anatha will complete payment."

"Is he to remain tethered?" St. Cyr nodded at her passenger.

"Your ship, your choice." Bruiser nodded to his men.

"Okay, then, put him with the rest of the cargo." St. Cyr shrugged as nonchalantly as she could fake. Her insides were anything but nonchalant. She needed to get this shipment delivered as soon as possible.

She needed to be as professional as she could pretend. She *needed*. She needed to distance herself form this man and pray her meds would be strong enough. If the nodig-sessu took hold of her while they were in space, alone? No, she didn't want to think about what would happen. Because what she wanted involved lips and skin and would only aggravate the nodig more.

She leaned on the button to raise the ramp, closing herself in the ship with the man who defined her every physical desire. Cargo, off limits. She wouldn't damage the goods. But she might let him damage her.

She walked up behind the man and began loosening his bonds. "Okay, dancer boy, what's the deal?"

He spun on her and grabbed her shoulders. The pain in his eyes felt like a knife wound in her gut. "You can't take me back there," he pleaded.

"I can. I'm being paid very well to do so." She glanced at the single document still in her hand. "This says I'm to take you to Kameros, and I've got to do it in two weeks. That planet is a week away, so I will deliver you early." St. Cyr refused to look him in the eyes again.

"C'mon." She sighed heavily and walked away from the man. "What's your name?" She couldn't continue to call him Blue-boy in her head, and she didn't want to call him that out loud.

"I'm called Dagon. Bayrrune Anatha is my mother's brother. I did not realize he had holdings on Fergus. I would not have come here." He followed after St. Cyr as she headed into the living quarters. Dagon continued. "He is treating me like a runaway child, simply because I embarrass him. If he hadn't made this into a big deal, no one would have known there was a family connection. I would have just been another Ma'achqwae minding my own business."

St. Cyr spun on her heel and faced Dagon. "Look, dancer-boy, I don't care for your whining. You're on my ship now, you're my responsibility. So shut up and stay out of my way."

Dagon stopped moving, and stared at her. His big golden eyes seared her soul.

She inhaled sharply as she realized she had barked more loudly than intended. His closeness was putting every nerve in her body on edge. Her skin was too aware that she only wore a thin dressing gown. Her nipples pebbled, and a pulse of want throbbed between her legs.

"You can have this room. The galley is that way." She pointed further along the corridor. "The head is that first door we passed, showers opposite." St. Cyr pulled her dressing gown tighter around her, lest she fling it open and invite Dagon to screw her right here on the floor.

She continued down the passage way. She heard Dagon move, and the door to his bunk close. St. Cyr tilted her head back and rolled her shoulders, trying to ease the tension that had settled into her neck and back. She untied the belt as she walked. First thing before launch prep was to get dressed. She slipped the robe from her shoulders before she stepped into her own room.

"Why did you jump that guard last night?" The voice had lost the whining tone and was smooth, just like she'd hoped it would be. "I recognize you."

St. Cyr turned. Startled, she dropped her robe. Dagon stood less than a pace away. His gaze raked her nude form. A smile twitched the edge of his lips. He could reach out and touch her if he wanted. She wanted. She didn't move. Their eyes held each other's gaze. Words failed her. As long as she didn't look at him she could pretend and treat him as cargo. But to see him? She attempted to swallow, but her throat was dry as dust.

She flinched as he leaned forward. He picked up her robe and handed it to her. "Get dressed, Captain. It looks like we have a week's worth of time in which to negotiate."

Dagon lay back in his temporary bunk. His head rested in his clasped upper hands, while his lower hands folded across his mid-section.

Well, this was going to be an interesting week. Interesting in the way a Phlexien opera was interesting—long, prolonged, and painfully discordant, unless he could figure this woman out. She either hated him or she wanted him. He could not tell. The confusion was agony. The captain was a paradox. It had taken him a few moments to recognize her as the screaming banshee from last night, all flashing eyes, flying braids, and curse words.

This morning she was the polar opposite, hair mussed and hanging down her back, eyes hooded with sleep, and pouty, kiss-able lips. He much preferred the woman from this morning. Especially the way gold clouds swarmed under her skin when her ire was up. At first he assumed she was Terran, but those whorls of gold gave her away as part Neryad.

Her words were sharp, dismissive, yet her body language oozed come hither. Was she even aware that she bit her lower lip in a way that made Dagon all too aware of wanting to kiss that mouth? His cock stiffened as he remembered how her chest lifted and fell after her robe dropped. Her body was beautiful, one of a fighter, and he wanted to taste every inch of it. The puckered blaster scar below her right shoulder did not detract from the perfection of her breasts at all. In fact, knowing she was a bit aggressive made her more attractive to him. Another faded scar, possibly from her childhood, followed the line of her hip. Three ragged lines more like a claw mark than any weapon Dagon was aware of.

"We launch in fifteen." Her sharply enunciated words from the comm cut thru his musings. He might as well stay put, no use trying to familiarize himself with the Milkmaid until they were underway.

Dagon closed his eyes. Mine. She had snarled 'mine' over and over as she'd attacked the men who had taken him into custody. Could that mean what he hoped?

St. Cyr slammed her fists against controls, not paying attention as she finalized the Milkmaid for takeoff. Takeoff and landing were the only times her ship needed operator control. The rest of space travel in the Milkmaid was preprogrammed guidance systems.

She should have insisted on knowing what she was transporting. Passengers were fine. But this Ma'achqwae male was a personal problem. The nodig pulsed in her veins like lava, thick and burning. Stupid genetics.

"Voice command," she said sternly to activate the system.

"Vol containers," a synthesized computer voice replied. "Let me look that up for you."

"You stupid interface," St. Cyr muttered. The vocal interface on the Milkmaid worked slightly better than fifty percent of the time. This was not one of those times. "Contact Enceladian Yaz Statman Aan and conference in Ionian Zora Herne."

"Contacting Enceladian Yaz Statman Aan. Records show Enceladian Yaz Statman Aan to be in the vicinity. Contacting Ionian Zora Herne." There was a pause. "Ionian Zora Herne is not in vicinity. Records showing she will exit space jump in three standard hours. Resume contact at that time? Confirm."

"No, continue with Enceladian Yaz Statman Aan only," St. Cyr directed.

"Contacting." The comm unit crackled with static.

"St. Cyr, are you feeling better this morning?" Yaz's soothing trill came through the speakers.

"Worse," St. Cyr grumbled. "How much is one of those mech units? Can I afford one?"

"You sound stressed. And no, I do not think you can afford a fully functional male mech." Yaz answered.

"My transport job is a person. It's that Ma'achqwae dancer."

"Oh. Oh my. How is your nodig-sessu? Or is that rude to ask?"

"The mech helped. Some." St. Cyr scoffed. "That's why I'm thinking it might be time to invest in my own. It would make situations like this one a little less delicate and easier to deal with."

"St. Cyr, isn't there a way to null the nodig-sessu in Neryad females? Aren't the meds enough?"

"The only permanent way to get rid of the nodig is to sterilize the female, rendering her completely asexual. I don't mind the sterilization part, it's the asexual part I mind. Besides, I think it has to be done in a female's youth. It wouldn't work on me."

As she spoke, St. Cyr watched the communication feed for approval to launch from Fergus control. The light held steady, indicating the Milkmaid was in queue. Uncertainty overwhelmed her, not a comfortable feeling, not a feeling she was used to.

"Yaz, I need counsel. What should I do?"

"Having sex with the male is the simplest resolution."

"I can't! He's my job." The sound of her distress grated on her own ears.

"Then double up on your meds and keep away from the male. Or let the male decide if he is willing to participate. They are typically willing when sex is involved."

"He's my passenger, so that's unethical."

"It is the nodig-sessu. There is unethical, and there is dead. Besides, it's only unethical if you are using your position of power as coercion. A willing male is not unethical. "

St. Cyr groaned. Yaz was right. This could kill her, especially with it being as strong and demanding as it was.

The light switched to a slow pulse, indicating she could launch. "I'm taking off, I'll be hitting my jump in a few. Comm me in a few days, will ya? Oh, and if you talk to Zora before I do, make sure to laugh about my predicament with her."

St. Cyr ended her link with Yaz before guiding the Milkmaid into the asteroid field.

She was not going to let this man and her biological need distract her. She may not be able to control the nodig, but she could distance herself from the man, avoid him. It was a small ship but it was possible.

Once clear of the asteroid belt St. Cyr set the ship to auto pilot. She stretched as she stood. Her breasts strained against the fabric of her shirt. Her nipples pebbled. This was going to be a long week. Stupid nodig.

St. Cyr stepped into the galley.

Avoiding him was easier said than done. Of course he had to be in the galley. His arm muscles bunched under the heavy load he carried. Why was a bulging muscle so sexy?

"What are you doing?" Her question was more of a bark than intended.

"Captain," Dagon acknowledged her with a lift of his chin. "I am moving the provisions from the cargo hold into the galley where they will be needed. Seemed pointless to leave food back there."

"Fine," she spat. The longer she was in his presence, the harder it was going to be to ignore him. She spun on her heel and went to hide in her cabin.

"Captain," Dagon spoke into the air. He looked around at the ceiling, uncertain if the comm unit was actually working. He was effectively abandoned on this ship. It had been six standard hours since he had last seen the captain. Most things he could find or figure out for himself. But he had no way of communicating with her without being in the same part of the ship. He had no idea where she was. She didn't respond when he knocked on her bunk door.

"Activate comm." He spoke to the room. There was no identifiable comm switch. He assumed the system was voice activated. No response.

"Captain!" he yelled.

"My name is St. Cyr." Her voice was a purr that licked straight to his crotch. He turned to see her languidly lean against the bulkhead. "What are you going on about?"

"First, how does the comm system in this place function? I can't keep shouting out and hope you hear me."

"Voice command comm," St. Cyr stated.

Dagon could hear the click and buzz of static as the comm unit activated.

"Thank you." He glanced at the captain. Was she even aware the way she bit her lip was enticing?

"End comm," she stated clearly, and the soft buzz of an open link ended. "Your first issue is taken care of. What's second?"

"Food." Dagon pulled two plates from the heating unit. "You do eat, right?"

He slid a plate across the table in front of her. St. Cyr slid into a chair and hummed as she picked up a fork. She must be hungry since she was smiling at the meal and making happy sounds.

However, he soon discovered the captain made eating difficult. Her moans as she ate, and the way she pulsed in her chair, was highly distracting.

"This is good." She hummed. "Will you cook for the entire trip?"

"If you ask nicely." Dagon raised an eyebrow at her.

She tilted her head to the side in defeat. "I have been brusque. I was not properly informed that I was transporting a live humanoid. I was…"

"You were cranky. My uncle has that effect on people."

She nodded. "I can see how he would. This little trip is going to take 112 standard hours. That's a minimum of twelve meals. I would appreciate it if you would be responsible for meal prep. I don't think you would like my cooking. I know I don't."

Dagon laughed at her self-deprecating remark. He was rewarded by a smile that lit up her face.

Mine. She had said mine. He was willing to be hers, even if only for the 112 standard hours she said this journey would take.

Dagon stretched his arms out and away from his torso. He inhaled deeply, bent his knees, and lowered his torso. He swept his lower arms in, keeping the upper pair outstretched. He breathed again and lifted back into a standing position, his arms extending out.

He centered his breathing and focused only on the movement of his body. He was not going to think about how his uncle found him again. He was not going to think about how he was being retuned to his home world like a convict. He might be confined to a cramped spaceship, but the cargo hold was empty, and it had atmosphere. He was going to use it. He was going to lose himself in movement.

He cleared his mind and lifted onto his toes. Centering his balance, he raised one leg behind him. He held the pose for thirty seconds before returning to his beginning posture. He bent his knees and spun.

The coloring under St. Cyr's skin swirled more and more every day as her agitation with him grew. He wasn't sure what to do to appease her. Yes, thinking about St. Cyr was far more pleasant than thinking about his family's plans for his life. Dagon practiced the spin again, this time holding the end pose. He shifted to the starting position of the spin and held the shape, reminding his body of the desired positioning of arms and legs. He adjusted and held the end pose.

This time when he spun, the forms he made with his limbs were closer to the desired shape.

He shook his long limbs. St. Cyr had been hiding from him. He was certain of it. She had stopped joining him for meals fifty four hours ago. He thought she might be Neryad, yet she didn't act like any he had ever met before. She was short tempered and hot headed.

He crossed his ankles, bent his knees slightly, and leapt into the air. When he landed, his feet had changed position. He repeated the small jump, counting each time. Focusing on keeping his body fit for dancing helped him to not think about St. Cyr, or what was waiting for him back on Kameros.

Dagon worked through standard dance drills until his body broke out in a light sweat. The cargo hold provided enough space he could move about. Now that he was properly warmed up Dagon allowed himself some play time.

He spoke to the empty space around him. "Voice command. Play music in cargo hold only."

A discordant squeal reverberated through the comm speakers.

"Voice command, play music, not Phlexian. Play something from Kameros."

The music changed, a rhythmic beat accompanied by soothing, shifting melodic tones.

Dagon began his impromptu performance with one of his practiced spins. He lunged across the open space, turning and lifting onto his toes as he reached the bulkhead. His feet shifted side to side as he swayed and spun and leapt with the music.

He landed awkwardly and stumbled. He heard a sharp intake of air on the walkway above him. He glanced up but quickly averted his eyes. St. Cyr watched. He wanted to let her think he didn't know she was there so that she would continue to observe.

"Voice command. Change music. Play something with a faster beat, popular social dance."

As directed the music changed. The back beat was stronger, the melody driven with a heavy bass line.

Dagon changed his style of dance. His entire posture lowered with a deeper bend in his knees. He floated across the floor, letting his feet glide with a rotation of his ankles. He smiled when he heard another gasp from his audience. Her noises told him she liked what she saw. He dove for the floor, catching himself at the last second with his primary hands. A body wave and a low spin repositioned his shoulders onto the floor. He kicked his feet up and under, lifting his torso at the same time, so that he landed upright and on his feet in a deep crouch.

He continued with low, grounded motion, catching glimpses of St. Cyr as he danced. Was she aware that she pulsed her hips in time to the music? She wasn't dancing exactly, but making small sexual thrusting motions. He spun and caught another glimpse of her. No, that was an involuntary movement.

Distracted by St. Cyr's hips, Dagon stopped. He breathed hard, having broken his dancer's concentration when he realized she was watching. He rested his upper hands on his thighs, letting his lower hands hang limp. His head fell forward. He could see her out of the corner of his eye. His hair had fallen into his face, hiding his gaze from her. He didn't move again until he heard her leave. She didn't need to know he was aware of her being there.

He smiled. She was physically affected by him. So why was she being so distant and bad-humored?

They safely parked, waiting for the planet to come into approach range. Predictable orbits made jumping further ahead along the orbital path and letting the planet come into range, rather than chasing after it, save on fuel. A navigation trick that St. Cyr learned early on and why she was able to make many of her deliveries ahead of schedule.

She was glad she had been able to think that far in advance. The nodig now clouded her thought processes. Extra injections were not helping. Self-satisfaction no longer existed for her.

It seemed like Dagon was doing everything in his power to be more attractive to her. She had followed the sounds of music coming from her cargo hold to find him dancing. His grace and fluidity brought her to tears. His visceral, grounded movements made her want to rip her clothes off and offer herself as a sacrifice to him. The sexiest thing he did in her presence was breathe.

She had to accept that his mere presence heightened the nodig in her.

She closed the cabin door behind her and administered a sedative. Her meds were not working. Maybe sleeping through the next few days would allow herself to survive this.

St. Cyr must have missed the knock in her agony. The door hissed open.

"You haven't been eating. Are you well?" Dagon asked.

St. Cyr groaned loudly before she was able to form words. "What are you doing here?" She panted, curled up into herself. Her physical need had become a cramping pain in her gut. Sweat beaded on her forehead. She had attempted to medicate herself into a sleep state for several days. It hadn't worked.

"You're Neryad?" Dagon asked.

Why didn't she have an onboard mech? Because the need had never been so strong before.

"You have the nodig-sessu, correct?" Dagon stepped into her cabin. He pulled his shirt over his head, exposing the contours of his muscular torso.

St. Cyr moaned and involuntarily reached out for him. "I can't. You can't. This is my problem. I can't ask you to do this."

"You don't have to ask. I volunteer. Besides, I need you."

Her heart skipped a beat with those words.

"I can't fly a ship."

The words twisted in her gut like a knife. Of course this wasn't emotional for him. She forgot herself for a moment. She stared at Dagon, shirtless, framed in the door. Yes, she would do this. She shouldn't but…

St. Cyr flew from her curled up position on her bed and wrapped herself around Dagon's body. Arms enfolded her. She couldn't tell who was doing the kissing. Her lips were being pressed as fiercely as she consumed his mouth. One hand was in her hair, holding her firmly. Another hand molded itself to her breast. Other hands scooped against her ass, pulling her hips close to his groin.

Dagon's body wanted her as much as she needed his. His arousal was hard against her lower belly. He had said he volunteered. Maybe her nodig was throwing pheromones that his body responded to. She didn't care about that at this moment. At this moment she needed to feel and not think.

She sank her fingernails into the flesh of his shoulders. She felt, more than heard, the moan he made as it rumbled through his chest.

Deities, his hands! She had fantasized about all the hands, and now she knew why. He unfastened her clothing with one pair of hands and was still able to touch and grab her with the other. She wished she had more arms. She had to stop touching him to pull at the drawstring on his pants. After loosening them, she shoved her hand down the front to cup his shaft. They both moaned at the contact. He was solid and hot. Somewhere in the back of her brain, St. Cyr registered that she had assumed his skin would feel cool to the touch because of his coloring. His skin was not cool, but burning, and felt like suede over marble. He was so hard under her fingers. Hard and thick.

She needed him, more touching, more mouth. She tripped and stumbled over her own pants around her knees as she pulled Dagon to her bunk. They fell in a tangle of limbs. His weight felt delectable on top of her as they continued to touch and taste each other.

She could no longer vocalize and only grunted and whimpered her frustration at how many clothes were still between them. Dagon, as eager as she was, extricated himself from her grasp only long enough to shuck his pants. He pulled her boots from her feet, peeled her pants the rest of the way off, and ripped her panties from her hips.

When he returned to her, she wrapped her legs around him. Driven by lust, fueled by the touch of his skin between her thighs. Dagon's fingers bit into the flesh at her hips as he clutched her up to him. She countered the move and tightened her legs.

She screamed with pleasurable need as he drove into her. That was where her body longed for him to be, cock deep, hip to hip. They ground their lust into each other. The nodig wanted to consume Dagon. Mechs had nothing on a live male.

After the initial penetration, St. Cyr's body tensed, preparing for a release. She moaned and cried out as Dagon serviced her with thrusts, groping hands, and a sucking, needy mouth. The nodig-sessu never allowed much thinking or finesse. The nodig was compulsive and carnal and basic.

St. Cyr could get tricky and show Dagon what she was capable of next time. Would he want a next time? Her brain dissolved into nerves again and thought abandoned her as the pressure built in her core. She saw stars behind her eyes. Her breathing was nothing more than pants and gulps for air.

She dug her fingers into Dagon's back and let out a guttural scream as her body peaked and she convulsed around his plunging member. The orgasm continued to throb and strobe through her as he continued to grind into her.

Dagon pushed up on two arms. He stroked her face as he looked deep into her eyes. St. Cyr continued to come as he slowed and gentled his actions. But the expression on his face seemed to inspire her body into another wave of internal convulsions.

St. Cyr broke eye contact and cried out as more convulsions claimed her body. The nodig-driven orgasm would milk at her lover up to ten times longer than a typical one. She looked up at Dagon as he chuckled. He stopped moving and held himself to her.

"What?" she managed to whimper.

"I'm enjoying the ride, but I'm not going to last much longer. And you've been going nonstop."

"The nodig-sessu," St. Cyr moaned.

"The nodig-sessu," Dagon repeated. He began to stroke into her. Her convulsions slowed and matched pace with his movements.

Dagon cried out as he reached his own release. The wet heat between her legs renewed St. Cyr's urgent need. Dagon wrapped a leg around her and twisted, rolling St. Cyr into position above him, straddling his hips. "I can't move. You have to take over." He laughed with a sigh.

St. Cyr smiled down into his face. He was beautiful, his eyes hooded with his spent desire. His lips curved into a satisfied smile. She rocked against him from her perch. The nodig persisted to drive her, but not at such a frenzied pace. Dagon continued to stroke and pet and touch her as her body pulled on his cock inside of her.

Finally St. Cyr collapsed against his chest, her breath heaving with exertion. Her leg muscles cramped in uncomfortable spasms. She felt enveloped in care as Dagon wrapped his arms over her and held her. St. Cyr fell asleep cocooned in his arms.

St. Cyr's light breathing and relaxed face were in direct opposition to her demeanor the past few days. Dagon trailed his fingers lightly over her shoulder, not wanting to wake her. She looked at peace, the pinch of pain that had increasingly furrowed her brow as the days passed finally gone.

The shifting gold under her skin chased after his fingers, as if it wanted to touch him back.

According to her calculations they would only have two more days together. If this took care of her nodig, would he be allowed to touch her again?

He adored the idea that this beautiful fierce woman had needed him. His own family didn't care for him. They only wanted to control him. Case in point, his uncle hiring St. Cyr to take him home to his mother. He would be delivered, and within a few weeks he would be married off like so much chattel. If they really wanted to be free of him, why didn't they leave him alone? Because he was worth money. His family's position could demand a high dowry. Would St. Cyr be pleased if he ran away and tried to find her instead?

She had cried out 'mine' when she attacked the guards who gathered him for delivery. She had called out 'mine' again as her body came around him. She had need for him. But did she want him?

Stupid, this wasn't about creating an emotional bond. He had to stop that line of thought.

Dagon sighed. Trapped under her soft warm body was not good for his heart. He kissed her temple lightly and shifted so he could ease himself out from under her.

The arm she had thrown over his chest tensed, and her hand wrapped around his shoulder. "Stay," she murmured.

Dagon tried to lift her hand from him.

"Please, this is nice."

"I should—"

"Dagon." His name sounded like a prayer on her lips. "Neither of us has anywhere to be or anywhere to go. I want you to stay." She sighed. Her breath caressed his chest. "I want you to want to stay."

Dagon closed his eyes tight. Did she have any idea what those words did to him? He wanted to stay. He wanted to stay for a very long time. He stroked her hair. It was soft and silky as it flowed between his fingers. "I'm not going anywhere."

Dagon woke to a raging erection and a hot sucking mouth on his neck.

"Ahhh." He exhaled and reveled in the feel of her touching him. She caressed and massaged at his pecs and shoulders. Her hands caressed and moved, as if she couldn't get enough of him under her palms. The gold of her skin moved in rapid patterns like a fast shifting storm. The color was so strong that she practically glowed

St. Cyr made mewing noises of frustration. Dagon reached down with one arm and extricated the blanket that had become tangled in her kicking legs. At the same time, he grabbed her leg and braced her hip as he guided her into a straddling position.

Her hips already rocked above him with the thrusting action she'd used when he was inside her. Dagon wasn't familiar enough with the nodig to know how long this would last. He had heard of it. To his young lustful ears, Neryad sounded like ideal women, driven by sex and nothing more. He had been a fool. He still was.

He should learn more about this, learn more about her, but not right now. Right now he needed her, too. St. Cyr slid down his length allowing him to penetrate her. Dagon only wanted to be here, with her supple body wrapped around him, grinding into him. Her muscles were already clenching and spasming in orgasm. He didn't care that he was a tool for her use, as long as she used him.

He held her hips hard so that he could thrust up into her. He caressed and kneaded her breasts. The expression of sheer ecstasy on her face urged him to pound harder.

St. Cyr's mews turned to a rhythmic chanting that matched the motion of their bodies. "Mine. Mine. Mine."

Dagon couldn't handle it, he exploded with a growl. His muscles seized up and he stopped thrusting. He could feel his cock pulsing and spilling into her. Her muscles an unceasing riot around him. He collapsed his hips back against the bed. St. Cyr continued to grind against him until she froze up in a final climactic spasm.

"Thank you," she panted against his chest after she, too, collapsed.

"Don't thank me. This is my pleasure." Dagon relaxed with his eyes closed. He felt her push up. "Don't say anything right now, please. Don't spoil this."

St. Cyr remained braced with her hands on his chest. He could tell she was staring at him. He mindlessly trailed his hands up and down her back and sides. She was slick with sweat. Four hands weren't enough to touch her with. He sighed when she finally lowered herself to his chest and let her fingers trace over his skin.

They ate in silence.

St. Cyr didn't know how to talk to him. She wanted to thank him for essentially saving her life, but he didn't want to hear that. He'd told her to stop thanking him. He said he'd enjoyed it. But she felt as if she'd committed a seriously unethical misstep, sleeping with her passenger.

There were no laws against it, and he'd come to her willingly.

She still had pangs of guilt. Maybe she should offer to take him anywhere he wanted to go. She would refund his uncle, and they would never speak again.

She looked through her lashes at him. Dagon concentrated on the soup he had made. It was hot, nourishing, and delicious. She would miss his cooking. She would miss sneaking into the cargo hold to watch him dance. She would miss the feel of his skin under her fingers and the way he caressed her entire body.

St. Cyr needed to admit to herself she would miss him.

"Kameros should be in orbital approach tomorrow," she announced.

Dagon said nothing, stood, and took his empty dishes with him. Uncharacteristically he tossed them into the cleaning unit and left. She was alone.

Alone with her thoughts, alone with the knowledge that she'd continued to make love to him under the pretense of the nodig, even though it had ebbed after the first twelve hours of their marathon intercourse session.

He didn't want to go to Kameros, and she knew it. She was an ass.

She left her dishes on the table and followed after him.

Arms out, one leg extended to the back, he stood in the middle of the empty cargo hold. He looked poised for a spin, but there was no music, and he held perfectly still. The first time she'd seen him, not even a standard station week ago, he had been dancing, and something inside her had snapped.

Dagon's knees bent slightly, and then he was spinning. One, two, three, four full rotations before he stopped. He grunted and began spinning again. St. Cyr lost count of rotations.

She slowly made her way from the walkway down to the floor. She stood in front of him, but he didn't see her. At least, he didn't look at her. His head was held straight, and his focus was somewhere slightly up and far away, past her. When she saw the rim of red around his large gold eyes, tears burned her own eyes.

She'd used him and hurt him. She didn't know how to make it better. She didn't know if she could.

Dagon continued to spin, stopping from time to time to adjust his position and posture. He never looked at her. Dejected, St. Cyr left him. The tears that had threatened earlier trailed silently down her face.

St. Cyr tapped on the open cabin door frame. Shirtless, Dagon's perfect muscular back was to her. She loved the color of his skin. It looked like he was shoving his few belongings into one of the bags that had been delivered as part of his provisions.

When she tapped, his shoulders tightened, and his double muscles bunched. No way to miss his body language—he did not want to talk to her.

"Kameros is still within range, you're here to tell me to get ready. Well, I already am." He still didn't turn to face her.

"I didn't come here to talk about that," she said quietly.

She stepped into the cabin and tentatively placed her hand on the center of his back. Now she could feel the muscles contracting. She glided her fingers across the tops of his shoulders. Dagon reached behind him and grabbed her hand, stilling her action.

"Do you need me?" There was a hitch to his voice that St. Cyr knew she'd caused.

"No." She answered with a whisper.

"Then why are you here?" His voice was thick with emotion. He still held her hand, still would not face her.

"I don't have the nodig-sessu anymore. I want you."

Dagon spun and captured her around the hips with his lower arms. His upper hands held her face. His eyes searched hers. "What is it you want from me, St. Cyr? Aren't I just a delivery fee, a convenient penis for your hormones?"

She tried to swallow, but her mouth was dry. St. Cyr wrapped her hands over Dagon's upper wrists. She had to face him and her own mistakes.

"The nodig was triggered back on Fergus. But it's never been like this before. Usually a mech can take care of things for me. That didn't work out so well. Then the package I was to deliver for Anatha arrived, and everything got worse." She drew in a ragged sigh. "Apparently you sparked something in me that only you can satisfy. I saw your performance. Moments later I saw you in custody. I lost control. I had to get to you, and I couldn't believe it when you were the item I was to deliver."

She closed her eyes. Dagon's thumbs began caressing her cheeks. She opened her eyes again. He was impossibly beautiful and he looked at her with such pain. Pain she had caused.

"Tell me where you want to go and I'll return your uncle's money. I don't transport people against their will. I made a series of bad judgement calls and you—"

Dagon's thumb covered her mouth. "Don't say I was one of them. Don't say I was a mistake. Did you ever wonder, at least once, why I was complacent about being transported by you? Were you capable of thinking clearly, or had the nodig already taken hold?"

St. Cyr pulled on his wrists until he released her face. His arms were still around her. She rested her hands on his chest, followed by her cheek. His upper arms enfolded her against him.

"Apparently I stopped thinking properly when I first saw you wrapped in that length of red silk, twirling around in zero-grav. My friends realized something was wrong, but they didn't realize it was the nodig-sessu. Hell, they didn't even know I'm part Neryad until that night. I used a mech. I should have been fine."

Gentle fingers stroked her hair. She felt his chuckle rumbling in his chest. "I recognized you after they put me on the Milkmaid. You tried to free me from my uncle's guards. Do you know what you said that night?"

She shook her head. "No."

"Mine. You said 'mine.' And you claimed me. And you kept saying it, and I wanted it to be true. Take me back to my mother's people on Kameros. Claim your payment. Give them no reason to find fault with your services. But stay in orbit, I'll come back to you. They can't keep me now."

"I'll take you anywhere you want to go." She owed him that, and he was willing to return to his planet so she could earn her transport fee. "I'm so sorry I did this to you."

"St. Cyr, you aren't paying attention."

She pushed out of his embrace to look into his eyes. "What do you mean?"

"I need you."

"Yes, to transport—"

He cut her off. "Not to transport. I need you. I want you to take me away, and I'll go wherever you go. And I can be here for you when you need me."

St. Cyr closed her eyes. She felt the hot sting of tears. "We're both idiots. Please tell me we're both trying and failing at saying the same thing."

"I want you to be mine. I want to be yours." Dagon's hands were stroking the side of her face again.

Tears spilled down her cheeks. "Yes, please. Be mine. I'm already yours."

Their lips met, and it wasn't the nodig that propelled them to remove their clothes but a desire and want of each other.

St. Cyr cried out as Dagon slid into her. His touch was perfect and took her to the edge immediately. It was what she longed for. She understood the nodig now. It wasn't simply for sex, but for completion, to be made whole, when she hadn't realized she wasn't.

He collapsed on the small bunk next to her after they had both screamed out their release. She snuggled into his multi-armed embrace. "Mine," she whispered.

Dagon pulled her close. "Mine."

NINE LADIES DANCING

*K*yra stalked into the dressing room carrying a styrofoam to-go box and a long-necked bottle of beer.

"What are you doing? You know Louie doesn't want us eating back here. You can smell the grease on that burger for miles," Femalé complained.

"I'm tired, I'm hungry, and I'm sick of people railing against me for things that are not my fault."

The other women in the dressing room made noises of agreement.

Kyra set the containers on her makeup table and began changing. The first thing she did was pull her hair out of the sedate low ponytail she'd worn for that horrific interview, before running her fingers through her hair, fluffing up her frizzy red curls. Fuck that man and his aversion to red hair. She liked it. She didn't want that stupid modern art museum job anyway.

She slipped her feet out of her sensible black pumps and changed from the functional below-knee skirt and floral blouse into a tiny pair of panties that could almost be called boy-shorts. They were boxy in shape, but they exposed more ass cheek than they covered. She hooked her bra over the hanger with the rest of her interview outfit before she pulled on a tight white tank.

She essentially appeared as if she were walking around in her underwear before getting dressed, instead of being completely outfitted.

Orangelo staggered into the room, sweat glistened on her skin. "Vagandria, you're up next, darlin.' You had better get a wig on that head before Louie sees you."

Kyra shook her head. No wig. "This is either going to be brilliant beyond compare or it's going to get me fired. Wish me luck." She tossed a large towel over her shoulder, strapped her feet into silver platform stilettos, and left the dressing room carrying her food.

Out on stage, she didn't pose or sashay. She walked with as much grace as she could muster in her seven-inch heels, which, after over three years of dancing, she did pretty well. She carried a folding chair and her food. She placed the chair at the end of the stage, balanced her food on the seat of the chair, and spread the towel out on the floor. Picking up the food, she sat back in the chair.

There was no poise in how she sat either. Legs splayed apart, as if she were a man, taking up as much room as possible. She placed the to-go box on the floor, opened it, and began eating.

The woman on stage was nothing that Duke had expected. She walked out like she owned the club. She radiated fierce command. She was in charge and she didn't give a fuck what anyone thought.

Duke assumed the strip club would have dancers in barely-there outfits, shimmying about while removing bits of clothing for his pleasure. This woman looked like she'd just rolled out of bed, with wild hair and the type of underwear his last girlfriend wore on her "messy days." She was beyond distracting; she had successfully redirected any blood flow from his brain straight into his cock. And all she was doing was eating a damned hamburger.

She ate slowly and deliberately. Every time she licked one of her fingers or wiped the corner of her mouth, his cock throbbed and strained against the front of his trousers.

After she finished the burger, she slouched back in the chair, took a long pull on the beer. She stared out at nothing and belched. She then tossed her head back and poured the rest of the beer over her chest. The white shirt turned to transparent tissue and plastered itself even more completely to her breasts.

Duke groaned and about creamed himself when he caught sight of pink nipples through the fabric.

Louie barged into the dressing room, close on Kyra's heels. His expressive bushy eyebrows meeting in the center, his mouth in a downed turned grimace. "I should fire you for that stunt, Vagandria." He never offered his dancers the courtesy of knocking, whenever they complained, he always countered with, 'It's not like I haven't seen you naked before.'

"What did I tell you about your hair?"

"Yeah, yeah, yeah, I get it, you don't like redheads, no one wants to see hair like mine. Tell me something I don't know." The man at this afternoon's interview had told her in no uncertain terms that she was intellectually inferior for having the color orange growing out of her head. He'd questioned the legitimacy of her college credentials all because he had a bad experience with an ex-wife and some red hair dye. Kyra started throwing the assorted makeup kits on her dressing table into the middle, preparing for a hasty departure. She expected Louie to start in on her not taking her top off next.

Louie insisted that boobs be shown with every performance. The wet T-shirt exposed as much as if she had removed the shirt. But he would fire her in a heartbeat.

The men in the main room had been more interested in their drinks than they were in her. It wouldn't have made a bit of difference if she had been dancing. No tips were still no tips, and those guys were not tipping. Hell, she could have gone full nude while eating that burger and the only person who would have noticed was Louie. And at that point, he would have commented on her personal grooming habits. The man was obsessed with coochie hair and tits.

"The Johns seemed have been inspired, and kitchen orders went up. You have three privates waiting for you in rooms one, two, and four. I still don't want to see a shit stunt like that again or I will fire your ass."

Kyra dropped her head and groaned. She should say no. She should renegotiate her contract to not have to do the private lap dances. Oh wait, she didn't have a contract. Lap dances out in the main room were fine, but the guys who paid extra for the private showing always seemed to think that meant she would also prostitute herself for them. She had come close more than once. She also ended up very drunk, very depressed, and harming herself after the fact. No, she couldn't, it was too far down that rabbit hole. She was afraid she wouldn't survive it. Besides, it would be her luck that the day she did accept a John, he would be an undercover cop and it would be a setup.

"Shit, gimme five and I'll be out." Three privates, just from eating a hamburger? Maybe she needed to do that more often. She shoved all her misgivings back into the little dark pit where she hid them away so she could survive. She picked up a large fluffy duster and began powdering herself down.

When she entered room four, she was prepared to find another overweight, sweaty, middle-aged man who didn't understand the hands-off rule. She had walked in the room on the defense, prepared to run down the rules, fight off advances, and tell the guy she didn't really care if he didn't normally like redheads. She stopped as she faced a distractingly tall, handsome man. His square jaw was clenched, his brow was furrowed, and he looked completely distraught. He wasn't sitting on the throne in the back of the room, rubbing himself through his clothes, as was typical. He paced back and forth.

"I'm sorry." He stopped walking, looked at Kyra, and showed her the chair. "Please, why don't you sit?"

"You're the one who should be sitting." She eyed him quizzically.

"I don't feel like sitting, and I can only imagine your feet must hurt in those shoes."

Kyra shook her head and sank into the chair with a flourish. The man didn't notice.

"I've never done this before."

"Do you need me to talk you through the process?" Kyra tapped one pointer finger with the other, ready to expound on her personal rules of lap dances.

"No, I'm not going to have you dance or anything." The man shrugged out of his blazer. He placed it around Kyra's shoulders. "Here, you look cold and not dressed."

Kyra laughed. "I'm a stripper. Of course, I'm not dressed."

"I should go." He bolted from the room before she even had time to stand up.

She tried to follow him, but he was long gone by the time she entered the main room of the club. Returning to the dressing room, she took off the jacket, found a hanger, and hung it on the end of the costuming rack. She buried her nose into the collar of the jacket before she hung it up. He wore expensive smelling cologne. She rummaged through the pockets to see if she could find anything about the man. No identification, only a brochure to the local fine art museum. Replacing the pamphlet in the pocket, Kyra smiled.

Duke drove fast, faster. He ignored the wet road conditions to cut in and out of traffic. He couldn't put enough distance between him and today. The funeral, while not a party was pleasant enough. Too many false condolences, too many hours with a false smile on his face.

What had he been thinking, going to a strip club? He wanted to cut loose after the restraints of the day. What had he been thinking, buying a private lap dance from that woman? That she would come strutting in and eat him the way she had that hamburger. One look at her face and he knew he had done everything wrong. He wanted to go back and see her, wanted to talk to her, find out why she did what she did. At the same time, he should never go back there, should wipe the image of her from his mind. He wanted…

Damn, damn, damn, damn, damn. He pounded the steering wheel in frustration. He would have to go back. He left his jacket.

Duke sat nervously on the throne provided for the private lap dances. He focused on his fingers, pushing at his well-manicured cuticles. It had taken him over a week before he found a break in his schedule, and the balls to walk back into the club and request a private with the wild haired, devourer of hamburgers.

"Well, hello there."

His head snapped up at the voice. She stood just inside the door wearing a revealing bathing suit. Strategically placed ties would allow her to remove pieces as she desired. Her hair was violet today. Maybe the mass of orange had just been a wig. Too bad—Duke liked redheads.

He couldn't talk. He had seen her number earlier, and when she took to the pole, he had thoughts of replacing it with his own throbbing erection. But that was the whole point, wasn't it?

"I have your jacket from last time." She sashayed closer to him, swinging her hips side to side in an exaggerated motion. "So do I get to dance for you this time, or you just want your stuff back?"

"Dance," Duke croaked.

She wiggled to the door. He watched as she turned a switch and pressed a button on a panel in the wall. Dance music filled the room with a bwah-ah-ah-ah. He felt the sound more than he heard it.

She spun away from him before bending over to touch the floor. This put her in a position that displayed her ass and her feminine sex. Duke shifted uncomfortably. Even though she was covered, she was very close, and only a thin piece of fabric protected her from being completely exposed to him.

"Can I touch?" he managed to ask.

"No, no, no," she said, turning around. "I can touch you, but you don't get to touch me." She started to crawl into his lap. Duke threw his hands out and away as if he were being held up. "And nothing below the belt, so you're safe. What's your name?"

"Duke."

"Here, Duke." She placed his hands on the arms of the chair. "I'm Vagandria." She said the name like Vah- tzandriah, emphasizing the first syllable and slurring the rest of the name together.

Duke grew more uncomfortable the closer she was."Stop. Don't. I can't do this."

Vagandria stood up and looked at him quizzically. "You've paid me twice for this, and what? Afraid the wife wouldn't approve?"

"I'm not married, and I'm not comfortable. Look I know I paid for your time. I don't know what I was thinking, but this is weird for me. Can we just talk?"

"Sure." Vagandria sat on the platform at his feet. "But if you are just looking to talk, you could find some homeless guy in the park for cheaper."

"True, but the company wouldn't smell as nice or be nearly as attractive." Or have eyes like a doe blinking up at him, or lips he wanted to kiss, or breasts that haunted his dreams.

The flashing siren style lights announced their limited time was up. Duke stood up, told her to wait before excusing himself.

"I paid for a second private session with you." he said when he closed the door behind him.

"Hey, I just dance. I'm not gonna suck you off or anything," Kyra announced, though the thought was in her mind. She wouldn't mind going home with someone as hot as Duke.

The man blushed. That was charming and different.

"God, no! I just wanted to keep talking."

Kyra smiled. Talking was a welcome break from having to peel unwanted hands from her ass for another fifteen minutes.

But, truthfully, his hands hadn't wandered and they wouldn't be unwelcome.

They talked until the lights flashed again.

"Well, my time is up. You wouldn't be interested in going out with me sometime, would you?"

Kyra shook her head. Never date the men from the club, ever. That was the first rule she'd learned. Even if it was tempting, just don't do it.

"That's a real nice thought, but not gonna happen. You can come back for a private dance if you want. Oh wait, let me get you your jacket." Kyra dashed off to retrieve his coat from the previous week.

Carrying it back to Duke, she noticed how it no longer smelled like him but stale smoke and club stink.

"You're gonna want to get this dry cleaned, it smells."

When Duke's hand brushed hers, Kyra felt a zing at the contact. She hoped he would come back again.

Louie stood waiting for Kyra when she stepped off the stage and into the dressing room. His eye brows were clenched tight, his mouth scowling. She hadn't done anything wrong, so why was he there glowering at her? She didn't do any more pole than she was capable of, no embarrassing incidents. She had ripped her top off, and the bra went next fairly early on in the song. And, because tips were flying, the panties came off as well. Since she was well groomed and had electric blue pubic hair, there was nothing Louie could complain about.

"Vagandria, your regular is waiting in room three," Louie barked before leaving.

Why couldn't that man have more than one expression, she had been worried over nothing.

"Your regular? You mean that tall glass of water you been telling us about?" La-a asked as she powdered between her breasts with sparkle dust.

"If he's comin' here too much, something's wrong," Pajamā added.

"Maybe he's really rich, Pashamay, and he wants to take her away from the world of stripping," Femalé replied to the other woman.

Kyra laughed. "Oh, wouldn't that be nice? But life isn't the plot of some movie. With my luck he's just got the looks, but no brain, and definitely no money."

"He hasn't gotten creepier than normal yet, has he?"

"I still haven't actually danced for him. He just wants to talk. He's mostly super nervous. Super hot and super nervous."

"Well, hot don't mean not creepy. Don't let him get weird on you, you hear me?" La-a got close to Kyra's face, looking her right in the eyes.

"Yes, Ladasha, I hear you." Kyra tucked her hair into a bright pink wig and pulled on a fresh pair of rhinestone panties and a tight tank top with no bra. If Duke decided to let her dance, she might let him in on a little audience participation and let him pour a beer down her front. It would be sexier with champagne, but this was the King Diamond, so beer was it.

"You again?" Kyra didn't hide her grin when she walked into room three and found the handsome Duke waiting for her. He was a welcome relief from the men who grunted and grabbed.

"I enjoyed our chat the other day."

"I did, too," Kyra said as she sat on the raised dais the chair occupied. "So what's up in your world, Duke?"

"I thought I saw you the other day, waitressing."

"It's possible. I do have other jobs."

"Why? I pay good money for fifteen minutes of your time, you should be making a pretty decent income based on my calculations."

Kyra cackled. "That's hysterical, you actually think I get paid all of that money?"

Duke nodded and made a positive sound.

"I hate to burst your bubble, but strippers barely make more than waitresses do. And that's not much. Everybody gets a cut of what tips I make." She started counting off on her fingers. "The house gets a cut, the bus boy picking up the tips takes a cut, I have to split with the kitchen, and then all the dancers split the rest of the take. I do get paid extra for private lap dances, but it's just a small percentage."

"Then why do it? You could make better money—"

Kyra cut him off. "What, if I were a welder? This isn't a movie, Duke. I could make better money if I could get a better job. Trust me, I didn't set out with this as a career goal. And if I had, I'd be in Vegas."

"I'm sorry, Vagandria. Could I maybe visit you at your other job? You are the most beautiful woman I have ever seen, and I don't know what's gotten into me. I went back and ate at the place where I thought I saw you. But you weren't there, and they said no one with your description worked there."

Oh crap, he had finally gone there: Creeperland. Kyra stood up. "Please don't do that. Look, you should go. And don't plan on coming back."

"I just want to see you again."

"You are freaking me out. If you really are a nice guy, you would realize this is not cool behavior. Do not try to find me at my other job."

"But..."

She stormed out of the room. Damn, she was going to need a drink. The handsome one turned creeper. She needed to remind herself, like she kept saying, life wasn't a movie.

Christmas music from a string quartet filled the air. Kyra stood quietly holding a silver platter. Dressed in black slacks and blouse with a small white apron, she was furniture with food. She smiled blandly at the patrons in their dresses and tuxedos that cost more than she made in six months. The holiday gala was too crowded for her to move about, so she didn't. When her tray was almost empty, she vanished to the kitchen to get a refill of finger foods and returned to her exact same position as a serving statue.

She caught a glimpse of the man from the disastrous interview, the one who had blamed her red hair for his wife's infidelities. It had been several weeks, yet it still rankled. She wondered if she would ever live up to the fiery expectations of her hair and blow up at the man? Granted, now was not the time. Especially since he was talking to one of her favorite people from the Fine Art Museum. And they were headed her way.

The shorter of the two bumped into her. "Oh, I am so sorry, too crowded in here. Kyra?" He apologized.

She offered the gentleman a genuine smile. "Hello, Mr. Jameson. Are you having a good evening?" She was saved having to acknowledge interview bully. His attention taken by another gala attendee.

"We have quite the turn out, don't we? I am pleased, and I think our benefactor will be as well. Why are you here, young lady, and with a tray no less?"

Mr. Jameson was in charge of the education outreach program at the fine art museum. Kyra donated as much time as she could afford to the museum as a docent. Since Mr. Jameson knew her name, so far it was paying off.

"I happen to work for the catering company, and honestly"— she leaned closer to him conspiratorially—"I pulled some strings so that I could work tonight's event. It's the only way I would have been able to see all of this." She indicated with a nod of her head the elaborate decorations and evening gowns that filled the lobby of the museum.

Mr. Jameson patted her on the upper arm. "Well, I am glad you found a way in."

Kyra bit the inside of her lip. If he would actually hire her for the education department, she could have been here enjoying the party and not working it.

"Champlain, glad to see you," Mr. Jameson called out, waving someone Kyra could not see over. "Kyra, have you met Duke Champlain? He is our largest supporting patron."

Kyra stared wide-eyed at the tall, good looking Duke. Duke, who talked to her in the private rooms at the King Diamond. Duke. He shook Mr. Jameson's hand. "I just manage the trust that's technically the museum's largest financial supporter." He hadn't noticed it was her yet, and why would he? She wasn't wearing any makeup, she had clothes on, and her hair was slicked back into a clean and respectable bun. She was a human platter.

"Duke, let me introduce you to Kyra, our most reliable docent volunteer."

Duke faced Kyra. His smile vanished. His eyes went wide. They were actually a dark blue. Kyra never could tell from the crappy lighting in the club. "You?" His voice was barely above a whisper.

Kyra panicked and ran, tipping the contents of the tray onto the floor in her haste to escape. Bile rose in the back of her throat. She crashed through the kitchen doors before stopping, before thinking. Duke, regular turned creep, was some kind of crazy money millionaire? Oh God, hopefully he wouldn't tell Mr. Jameson he saw her at a strip club. Mr. Jameson would never hire her if he knew.

Then again, would Mr. Jameson hire her after she tossed her tray to the floor and fled in the middle of an introduction?

A firm hand grabbed her upper arm and spun her around. She looked up into Duke's face. His brows furrowed and his eyes blazed. "What are you doing here? You told me to stop bothering you, so why are you here? Why is it okay for you to follow me?"

"I'm not following you. How was I to know you would be here? I work for the catering company." Kyra tried not to sound as terrified as she was. She wasn't afraid of what Duke might do to her in his anger, but at what he could do to her future with a few choice words to Mr. Jameson and the board of the museum. "And I volunteer for the museum."

"Why?" The question was a bark.

"Because I don't want to be a..." Kyra looked around her and dropped her voice to a whisper. "Stripper for the rest of my life, okay? Because I have an expensive degree in museum studies and outreach education. I want to work here. I volunteer so they have a face and a work ethic to go with my resume. Is that okay with you?" She yanked her arm from Duke's grip.

"I thought your name was Vagandrea. I stopped coming to see you like you asked."

"Are you daft? Think about it. Vag-Andrea. You really think my parents named me after a va-jay-jay?" She rolled her eyes

"Wendell! Get out of here. You're fired!" Kyra turned to see her boss charging towards her like a rhino on a mission.

She sagged. "Come on, Gerry." She whined.

"I knocked the tray out of her hands, that was my fault," Duke said, addressing the raging caterer.

Confronted with a tuxedoed guest, Gerry settled. "Don't mess up again, Wendell, or you're out."

"Thanks, Gerry."

They watched in silence as Gerry retreated over to the far side of the kitchen.

"Look, this isn't the club, and Jameson just introduced us. Will you go out with me?" Duke spread his arms wide.

"I don't date guys from the club," she said, more to remind herself than anyone else. But he did look good in a tux.

"I never met a Kyra Wendell at some club. We met here, tonight. Jameson just introduced us. You can ask him yourself. I'm sure he'll remember, since you spilled finger food on him."

"Oh God, I did, didn't I? I need to apologize." Kyra blinked back her frustration.

Duke leveled a stare at Kyra. "Go out with me and I'll make sure all is good between Jameson and you."

She huffed, equal parts frustration and resignation. "We met at the museum's gala holiday shindig? You've never seen me before?"

"I would remember with searing detail the first time I met you. You belong in a fine art museum. You are very unforgettable." Duke's eyes narrowed, and Kyra caught her breath. This was a very different man than one she had met in the club. Here he was the one in control, and he knew it. "Let me take you out after this is all over, give me a chance to explain myself."

"I'll be here late, cleaning up." Kyra sighed.

"I'll wait. I have a feeling it will be worth it."

Kyra slid into the booth across from Duke. He still wore his tux from the Gala, but the bow tie had long since disappeared. He had a nice neck. She could imagine doing things to that neck with her mouth. The ride over here had almost been the beginning and the end of their date. She had nervously watched him during the trip across town. The chill of the night had kept her awake, and she was used to working nights. Duke was clearly not a night owl, or he was lulled by the warmth of his cashmere overcoat. He fought to keep his eyes open, the late night/early morning hour wasn't something he was used to.

He had waited an hour after the end of the event for her. She gave him kudos for that. He said he would, and he did, all without complaining. If he didn't start talking soon, this was going to be a very short date.

"Kyra." He nodded and said her name again. "Kyra. It suits you better. I don't know where my head was to think the other one might be anything other than a performance name."

"So now that you have me out on a date, how do you plan on impressing me?" Kyra asked as she eyed him over the top of her menu. It wasn't going to take much. Duke Champlain was impressive all on his own merit. She already considered him to be incredibly handsome. As a volunteer for the museum, she was familiar with the fact that he had taken over running the family foundation after his father had died. The Champlain Foundation was a major contributor to area museums and the local PBS stations. It was nice to be able to match the impressive philanthropic support to a good looking face.

So here she was sitting across from him, and she wondered how he was going to dance for her.

"Look, Kyra, I need to apologize."

An apology right out of the starting gate was not what she expected.

"After that last time I saw you, I really thought long and hard about what you had said. And I was a total asshole."

Kyra placed her menu flat on the table and raised her eyebrows.

"That first night I saw you..." Duke wiped his hand over his face. "Damn. You just sat there eating a hamburger and you gave zero fucks. I wanted that. That attitude was the sexiest damn thing I've ever seen. We'd buried my father that day. I had no chill what so ever, rationality was out the window. I went out to do something that would embarrass the crap out of the old man."

They were interrupted by the waitress asking if the were ready.

Kyra ordered a sundae. She wanted something light and sweet. Fried food this late would make it difficult and uncomfortable to sleep. The waitress left. Kyra leaned towards Duke. "Hitting a strip joint would piss your father off, so you came to one after he died?"

"Yeah, I'm stupid. I do things in the wrong order. As a kid, I never took responsibility for anything. Dad cut me off financially once. Freaked me out. I thought I couldn't survive."

Kyra scoffed. Poor little rich boy.

"So I straightened up my act, and I learned finance. Proved to myself I didn't need his money. I made my own. But by then, acting on the straight and narrow had become so ingrained that I never did anything that could be a disappointment. I felt the need to cut loose."

"And what did you think would happen at the club?"

"I have no idea. But I do know you were not in any of the preconceived notions I had of what would be going on once I walked through those doors."

Duke paused again as the waitress delivered their orders.

Kyra spooned the cold ice cream into her mouth, slowly, deliberately licking the spoon clean. Making sure Duke got a good look at her pink tongue toying with the utensil. Her message was clear. Duke's eyes popped out of his head before he managed to regain his composure. Kyra smirked.

"So then what? You walk in and instead of some T and A, you get some moody bitch eating."

"And I never wanted to be a hamburger so badly in my life."

He stared at her with an intensity that made goose pimples rise on her arms. Kyra shivered. "What's the next step, Duke?"

"The way I see it, we have two options. Option one, not my favorite, I thank you for an intriguing late night, make arrangements to see you again, get you a car, and send you home."

"And option two?"

"This is my personal favorite, and I think the odds are heavily leaning in this direction. Option two, I take you home and I make you scream, and you make me feel like a fucking hamburger."

Kyra did not attempt to hide her smile. "What about option three? We say goodnight and never speak of this again?"

"That's not really a choice here, and the way you keep fingering that top button on your shirt and licking that spoon, you really aren't considering it, either."

"So why did I bring it up?"

"To prove to me that there is more to the big picture here, and I clearly wasn't weighing all possibilities." Duke paused, drained his coffee, and stood up. "I think it's safe to say we can both agree that the third one is off the plate."

"Then it's option two, I guess." Kyra put down her spoon.

He tossed several bills on the table. It was substantially more than what their total would have been.

She stood, leaving the rest of her sundae to melt.

Duke pressed her against the wall of the stair landing.

The car ride to his apartment had been quiet, sedate. Kyra began to wonder if he really intended those professed deeds. His public behavior contradicted the words he'd spoken.

She'd been wrong.

Kyra let him dominate her, pressing his body against hers, urgently consuming her lips. Now his actions matched his promised words.

He pulled away and led her up another flight of stairs. She was in his arms again. He tried to wrap himself around her and walk at the same time. She giggled and pushed away from him. "Get us inside." She shoved at him to encourage him to continue moving towards his apartment.

Duke led her down the short hall and fumbled with keys.

Behind him, Kyra reached around his back and caressed his chest. Duke dropped the keys. He turned and crushed her against him once more.

"Inside," she demanded.

Duke retrieved the keys and finally opened the door. The keys landed on an entry table right before he closed the door and trapped Kyra in his arms. He nuzzled her neck as he flipped the locks on the door.

His lips left her breathless. It was hard to remember what she needed to do. She managed to kick off one shoe. She unbuttoned random buttons on her blouse, shrugged off her light jacket, and floundered over other random buttons on Duke's dress shirt.

Duke grabbed her hands as they scrambled for his belt. "Come." He bent and scooped her into his arms.

Kyra snaked her hands around his neck. She kicked off her other shoe as he carried her.

The bed he placed her on was already unmade. Somewhere in Kyra's brain, she registered that he was a little sloppy. Good. She didn't like perfect men. Now he had a flaw.

Duke kissed the palm of her hand before stepping away. She managed to get the rest of her buttons unfastened as he walked across the room and turned on some low music. It was smooth and soft, not the bow-chikka-boom-boom kind of dance music she stripped to. This was music for seduction, music for making love.

Duke pivoted back to her. He removed his overcoat and tux jacket and pulled the tails of his shirt out of his pants.

Kyra didn't wait for him to make it all the way to the bed. She was up and back in his arms, trying to pull all of him into her through his lips.

Slowly Duke ran his hands over her shoulders, skimming her shirt all the way off. She wasn't aware of his exact motions, but suddenly her bra was missing and his nude torso pressed against her. He backed her against the bed, and then they were down. Legs tangling, arms touching, lips and tongues tasting.

Her pants were gone, strewn together with his somewhere on the floor. He reached for his bedside table and knocked around in the drawer, pulling out a foil condom packet. Duke paused when he turned his attention back to Kyra. "Most people dye the hair on their heads interesting colors. I wasn't expecting that." He stared hungrily at her sex.

Kyra tossed her head back and laughed deep in her throat. "Louie can't stand hair that's natural colored of any kind. So it's shave it all off or..." She indicated her fire engine red pubic hair with a wave of her hand. "Last month it was blue. I decided red was a little more festive."

Duke leaned in, capturing Kyra's lips. "I've always been fascinated by redheads. I guess this just makes you more so of one."

Kyra pulled Duke closer, and wrapped her legs around him. "Put that condom on and find out."

Duke kept his word. When he penetrated her, Kyra cried out with pleasure. When he made her come, she screamed.

Duke woke, entwined around the most passionate lover he had ever had. Kyra had urged him on with her caresses. The noises she made brought him to the verge of his own orgasm more than once. When she came, he couldn't hold it any longer, and he thrust out his own release into her receptive body.

She slept snuggled in his embrace. Her warm, supple body fit so nicely. He didn't want to let her go when she woke up, but they would have to return to the world. He wanted to keep her with him in his bed.

He gently stroked the side of her face. She looked just like a Botticelli. He hadn't told her because it sounded like a cheap pick-up line. She stirred. He pulled his hand back, not wanting to disturb her. It was difficult. He needed to continue touching her.

"That felt nice, why did you stop?" Kyra's soft voice caught him off guard.

"You're awake."

"Hmm. It's hard to sleep with you staring at me. I've been awake for a few minutes. Long enough to enjoy you petting my skin." She wriggled deeper into his embrace.

"Your skin is so soft and touchable."

"Then please, keep touching."

Kyra padded back into his bedroom, wearing only his shirt from the night before. Her flaming red hair was a riot on the top of her head. The fire engine red hair below, hidden by his shirt which reached her thighs, caused him to smile and the blood in his body to redirect to his cock.

She slid back under the covers and tucked in close to him.

"How long can you stay?" he asked. He hoped she would say forever.

"I don't have to go to work until tonight, so we can play for hours and hours if you like."

"It's Christmas Eve. You have to work?"

"Yeah, the club. Lots of guys come in around the holidays. In order to get last night off for the gala at the museum, I swapped tonight with Dildora."

Duke grunted and turned away from Kyra. He was going to need to do something about her job, like get her to quit.

"Hey, don't go acting like my job is distasteful to you. It's not like it's a surprise. I get good tips this time of year. Besides, it's not like I can call in sick and expect to still have a job."

"I'm gonna not say anything before I say something stupid," Duke huffed.

Kyra slid her arms around him and pulled him back into her embrace. His head rested against her belly. She looked down into his eyes. "You are an amazingly smart man, Duke. That has to be the most understanding thing anyone has ever said to me about my job. It's easy to spout judgmental quips cause I'm a stripper. I know that, but it keeps me from being homeless, and that's worth it."

He reached up and twined his finger into her hair. "How have your boyfriends before dealt with this? I've never been in this situation before."

"Situation?"

"Yeah, all those men having access to the woman I'm seeing."

She smiled and stroked along his jaw. "First off, no one has access to me. It's eyes only. You want to know one of the reasons I don't mind having to dye my hair? Cause then no one sees the real me. Maybe Louie is smarter than he lets on. It's all wigs and insane colors. So no one sees any of the dancers the way we look outside. And no one ever recognizes us with our clothes on."

"I recognized you immediately."

"Well, you're different. I can't figure it out."

"It's easy. You're beautiful."

She leaned over him to reach his lips. "I think you're beautiful, too."

Duke reached up to hold her in place. He twisted so that he was facing her. He pulled her down and close. He leaned his body against hers, her head cradled on his arm, his head next to hers. "And the men in your life, how have they dealt with this?"

"Dealt with what, exactly?" Her breath felt soft on his cheek.

"I want to hide you away from those eyes. I have a need to stake a territorial claim."

"I like that. Can I have a territorial claim on you as well?"

Duke hummed in reply.

"I haven't had a boyfriend for a very long time. I've had a few hookups, but only with guys who worked at my waiting gigs. Cooks, other waiters, those types. Nothing long-term, and I don't think any of them knew about my job at the club."

"Would you give it up?"

"In a heartbeat, especially for a steady job that pays better and has benefits. It makes more consistent money than waitressing since it's not all tips. I really can't just give it up."

"Would you give it up for me?"

Kyra lifted up on her elbow. "That's a real nice thought, Duke, but one night of mind-blowing sex isn't going to cover my bills. And before you make promises, I'm not going to be some kept whore. That's not my modus operandi, and I'm not about to change it."

"Okay, fair enough." He brooded for a minute, staring up at Kyra. "Would you give it up if we got married?"

She smiled and his heart melted. "If I were so lucky as to marry you, Duke, I would definitely give it up."

He leaned into her, his lips finding hers, and began removing his shirt from her.

❄

"Girlfriend, you are purring, what gives?" Clotores draped herself across Kyra's makeup table.

Kyra smiled a soft little I-could-not-be-more-pleased-with-myself grin. She sighed as she dusted her chest with body glitter. A bad combination that started her coughing.

La-a poked Femalé. "It's a cover-up. She's coughing so she doesn't have to tell us."

Femalé laughed. "A sure sign that gurl got laid last night."

Kyra stopped coughing and stretched like a cat. "I didn't just get laid, I got thoroughly and completely worshiped. I met someone."

"Honey, worshiped sounds like a bit more than just met somebody." Clotores waved a long nailed finger at Kyra.

"No, I mean he's planning on sticking around 'met some-body.' He wants to keep me around 'met somebody.' Might have to introduce him to the parents 'met somebody.'"

"Oh, that's serious," La-a said.

"Tell us about him, and make it fast. Pajamā is almost done, and you're gonna have to git."

"It's Duke." Kyra sighed again.

"Oh no, you didn't. What have we told you about dating men from here?" La-a growled at Kyra.

"I met him at the museum. The docent manager introduced us last night at the gala event."

"Is that the one you swapped last night with Ariola for, so you could be a waitress at?" Clotores asked.

"I swapped with Dilly," Kyra began.

"She swapped with Yany, who swapped with Ariolah," Clotores explained

Kyra's brow furrowed and her eyes moved back and forth trying to figure out who switched nights with whom. She switched with Dilly, but then the other dancers managed to juggle the shift, and now Kyra owed Ariolah and big favor. "Yeah, that one. Anyway, I was completely covered neck to toe in black, my hair was slicked back, I'd worn no makeup, and he knew me on sight. He didn't give anything away. Actually saved my butt cause I fucked up pretty bad and was about to get fired."

"Vagandria, you know better." Femalé stood next to La-a.

Both women crossed their arms and glared at Kyra with disappointed expressions.

"I know, I know." Kyra threw up her arms, wrapping them around her head. "But I really, really like him."

Pajamā sashayed through the curtain into the back. "It's dead out there, Louie is probably gonna send one of us home." Her skin glowed with glitter and sweat.

"Oh, please be me," Clotores muttered.

Kyra rose and made her way towards the backstage curtains.

"Hey, Vagandria, your tall, good looking regular is out there," Pajamā said just as Kyra was slipping through the stage curtains.

"What?" Kyra stumbled onto the stage, looking back at the other dancer, what did she mean Duke was out there?

Lights strobed and music blasted. Kyra staggered more than strutted as she walked around the stage trying to see if Duke really was out in the audience.

The lights made it hard to see. The thought that Duke was out there and she couldn't see him made it difficult to focus. She tried to ignore all of that and be a professional and dance.

She grabbed onto the pole and began lazily spinning around. After a few turns, she pulled herself up and wrapped her legs around the pole, climbing higher.

Suddenly loud crashing sounds and yells caught her attention. Duke jumped onto the stage in front of her.

She slipped a few inches before regaining her grip. She looked down at Duke from her perch on the pole. "I thought we agreed it wouldn't be a good idea for you to come see me at this job anymore."

"And I thought we agreed if I married you that you would quit," Duke countered.

Kyra scoffed. "Yeah, we did, but..." She gripped the pole with her thighs, crossed her ankles, and extended her left hand. "I don't see a ring on this finger. Do you?"

Duke grabbed her hand and slid a ring on her finger. "Yes, I do."

The ring winked and sparkled better than any disco globe under the stage lights. All of her attention focused on her finger. She let out a gasp and lost her grip. Her feet landed on the stage with a thud. Before she realized what was happening, she'd been lifted and tossed over Duke's shoulder.

"Duke, what are you doing?" she yelled when she got air back in her lungs.

"I know a judge," he said as he carried her off the stage and through the front doors of the club.

"Put me down." Kyra began to kick, more for emphasis than real effect.

Duke slapped her exposed ass. "Stop squirming or I'll drop you." He placed her on the ground, and then dropped to one knee in the parking lot.

Snow slowly drifted down around them. Kyra began shaking with chill and nerves.

La-a, wrapped in marabou and satin, ran out of the club carrying a robe. The other dancers followed close behind. They all froze as they saw Duke on his knee.

"You had better say yes, gurl," La-a whispered, wrapping the robe around Kyra's shoulders.

"Oh, it is just like the movies!" Female clapped her hands.

"Damn, I ain't gonna get to go home now," Clotores complained.

"Do you have a brother? Or a cousin?" Pajamā asked.

"Option one, not my favorite, you tell me to fuck off. Option two, and for me, there is no other choice, you say yes and we get married right now." Duke looked at Kyra with a no-nonsense business expression. But she knew the passion behind his words.

"Option three?" Kyra asked. Her stomach was a riot of nerves.

"There is no option three." Duke raised his eyebrows at Kyra, an indication that he was waiting for her to agree.

Kyra laughed and lifted her gaze from Duke to her friends. "I guess you can tell Louie I quit." She returned her gaze to Duke. "Do I have time to change first, or is this judge of yours in a hurry?"

Duke stood, wrapping his arms around Kyra. "I'm sure he can wait long enough for you to get dressed, but don't put on too much. I'm going to be in a hurry to get you undressed as soon as you say 'I do.'"

"I haven't said yes yet," Kyra teased.

"She says yes!" her friends yelled as a reply for her.

"Oh my God, will the two of you get already, before Louie comes out here and fires us all?" La-a started pushing on Duke's shoulder.

He laughed and swung Kyra into his arms. "I don't really see that we have any other choice."

"I have to agree. Option two, it is."

10

XXLL X-TREME X-RATED LASCIVIOUS LORDS

*C*lary's eyes widened as the waitress set the margaritas on the table. The drinks were huge.

"I'm gonna be so wasted," she said. "Maybe I should have started drinking earlier today. I'm feeling so much better just looking at this deliciousness." Her day had not started off well—an empty bed, an aching heart.

"Good thing Britt is driving, but seriously," Tanya agreed as she took her first sip. "I think we might need something to eat with these. Can we get an order of nachos?" she asked before the waitress left. "And fried cheese sticks."

"Ladies." Clary lifted her glass with two hands. "A toast to friendship and shenanigans with my bishes." She desperately needed entertaining, especially after canceling her afternoon of dress and invitation shopping for her upcoming wedding.

They all delicately clinked their classes together, careful not to spill.

"I mean it," Clary continued. "Thanks for understanding. You know you're the first people I'll tell if we break up or if we are moving forward. I just hate how I feel like I'm stuck in limbo. I wish he would talk to me. All he does is work. He doesn't—"

"Ah, ah, ah." Britt pointed and made noises at Clary. "No more talking about Josh or your relationship tonight. It's all bishes and strippers from here on out." Tonight's show was to be the culminating event after a day of wedding planning fun. Britt was Clary's best friend and future matron of honor and sister-in-law. Shocked at the announcement that Clary thought Josh was having doubts and couldn't face trying on white dresses until she knew for certain, Britt rallied and made sure that Clary had a distracting day despite canceling their original plans.

"Yeah, shut up, look how close we are to the stage. You'll be able to count chest hairs from here." Jen gushed with lusty excitement.

Clary did have to admit that Britt had gotten them prime seating when she'd purchased the VIP experience tickets for XXLL: X-treme X-rated Lusty Lords. Apparently it was the premier touring male strip show. The stage may have only been a small raised area tucked into the corner of the bar, but they were right in front of it.

"Strippers don't have chest hair, they shave." Tanya retorted.

"Fine, you'll be able to count their sweat drops from here," Jen corrected.

The house lights dimmed and multicolored spots of light danced over the audience.

Jen squealed. Tanya bounced in her seat and clapped. Britt cackled in delight. Clary managed slightly better than a weak smile. This was fun, but gloom still permeated her being, her depression wrapping around her like a smothering blanket. She took another sip of her margarita, maybe she could displace the depression with alcohol.

The colored spotlightss stopped swarming over the audience. Smoke filled the small stage. Bright white backlights lit the smoke. Large, looming dark shadows began moving around on stage.

Music blared, the smoke machine stopped, and five fully garbed combat soldiers stepped forward. The music was drowned out by the roar and screams coming from the crowd in the bar.

Clary didn't consider it to be dancing as the costumed men strutted around and removed pieces of clothing as they went. First came the helmets. The dancers all had a similar look about them—chiseled features, long, straight noses, shaggy hair. They weren't bad looking, Clary just didn't think they had any individuality. She liked a super clean-cut hair style and a prominent nose with a little character.

Next the jackets came off, revealing tank style undershirts, suspenders, and bulging arm muscles. Clary stopped thinking. When the shirts disappeared and pecs and abs were revealed, she joined in the cat-calling and hollering.

The first number ended, and the MC's voice filled the bar. "To our special ladies with A tickets."

Someone called out a heckle about A cups not being filling enough.

"That's tickets, ladies, not cups. Don't go dissing my ladies with the A-cups. Those are perfect mouthfuls. But right now I need A tickets."

Six women giggled their way up and into the chairs that Clary hadn't previously noticed lining the back of the stage.

The lights dimmed again, more music started, and another group of dancers emerged. This time they wore full-headed animal masks and tuxedoes. By the time their clothes were gone, it was bow ties, G-strings, and the crazy masks. Clary had to admit, with their faces hidden, the fantasy became harder to avoid. She could picture those abs, those arms, but with a face she preferred. Tanya had been wrong, not all of the guys had shaved chests.

Tanya leaned over, smacking Clary in the shoulder. "Hey, that guy has a shark tattoo like Josh, doesn't he?" She pointed to one of the taller men on stage.

Clary nodded, she had noticed. "Lots of guys have tats on their arms like that." She had thought Josh's ink-work was custom, but now it looked like it was just flash, the same thing anyone could get by picking out the pictures posted up on the walls of a tattoo parlor.

It didn't matter, no more thinking of Josh tonight. Josh had a good body, but nothing like what was gyrating on stage right now, and Josh didn't dance. Of course, she had to admit, some of these guys really couldn't dance, either. Clearly, they were hired for their build and willingness to take everything off. A few of the masked dancers left the stage, and the rest switched from performing for the crowd to personalizing the show for the ladies with onstage seats.

The individual lap dances and clothed sex show made Clary's jaw drop. The show was definitely called X-rated for a reason. Is that what they were in for when it was their turn on stage? She blushed just thinking about it.

"You know the drill by now, ladies. Who are my Beautiful Bs?"

Britt tentatively stood up. Jen jumped out of her chair. Tanya pulled Clary to her feet. Four other women also stood up.

"Ladies, will you please take a seat on the stage."

She stepped up onto the stage when the MC asked, "Which one of you is Clary?"

Clary waved her hand. Why did he know her name? Nerves and anxiety joined the party with Clary's dread and depression. She smiled nervously. She really just wanted to sit in the corner and ogle the men, not become part of the show.

"Oh shit, I forgot to tell them not to do this," Britt whispered in Clary's ear.

"Do what?" Clary asked.

"Just play along and forgive me, okay?"

"Forgive you for what?"

The MC continued. "Clary is getting married. Are you sure you want to give up access to all of this fine male anatomy and be stuck with one, just one dick for the rest of your life?"

Clary blushed under the attention of the audience. She nodded. This was what Britt needed forgiveness for.

The first dancer who pranced out onto the stage carried a large penis and testicle shaped plushie in front of his G-string. He rubbed the toy on Clary.

"Are you sure Clary? Just one for the rest of your life?" the MC's voice boomed.

Clary covered her mouth with her hand, hiding from embarrassment and the fact that she was not laughing. The next dancer came out with another plushie penis and repeated the same shtick, this time rubbing the toy over her hair. She started to giggle from nerves. The third dancer out didn't carry any stuffed anatomical pillows, but he did guide Clary's hands over his chest. He was slick with sweat. Her finger tips grazed across the stubble of his shaved chest, it was not appealing. She grimaced but tried to make it look like she was enjoying herself.

When the MC asked her again if she was ready to get married, even after all of this attention, she laughed and nodded her confirmation.

The original three men were now joined by two others on stage and began a choreographed routine, all five doing the exact same moves at the exact same time. The two new men wore jeans and the crazy animal masks from earlier. From her vantage point, Clary could see their defined asses as they gyrated to the music. The music changed, and the dancers targeted the women in the chairs for the somewhat embarrassing bump and grind in front of the entire bar.

Clary's dancer wore a zebra mask. She laughed and clapped for him as he began pulsing his hips at her. He was the tall one with the tattoo like Josh's. She liked tall men, and even though he wasn't the best dancer, he had an amazing body. It was like Josh's but better. He grabbed her hands and ran them over his skin. This one hadn't shaved, and his chest hairs tickled her fingers. He felt familiar.

Clary knew that was tequila in the margarita finally kicking in. He spun and began grinding his ass back towards her in an awkward twerking motion. *That birthmark, just above his waistband.* She stopped laughing. *The same mole on his shoulder. The tattoo was exactly the same. Exactly.*

The dancer turned to face her and lifted her from her chair. Clary jumped into his arms, wrapping her legs around his waist. The dancer grabbed her ass and held her close.

Clary ripped the mask from him. She smiled into his ruggedly handsome face and tapped the bump in his nose. Wrapping her arms around his head she planted her mouth on his.

Josh.

Clary was vaguely aware that the screams of the crowd grew louder, then quieter, as she was carried from the stage. She didn't stop kissing Josh. The lights changed, a door closed, and her back was supported against a flat surface. Josh pressed his body into hers, returning her kisses with a fierce ardor. The depression Clary had felt was burned away by his presence. His hands shoved her skirt up, and he yanked her panties to the side. Clary gasped as Josh slid into her and thrust her against the wall over and over again.

Clary breathed heavily as Josh sucked on her jaw and plowed into her with a fervor she hadn't experienced from him in months.

A loud banging on a door brought their attention away from each other temporarily. They paused long enough to look at the door. Someone yelled curse words. Clary and Josh returned to ignoring the voice and continued with their own pounding.

Clary cried out and thrashed her head, banging it against the wall behind her. "Ow, crap. That hurt."

Josh froze and gently stroked her hair where her hand held her head. "Hi, baby, are you okay?" he finally said as he eased himself from Clary, lowered her back to her feet, and smoothed her skirt down.

"I think you have some explaining to do," Clary said between breaths. "What's going on?"

"I can explain everything. Let's get out of here." Josh adjusted his jeans, took her hand, and led her back through the room behind the stage. He threw on a T-shirt and grabbed his jacket. They went around the back of the bar. Josh pulled her out the front door and into the cold.

Clary wrapped her arms around herself, and then Josh's arms were around her as he guided her to his car. "Get in, I'll turn the heat up." He closed the car door behind her before climbing in on the driver's side and starting the engine. He handed her his coat. "Britt will get your stuff. Don't worry."

"I'm not worried. I'm confused." Clary turned to glare at Josh. He kept his focus forward as he drove through the half-melted snow and slush. "What happened back there? What's been happening to you? To us?"

"I promise to explain everything. First, can we get some burgers? I'm starving."

Clary sat in silence, trying not to fume as Josh navigated the car to a drive-thru and then back to their apartment.

Josh tossed the bag of food onto the kitchen table and gathered Clary into his embrace. "I love you. If tonight didn't work, blame Britt."

"What does that even mean?"

"She arranged it all," he said. "Britt told me you once mentioned having a stripper fantasy and that I wasn't romantic enough. She said this strip show was coming to town and I should be in it, how that would show you I am your fantasy lover and all that crap. It would be a huge surprise for you. Stupidly I told her I'd do it if she did all the foot work. I didn't think anything would happen."

Clary pushed out of Josh's arms and stared at him incredulously. "What?"

Josh unwrapped a hamburger and shoved half into his mouth with one bite. Clary watched him chew. The depression was trying to seep its way back in, like fingers of darkness wrapping around her head. But Josh was talking to her. He had made love to her like he was starving for her as much as she hungered for him. That thought kept the fingers from closing tight around her.

"I had to send them a picture of me without a shirt on," he explained. "And they said yes, if I worked out more. I had to take a dance class. I had to learn three dance numbers. They sent me videos to follow. And I had to keep it a secret. It practically killed me."

"No, Josh, it practically killed us," she corrected. "You wouldn't tell me what was going on. You stopped being you. I thought you no longer were in love with me. How long has this been going on?"

"Weeks, " he admitted. "I had to drop weight fast. They said I needed to be more cut or everyone in the audience would know I was some kind of joke. I had six weeks to do it. I have been cranky and hungry and tired. Baby, never go on a diet again. That was torture. I never want you doing something like that to yourself."

"Why did you stop touching me? It's been weeks."

Josh nodded. "I didn't want you to recognize me when I was up there. The surprise, you know?"

"I blew off my dress appointment, and I did not go shopping for invitations. I seriously considered this was the end for us." The familiar sting of tears burned her eyes. *Stupid response to anger.*

"I know. Britt texted me. I wanted to call it off at that point, but she said it was even more important. I'm sorry. I am so sorry." Josh sank to his knees in front of Clary. He reached for her hands, clasping them in his. "I love you. I will make this up to you. I will do stupid things for you. Can you forgive me for ever causing you doubt?"

"Was this why you wouldn't go to my parents for Christmas?"

Josh nodded.

"You practically ruined Christmas so that you could be a stripper for me?"

"I somehow thought that this would make up for not being there on Christmas morning, that it would be a big surprise gift. I'll make it up to you. There are twelve days of Christmas right?" Josh calculated quickly. "Today is day ten. I still have two days left. Two days and the rest of your life to make up for my stupid mistake."

"Well, it was a good surprise," Clary said. "But damn, the lead up sucked."

"I know, baby, I know." Josh pulled Clary out of her chair, and into his arms. "Will you still marry me?"

"One dick for the rest of my life?" she mused. "You know, I'm missing the rest of the show. And what you did was kind of an asshole move."

Josh guided Clary's hand over his chest. "I'll make it up to you. I've got some new dance moves to show off, and we didn't finish things properly back at the club. And," Josh pulled something out of the back of his shirt. "I kept this." He said as he slipped the zebra mask back on.

Clary giggled as Josh lifted her and carried her to their bed.

11

PIPER'S DAUGHTER

*R*ose stared into the pit. The open hole of her father's grave. He had always taken care of everything. All she needed to do was cook, do what he called cleaning, and not argue much. He had always taken care of everything. She had never even had a job. She didn't know what to do next. He wasn't there to tell her what she should think, how to feel. Maybe now she could be angry. Who was going to stop her?

She tore her gaze from absently staring at the hole that held her father's coffin, realizing everything had gone quiet. Snow fell, muffling the sounds of the world. No one, not even the groundskeeper who would later fill in the grave, was around. Alone. Alone with her thoughts; alone with the ghosts.

He had always taken care of everything, except for me. Well, that was typical. She hadn't needed to decide a single thing regarding the funeral. All of the arrangements had been finalized years ago. He even specified what types of flowers he wanted. No roses, never roses.

A car had picked her up from the house, driven her to the church, followed the hearse to the cemetery for a graveside service, and promptly left as soon as she'd stepped out.

Now everyone was gone. Had her father done this on purpose or had he assumed one of the members of his church would take her home? She shook her head, the tight bun, a heavy counterweight to the slight movement. To have done this on purpose would have required that he actually considered someone other than himself. This was an oversight, a mistake, but then again, he never had cared what happened to her.

Rose pulled the pins from her hair, letting the thick, golden locks fall in waves down her back. She ran a hand through the strands, tugging every few inches as tangles trapped her fingers.

First things first, she was going to cut her hair. It was too heavy, too unruly to manage at this length. Father had never let her. She would make appointments and he would find a reason not to drive her into town, or he would conveniently be out of money. He could no longer sabotage her, he could no longer threaten her if she cut it herself.

Rose sighed. Second things second. First, she had to get home, then she could worry about a haircut. She leaned against a headstone and dusted snow from her shoes. No reception, no reason for anyone to come looking for her. No family, and no friends. She was going to have to walk. She hiked up the hated pantyhose. They weren't good for anything and they certainly didn't keep her warm against the cold. Her shoes, basic black pumps, were only suitable for looking pretty. She would have to walk in the middle of the road to avoid slipping in either the snow melt in the sun or the ice patches in the shade. It was a few miles into town and another three or four to the house. The day was cloudless so she would have light, and maybe some warmth, whenever the sun broke through the redwoods and other conifers that blanketed this part of the Sierra Nevada. Even with the unusually low snowfall they'd experienced this year, she'd be cold, wet, tired, and blistered by the time she reached home. There was no reason to delay getting started.

The winter sun beat down on Jimmy's back, making this hot work even hotter. Fool that he was, he hadn't taken off the black suit jacket until he had already started sweating. He hated hand jacks. Foot jacks were more effective and faster, but he hadn't found one. He cranked and cursed as the vehicle jerked, and lifted off the tire.

"Crap," he grunted as he pulled the spare from the hearse. He slid backward on the steep embankment as the spare overbalanced him. He managed to keep to his feet. He needed to keep his mind on the task at hand before he ruined his suit or injured himself.

However, his thoughts were on the young woman whose father they had buried. When he'd left the cemetery, there had hardly been anyone left but her, and she'd looked so frail and serious. The oversized bun on the top of her head reminded him of a little bitty thing playing dress-up.

But the resemblance to a child ended there. She was petite, but she was no little girl. Those were a woman's curves, and a woman's lips, and man-oh-man, if Rose St. John hadn't grown up well. In high school, she had been a mousy little thing. She sat in front of him in World History. Cheating off her tests had probably been the only thing that kept him from failing. He hadn't even remembered her name until he saw her today as they loaded the coffin into the back of the hearse.

She stood somber and quiet during the service. Probably in shock since her father had just died. Jimmy hadn't wanted to desert her at the cemetery, but Tobey ordered him to deliver the coffin and leave.

Jimmy hadn't felt right in his gut driving away and leaving Rose alone. In fact, his current situation had been caused by his guilt. He'd swung the hearse into a wide U-turn to go back and make sure she had a ride home, and that was when the tire blew.

Jimmy wiped his hands together, as if he could clear away the grease and not just smear it around. A familiar movie tune wafted past on the breeze. He looked down the road, trying to locate the source of the off-key singing. A cloud of thick golden tresses swirled around a tiny black-clad figure in the freezing wind. In shoes not fit for walking, she high-stepped and skipped her way over the ice and rocks on the side of the road.

❄

"Is that you, Rose?"

When she heard the man's voice, Rose froze. Focused on the road and watching her step, she hadn't noticed the hearse on the shoulder until he called out to her—the tall, good-looking one, the one who'd cheated off her tests in high school. The one she'd always hoped would talk to her since she had let him cheat, but nope. Boys didn't talk to her in high school, and men didn't talk to her now, seven years later.

James. What was his last name? He'd played football and basketball, a total jock. Even as a teen, he'd been broad and muscular. And now, his white dress shirt showed off his even broader, adult shoulders, the rolled-up sleeves emphasized the unseasonal tan of his strong forearms.

Clearly he now worked for the funeral home, he'd helped to carry the coffin earlier and here he was with the hearse. The butterfly flutters in her tummy proved she still had a bit of a crush on him.

"Oh, hi. Did you get a flat? Need some help?" Not that Rose could do anything, but she had been well trained to at least offer assistance.

"No, I'm good. Just finished. You aren't walking home, are you? Where's your ride?" he asked.

Rose threw back her head and cackled. "You're funny. Why would I have a ride? I'm pretty sure that damned old bastard made sure that I would be stranded at the cemetery after the funeral. So no, I don't have a ride, because my father was a selfish prick." Her voice was thick with knives and resentment. She bit her lip, shocked at her own audacity, speaking ill of the dead. Speaking ill of her father to James, who was essentially a stranger.

"That would explain why I heard you singing 'Ding Dong the Witch is Dead'?" He smirked.

"Busted." Rose grinned sheepishly, relaxing because he hadn't criticized her musical selection at such a time.

"Can I give you a lift home, Rose?"

Her heart sped up and her breathing caught in her throat. James-the-test-cheater knew her name. "I would love that. It's James, right?"

He nodded. "Jimmy Erickson."

"Oh, right." She completely remembered everything about him now. "Could you maybe give me a ride to a place that cuts hair?" She held up the long, weighty mess like a dead fish. It felt like this was the one thing she needed to do now that her father was dead. She hoped that once the hair was gone, the memories the hair held would disappear, too.

"You want to cut all that off?" Jimmy asked. "It's pretty."

It was nice that he thought her hair was pretty, but it was too late to change her mind. It was her hair and she was finally able to do what she wanted with it. Rose scoffed.

"Then you can have it. I want it all gone."

James leaned against the hood of his own car waiting for Rose. He wanted to make sure she saw him when she got out of the beauty salon and didn't try to walk the rest of the way home. She had insisted that she would be fine and could walk from downtown, but now that he'd busted a tire on her behalf, he felt somewhat responsible for her. She'd been super shy in school, but this afternoon on the ride back to town, she was different. She chatted nervously, the small, solemn figure by her father's grave completely gone. He had managed to find out she wasn't seeing anyone, but he hadn't been able to get a word in edgewise to ask her out.

He dropped her off at Sally's Shears before swinging by the funeral home to pick his own car up, a classic fastback Mustang. Jimmy was slowly restoring the vehicle. It was still a beater, but it was a beater with good bones.

He saw her before she saw him. Lithe and waif-like, she looked around for him, before breaking into a broad bright grin when they made eye contact. Rose flew into Jimmy's arms. She wrapped her arms around him and pressed her lips to his. As soon as the initial wave of shock washed over him, he began kissing her back. Lips, tongues, arms. He pulled her into his chest and let her consume him with her passion. Rose kissed him as if she had been kissing him for years. She knew what she was doing, without hesitation.

"Thanks," she said breathlessly after she stepped back. "I feel so much lighter now."

Jimmy smiled at her. He didn't know what had brought on the lip lock, but if that was what driving a beautiful girl to the hair salon did, he would drive her here every day.

As for her hair, it was gone. The golden waves were now close-cropped on the sides and back with a long curl on the top of her head, falling into her face. Maybe it was the hair or the makeup she had applied while in the salon, but he hadn't noticed how big her golden eyes were before, or how delicate and pointy her chin was. She looked like a fairy. Now he understood the term pixie-cut.

Rose spun in a circle on the sidewalk in front of him, arms wide as if she tried to grab onto the world. She giggled and smiled brightly. Jimmy laughed. Rose's joy was contagious. And right now, Jimmy would do about anything for her to kiss him like that again. "I like your hair. Now what?"

When she stopped spinning, she said, "I want to have sex, and I want pie. And jeans. I want to wear pants again." She clapped her hands over her mouth and blushed.

Jimmy was pretty certain his eyes popped out of his head at her comment.

When her gaze fell on his face, she stammered, "Not necessarily in that order. Jeans first, then pie. I want to get out of these dreary funeral duds, and I want to eat something sweet and bad for me. Do you like pie?"

"Sure." Jimmy couldn't help but smile at her. Whatever Rose wanted to do today, he was here to help.

Jimmy stood awkwardly in the middle of Rose's living room. He rocked back and forth, hands shoved deep into his pockets, as if he was afraid to touch anything.

"Hey, I'm really sorry about this." Rose stepped back into the living room. She gestured at the piles that dominated the room.

She knew it looked like nothing had been thrown away in years. Nothing had. She pressed her palms against the thrift store jeans. She hadn't owned any for years. She was much more comfortable in the pants and a sweater. Her feet were finally warm and toasty in her favorite thick socks and boots.

"My father was a classic hoarder. I wasn't allowed to throw anything away. It got worse this past year. I never realized it was a symptom of a more serious illness. And I should apologize for kissing you like that. I let my enthusiasm run amok."

"No apologies. You can run amok with me anytime. I am a bit confused. Shouldn't you be sad, you know, in mourning? You did just bury your father."

Rose shook her head. Her neck moved like a wobble-headed doll now that she wasn't wrestling with the weight of all of her hair. The tension in her shoulders released from invisible burdens. "I buried my abuser today. Today I am free. I don't know what's next, but he cannot manipulate me anymore. He cannot keep me from living anymore."

Rose's heart thumped hard when Jimmy sidled up to her and pulled her to into his embrace. "So that means you want pie?"

She rested her hands against his chest. It felt firm and muscular through the thin fabric of his shirt.

"I want to live, James. And that means being able to have pie whenever I choose. That means being able to kiss a man because I can. It means being able to cut my hair because it's *my* hair on *my* head. He is probably spinning in his grave because I've cut it off, I'm in pants, and I'm alone in the house with you, contemplating how to throw out all this crap."

Jimmy nuzzled against her ear. "You never brought any of your boyfriends home when the old man was out of town?"

Jimmy's lips tickled. A soft moan escaped her lips. Jimmy's tongue was doing evil things to her ear. His lips on her neck made her want his lips everywhere. "He never went anywhere. And I wasn't allowed boyfriends," she said softly. "You're the first boy I've ever kissed."

Jimmy stopped kissing her. The temperature dropped as he stepped away.

"Oh, hell, you're a…" He paused, running his hand over his face.

"I'm a what? Say it," she taunted. He couldn't call her anything worse than what she really was. "A sorry sad case, a shut-in, an ugly old maid?"

"A virgin," Jimmy stated.

"Yep, that, too. A virgin. Is that so bad?" The sting of tears rimmed her eyes. She blinked the sensations away. If her dead father ruined her shot with Jimmy, she… Well, she couldn't kill the old bastard, could she? Jimmy stared at her. She stared back, pleading with her eyes for him to hold her. A tear slipped free when he finally wrapped his arms around her again.

"No, Rose, it's not so bad. It means I need to cool my jets a whole lot."

Rose cried into Jimmy's chest. She cried out all of the frustration of allowing her father to control her for years, all of the grief she actually did feel over his loss, all of the uncertainty for her future.

Rose blinked awake, darkness surrounded her. She was warm under a blanket and snuggled against Jimmy. She didn't remember him moving them to the couch or wrapping a quilt around them. The air in the living room was sharp, cold. She needed to turn on the heater.

Jimmy's head listed to the side. He snored gently. Apparently, her emotional outpouring had exhausted him as well. She burrowed back into his embrace. This was nice. Why had her father been so set against her having this? Not that she knew what this was. But being in Jimmy's arms was nice.

Jimmy snorted, gasped, and lifted his head. He looked at her bleary-eyed. "Did I fall asleep?"

Rose nodded. "I have no idea what time it is."

Jimmy checked his watch. "Dinnertime. Do you still want pie? There's a great diner between here and Tahoe."

"That sounds good." Rose stood and stretched with a yawn. She followed the path between mounds of detritus into the kitchen, pushed a stack from the kitchen counter onto the floor, adding to the existing piles, lifted up on her arms, hiked up a knee, and then stood on the counter. She opened one of the top cupboards and flailed around inside. "Father hid money up here all the time. Got it." With a large round tin in her hands, she sat on the counter and pried the lid open. Instead of the promised butter cookies on the label, it held a small stack of dollar bills. "Let's see just how much he left me before I starve."

She began counting. Her jaw clenched as she realized that comment was a little closer to reality than intended. As far as she knew this was the only cash her father ever kept in the house. He'd probably forgotten about it last year, before he had gotten so bad. She hadn't heard him clamoring onto the counter to hide it in a long time.

"Don't you have a savings or anything?" Jimmy asked.

Rose shook her head. "The house is paid off, so I should be okay there. Even with Father only getting disability for the last few years, he wouldn't let me work. I'll have to figure out how to get a job." She gestured to the piles. "He would have fits, and things would get moved around, book shelves emptied. I was never allowed to touch anything. Maybe there's something of value underneath all this that I can sell. Not the car, though. I want to learn how to drive. Kind of hard to get around without one."

Rose folded a few of the bills and put them into her pocket. She didn't want to think about everything she needed to do. For now, she wanted to focus on getting a piece of pie, and maybe getting Jimmy to kiss her again. She closed the lid to the tin and looked up at Jimmy. "Shall we?"

The diner was bright with neon colors. Chrome features reflected color like all of the Christmas lights that were already coming down around town.

Three kinds of pie were arranged between Rose and Jimmy. Rose waved her fork around, conducting along with the music playing on the jukebox.

Jimmy stared at her. Her father had died, and she was sucking in everything good about life she could. Anyone else would be wrapped in doom and gloom. She found her old man dead in his recliner the day after Christmas, which had to put a damper on anyone's holiday. But from the look of her house, she hadn't had much of a celebration anyway.

"You told me you father was your abuser. Did he hit you?" Jimmy finally got up the nerve to ask.

"He was emotionally abusive. First of all, you've seen the conditions I was forced to live in. That is disgusting. I had to clean that." She gestured air quotes around the word clean. "I had to dust the piles." Rose took a bite of the cream pie. She closed her eyes as she clearly savored the flavors in her mouth.

Jimmy's body reacted to her satisfied grin. Blood left his brain as he thought about what he would give to put an expression like that on her face.

"He'd gotten so bad towards the end he would yell at me for switching something from one pile to another."

As she described her life, blood returned to his brain, allowing him to ask questions. "How did you realize this wasn't normal, that he was abusive? I thought that a lot of victims think that's just the way things are. They don't realize they are being abused. I can't imagine he would let you watch Oprah or Dr. Phil where they would talk about all of that."

"It wasn't always like that, but it was just us. I had to take care of him after Mother died. He watched TV all the time, but I wasn't allowed to. It got worse after he joined the Brotherhood of Jesus. After that, I wasn't allowed to read certain books, and I couldn't wear pants. I wasn't allowed to talk to anyone he didn't know. I couldn't go to the grocery store alone unless he was sick."

"Is that the super fundamentalist cult church? You're not—" Jimmy cut himself off. "How did you get around? What were you allowed to do? I mean, well, you seem pretty darned spirited, and not terribly beat down," he observed.

According to Rose, her father had kept her subjugated, and hidden from the world. She seemed to fly, even though she was sitting.

"I walked, a lot. Father had arranged for someone from the church to give me ride into town once a week. I could shop and go to the library. I was allowed to work at the church, and you know what happens when you volunteer to do office work?" Rose leaned forward on the table, fork full of cherry pie gripped tight in her hand. "They teach you how to use the computer. Librarians know how to help you answer questions. So I started looking up the hoarding thing. I didn't even know that's what it was called. I just knew it was gross, and I wanted to see if there was a way to convince him to let me toss it."

"Why did you stay Rose, why didn't you run?"

She sighed. "I though about it. I thought about running away a lot. I came close more than once, but I was scared. Then the more I learned the more I figured he couldn't help it. You don't run away from someone who is sick. He was sick."

She shoved the fork in her mouth and continued talking around the mouthful of pie. "It's a mental illness."

Jimmy couldn't help but smile. Her world had suddenly changed, and clearly for the better. He had never met anyone so hungry to live. Jimmy didn't have a clear goal for his own life. He always tried to be useful. He had a handful of odd jobs because he "could help out." And now here was Rose, embracing all of the life she had been denied. He definitely wanted to help her meet her dreams. He wanted to be a part of them.

"What does day two of your to-do list include?"

"I have to find out about getting a dumpster so I can start cleaning out the house. That's going to be a lot of work."

"Won't people from the B... your church help out?"

Rose shook her head side to side, a look of disgust twisting her face. "I'm not a member, and I don't want to have anything to do with those people now that I don't have to. I should prob-ably call Mr. Staussan, too."

"The lawyer with the fancy building downtown?"

Rose nodded. "I need to find out if there is any money and how I do basic stuff like pay bills. I'm hoping my father gave him my birth certificate or that he might know where to look, or how I get a copy. I'm going to need that to get a driver's license and a job, right?"

For someone who had been cut off from the world, she seemed to be aware of what she needed. He wasn't sure he would be so tuned into the responsibilities of functional adulthood if he had been in her shoes. Rose was coming out of a forced seclusion and already knew more of the world than he ever had, and he'd been living on his own since he graduated high school and his mom started charging him rent. Rose may have it figured out, but he still wanted to be there.

"I can come over and help you clean in the morning if you'd like, but I gotta work tomorrow night."

"You got an evening funeral to drive for?" Rose asked.

He grinned, unsure how much to reveal. "Naw, that's only one of my jobs. I work at a club up in Tahoe one weekend a month. You like dance music? You should come with me. You can hang out while I do my thing. It will definitely introduce you to the wilder side of life."

Rose beamed. "Really?"

"You think you can handle it?"

She laughed as she nodded.

Yeah, she was grabbing life by the horns. Jimmy definitely wanted to be along for this ride.

Rose leaned into the mirror. Putting on makeup was a lot harder than Sally at the salon had made it look. Rose bugged her eyes as wide as she could and carefully swiped the fuzzy bristles of the mascara up and out, coating her lashes. She counted to thirty with her eyes as wide as possible. She needed to blink, but Sally had said no blinking for at least thirty seconds to let the mascara dry.

She let out a ragged sigh. One eye done.

The crackling rattle of car tires on the gravel drive demanded her attention. Jimmy had mentioned he would come over to help. A flutter of excitement took her breath. She tried to focus on finishing her makeup quickly, wanting to look good for him. She was both surprised and flattered he hadn't changed his mind. He seemed to have grown up into a genuinely nice man.

Excited, she stuffed the mascara back into the tube to do the other eye. A shuffle and a crash thundered through the house as a pile in the living room collapsed.

Rose froze with the mascara wand less than an inch from her lashes. She took a deep breath before she continued sweeping the makeup on. He must have let himself in.

"This place is a sty Brother Carter. How will we ever clean up this filth?"

Rose blinked. That most certainly was not Jimmy's voice. And now there was a black smudge of mascara under her eye. She didn't recognize the female voice, but Brother Carter was the head deacon from the Brotherhood.

"Excuse me?" Rose called out as she entered the living room. "What are you doing? Can I help you?"

"Who are you?" Mrs. Cuthbert, one of the busybodies from the church, asked. The woman never had time for anything but sticking her nose where it wasn't needed.

"I'm Rose St. John, and this is my house. Is there something you need? You should have knocked. As you can see, the living room isn't in any condition for guests." While inside she felt like yelling and screaming, letting the new Rose loose, she remained cordial and mannerly.

"Ah, Rose, I didn't recognize you. You have changed so much since the last time I saw you."

"I've cut my hair since the funeral," she responded flatly. Mrs. Cuthbert knew damn well who she was. This was one of those annoying games the woman played whenever Rose volunteered at the church office to trick her into doing the old bat's work.

"This will just not do. Your daddy gave this house to the church. I can see why now, seeing how you've taken care of it." Mrs. Cuthbert huffed.

"What do you mean he gave the house to the church?"

"Rosie, dear." Brother Carter took her hand. Bile burned the back of her throat, but she tried to remain polite. She had never liked Brother Carter. He seemed dishonest and slimy.

"We take possession of the property with the new year. I'm sure I can work it out with the elders to allow you a few weeks to gather your things and find other accommodations. I am only too happy to help you out." When the old man started stroking the back of her hand, she snatched it free of his grip. She stared at him, incredulous.

"You must be wrong."

"Oh no, Rose, he gave the house to the Brotherhood. It was in his papers," Mrs. Cuthbert said with a sneer in her tone.

Of course, her father gave the house to his church. He took care of everything, just not her. Why on earth had Rose thought things would be any different after his death? She closed her eyes against the pain. Pain she should have seen coming.

"Go away." Rose's voice quavered. "Get out. This is my house. Get out of my house!" She screamed and kept screaming until Brother Carter and Mrs. Cuthbert rushed out the door, jumped in Mrs. Cuthbert's paneled station wagon, and sped back down the driveway.

The next time tires crunched on her unpaved driveway, Rose ran to the front window and peeked through the curtain. Nerves danced in her stomach. Was it Jimmy? Because if it was Brother Carter again, she was calling the police.

But when she didn't see the Mustang, the nerves stopped dancing. A large gray luxury vehicle slowed to a stop in front of the house. Jimmy's car rumbled in behind it. Rose's nerves began dancing again. Mr. Staussan, silver haired and in an expensive suit, exited the big car. It was a striking visual contrast to Jimmy in a hoodie and tight jeans getting out of his beat up old Mustang. Rose hadn't expected the lawyer to actually come over today. The receptionist at his office had said he would return her call, not show up on her doorstep.

Maybe she needed to sign papers. He knew she didn't drive.

"Hello, Mr. Staussan. This is a surprise. Won't you come in? Excuse the mess, my father wasn't well." She smiled politely at him as he passed her into the house.

Jimmy kissed her lightly on the cheek in greeting and followed the lawyer into the overcrowded living room. "Bad timing?"

She shrugged before closing the door behind him.

Staussan looked around. "Rose, I had no idea it had gotten this bad."

"It's been getting worse the past few years. But," she added with a sigh, "now I can start cleaning up and taking care of things properly."

Staussan shuffled in place. Awkwardly, he opened his briefcase while standing in the middle of the living room. "You might not want to do anything, Rose. We have a situation."

"I know. Brother Carter came by and said Father gave the house to the BOJ. How could he do that? He wasn't well."

"Maybe you two should sit down," Jimmy stepped into the kitchen and quickly cleared off the table with a broad swipe of his arm. He dumped the contents of one chair onto one of the piles.

Staussan mumbled a thank you as he eased into the cleaned off chair. Jimmy stood behind Rose as she sat, placing a hand on her shoulder. The lawyer laid a thick, bound document in front of Rose, and she stared at it.

Staussan cleared his throat. "You see, Miss St. John, I received a call from the BOJ."

Rose grabbed for Jimmy's hand. Mr. Staussan was not calling her Rose. This was not good.

"I went over your father's will again this morning, and it seems he expected that you would already be taken care of. I gather he thought you to be married by now. "

Rose gulped, she felt light headed. "What? How could I be married? He never let me talk to anyone. Did he make arrangements and forget to tell me?" Her voice turned shrill as panic set in. She clenched Jimmy's hand tightly.

The lawyer flipped calmly through the pages of the document, until he reached an official-looking form. "Because of your situation, according to the will the Brotherhood of Jesus is to get, and I am sorry, all properties, including vehicles and bank accounts."

Rose stared blankly at the man. Was she even breathing? If her father had ever cared for her, ever thought about her, it was clear that part of him had died years before his body had.

She had been so relieved at his death, so eager to move on with her life, that she hadn't for a moment considered she wouldn't even have somewhere to *live.*

"Where am I supposed to live?" Her fortitude deserted her as she collapsed in tears. He had managed to destroy her life even after his death. She wasn't free of him. She would never be free.

Jimmy leaned over Rose. "We'll figure something out," he said softly as he stroked her heaving back. "Mr. Staussan, there has got to be something in that will for Rose. What did you mean by her situation?"

The man nodded. "I'm referring to Rose not being married. All properties would have been handed to her husband. Her mother's collections are hers. There was a figurine set specifically mentioned, and some musical instruments." He flipped through the document. "Flutes and other woodwinds. But who knows how long it will take to find them?" He gestured at the hoarding mess. "There is one thing, but it's so far-fetched, and, well, it has to be done in the next twenty-four hours."

Rose lifted her head and blinked through tears at the lawyer.

"The will stipulates that if you are unmarried when your father dies, you have until the end of the same calendar year to marry. At which point your husband becomes the sole benefactor. With exception of your mother's collections. Those are to remain yours."

Rose gasped in disbelief. She stared at the lawyer in numb shock. "My husband gets everything? Not me? I don't have a husband."

"It's December thirtieth, Mr. Staussan. Surely her father made some kind of contingency for that?" Jimmy asked.

Staussan ran his hand through his hair. "I'm sorry, he was very clear."

"Well, all right. We can get married this afternoon," Jimmy stated.

Rose turned and blinked up at him. The nausea caught in her throat settled. "Jimmy, I can't ask you to do that."

"Son, are you trying to rip this young lady off?" The lawyer sounded stern, ready to protect Rose. But it was the church and her father ripping her off, not Jimmy. Mr. Staussan hadn't exactly offered other suggestions. If they didn't do something, she would be homeless and helpless. Her father had clearly seen to that.

Jimmy scoffed, telling the lawyer exactly what was in Rose's head. "You're telling her she has to give up her home, and you're asking me if I'm ripping her off?" Jimmy squatted down in front of her, staring into her eyes. "Look, it's the only way so you don't lose everything. You think the BOJ is going to let you take the time to sort through all this crap to find your shit?"

Rose shrugged.

"No, Rose, they aren't. It's the same group of people who left you to walk home in the snow from the funeral. They're going to want to empty this place out and sell it fast." Jimmy turned to Mr. Staussan.

The old man rubbed his chin, a thoughtful expression crossed his face. "You'll have to drive into Nevada to get it done in time."

"Fine, we can do that," Jimmy agreed.

"What?" Rose looked from the lawyer to Jimmy, her mouth open in shock.

"C'mon, Rose, we'll be right there anyway since we planned on going to Tahoe tonight. We can leave early or, instead of coming back here, we'll head on over to the Nevada side, get a room, and get married in the morning."

"Isn't there another way?" She turned to the lawyer, waving at the papers. How would such a ridiculous legal document stand? How was this happening to her in this day and age? She'd dreamed all her life of finally getting to be a free woman, and now, to keep her home, she would have to marry?

Staussan shook his head. "You should have a few years to contest this, but the BOJ isn't going to sit around and wait for that to happen. Legal or not, they will move on the property as soon as they can. They aren't popular around here for many reasons. They have done this before, get a clause like this in your father's will and pull the rug out from under the grieving family, leaving them with nothing."

"It's not how I thought I'd get married, either. And it's not like we have to stay married. Right?" Jimmy stood, shifting his attention back to Mr. Staussan.

"You'll have to stay married through probate. I don't know how long that will take. It could be anywhere from months to years if this is contested."

"How soon would Rose be able to have access to any assets? Like money? She's going to need something to live on."

Rose watched the conversation between the two men, shifting her attention back and forth. Her future was once again in the hands of someone other than herself. She felt numb. At least this time they both seemed to be making sure she was cared for.

"Accounts will be locked up in probate. Rose won't have access for quite some time. My office can issue a loan against the available balance that will be on hold."

Jimmy crouched down in front of Rose again. "I'll sign a promissory note that I'll turn everything over to you as soon as legally possible. Rose, it's the only way to save your house and your inheritance." Jimmy held her gaze for a few tense seconds. He stood, grabbed her hand, and pulled her outside into the frozen air on the front porch.

"There isn't much room do this in there." Jimmy sank to one knee. "Marry me, Rose. Let me help you."

Rose grinned down at him, grateful for his kind-hearted gesture. "You're giving me a proper proposal on one knee and everything. Yes." She sighed and held on to his hand.

Mr. Staussan stood, framed in the doorway. "Congratulations. I'll get the appropriate documents in order. Call me once you're married. I will need that certificate as soon as possible. And it must have this year's date on it to avoid any problems from the BOJ."

Rose leaned against Jimmy's arm as they watched the lawyer pull out of her driveway.

"You handled that quite well." Jimmy spoke softly.

"I was a blubbery mess." She tried to laugh it off, but Jimmy was right. Everything had imploded around her, and she hadn't reacted at all. She couldn't react. She didn't know how to fight any of this.

"Yeah, but you held it together. You didn't throw things or scream. And you certainly had every right to." He ran a thumb across her cheek. To Rose, it felt like he smeared fire, because his touch burned. "Your makeup is all smeared."

"I know." She sighed and sank down onto a slumping bad posture. "I don't know how to get it off."

"Come on, I'll show you." Jimmy squeezed past her to avoid knocking over anything and guided her back into the bathroom.

Rose watched him rummage through the medicine cabinet and under the sink. He straightened triumphantly with a large jar of petroleum jelly. Wrapping an arm around her waist, he leaned against the sink and tugged her into his personal space. "Look up."

His thighs pressed against hers as he settled her between his legs. His chest lifted against her as he breathed. He smelled of mint gum. She had been next to him before, but not intertwined like this. Her stomach flipped. Gently, Jimmy wiped a tissue of ointment under her eyes, then even more gently he began stroking the makeup from her cheeks.

"There," he announced when he finished. He didn't adjust position.

Neither did Rose. She stared up at Jimmy, into the depths of his eyes. At some point, his hands fell to her hips, pulling her closer.

Rose didn't want Jimmy to stop reeling her in. She continued until their lips pressed together. She forgot everything as the warmth of his mouth played against hers. Her fingers grasped the fabric of his shirt.

Jimmy cupped the back of her head and slid his tongue against her lips. She parted them and tasted him. All she knew was her mouth wanted his, and her hands wanted to be on his body. She pressed into him. His firm chest flattened her breasts while her belly brushed against a firmer bulge in his jeans.

Rose tensed and scrambled out of his embrace at the realization that he had gotten turned on, and she had rubbed against him, against 'it.' She blushed and stammered. "Uh...so you came over to help me clean?"

The bathroom was suddenly too small for the two of them. Rose tripped over Jimmy's leg escaping from its confines and her own arousal.

"Rose?" Jimmy followed her out into the living room.

"I need to get all of this cleaned." Her voice was barely above a whisper.

"I see." Jimmy sighed. "I brought garbage bags like you asked. We should be able to get some work done before it's time to head out. I have to be at the club by seven."

"I guess we had better get started." Rose began picking up papers from one of the piles, unable to look Jimmy in the eye.

"So what's the plan?" he asked.

Rose relaxed. He wasn't going to make her talk about it. Oh God, she was calling it 'it.' He had an erection, and she was all nerves. She swallowed, trying to get moisture into her dry throat.

"I want to clean up the front part of the house before I do the other rooms. My bedroom is fine, my father's not so much. And then there is the room I can barely open the door to." She gestured at all the piles, still avoiding his eyes. "I can keep the doors to those closed for now, but this needs to be taken care of."

"Are we sorting or shoveling?"

"Sorting. Somewhere in all of this are my mother's collections. The top layer is all garbage, but a few years back Father emptied the attic. I think all of that is in here somewhere." Rose talked through her mental to-do list, such as getting a dumpster.

"Why don't you make your calls and I'll go get some sandwiches for lunch. Okay?"

Rose nodded. Her nerves still jangled from the confrontation with Brother Carter, the bad news from the lawyer, and Jimmy's lips, as well as that other part of him. He was going to marry her. He would probably expect her to deal with that other part of his anatomy. She wanted to, but she didn't know if she was ready yet. She was just getting used to the idea of kissing him. His car rumbled out of the driveway.

Rose stood in the middle of her living room surrounded by stratified layers of garbage--papers, random clothing, bits of broken stuff. She wasn't planning on losing any of it to the BOJ. Jimmy was helping her make sure of that. Panic that she was going to be homeless washed over her, despite Jimmy's assurances. Slowly she turned in a circle, staring at piles of junk. A path through the stacks led into the back of the house. Her father's recliner was cleared off, as was half the couch. The living room looked more like a landfill, with garbage piled everywhere.

Step one, get that dumpster. She picked up the phone and realized she didn't know who to call.

If there was a phone book in here, she would never find it. What did she do when she had questions she couldn't answer?

"Mid-county Library, this is Miss Clark," a friendly voice said over the phone.

The librarian helped Rose locate a number for the county waste management. Rental of a dumpster was more complicated than Rose anticipated. She was going to need to get the biggest dumpster they offered, and she didn't have that kind of money. She released a heavy sigh. Time to find out about how much her father had and snag a loan from the lawyer.

"Um, Jimmy, this is a strip club," Rose announced as they got out of the car. She pulled her coat closer. She looked from the neon sign of kicking legs to Jimmy. Confusion crossed her brow. She didn't think she was going to be very comfortable hanging out here.

"Yep, and the last weekend of every month is Ladies' Night." Jimmy pulled a large duffel from the trunk.

"So you bartend on Ladies' Nights?" Rose asked hopefully. She didn't want to entertain any other possibilities

"C'mon." Jimmy nodded his head toward the club, giving her a sly smile.

Rose followed him into a dark, enclosed space. A runway stage, with a pole at the end, glowed under lights. Jimmy led

Rose to a stool at the end of the bar that ran the length of the back wall.

A busty woman approached them from the other side of the bar. "S'up, Jimmy?"

"Claudette, meet Rose." Rose reached across and shook Claudette's hand. "I need you to take real good care of Rose for me. Everything she orders is on my tab."

"Sure thing." Claudette turned to Rose. "You his new girl?"

Jimmy stepped so close his heat radiated against her back. The arm he threw over her shoulder felt protective. She wanted to lean into him, let him keep her safe. Instead, she sat ramrod straight, too nervous to move at all. "Rose and I are getting married in the morning."

Startled, Rose looked up into Jimmy's face. He beamed with pride. It radiated off him.

Sex, it had to be he was excited because they were going to have sex. Rose's stomach flipped. She felt like a nervous bride. She was a nervous bride. Never been kissed until yesterday and now she was going to get married and have to do all the married things. Why was this so hard? If she thought about it, she became a mess. If she didn't think, and he kissed her, her body got soft and happy, and she wanted to touch his skin. He got all hard. Her throat dried up as the reality of Jimmy having a penis flooded back into her brain.

"Wow, congratulations. That's…" Claudette paused. Rose could tell that she searched for a word that wouldn't be offensive.

"Unexpected. But we decided not to wait. No time like the present, right?" Rose replied, her voice brittle and fake.

Claudette nodded. "Whatever you say. Let me know if you want something."

Oh God, she thinks I'm pregnant. "Thanks," Rose said, her voice returning to normal.

"You hang out here," Jimmy told her. "I need to head back. Stay here until after the show so I can find you." He kissed her on the cheek, picked up his pack, and strode toward the opposite side of the stage.

"Jimmy." Rose ran after him. "What do you mean stay here? Aren't you bartending?"

Jimmy shook his head. "Claudette's the bartender. I'm part of the show."

Rose's mouth opened into a silent O and her eyes bugged out. She blinked a few times. She was about to see Jimmy naked a whole lot sooner than she'd expected.

"You're a stripper?" she finally managed. Nerves along her upper arms tingled strangely. The skin across her shoulders tried to migrate to the back of her neck. She felt a tic pulse under her eye. She had to stop freaking out about this.

Jimmy chuckled. "Exotic male dancer, but only on the last weekend of the month. Don't worry, you won't see anything you aren't ready to see." He winked before he disappeared behind the curtain and into the backstage area.

Rose's stomach did an uncomfortable flip.

The curtains swung shut behind Jimmy. What the hell was he doing? He'd started off wanting to help Rose out, and now, this had gotten serious fast. Too fast. He decided at the diner that he was all in, but he hadn't realized that included getting married right away. He grinned. He would have gotten there eventually, maybe in a year or two, just not tomorrow.

He opened the door to the dressing room. The combined smell of stale cigarettes, alcohol, sweat, and too much cheap perfume assaulted his nasal passages.

"Hey, Jimbo," several of the other performers called.

"Okay, guys." Jimmy planted his feet inside the entrance to the room. "The girl in the back corner of the bar is hands off."

"Why, she your date?"

"Is she loaded, and you want all the tips?"

"Yeah, what gives?"

Jimmy cleared his throat. "That's my wife, and I don't want you trolls freaking her out with your smelly asses."

"Dude, you got married?" A hand smacked Jimmy across the back of his shoulders. "Congratulations."

"I am in the morning," Jimmy clarified.

"So she's fair game!" one of the men said with a laugh.

Jimmy growled, not surprised by his own protective reaction. "Only if you want to go home without any balls. Like I said, off limits. She's kind of nervous about being here, so play nice."

"Chill out, man. No one is going to hump all over your woman but you. You had better give her one hell of a lap dance, though. Just saying."

Jimmy sighed. He wanted to give Rose all of the lap dances. She was going to become his wife and they hadn't even properly started dating. He didn't want to scare her, but he did want to give her all of his attention. But he still needed to show off for the other women in the club. He was paid in tips, and he needed the income, especially now he was going to be a married man.

Rose huddled in the corner drinking ice tea and eating nachos.

Droves of women noisily filled the bar without a man in sight. They were screaming and hollering before the show even began.

When the house lights dropped to signal the beginning of the show, the noise level increased.

Rose's eyes bugged out when she watched three buff, half-naked men in tight blue jeans strut onto the catwalk. The first one spun around the stripper pole. Women lined the stage and threw money at the dancers.

Holy cow, if Jimmy was one of those… She blushed deeply as she realized how buff Jimmy had to be. He had kissed her, and she was going to marry him. It was a marriage of convenience, but, dang, if she wasn't interested in making it completely legal, consummated and all.

Her blush roared back across her face as she thought about sex. Her flush grew hotter the second she spotted Jimmy on stage. When his shirt flew off, the women in the audience screamed with hoots and laughter. Rose sucked in her breath. She had rested against those shoulders. Those mile-wide shoulders.

On the third dance number, the dancers jumped off the stage to the main floor. Rose hid her eyes behind her hand as the dancers began bumping and grinding on the women in the audience. It was all too raw for her. Driven by curiosity, she peeked and saw the dancers strutting around with money sticking out of their G-strings.

Not wanting any of the embarrassing bump-and-grind attention, she avoided looking at any of the men whenever they strutted near. She breathed a sigh of relief as each one of them passed her by.

The lights dimmed, and the men disappeared behind the backstage curtain. Another stage number. This time Jimmy and another man took turns showing off their upper body strength on the stripper pole. They spun and did stunts on the pole. The other dancer had more grace and skill as he twirled around the pole, but Jimmy was far better looking.

The men hit the main floor again, and again, Rose diverted her eyes. She risked furtive glances, but was too embarrassed to watch.

A warm presence against her arm brought her attention away from her nachos. She caught a glimpse of skin and turned away. She attempted to hide by making the dancer think she was more interested in eating than watching him. She could feel the air shift as the dancer moved around her.

"Oh no, no, I don't want..." she protested as she turned to look the man in the eye.

She froze. Jimmy smiled at her. She couldn't break eye contact with him. She could sense his body move around hers, but she couldn't take her eyes from his face. When he grabbed her hand and rubbed it over his chest, she closed her eyes. His skin was hot and slick with sweat. She didn't want to think. She only wanted to feel, to enjoy him under her fingers. If she thought too much, she would panic. She was too aware there were people in the bar who could see them touching.

Oh God, people could see them. All of her muscles tensed up and her eyes flew open. Dropping her hand, Jimmy winked at her before he spun away to cavort for another woman.

Waving a napkin in front of her hot face, she remained on

her stool and stared at her nachos while she listened to the music and the shrill screams of the women around her. Her eyes never wandered too far from her food, or from looking at all the different liquor bottles along the back wall of the bar.

"Can I have another one of these?" she asked the bartender as she held up her tall narrow tea glass. It was a different woman than Claudette.

"Long Island?" she asked.

"Iced tea," Rose corrected.

The refill tasted a little sweeter than she was used to, but it went well with the nachos. She continued to focus on the food even after the music ended and the audience slowly filtered out of the club. She wasn't sure how long it had been or how many nachos she had ordered. Rose found it hard to keep her balance on the stool. The bar swam in her vision. She closed her eyes and waited for Jimmy.

"Rose, you ready?" Jimmy gently touched her on the shoulder. She looked pale, terrified. Maybe bringing her here tonight hadn't been the best idea he'd ever had. When she tried to stand, her legs collapsed out from under her. Jimmy caught her in his strong arms.

"You're really handsome." Rose's words slurred together. "We're gonna get married."

"Yes, we are." Jimmy tried to stabilize her, but she melted against his chest.

"You're a stripper," she garbled. "I'm gonna marry a stripper and have sex."

Not tonight, you aren't. "And you're intoxicated. What the hell have you been drinking?" Jimmy asked.

"Ice tea." It sounded more like 'eyesh tuh.'

Jimmy picked up her glass and sniffed. "Crap. Claudette, what have you been giving her?"

"She's just been drinking tea all night. And eating nachos, may I point out, not watching your show," Claudette said as she sauntered over.

He handed the glass to Claudette. "Does that taste like tea to you?"

Claudette barked out a laugh. "I guess Lydia thought she was drinking Long Island Ice Teas."

"Not funny. I don't think she's ever had alcohol before, and now she's drunk off her ass." Jimmy looked down at Rose's sweet face. She was crushed into his chest. Her mouth gaped open and she made soft snoring noises. "And asleep. Great."

Jimmy hefted his duffel over one shoulder before bending to lift Rose into his arms.

"I'm supposed to carry you over the threshold after we're married, not before," he said as he carried her out to his car. "I promise I'll carry you over your threshold tomorrow, when you'll remember it."

She replied with a snort and a loud snore.

Rose balanced with one hand pressed against her forehead and the other reaching for the counter. Her head throbbed. She couldn't remember anything past a certain point last night. She remembered the show and Jimmy's naked torso. She remembered wanting to touch him and have him touch her. She remembered panicking.

The officiant in the quickie wedding chapel droned on about some nonsense regarding the sanctity of marriage. Whatever. She wanted the noise to stop. He asked her a question; she said yes. He prompted her to a more particular response; she said what she was directed to say.

Jimmy's soft lips brushed against hers. Had he kissed her last night? Had his lips been soft or seeking? She was afraid of what she might have done. Her body hated her this morning. Did her stomach hurt because she was nervous? Sick? Hung over? Or were those cramps from sex? She couldn't remember anything after the show and was too nervous to look at him. Too terrified to ask.

A pen was pushed into her hand and she signed her name. More noise, more jostling.

Jimmy whispered, "you okay?"

No, she was not okay. "Please just make it all stop," Rose managed to groan. She had never felt this sick in her life. Even the air hurt her hair.

She was hung over, getting married, and completely unable to remember if she had thrown herself at her new husband last night. It was not a pleasant combination.

"Can I go to bed now?" Rose whined. Sleep would make the dull throbbing pain stop.

"You can sleep in the car. I need to get this marriage certificate over to Mr. Staussan and take you home," Jimmy answered in low soothing tones. His car wasn't soothing. The rumbling of the engine beat her up until she managed to fall asleep again.

With the wedding papers in hand, Mr. Staussan declared Jimmy the heir to her father's fortune and promptly issued Rose a partial loan against the balance in her father's bank account. It took less than a week for her have access to the funds and order a dumpster.

"I found another figurine!" Jimmy called out from the living room. He turned the figure around in his hand. Another guy playing a flute, probably the Pied Piper of Hamlin, based on the line of children dancing after the man with the instrument.

Rose rushed from the second bedroom, setting a long narrow box down as she entered the room. "Really?"

"Yeah, it's a nice one too. Look." Jimmy held up the porcelain figure for Rose to examine.

"I wonder how many there are." Rose carried it over to the mantle to place next to the other pieces they had already found.

"I get the connection between the figures playing flutes, like the drum and fife one, that Pan, and this new one. But I don't get the airplane."

"It's a Piper Cub. They are all pipers of some kind or another. That was my mother's nickname. Piper."

Jimmy nodded. "Oh."

"Look, I found another recorder." She opened the box to show him.

Jimmy picked up the instrument. "This one makes nine total, flutes, piccolos, and recorders. Your mom must have played a lot."

"I don't remember her playing anything, but she made me take lessons."

"You play?" He dusted his palms on the back of his jeans. "Play something."

Rose rolled her eyes. "Oh God, no. You'll run screaming and never come back." She laughed.

Jimmy stood solemnly holding the recorder out to Rose. "Please. I'm not going anywhere."

Rose grimaced as she removed the instrument from his hands. In shape, it was a basic recorder, except this one was not clear red plastic like the one he had been tortured with in the fifth grade. This instrument glowed with the rich golden color of the wood it had been carved from.

He winced as Rose blew an ear-splitting note.

"Sorry," she muttered and repositioned her fingers. She closed her eyes, inhaled, and placed her lips around the mouthpiece. A clear, pure note emanated from the recorder.

Jimmy's body reacted to everything. His ears welcomed the rich tones of the music. His body began to sway to Rose's choice of "The Snake Charmer." And his cock stiffened at the sight of her lips wrapped around the mouthpiece.

He tried to ignore his growing desire and let the music enchant him into an impromptu performance of undulations and sinuous movements. He crossed his legs and pivoted, wrapping his arms and circling his wrists in snake-like motions.

One of his feet slipped out from under him. He staggered before awkwardly regaining his feet. "Damn it."

Rose stopped playing. "You okay?"

"Yeah, there's still so much crap on the floor." Jimmy kicked around to see what had unexpectedly ended his performance. It looked like petals of some kind. "Check this out." Jimmy kneeled down and brushed at a crushed pile of twigs and dead leaves.

Rose sighed. "More dead plants. I guess those are from

around when my mom died. I can't remember any plants in the house after that."

"But look." Jimmy pointed at a few desiccated blossoms. "They were roses. I thought you said your dad hated roses."

"He couldn't stand them."

"Most of the flowers we're finding at this level are all roses. They were your mother's favorite, weren't they?" He lifted his eyes to her.

Rose's shrug let him know she'd never made that connection. "No wonder he hated me."

"I don't think your dad hated you. It's like we hit an important layer of history here, the flowers, and I'm finding more of the figures and your mother's flutes. When did you mother die?"

"I was in the eighth grade."

"Look at the date on this." Jimmy handed her a yellowed, brittle newspaper.

"Same year." Rose glanced across the living room. "You're right. This must be when all of this mess started, with Mother's death. I guess he couldn't handle it."

"How did you?" he asked.

"Honestly? I didn't. I was shuffled off to relatives that summer. When I came back I was in survival mode. I think I've been in survival mode ever since." Rose kneeled beside Jimmy on the floor. They had successfully cleaned a large section of the living room. Day by day, they recovered more space in the house.

"Losing her must have broken him," he said softly.

Rose sighed. "I didn't survive my mother's death. She left me with him. He was so angry. I was never allowed to visit her in the hospital. I had no idea my father wasn't coping. I was mad at her. I don't know if I was following his lead, or if I had my own emotions. After she died, I thought he hated me. I didn't have time to miss her. I was too busy trying to be good, trying to avoid his wrath. He would always tell me how much he hated roses. I figured that included me too."

Tears fell from her eyes. Jimmy reached over and wiped one away with the pad of his thumb. Rose collapsed in a heap. "Her favorite flowers were roses. I never got to say goodbye. I was just mad all the time. And now Father is dead, and I'm all alone." She sobbed and gulped for air.

Jimmy wrapped his arms around her, making soothing noises.

"You aren't alone, Rose. You have me now," he reminded her.

"But this isn't real, Jimmy," she cried against his chest.

"Don't say that. This is as real as it needs to be. It's as real as you want." He stood, pulling Rose to her feet. He scooped her up and waded through the rest of the living room, carrying her back to her bedroom.

Rose cried into his chest. Jimmy lowered her to her bed and lay down next to her. This fragile woman had endured so much. He stroked her hair as she continued to cry over the loss of her mother, possibly for the first time. And for the loss of her father, who she'd really lost when her mother died. Once her breathing steadied, he continued to hold her until she fell asleep.

This was real for him. She already had a firm hold on his heart. It would just take time to woo her.

A loud banging rattled the front door. Jimmy sighed with aggravation and rolled out of the small bed. He stomped through the house and opened the door to find Mrs. Cuthbert on the porch, her face so pinched it looked like she was constantly smelling something bad.

"Where is Miss St. John?" Mrs. Cuthbert demanded.

"My wife is resting. She's had an emotional morning. Why are you here?" Jimmy asked.

"I just came here to tell her that we know what you two are up to and this house will never be hers." Mrs. Cuthbert spit her words at Jimmy. "You haven't even moved in here properly, like a husband should."

"I don't have to explain myself to you. But for your information, I am moving in here. We got married in a hurry, and I had to give notice to my landlord. Got a problem with that?"

"James Erickson, I found out about you and your so called jobs." Mrs. Cuthbert sneered the words like it left a bad taste in her mouth.

Jimmy crossed his arms. "So?"

"You're just a common man-whore, and you're taking advantage of that poor girl."

"You and that church are trying to toss her out on the street. Don't get all morally righteous on me. As her husband, the property is mine, and I will make sure your cult never gets its hands on it. Now take yourself and that junky-ass car of yours off my property. And the term you're looking for is exotic male dancer, not man-whore."

Jimmy shifted into a dancer's posture, bending his knees, and began thrusting his hips toward Mrs. Cuthbert. With each thrust, he jumped toward her a fraction.

Mrs. Cuthbert croaked out a sound of horror in her throat and scrambled off the porch.

Jimmy laughed at her loudly to be sure she heard before closing the door.

Rose shuffled out of her bedroom. "Who was that?"

"Nothing, baby, go back to bed. You need the rest." Jimmy wrapped an arm around Rose's shoulder and guided her back to her room.

"Get in with me. I feel better with you there."

"Of course." Jimmy lay down next to Rose. She snuggled into his chest. He shifted so that she wouldn't feel the raging erection that had sprung back to life when she invited him into her bed.

Rose sat in Mr. Staussan's office. He had called her requesting a visit. She hoped he could do something to get the BOJ to leave her and Jimmy alone. It had been a long three weeks since they'd got married, and Mrs. Cuthbert and Brother Carter seemed to be at the house on a daily basis with some complaint or threat. This time they threatened a court injunction against Jimmy being the rightful heir as her husband.

"I was hoping James would have accompanied you," Mr. Staussan said.

Rose shifted in her seat. The hard wood and her nerves made it an extremely uncomfortable chair. "He had to work for the funeral home today," she explained.

"How many flutes have you found so far?"

"We've found eleven. And eleven piper figurines. I don't think they're worth anything, but some of the instruments might be." Rose shrugged. She didn't want to sell off her mother's figurines. They were triggering memories she had long ago repressed, memories of a happy childhood she had forgotten in her misery.

Staussan cleared his throat. "The church elders are becoming more and more aggressive regarding their claim to the property and bank accounts. You may need to sell the instruments until we can get them to accept that the inheritance goes to you and James. We finally located all of the bank accounts. You need to see this." He slid a sheet of paper across his desk to her.

Once Rose saw the account totals she understood. The house was inconsequential. The BOJ was after the money.

Staussan nodded, his expression grim. "This is awkward for me, but the church is trying to demand that a doctor certify that you are indeed married."

Rose blushed. Her mouth gaped open.

"They can't, and I'm not even suggesting that you volunteer for such a thing. I'm warning you that they are going to drag this out for as long as they can."

"Mrs. Cuthbert won't be happy until she's in my marriage bed!" Rose cried.

"It's not her who is making the claims, it's Carter Trace. He seems to be the driving force with the court."

"That's Brother Carter. He does everything that Cuthbert woman tells him to do. It's been barely a month, and they're at my house every other day. Why can't they leave me alone?" Rose's face grew hot with anger and embarrassment. Could they just look at her and know she'd only done it once when she was really drunk and that Jimmy didn't think of her that way, no matter how often she now thought about him?

"I'm afraid they aren't going to let this drop until you've spent all the money in those accounts on legal fees. We can file a restraining order against them for now. I'm sorry I didn't recommend that earlier."

Mr. Staussan's words bounced around in her brain as she

trudged her way to the funeral home. She needed Jimmy. He would have good advice, and even if he didn't, being with him was soothing. She found him in the garage, running a polishing cloth over the hood of the hearse.

"What's the matter, baby?" Jimmy's arms wrapped around her in a protective embrace as soon as she approached, but he didn't kiss her.

"Why don't you kiss me? We're married. Married people kiss. We should kiss."

Rose's lips tingled as Jimmy's lips caressed them. Her mouth opened in pleasure and Jimmy's tongue teased hers. His lips pulled at something in her, and her body reacted, wanting more than only his kiss. He lifted his head away from her, ending the embrace.

"I'm happy to kiss you, especially now that I know you want me to. So what's with this gloomy face?"

"The elders are gonna ask the court to request proof that we're really married."

"Huh?" Jimmy furrowed his brow at Rose's statement. "That's what the marriage certificate is for."

"They said they wanted to examine me. For evidence that we, you know, had sex." She whispered the last words.

"That's not going to happen, Rose. They can't do that. Who said they were going to do that?" Jimmy asked.

"Mr. Staussan."

"He's being a pervy old man and trying to find out if we've done it. The wackos at that church wouldn't do that. They are rude and greedy, but they're from a church."

"Don't underestimate them, Jimmy. They want my father's money. I saw the figures today. It's a lot more than we realized."

"It's never going to happen." Jimmy shook his head.

"But it's okay, right? Didn't we already do it? You know, the night before we got married?" Rose stammered, the thought of having to undergo an exam for this particular reason made her stomach turn.

"You got drunk and fell asleep. I didn't touch you. You're still, you know, a virgin." Jimmy whispered the last word. "I wouldn't take advantage of you like that."

Rose gulped. He hadn't touched her. He didn't like her enough to touch her. She had to ask him to kiss her. She felt so alone, even while still in his embrace. "I know you aren't interested in me, but…" She swallowed again, trying to dissolve the tightness in her throat. "Will you sleep with me in case they do get a court order?"

Jimmy looked over his shoulder. "No, Rose, I won't have sex with you to appease those church biddies." He kept his voice low.

His statement punched her in the gut. She pushed out of his embrace.

"Hold on." Jimmy caught her hands and held them with his larger ones. "I will make love to you as my bride and my wife."

Rose gaped up at Jimmy. "You'll what?"

"Rose, when I married you, it was for real. I'm married to you here, where it counts." Jimmy placed her hands over his heart. "I plan on winning you, no matter how slow I have to go, no matter how long it takes. I don't want to pressure you if you aren't ready." Jimmy paused. "Hell, Rose, we never discussed our feelings for each other. I had already decided I wanted to date you, but you needed to get married. It never really went any further than that. And we haven't really talked about it since. You get so skittish whenever we get close."

"I'm your wife and you still want to date me?" Rose asked, confused.

"Honestly, I want to skip all that dating stuff, all that will you or won't you crap, and be married to you. I want to have my wife in my bed, have a nice little home to raise kids in. And yeah, I want to woo my wife. I want to date that girl who cut off all of her hair and told me she wanted to eat pie and have sex for the first time."

"I want to do that, too." Rose's voice was small, almost a whisper.

Jimmy sighed, staring into her eyes. "I want to be there for all of it, Rose. I would like to take you on a date, and I would like to make love with you."

❄

"I really married a stripper," Rose joked as Jimmy drove into Tahoe for his monthly dance gig.

"Exotic male entertainer. You gonna watch this time or hide in the corner again?" Jimmy didn't take his eyes off the road, but he smiled broadly. He was in an incredibly good mood ever since Rose asked if she could come with him tonight, even after the heavy lifting he had done today from moving his furniture into the other bedroom.

"I'll try to watch, at least you. I want to watch you." Rose let her breath out slowly. She wanted to watch him, she wanted to touch him, she wanted all of him, and she was pretty certain tonight would be that night.

"I'll make sure to dance just for you."

When they reached the club, Rose found the same corner seat in the bar while Jimmy disappeared backstage.

"Hey, Jimmy's wife!"

Rose pointed at her chest. "Apparently last time I got wasted. Sorry about that."

"Yeah, you must have had one bitch of a hangover." Claudette laughed.

Rose nodded slowly. "Most definitely. Tonight I'm sticking with soda."

The bartender was still laughing when she returned with Rose's drink.

The lights dropped and the music got loud.

This time, Rose watched. It was the same dance routine as last month, three buff men and a stripper pole. It sounded like the opening line to a joke, only the blush that lit up her face was anything but funny. Jimmy hadn't come out yet, and she didn't know if she could watch the entire show. All these mostly naked men, all these screaming women. She swiveled around and made eye contact with Claudette.

"Aren't you gonna watch your man this time?"

"It's all so... so much skin," Rose confessed. "How can I be special when he does this?"

"Of course you are. This is for fun and tips. Besides, you get to go home with him," Claudette explained.

Rose spun back around as the music switched. Jimmy was

out on stage in tight, faded jeans and a plain white shirt. She could imagine that Jimmy performed for her alone. She could touch all of that if she wanted. He'd said so. He said it was up to her, her decision. He would wait because he was falling in love with her. And she was stalling because she was already in love with him, and afraid.

At the end of the night, Rose followed him back to the car. He had kissed her on the cheek, but she didn't know how to get him to start kissing her on the lips. She didn't know how to start the touching.

"Jimmy?"

He stopped on the top stair to the porch, turned, and looked at her.

"Claudette said something at the club to me."

"Uh huh?" He continued into the house.

Rose followed. "She said I get to go home with you at the end of the night."

"Yeah?"

"Did she mean that of all the people there, I'm the one who gets to have sex with you?"

"That's exactly what she meant." Jimmy dropped his duffle in the middle of the now clean living room and pulled Rose into an embrace. "What's this all about, baby?"

"I've come home with you. Can we?"

His eyes lit up like starlight. Rose let out a loud giggle as Jimmy swept her into his arms and carried her into his bedroom.

He searched her face. "You know I love you, right? If you aren't ready…"

She rested her palm against his cheek, trying to get him to look her in the eye. Her throat was dry, and the words came out in a raspy whisper. "I love you. I think it's time I became Mrs. Erickson properly."

When Jimmy's lips found Rose's, she melted into him. She stopped thinking and let her body feel. She was aware of the bed being soft and her clothes being removed, but she didn't think about it. She focused on the feel of his skin against hers, the heat of his body, and the need in hers. He kissed her constantly, and she him.

It didn't hurt as she had been led to believe it would. It felt like pressure, glorious, wonderful, amazing pressure. His touch was gentle and loving. She explored all the planes of his body with her fingers. Now that she had started touching him, she never wanted to stop. Rose merged into Jimmy, and she understood how two could become one.

After it was all over, arms pulled her back into bed when she tried to get up. "Where do you think you're going, my wife?" Jimmy's voice was a rumbly purr.

"I was going to go to bed, in my room," Rose explained.

"This is our room. This is our bed now. I want you with me."

"But I need a nightgown." Rose squirmed as Jimmy nibbled at her ear.

"No, you don't. It will only get in the way." His arms tightened around her.

"Oh," was all she managed before his lips claimed hers again.

Six weeks later.

"Hey, baby!" Jimmy called out.

Rose came out of the bathroom, her hand a clenched fist. "What?"

She ignored her nerves as she pushed into the back room of the house. A room that had been shut up and used for collecting more of her father's garbage. She hadn't been able to open the door to this room for years. She hardly remembered it ever being used for anything other than a dumping ground.

"Did you know there's another bathroom back here?"

"A what?" she asked as she stepped around more piles of junk, and towards where Jimmy worked.

"Yeah, this was a big bedroom with its own attached bath. There is a closet behind the big pile in the far corner."

"I was never allowed in here. I wonder if this was my parent's bedroom."

"Once I get it all cleaned up, it will be ours."

"Good." Rose inched around a few remaining stacks of trash to peer into the bathroom that Jimmy had discovered. It wasn't large, but it was a full bath. "Two bathrooms is definitely better than one. We'll need the space."

Jimmy looked over at her. "What's that supposed to mean?"

"It means…" Rose held out a marker-sized piece of lavender and white plastic. A small window in the top of the plastic piece showed two pink lines. "I think the BOJ is finally going to leave us alone."

Jimmy tripped over his own feet and a stack of garbage as he scrambled to get to Rose.

"Are you serious? This means what I think this means? A baby? I'll drop this off at the lawyer's on my way to work this afternoon. That'll show them, trying to claim we aren't really man and wife." He set Rose down. "Have I mentioned how much I love you?"

Rose giggled. "You've said it a few times today, but I'll let you say it again."

"I love you, Rose."

Rose pressed her lips to Jimmy's. "I love you, too"

12

BANG A DRUMMER

*F*ive men and two women walked in formation through the fair. Their presence demanded attention. The women in the front were pretty in a wild Highlands fantasy sort of way, while each of the men was better-looking than the one before. All exuded power and sex appeal.

Bucky grabbed Lettie by the scruff of her wool cape and pulled her out of the way.

Annoyed with being jerked backward, she began to complain. "Wha—"

The words stopped in her throat as she glimpsed the group. A wave of male dominance and testosterone washed over her as they approached. She held onto Bucky for stability. She couldn't take her eyes from the man just behind the female leader. He was tall, with a mane of dark golden hair falling to his belt. His broad chest and shoulders strained the lacings across the front of his shirt. His kilt exposed his knees and shapely calves. Bunched up socks and black combat boots with extra buckles completed his wardrobe.

Kilts. Lettie went weak in the knees. They were all in kilts, and they were all so damn hot. But this golden lion of a man made her heart flutter. When he looked at her, and they made eye contact, the electricity triggered internal pulses in her core.

Lettie gasped loudly. Eye contact and she was wet. Eye

contact and she practically came. "Damn. I wish I had known they were going to be here."

"Why?" Bucky asked.

"I would have dressed like a girl." She adjusted her doublet and fell into the growing horde following behind the band *There Be Dragons*.

"Where are you going?" Bucky hitched up the velvet skirt to his dress and followed after her.

"With them!"

By the time Lettie and Bucky reached the stage, the men of the group were stripping off shirts and strapping on drums. Then the shouting began. Shouting and drumming and hair tossing.

There Be Dragons was a crowd favorite, and they always made an impressive entrance to the Renaissance Fair. This small winter Twelfth Night Festival was no different. They entered like they owned the place. They lured an audience with their magnetism, and they entertained the hell out of the people who came to their show.

"I forgot how hot they were," Lettie yelled in Bucky's ear. She breathed heavily, practically panting as she watched *There be Dragons* pound out rhythms and chant the words to their songs. The women, petite compared to the men, danced onto the stage playing fiddles. The sound combined with the drums and the pipes was magical.

Transported in time, Lettie watched a fairy performance. The fair always took her away from reality for a few hours. She focused on the man who'd caught her stare earlier. He couldn't be real. He was too perfect. She didn't recognize him from previous times she'd seen this group, he must be new. She would definitely have remembered him because he was too good looking to forget.

When the curly haired ginger girl began flirting with the golden man, Bucky's fingers bit Lettie's shoulder. She spared a glance for her brother. He was squinting daggers at the man the redhead flirted with. She smiled. Seconds ago, Lettie had been glaring at the woman for the same reason.

"I don't like that they've added the redheaded bitch. It brings them down." She knew the insult would aggravate her brother.

"Don't talk about the mother of my children that way." Bucky practically growled. "He looks like he would snap her in half if they had sex."

"Maybe she likes really big guys."

"I'm big," Bucky said.

"You're tall, not big. You aren't buff like that. Damn, he could break me. Anytime." Lettie said the last part with a wistful sigh.

"I'm big where it counts."

"Ew, I've seen you naked, and no, you're not." She shoved Bucky on the arm.

"You've never seen me primed for action. They magically inflate, you know."

"I do not need to know that about you. TMI."

Bucky smiled at her reaction, but Lettie noticed his eyes never left the redhead girl on the stage.

"You're just jealous because she's up there playing with that guy and you aren't." Bucky chuckled.

"Shut up. I could say the same for you."

Bucky continued to laugh at her pain. "Let me guess, you want Mr. shampoo-commercial hair, the blond one?"

"God, please." It was practically a moan. Lettie's lust was thick.

Her anticipation grew. She hoped the drummers of TBD would do their usual schtick, even in this cold. If they did, she would get to see more of her man. Their shirts were already gone, and even though it had started to snow teeny tiny flakes, the performers were sweating.

When the last drum beat was forcefully smashed and the men of *There Be Dragons* shouted one last time, they did it! They pulled their kilts off. The men were left standing on stage wearing drums to cover their privates. The audience screamed in delight. Lettie moaned wantonly while Bucky groaned in distaste. When the band turned to exit, they exposed the crowd to well-defined, completely naked asses.

Lettie had a hard time not drooling. Her eye-candy favorite

had a perfect ass. "Damn, you could bounce a quarter off that and get back two dimes and a nickel."

"Are you objectifying those men?" a woman standing near Lettie asked incredulously.

"Oh, yes, I am," Lettie said with a throaty, lustful sound.

"Disgusting. Keep that to yourself." The woman glared at Lettie.

Lettie looked with confusion from the woman to her brother, then back at the woman. She blinked a few times before realization dawned on her.

Lettie guffawed and began slapping Bucky. "She thinks..." But she couldn't speak for laughing.

"Oh, that's good." Bucky began laughing with Lettie.

"Young man, you are incredibly rude," the woman chastised Lettie before stomping off in a huff.

"She thinks you're a gay guy. That's brilliant." Bucky continued laughing.

"Laugh it up, princess, that means she really thought you were a girl in that dress."

"Yes!" They high fived each other over their cross-dressing success.

To see them dressed as they were, it was impossible to tell they were the same age. When in mundane clothes they clearly looked like the twins they were. Today, in historical costuming, they did not. They were garbed in the spirit of the Shakespeare play they were about to see. Lettie was dressed as a young Elizabethan man, complete with starched lace collar, puffy pantaloons, and a doublet in a dark amber that set off her eyes. Her short, dark hair was gelled tight to her scalp, pixie style. With no makeup on and her natural shape hidden by the clothes, she looked like a fifteen-year-old boy, not the twenty-three-year-old woman she really was.

Bucky, on the other hand, wore her red velvet gown. The corseting forced his slender build into a more feminine shape. A wig with long, smooth curls fell to his shoulders. A heavy application of makeup made him look like a tired young woman. Together they still looked like any brother-sister pair attending the festival, except Bucky was the taller, older sister, and Lettie the shorter, younger brother.

Lance followed the other guys backstage, his kilt draped over his shoulder. He wrapped the heavily pleated garment around his hips before unstrapping the large drum that protected his modesty for the audience.

"Oy, what was that all about?" Olive, his sister, came up and slapped him on his arm.

He mock-flinched at her barrage.

"You missed cues, and you didn't do my choreography," she complained.

"No one noticed," he huffed, glaring at nothing in particular. His gaze landed on a stack of hay bales placed in the corner to keep the wind from tearing through the tent. One of the bales had broken and spilled out over the floor. Olive was right. His performance hadn't been up to par. He had been distracted. He sat heavily on one of the benches in the middle of the tent.

When they'd entered the festival, the crowd had scattered out of their way like the parting of the Red Sea. Lance had eyed the crowd, looking for some willing young wench. So far Renaissance Fairs had been good for unencumbered hookups. Why should the weather and time of year make any difference? Lance typically spotted one or two candidates right away. But not this afternoon.

What he'd seen instead had shaken him to his core. Undermined the foundation of his very self-identity.

He'd seen the mate glow.

The soft aura surrounded an ideal person for him to spend the rest of his life with. He could love this person until death they do part. They would be able to carry on their gift to another generation. While not a limiting magic, ignoring the mate glow could lead to reduced interest in other relationships. Not even hookups would be appealing. He would experience a constant longing for the one that got away.

Lance could ignore it. He should ignore it. He needed to find out more about it, especially since the soft, pulsing glow had surrounded a young man with soft, feminine features. He groaned and buried his face in his hands.

"C'mon." Bucky pulled on Lettie's arm. "The play is going to start. It's too cold out here."

The temperature was steadily dropping. Sitting mournfully on a bale of hay was not going to make her dream man reappear from behind the stage. Besides, what would she say? She was dressed like a man and, apparently, it fooled people.

She followed Bucky into the theater and jostled into their seats. The cornerstone feature of this festival was a performance of the Shakespeare's *Twelfth Night*. If Lettie liked pretty androgynous men, she could see how a little cross-dressing confusion could happen. But she didn't, and she was surprised how she could ever be confused for a boy, even if she was dressed as one. Now, Bucky in that dress was definitely turning male heads. Bucky made a nice looking female.

Could Lettie fall for a man who got the hots for her while assuming she was male? Wouldn't that confuse things? She was open to gender-fluid concepts, but she considered herself cisgender female and heterosexual. Nothing wrong with any other identities, but that was hers. What if the man she fell for was the fluid one? Wouldn't that make her fluid, too?

The confusion on the stage in *Twelfth Night* added to the confusion in her brain. She thought she had accepted that love is love. But she had to admit she loved men and sex with men, so while identity fluidity was definitely an option, fluidity with body parts, maybe not so much.

"That was great," Bucky announced as they exited the theater. "Sebastian strolls up, gets the hot babe, and didn't have to do any of the work. I feel sorry for Viola, though."

"Why?"

"She ends up with the poor, sexually confused Orsino. Does he like girls or does he like boys? I bet twenty years in their future after the kids are all grown up, he moves in with the stable boy."

They both laughed as they followed the crowd onto the festival's main street. The sun had set, and many of the booths had already closed up shop. A few hot meat pie vendors were still hawking their wares.

The pastie vendor had a serious line forming in front of their stand. "Smells good. I'm starved." Lettie sighed.

"The feast starts in a few minutes. Let's head over that way. Maybe we can get in early, get good seats."

"Which way is it? I'm all turned around."

Bucky indicated a passage between shops and headed in that direction.

A large, shaggy dog glowered at them from the shadows, only its glowing blue eyes clearly visible. Bucky stopped and threw a protective arm in front of Lettie.

Lettie pushed his arm down. "He's probably just cold, sitting out here in the snow." She turned to the animal. "You're all right, boy, aren't you? You aren't going to eat us?"

The dog stepped into the light. His tail started to wag back and forth.

"See? His ears are up, and his tail is wagging." The huge dog sported a thick, light brown coat, while heavier, darker fur covered the animal's shoulders and chest. To Lettie, he looked like a wolf, only bigger and fluffier. He reminded her of some type of mastiff breed, but with a longer face.

The dog trotted straight for Lettie. "Whoa, there, boy."

The dog didn't stop. He reared up on his hind feet and planted his front paws on her shoulders. She bent under his weight. "Uff." She adjusted her stance so she wasn't knocked on her ass.

He sniffed around Lettie's neck.

She flinched away from the dog's wet nose as it tickled her ear. Unable to lift his paws from her, Lettie struggle under his weight. "Damn, he's heavy. Okay, big guy, time for you to get down." She finally managed to get the heavy animal off her. Once on all four paws, he thrust his nose into her crotch.

"Seriously, stop." She tried to push him back, but the beast was strong and determined to sniff. "You could at least buy me dinner first." She laughed as she continued to back away while pushing him out of her legs.

"You stupid brute," a voice called behind them.

One of the women from *There Be Dragons* approached. Her orange curls bounced in a way that Lettie expected would cause Bucky to ruin the drape of his dress with his "magically inflatable" body part.

"Does this belong to you?" Bucky asked, indicating Lettie and the very persistent, sniffing dog.

"My brother's." The redhead grabbed the scruff of the dog's neck and pulled him back from Lettie. "Get off, you rude beast. That is no way to treat a person."

Freed from the dog's probing nose, Lettie released an embarrassed giggle. "Was he a gynecologist in a previous life? He can send the bill to my insurance."

The dog leaped back up onto her shoulders and licked the side of her face before loping off.

"I guess that was thanks and goodbye." Lettie rubbed her hand over the lick, wiping the slobber away. "I hope it was good for him. Typical male. I found it a little less than satisfying."

The redhead failed to contain a laugh. "I am so sorry about that." She gestured after the dog. "He must have gotten out. He needs a keeper. I'm Olive."

"I'm Bu—" Bucky began.

"Buffy, and I'm Lot," Lettie cut in before her brother gave away their game. She eyed him knowingly, hoping he clued in. "We recognize you from *There Be Dragons*. You're new, aren't you? You guys are really good."

"Thanks. It's fun. My brother and I have only been with them for a few months. We're glad to hear that people enjoyed the show. Look, there's a big feast in about fifteen minutes. Do you have tickets?"

Olive, Lettie noticed, was definitely directing her conversation to Bucky. Her brother responded to the attention, his posture straightening, his chest puffing slightly. Of course being corseted in, he looked like a flirting girl lifting her boobs, but he wasn't acting very girlish, trying to posture like a man, despite his dress.

"We got the full package deal—fest passes, play tickets, and tickets to the feast," Bucky answered.

"Good, I'll see you there." Olive twirled dramatically and flitted away.

"Oh my God, was she flirting with you? I swear I saw her fluttering her eyelashes." Lettie teased.

"So what if she was?"

"You look like a girl, so if she thinks she was flirting with a girl, you have a crush on a lesbian."

Bucky deflated. "It won't be the first time. She's cute, maybe I should tell her I'm a guy?"

Lettie watched Bucky stare after the young woman.

"What are you thinking?" Lettie could tell there was more disappointment in his expression than finding out Olive batted for the other team.

"She didn't have an accent," Bucky said sadly "In my little fantasy of her, she's got a lilting Scottish accent."

"Poor baby." Lettie petted his arm in mock sympathy.

"Oh, shut up, you and that live sex act with a dog out in the middle of everything."

"That was so embarrassing. I'm glad he didn't start humping me. What kind of dog was that, anyway?"

Bucky shrugged. "Don't know, but now I have a good excuse to talk to Olive at the feast."

"Are you going to tell me what that was all about, or are you purposefully out to destroy my future?" Olive railed at Lance.

Lance sat, elbow on thighs, studying his hands and contemplating the information he had gathered. Not a male. Men didn't smell like that, and there had been no male genitalia hidden under all those folds of fabric. The amount of relief he felt was immeasurable.

He looked up through his hair at Olive. "What are you going on about?"

"That boy you violated."

"Girl, not a boy," Lance stated.

Olive flounced down next to him on the bench. "Oh, really? Now that makes things a whole lot more interesting."

"What's that supposed to mean?"

"The tall one she was with was not a girl."

"How could you tell?" He swept his hair behind his shoulder as he sat up.

"Women don't have Adam's apples, and his five o'clock shadow was starting to be visible under the makeup," Olive explained. "Are you going to tell me why you were so impolite? I've never seen you be such a dog like that before."

"She glows, Olive. I thought she was a boy. I was having issues."

"Well, that's a fine howdy-do," Olive said.

"Why do you say that?"

"Because the man in the dress was glowing for me," she explained. "It's why I looked twice, otherwise, there was no real reason to pay too much attention to him. I thought he was a girl."

"Damn." Lance looked back down at his hands.

"Tell me about it."

"This changes everything. Doesn't it?"

"It will for me," Olive answered "I'm not going to ignore it. Hopefully, he's open to a relationship because I plan on starting something tonight."

Lance chuckled. "This gives me a great deal to think about. Not in the least, how do I go about wooing her while she's dressed as a boy?"

Olive cackled. "You'd better find out how old she is. Someone will think you're a pedophile if they see you going off to bang that boy in the camper."

"Add that to the list. Hasn't that thought hasn't crossed your mind? Sneaking off to screw a girl?"

Olive stood, hands on her hips. "First of all, I don't give a rat's ass what anyone else thinks. If I want to make out with a girl, I will damn well make out with a girl. Secondly, that's not really going to be an issue, I'm hardly likely to sleep with him tonight."

"You just met your mate, and you aren't going to do your best to get up his skirt right away?" Lance asked.

"I've been saving myself for my mate, so maybe I will maybe I won't. I don't know. A lot is going to depend on him."

Lance stared at his sister, his brow furrowed. "Really?"

"Don't be so shocked," Olive replied. "When you've been told your whole life that there is one special person out there just for you, and you will see them glow with love, why the hell complicate things? So yeah, I've waited. I do have plans to throw myself at that man in drag. I just hope he's receptive." Olive smoothed down her dress. "Do I look presentable?" She turned and glanced at Lance from over her shoulder.

"You look fine, kid. If he's glowing, he'll think you're a fairy princess. That's typically how this thing works. The mate glow indicates an ideal mate, so he'll be super interested in you, too. I'm not going to have to issue threats or warnings and do the grouchy big brother thing, unless you want me to."

"Please don't. Now put your kilt back on."

"Jeans are warmer," Lance grumbled.

"And Ren Fair ladies swoon over kilts," Olive said.. "Come on, we should go properly meet these people we're planning the rest of our lives with. That would only be fair to them, don't you think?"

Lance stood behind the young woman dressed as a boy. Her attention was on the male in the red dress having what appeared to be a deep conversation with his sister across the room. This was a girl, he reminded himself.

He swept his long hair behind his shoulder. This would be easier if she was dressed like a girl. Was he supposed to pretend he thought she was a male or was it okay to talk to her like he knew she was a female? Hell, he first needed to find out how old she was. If she wasn't over eighteen, he was going to back off and drown his enthusiasm in too many beers. As a boy, she didn't look much older than sixteen or so.

He lifted his head to watch Olive across the room. Her red

curls were bent close to her mate's long dark hair. The two of them looked like girlfriends planning a conspiracy. He expected them to start giggling at any moment.

"Our sisters look like they're new BFFs," Lance finally said.

The girl twisted in her seat and gazed up at him. Lance stopped breathing. How could he have ever seen her as anything but a beautiful young woman? Her large golden eyes claimed his soul. Her perfect, pert nose was covered in a smattering of delightful freckles. And her full lips formed a delicate O.

Blood rushed away from his brain and into a throbbing hard-on. He would give anything at this moment to see those eyes peer up at him like this while her mouth was wrapped around him.

Lance lost himself in her eyes for what felt like an eternity, an eternity that ended a split second later. He sat in the empty seat next to her. "Mind if I join you? Us brothers have to stick together." He awkwardly slapped her on the back.

She wasn't talking. Crap. He was going about this all wrong. "I heard from Olive that my dog misbehaved. I hope he didn't scare your sister too much."

Lettie couldn't talk. Her mouth was completely dry. The gorgeous blond from the drum band was talking to her about Bucky, as if he were her sister. *Oh, God, he thinks I'm a boy and he's interested in Bucky as a girl. This is messed up.*

"We met your sister after your dog played proctologist. I hope he gave you my test results. He sort of ran off before letting me know how I checked out." That was so stupid that Lettie groaned, then coughed to cover her distress.

"You okay there, buddy?"

This was worse than horrible. Her insides quivered. If she could have an erection, she would, just because he was talking to her. But he thought he was talking to a man. The golden man handed her the drink that sat in front of her. She took a long pull on her beer, hoping it would steady her nerves.

"Name's Lance." He extended his hand.

Lance. Lettie let the sound roll around in her brain. She liked it. It suited him. "Le— Lot—" She cut herself off before completing her name.

Lance nodded at her beer. "You must look younger than you really are."

"How old do you think I am?" She may have said that a little more saucily than intended. She bit her lip.

"You look like you're about fifteen, but you're drinking a beer, so you're at least twenty-one." Their eyes met again.

"I'm twenty-three," she said, swallowing hard.

No, no, no, no, no. That look, that was a smoldering look, and he thinks I'm a boy.

Oh crap. She froze as Lance moved toward her. He leaned back and flipped his hair over his shoulder. Lettie wanted to bury her face in that mane. She relaxed slightly as he focused more on the space in front of him than on her.

"You do the fair circuit often?" his voice rumbled.

She closed her eyes and breathed in the sound, letting it roll over her.

"When it's in town. Do you play a lot of fairs?" Lettie stared into her drink. He wasn't flirting, just talking while her brother monopolized his sister. He probably was only over here to keep an eye on them.

"Yeah, it keeps us on the road a good bit. More places are having winter events like this one, so I guess we'll be traveling year round soon."

"Life of a Renaissance rock star."

"Sure. The guy I replaced decided he wanted to get married and have a steady lifestyle. This isn't very steady."

The guy sounded as if he was already beginning to question his life choices. "Is it fun?"

"It's fun until it isn't."

"That sounds like secrets underneath. I'm not drunk enough for a philosophical discussion, Lance."

"The best discussions happen when you aren't drunk, just reflective. What secrets did my beast uncover from you, Lot?"

She slowly moved her head side to side. "Speaking of beasts, what kind of dog was that?"

"He's a wolf."

Lettie gulped. "Oh shit." So he could have eaten her in one bite.

"I know he found something out about you, but it's best if you tell me." Lance looked across his shoulder at her. She felt his eyes pierce her in place.

"I...I'm a girl," she whispered.

"I knew that." Lance flashed a grin that turned Lettie into a human puddle.

He knew. He had been flirting but covering it up. *Damn.*

"Tell me something I don't know. And yes, I know your sister is a male. Boyfriend?"

"Brother."

Lance's smile widened. "That, I didn't know."

The electrical zing she'd felt from him the first time they'd made eye contact hit her again.

"Seems to me that neither of us is up for social norms," Lance stated.

Lettie creased her brow. "Explain yourself."

"You have short hair, while mine is long. You're in pants while I'm in a..."

"Kilt. You're in a kilt. Don't you dare say skirt. Men in skirts aren't hot, but men in kilts are."

Lance laughed. "My sister might argue with you over that." Lance nodded to the side, indicating that Lettie should look at their siblings.

He was right. Olive looked like she was about to climb in Bucky's lap and start making out.

"Your turn. Tell me something that I don't know." Lettie crossed her arms as she turned to face the large man next to her.

"I want to see your mouth on me, Lot." Lance winked at her as he took a drink.

"Lettie," she said with a furious blush. "I said something I don't know." Most lewd come-ons involved blowjobs and her lips. Typically it annoyed Lettie. Coming from Lance, she agreed with him, she wanted her mouth on him too. Emboldened by her own emotions, still flushed, she leaned into him. "Let me guess" She couldn't think of anything, so she made something ridiculously wild up. "The wolf is you."

Lance coughed and spit his beer out, dropping the mug, spilling its contents down the front of his shirt and into his lap. "Shit!" He stared at her.

His eyes flashed bright blue. Lettie backed away. Lance stood, grabbed her wrist, and dragged her from the feast. She stumbled after him in silence. He pulled her down the main festival street, past painted canvas tarps, and into a behind-the-scene area. Near a large canvas tent, he dropped her wrist and ripped his wet shirt off. Lance stopped, though the movement of his back showed he was breathing heavily.

Lettie stared at his muscles. He was so angry that he'd growled. She stepped closer, tentatively placing her hand on his skin. "What did I say?"

"Wait here," he snarled before stepping through into the tent in front of them.

Lettie pulled her cloak about her to keep warm in the freezing weather. She should just leave. Lance had just gotten very weird and creepy, and she didn't need weird, not when she wanted hot and flirty.

Determined to disappear before he emerged, she trotted a few dozen yards before she realized she had no idea how Lance had found this area of the grounds. She continued through the maze of tents and canvas tarps trying to find her way back to the feast. A couple of figures were warming their hands over a barrel fire, so she walked in their direction

When she got close enough, she realized she was no longer in the festival area but by a freeway overpass near the far end of the fairgrounds. Scraggly, bearded, dirt-encrusted faces smiled with rotten teeth at her.

"You're too pretty to be a boy," one of the men slurred.

They were drunk. She needed to go back to find Lance. He may have gotten weird on her, but he was definitely safer than these two. Before she could leave, one of them snatched her cape and tugged her toward him. "That's a mouth that belongs on a girl, doing girlie things."

Lettie swallowed down bile in her panic. What had she

gotten herself into? It didn't matter that she was dressed like a boy. Either these two could tell she wasn't, or they didn't care.

"Like sucking on my dick."

Both men cackled.

"Boys, boys, boys," a deep, gruff voice said in the darkness. "What have I told you about mishandling the ladies?"

"It's no lady, it's a pretty little fairy lad from the festival," one of the men said.

"Let him be, Tommy."

Lettie's shoulders relaxed slightly. It sounded like this newcomer was going to actually help her. When he stepped into the circle of light created by the fire, she saw that he was a large man, although he remained far enough out of the light that she couldn't make out his features. His large beefy hand slapped Tommy on the shoulder, and Tommy let go of her cape.

Lettie stumbled backward and dropped onto her ass, a scream escaping her lips as she fell.

The new man helped her up. "Come with me. I'll see to it you're taken care of." He started to lead Lettie even further away from the festival grounds, toward what appeared to be a tent city, based on what Lettie could make out in the dim light.

"I need to go over that way." She tried to head back in the proper direction.

"No, boy, we're going to go this way first." The hand that had steadied her earlier now gripped the back of her neck in a pinching vice. She cried out in pain. Fingers bit into her neck even more, making resistance almost impossible. It felt like he was going to crush her bones.

"Let me go," she managed to whimper, too scared to make any louder noise.

"Not until..." He stopped talking. A very large dog charged into their path and crouched down, teeth bared and ready to attack.

Wolf, Lettie corrected herself. The same one who'd been overly friendly, the same one that Lance claimed was his. Lance had acted strangely when she jokingly called him a werewolf. But there the wolf was, again, with the same glint in his eyes that she'd noticed in Lance's, a bright blue fire.

"I said…" Lettie donkey kicked the man, who still had a hand on her neck, though his grip had lessened. "Let me go."

The wolf lunged, snarling at the large man, but not attacking. Lettie rushed toward the creature, hoping he was safer. She buried her hand into the thick mane around his neck. "Get me outta here, boy."

Lettie followed the wolf back to the tent where she had deserted Lance. She sat on the bench in the middle of the room with a loud whoosh. "Where is your person? Where's Lance?" she asked the wolf.

In response, he sat down and dropped his head forward. Lettie swore as she watched the hair grow long and lighten, fur melting away to pale skin, paws lengthening to fingers. When he lifted his face to her, it was Lance's visage and not the long snout of a wolf that faced her.

Lettie screamed and then slipped from the bench onto the ground in a faint.

Her lungs expanded fully for the first time in hours. Lettie blinked, before focusing on Lance's face above her.

"There you are. I had to unwrap your bindings. You were having a hard time breathing."

Lettie lifted her hand and twisted her fingers into his hair. The smile Lance gave her made her heart skip a beat.

She pulled the hair, bringing his face down to hers. He didn't resist. Their lips met. Lance pulled her in closer. Her other arm wrapped around his neck. His face felt warm against hers, his lips like she had been missing them her entire life.

Lance carried her over to the spilled hay, where he placed a blanket before shifting Lettie onto the makeshift bed. His hands slid along her side. He adjusted himself over her, so she skimmed her leg over his.

"I'm wearing too many clothes," she said against his kisses.

"Hmmm-mmm," Lance growled in his throat.

Her doublet had already been mostly unbuttoned. Now,

Lance pulled the few buttons off in his haste to gain access to her skin.

Lettie groaned into his mouth as Lance's hand cupped her freed breast and his fingers found a nipple. Her hand fisted in his hair as he trailed kisses down the center of her chest. As he sucked a dark nipple into his mouth, she gripped his hair harder.

He gently tapped the back of her hand. "Don't pull it all out, or you won't have anything to hold on to later."

"Want you," Lettie panted. "Now."

"Condom." Lance pushed up and reached for his kilt, fishing in the pockets for his wallet.

Lettie kicked her way out of her pantaloons and tights. "You're beautiful," she said as Lance kneeled above her. His hair spread across his broad shoulders like a golden cape. Crisp, almost ginger hairs curled in a V-shape between his pecs and trailed down his abs.

"So are you." He handed her the foil pack.

Lettie, with her lush dark skin and darker curly hair on the top of her head and between her legs, stared up at him. She glowed. She made him feel like a superhero, and she was about to be his. When she hadn't been in front of the tent after he'd changed his shirt, he'd almost gone mad. When he heard her scream, he'd been ready to tear those men to pieces. But then, she had defended herself with that kick. God, what a turn on.

Her touch on his cock as she slid the condom on brought him back to the here and now, to the reality that she wanted him as badly as he needed her. He stopped thinking and lowered himself to her. She gasped as he slid into her, completely claiming her. She was his; details and logistics could be determined later. For now, she enfolded him in her body, wrapped her legs around him. She scraped her nails up his back. At that point, Lance stopped thinking at all and began thrusting, losing himself in her warmth.

With each stroke, Lettie made small, needful noises. Her

sounds drove him to a frenzied pace. Lance thrust harder, deeper.

"More, oh yes, more." Lettie urged him with her words and the lifting of her hips in time with his actions.

Lance lowered onto one elbow and rolled, pulling her on top. She had fabulous breasts. From below, he could better enjoy and touch them from this angle. Lettie shifted, bracing her hands on his shoulders before she began rocking against his length. He cupped her breasts as they bounced, playing with her nipples.

"I...I can't, oh!" Lettie froze. Her actions stopped as he felt her internal muscles spasm around him. Lance grabbed her hips and retook the responsibility of thrusting. His brain seized as his body exploded into her. Lettie began rocking again, encouraging Lance as he spent himself.

She collapsed against his chest. He fumbled around beside them and hauled his kilt to cover her. Soon enough, they would notice the cool air in the tent.

As Lance trailed his finger over her skin, he noticed she had freckles on her shoulder, too. He had never realized darker skin could freckle. Either way, her skin was the most beautiful color he had ever seen, ever tasted.

She twisted her fingers in his hair, which he liked, as if she wanted to capture him somehow. At least until Lettie yanked hard on the hair in her grasp, sat up, and scooted away from his embrace.

"What the hell was that for?" Lance rubbed at the sore spot near his temple.

"You're a fucking werewolf." She clutched the kilt in front of her, protecting her nakedness from his eyes.

"You said you knew." He rubbed his head above his temple, where she'd pulled his hair.

"I was joking. I didn't know. Werewolves don't exist."

"Yes, we do." Lance sat up. Lettie retreated to the bench and began pulling on her clothes.

Lance didn't follow her. Yet. "Are you okay?"

"What the hell? A wolf?"

He nodded and moved forward, closer. She didn't seem overly upset, and she wasn't scared.

Lettie leaned forward and slapped him across the face. "That's for sticking your nose in my crotch, you lech. What the hell was that all about?"

"You didn't seem as mad when you thought I was a dog." Lance grinned as he placed his palm over her slap.

"Dogs don't know any better. Stop grinning and explain yourself, perv."

"I thought you were a boy, and I was drawn to you."

"And?"

"I don't do boys. It was causing me issues."

"Aw, poor macho man, finds a brown boy a little attractive and—"

Lance stood, pulling Lettie into his embrace and crushing her to his still naked body. "Not a little attractive. The most beautiful creature I've ever seen. I'm distractingly drawn to you and I got an instant erection just because we made eye contact. Ready to slay monsters just for a smile. Ready to lay down my life for you. And if you were a man, I was going to have to make some adjustments in my way of thinking, and I honestly didn't know how to go about doing that." Lance ran a hand through his hair, and paced in a circle. "The first thing I did was to find out for certain if you were a boy, after that…. You look so young, and I'm not a cradle robber. Thank God you are female and over eighteen." He stopped pacing and wrapped Lettie back in his embrace. "I was thrilled when you smelled of arousal. I could only hope I did that to you, that I had the same effect on you as you had on me."

Lettie rested her hands on his chest. "You do have the same effect on me." She lifted up on her toes and kissed his chin. "It's cold in here. Get some clothes on before someone walks in." She pushed away from him.

Lance pulled her back into his grasp. Her fingers twisted into his hair. "When you were out there, alone, I was ready to tear that man's throat out for having his hand on you. And then my fierce little pixie kicked the shit out of him. I couldn't have been more proud." He glanced at her hand knotted in his hair.

She dragged him close for a deep kiss.

"I live with my parents. I can't bring you home tonight."

Lance's chest lifted against her as he laughed. "I'm sharing an RV with my sister. You can't come home with me tonight, either."

Lance stared at her, wishing for a way he could have her all night. He didn't want to let her go to get dressed, but she was right. Sooner or later people would come in here to gather their things. "You are so beautiful dressed as a boy, and you're the queen of all my fantasies when I see you like a woman naked and wanton before me. We'll figure this all out."

Lance pulled on jeans, strapped on his boots, and found a dry sweater. Lettie stood in front of him, looking very much like a smug young Elizabethan man. The smug was new. He had given her that, and he liked the way it looked on her.

He laced his fingers with hers and kissed her knuckles. "My Lord, shall we return to the feast?"

She giggled. "And then what?"

"And then I will strive to find a way to please you every day for the rest of your life."

ABOUT THE AUTHOR

 Bio-engineered to be the only redhead in a generation of blonds, Lulu feels that "aliens" may actually

be the best answer for a life-time of being asked, "Where did you get that red hair from?"

She did not come into writing from years of scribbling words on paper. Her background is rooted in visual arts and making pictures. Encouraged to make those pictures out of words Lulu began writing

just to see what would happen. What happened was two full-length manuscripts in three months.

Lulu cannot ride a horse, a motorcycle, spin a hula hoop, or play roller derby. Yes, she has attempted

all of those, even if it has been decades since she's been on a horse or a motorcycle. She embraces the

crazy that comes with that one little genetic mutation, and attempts to live up to the reputation that

proceeds her. Lulu would like to apologize for her contribution to the hole on the ozone layer from her

use of hairspray in the 1980s.

For more information, visit:
www.LuluMSylvian.com